A BREW FOR CHAOS

Also by Esme Addison

The Enchanted Bay Mysteries

A SPELL FOR TROUBLE
A HEX FOR DANGER

The Secret Society Mysteries

AN INTRIGUE OF WITCHES

A BREW FOR CHAOS

Esme Addison

SEVERN HOUSE

First world edition published in Great Britain and the USA in 2025
by Severn House, an imprint of Canongate Books Ltd,
14 High Street, Edinburgh EH1 1TE.

severnhouse.com

Copyright © Esme Addison LLC, 2025

Cover and jacket design by Piers Tilbury

All rights reserved including the right of reproduction in whole or in part in any form. The right of Esme Addison to be identified as the author of this work has been asserted in accordance with the Copyright, Designs & Patents Act 1988.

British Library Cataloguing-in-Publication Data
A CIP catalogue record for this title is available from the British Library.

ISBN-13: 978-1-4483-1263-4 (cased)
ISBN-13: 978-1-4483-1264-1 (e-book)

This is a work of fiction. Names, characters, places and incidents are either the product of the author's imagination or are used fictitiously. Except where actual historical events and characters are being described for the storyline of this novel, all situations in this publication are fictitious and any resemblance to actual persons, living or dead, business establishments, events or locales is purely coincidental.

No part of this book may be used or reproduced in any manner for the purpose of training artificial intelligence technologies or systems. This work is reserved from text and data mining (Article 4(3) Directive (EU) 2019/790).

All Severn House titles are printed on acid-free paper.

Typeset by Palimpsest Book Production Ltd., Falkirk, Stirlingshire, Scotland.
Printed and bound in Great Britain by TJ Books, Padstow, Cornwall.

The manufacturer's authorised representative in the EU for product safety is Authorised Rep Compliance Ltd, 71 Lower Baggot Street, Dublin D02 P593 Ireland (arccompliance.com)

Praise for the Enchanted Bay Mysteries

"Magical mysteries, romance and a Harry Potter-like storyline add up to an enchanting read"
Kirkus Reviews on *A Hex for Danger*

"Close family relationships, friendship, a lovingly portrayed coastal setting – all framed by details of running an herbal apothecary – distinguish this cozy"
Booklist on *A Hex for Danger*

"This cozy, with its well-developed characters and charming seaside setting, and framed by plant and mermaid lore, will appeal to those who enjoy stories with a touch of magic"
Booklist on *A Spell for Trouble*

"Sparkling"
Kirkus Reviews on *A Spell for Trouble*

"Fans of Ellery Adams's mysteries will want to try this one"
Library Journal on *A Spell for Trouble*

"A crafty plot, distinctive characters, and a quirky small-town setting . . . Cozy fans will be more than satisfied"
Publishers Weekly on *A Spell for Trouble*

About the author

Esme Addison is the Amazon bestselling author of the Enchanted Bay Mysteries, the first of which was nominated for an Agatha Award, and the new Secret Society Mysteries.

Esme lives in Raleigh, NC with her family and is a member of Sisters in Crime, International Thriller Writers, Mystery Writers of America and Crime Writers of Color. When she's not writing, you can find her reading, traveling, and indulging her love of history at museums and historical sites.

Twitter/X: @EsmeAddison
Facebook / Instagram / YouTube: @EsmeAddisonAuthor
esmeaddison.com

To my father (who is no longer with us) who always told me I was a writer – because of him and my mother, I never had any doubt. And to my mother who shared her imagination, and love of all things whimsical and fanciful.

Rodzina nie jest czymś ważnym. Jest wszystkim.
The family is not important. It is everything.

—A Polish proverb

ONE

Aleksandra Daniels stood at the edge of the crowd.

It was standing room only for her Aunt Lidia's presentation on the history of beer as medicine. Before her were rows of wooden folding chairs filled with customers of their family's herbal apothecary, Botanika located on Main Street, in a historic brick building.

But she couldn't focus on the success of the program, distracted as she was by her watch. It was almost over, and yet she was sure if her cousin Minka just showed up to support her mother's lecture, even at the last minute, her aunt would take the next step to patch things up between them.

Alex looked up from her phone to watch her ciocia Lidia, a woman in her sixties with long black hair streaked with silver pulled up into a topknot. Though she was a vibrant spot of color in the otherwise wood and brick interior with her denim jumper and cardigan color-blocked with hues of autumn over a burgundy turtleneck, Alex was distracted, barely hearing her aunt's words. *Ancient Sumerians. Medicinal beer. Healing herbs.*

It was all a jumble as Alex's thumbs flew over the keyboard. **Minka, where are you? It's almost over.**

'And that is the history of beer as medicine.'

Alex stuffed her phone into her purse and clapped along with the rest of the forty or so audience members.

'Thank you so much for listening to my presentation tonight. Pepper, I'm handing it over to you.' Lidia stepped away from the podium, scanning the crowd as she went.

Pepper Bellamy, a young woman in her late twenties, didn't need to be told twice. With her red hair slicked back into a high bun, she made her way to the front. Dressed in designer jeans and a silk blouse paired with a burgundy leather blazer, the high heels of her brown leather boots clicked against the oiled wood floors. She hovered over the microphone.

'I want to thank Lidia Sobieski, the owner of this fine establishment.' She waved a hand around the herbal apothecary. 'The presentation was a wonderful program brought to you by the *Bellamy Bay Bugler*.' Pepper peered into the crowd then pointed. 'I'd also like to thank my boss, the editor-in-chief, Jonah Fox. There he is.' She pointed to a tall man in his sixties with cropped brown hair thinning on top, gold wire-rimmed glasses and narrow, amiable features.

The man threw up a hand and waved.

'Jonah, do you want to say a few words about what we're working on?'

When he effected a bashful expression, Pepper persisted. 'You guys, we're doing a follow-up piece on the serial killer that stalked our town in the 1980s. Jonah, come on up and give everyone a preview.'

Serial killer? Alex frowned. *Here in Bellamy Bay?*

He made a gesture of looking embarrassed, stuffing his hands into his khakis but, in a practiced move, smoothly arrived at the podium. 'Good evening, good people of Bellamy Bay,' he said in the same folksy tone he wrote his op-ed pieces in, then cracked a grin. 'Pepper's right. We're working on something interesting for the paper, but I'd much rather use this time for something else. Once again, the *Bellamy Bay Bugler* is co-sponsoring the local Oktoberfest party and craft beer contest.'

'Serial killer?' Alex whispered to her aunt, who'd come to stand beside her.

'It was a long time ago. We've tried to put it behind us. Personally, I'd prefer he not dredge up that dark period of our town's history.' Her aunt shrugged, eyes on the crowd. 'Minka didn't come?'

Alex frowned. 'Sorry.'

Her aunt exhaled slowly but didn't comment.

'It's going to be the biggest party of the year,' Jonah continued. 'And if you're a home brewer like I am, you'll want to enter your brew into the contest for bragging rights and a cash prize and your beer stocked at all of the restaurants in town.'

There was an exaggerated cough from the crowd, and Jonah reluctantly turned to look in the direction of the sound. It had come from a woman in her early fifties.

A Brew for Chaos

She was tall and thin, her blonde hair cut into a short, layered style. 'Forgetting something, Jonah?' she called out, cupping her hands over her bright red lips like a makeshift megaphone.

'Of course.' His features stretched into a mock apology. 'Please note: The Colonial Brewery & Tavern is the second sponsor of our Oktoberfest and their owner, Spencer Francis, will be co-chairing the event . . .' He couldn't hide his frown. 'Along with me.' He looked at her with an *are-you-satisfied* look.

She smiled, and he doffed an imaginary hat and returned to the crowd.

More applause and Lidia returned to the podium. 'There are samples of non-alcoholic and alcoholic medicinal beer that I brewed for you all in the back of the shop. Please enjoy.'

Pepper was moving towards Alex, Jonah in hand, and embraced Alex when she reached her. 'Tonight's event was amazing, right?' When Alex agreed, she turned to Jonah. 'You're still entering your award-winning beer in the contest?'

'You know it. Can't let some interloper steal my title. Or my secret recipe.'

Alex noticed he eyed Spencer when he said that, and she regarded the woman with interest. She nudged Pepper. 'What's the deal with that woman?'

Pepper glanced at the blonde. 'All I know about her is that she's the absentee-owner of the brewery and tavern and they have a beverage company that produces and distributes beer all over the world. For as long as I can remember there's been a manager running the place while she lived in Europe for the last decade. This year she lobbied the town's planning committee aggressively to become not only the sponsor of our Oktoberfest but the site for the event. At least that's what my dad said was discussed at the last town council meeting.'

Pepper's family was descendant from the founder of Bellamy Bay, and her father was mayor. Alex knew not much happened that he didn't know about. She watched as Spencer paused at the door, glanced around and then slipped out. Odd, Alex thought, wondering at the woman's cagey behavior.

Twenty minutes passed, with Jonah and Pepper discussing the difficulty in procuring tents for the parking lot when Jonah checked his phone. Forehead creasing slightly, he sighed. 'My house alarm's going off.' He looked up. 'I need to go and meet the police there.'

'Let's hope it's a false alarm,' Pepper said. 'When you're done, want to meet up for a drink and discuss the Fisherman serial killer case?' She turned to Alex. 'You can join us. I've told Jonah I want you to help me research the case.'

Alex laughed. 'You do?'

'Sorry, Cubby. I've got some work to catch up on.'

Cubby? Alex mouthed with a smirk.

Pepper laughed. 'Cubby as in Cub Reporter. I got the nickname when I was an intern, and it just stuck.' Then her frown returned. 'But if you're working on the Fisherman case, shouldn't I be with you?'

Jonah chuckled. 'You've got plenty to keep you busy. For now, I want you to cover the golf event coming up.'

Pepper sniffed. 'Surely an intern could write that up.'

'And then there's Oktoberfest. You have plenty to do since you'll be assisting me on the planning committee.' He grinned at her. 'Which I really appreciate. With the anniversary of the Fisherman case, I'm too busy to really devote time to party planning.' He glanced at Alex. 'You can let your aunt know I'll be by for my delivery of hops . . . and other things.'

Pepper shot Alex a rueful look. 'I better head out too. I want to write about tonight while it's fresh in my mind. But I'll see you soon?'

Alex stood in the middle of the shop floor as lines of people moved around her, inspecting the bars of soap, glass jars of candles, herbal tonics and dry tea blends.

Dressed in an ironic t-shirt and worn jeans, Tanner sidled up beside her. 'Your aunt never fails to impress, huh?'

'You made it.' Alex grinned at the lanky teenager who worked after school in the shop with her. 'Get all your homework done?'

His brown eyes lit up. 'Still on the A and B honor roll.'

'That's good to hear . . . But are you okay?' Alex's voice softened. She suppressed the urge to ruffle his spiky brown hair. He seemed to be handling his grief well after losing both parents, but she couldn't help but wonder.

He shook his head. 'Don't look at me like that. I'm fine. I'm exactly where I want to be. And keeping busy.'

But Alex still felt guilty since she was the one who figured out who killed his father, the anonymous writer behind a blog that chronicled paranormal activity in their town. At seventeen, Tanner Robinson was now the writer behind *Bizarre Bellamy Bay*, an unassuming teenager who fielded emails from government and military whistleblowers and the only non-Magical Alex knew who was aware of her true heritage.

He looked around the shop. 'Crowd's thinning. I'm going to help Ms Lidia close up.'

A couple hours later, Alex and her aunt sat in the living room of the Sobieski home, a large, historic seafoam Queen Anne house with a wraparound porch centered on a large grassy lot filled with pots of orange and burgundy mums. Not too far from Main Street, Alex could walk to work when the weather was nice.

They were drinking Calm Down tea, a blend of calming herbs and adaptogenics that they could barely keep in the shop. Alex's shorthaired German Shepherd, almost three years old and named Athena, lay at her feet, big brown eyes trained on her.

'Tonight went well,' Alex commented, pulling a soft, fuzzy yellow blanket over her legs. 'We couldn't have fit another person in the building.'

'True. But it would've been nice if Minka had joined us.' Lidia glanced at the hardwood stairs. 'When she came home tonight, she went straight upstairs without a word.'

'She's still hurt,' Alex said gently.

'She's been gone for three months . . .' Pain crossed her face. 'It's always been her and me in the shop ever since she was a little girl. I've always known Kamila didn't care for the family business and that's fine. She's always said her calling is to serve and protect and I believe that. But Minka . . . she's a healer like me. Like you . . . I assumed she'd take over the shop one day.'

'You've got me, Ciociu.'

'And I'll always be grateful you returned to us, my kwiatuszek.' *My flower.*

After Alex's mother died, her father, a former detective turned police chief, a good and decent man by all accounts, had kept her from her mother's family: Aunt Lidia and her two cousins Minka and Kamila.

Growing up in Connecticut, she was separated by the family in more ways than just geography. She never knew her father's reasons, only understood that the Sobieskis were different and to be avoided. It was only after he died from heart issues earlier in the year that Alex had accepted an invitation to visit her mother's sister in Bellamy Bay, a small coastal community in North Carolina, and discovered they were a loving, supportive family descended from the Mermaid of Warsaw, known to most as a centuries' old Polish myth.

But Alex had discovered the mermaid had been real with descendants who'd lost their ability to shift into their Mer form and looked like everyone else. All that was left of the legacy was a genetic marker, and certain abilities that most humans did not have. Alex was still learning how to use her powers that centered on the manipulation of water or any type of moisture.

So far, the most useful ability was telepathy. Her telepathy was fueled by her ability to manipulate the water in the brain and body, using it to transmit and resonate with electromagnetic signals, allowing her to connect with others' thoughts and emotions.

Better than texting, she could be in constant contact with her family members if she wanted. She could manipulate a person's behavior, and also dive into anyone's thoughts if she desired. But for ethical reasons she tried never to do that. Even though most Magicals knew how to block another from searching their mind.

Probably the most gratifying skill of all was her gift of healing, a regenerative frequency that flowed from her palms when she willed it to. The Mer's healing ability stemmed from their control over the body's water – approximately sixty per cent of the human body – allowing them to accelerate cell regeneration, balance fluids, and promote rapid recovery by manipulating the water within tissues and cells.

But just as she could heal, she could hurt. Rather she could protect herself by generating electricity just like an electric ray and directing it at an opponent.

'Your decision to turn a visit into a permanent move was the best thing to happen to us all in a very long time.' Lidia leaned forward and patted her niece's cheek. 'By the way, creating those mini apple cider scented candles was a great idea, Aleksandra.

A Brew for Chaos 7

And then placing them by the front door? The best impulse buy. You're a real natural. Your mother would be so proud.' The smile on Alex's face fell away. She didn't want to talk about her mother, not even about how happy she'd be if she was alive. Her mother had drowned in Bellamy Bay when she was seven and it still hurt to think about her.

Athena stood and moved to Alex's side, nuzzling her thigh with the soft brown-black fur on her head. Alex smiled down at her and gently rubbed between her ears. 'Jonah said something about receiving a hops delivery.'

Lidia acknowledged the conversation change without comment. 'Good. I provide him with most of the herbs and spices he needs to make his craft beer. He's been one of my most loyal customers, beginning when he first arrived in town and hired me as a consultant.'

'We consult?'

Lidia laughed. 'No, *we* don't. But I do, on occasion. Jonah hired me when he first moved to town and began his position at the paper.'

'And what did he want to know?' Athena plopped down on the floor again.

'Not sure if you know anything about craft beer, but you can add herbs and spices to change the taste. As I recall, he was fascinated by the chemistry of it all. And he wanted to know the best ways to use ingredients to create the tastes he desired.'

'And he just brews for himself?'

'No, I think he sells locally to some of the shops. As he explained it to me, just something fun for him to do.'

'Speaking of beer, your presentation tonight . . . Beer as medicine? Is that for real?'

'It is.'

'I get that the herbs and fruit have a medicinal benefit, but beer?'

'Yes. Due to the presence of tetracycline, an antibiotic, high phytoestrogen content, and various minerals, beer has been used in herbal medicine since the time of the ancient Sumerians.'

'That's kind of amazing. And surprising.'

'This is all drinking beer in moderation, of course, or as a prescribed tonic historically.'

8 Esme Addison

'I'd love to learn more about this.'

'There's a reference guide on the kitchen bookshelf you can read.'

'Still, I wonder why Jonah was so fascinated with medicinal beer.'

Lidia shrugged. 'Tetracycline in particular was an interest of Jonah's as I recall. Not sure why, but it is known to bind with calcium before being deposited into the bones. It's in osteoporotic treatments. Perhaps he has a history of weak bones or bone fractures. It's genetic, you know.'

'Osteo-what?' Alex laughed. 'I feel like I should be taking notes.'

The next morning, Alex planted her hands on her waist and inspected the shop floor.

Botanika was ready for fall. She had festooned the ceiling corners with streamers of silk leaves in bright yellow and orange. Pumpkins of all colors, cream, blue, green, orange and pink, were artistically stacked in various corners of the shop and cornucopias overflowing with gourds and corn that shimmered with deep blue, purple and burgundy kernels accented tabletops and counters.

The front door jingled, and Jack Frazier entered the shop.

Alex smoothed her hair back when she saw her boyfriend heading towards the counter. A detective in the Bellamy Bay Police Department, he was dressed for work in his usual tan chinos and light blue button-down chambray shirt, with his shield and firearm peeking from around his waist. At six-foot-one Jack was about five inches taller than Alex, but that didn't stop her from coming around the counter, standing on her tiptoes and wrapping her arms around his neck. 'Hey you.'

'Hey yourself.' He leaned forward and lifted her off the ground in a bear hug before planting her down gently and kissing her on the lips. He nuzzled his nose into her shiny black hair and sighed. 'Lemongrass?' he guessed.

'You're getting better at identifying your herbs,' Alex noted. 'But there's also vanilla, sweet orange and sugar cane. Nonetheless, I'm impressed.'

'Don't be.' He chuckled. 'Still not a fan of all this . . . *hocus pocus.*'

A Brew for Chaos

'Still progress. Like what I've done with the place?'

He studied her expression. 'Not mad about last night?'

'What, that you didn't show up again?' She forced a wide grin. 'Nope, I'm totally used to you flaking out on me.'

He winced. 'I'm a cop, Alex. Criminals don't—'

'Sleep,' she finished for him. 'Yeah, I know. My dad used to say the same thing when his work made him miss important events in my life.'

She held her smile in place until he stopped watching her with his suspicious cop eyes, trying to ferret out the truth of how she really felt.

He grinned, looking around the shop. 'Very fall . . . harvest-y – is that a word?'

She softly exhaled. Good, he was letting it go. She didn't feel like getting into it with him. She followed his gaze, proud of how pretty the shop looked. 'Probably not. But I'll take it.' And this time her smile was genuine.

She really did try to not take it personal. The fact that Jack either bailed on dates with her or was late to see her and could never explain why. Even though it bothered her, what could she really say? Don't investigate that crime? Don't go to the aid of a person in need? She was a cop's kid. She understood the challenges of dating someone in law enforcement.

'And you've got all new stock since I last visited.' Jack picked up a bar of purple soap studded with dried black flowers and inspected the label. He grinned when he saw the surprised look on her face. 'I pay attention.'

Alex's smile widened. He was trying, and she appreciated that.

Jack began to read the soap label. 'Lavender for sweet dreams. Crushed juniper to keep bad dreams away—' He set the soap down with a thump. 'If I recall, juniper berries were the reason I had to arrest your aunt earlier this year. Didn't you Sobieskis learn your lesson?'

And just like that, the smile was gone. Alex rolled her eyes, not liking the way he called out her family. 'It's soap. Our customers know not to eat it. And you also know that Bryn Wesley poisoned Randy Bennett over a land deal – it had nothing to do with my aunt or herbal soap.'

He glanced around the shop. They were alone, and he gathered her in his arms. 'I know. I'm glad your aunt wasn't involved and I'm also glad you've found family since your father passed . . .' He pulled back slightly, staring into her green eyes. 'I just can't help but think your father was on to something when he kept you from them and this town for so many years.'

Alex stiffened in his arms, wondering where this conversation was going. 'What do you have against my family? As you've pointed out, they're all I have left and the only link to my mother.'

He pulled away from her, rubbing a hand over his blonde crew cut that was just beginning to grow out from the summer. 'I'm sorry. I don't mean to upset you.'

He watched her. She focused on the jars of spicy apple cider candles that were displayed beside the register. Fidgeting with the glass jars filled with red beeswax might prevent her boyfriend – the human lie detector – from seeing any of the tells – signs that she wasn't telling the truth.

'I just don't want you to get hurt. That's all. I care about you.' A look of concern flitted across his face. 'I hope you know that?'

'Honestly, it's hard to know where I stand with you . . .' Alex swallowed the lump in her throat. 'It can be difficult to feel connected to you sometimes, Jack. You keep so much of yourself—'

'I know that too,' he said a bit too forcefully, then smiled. 'It's just part of the job. I've kept my distance from people for so long it's hard to turn it off sometimes. But I want to fix that. Now, actually. I want you to meet my mother.'

Alex's hand stayed on a bottle. Really? His mother? She'd been dating him for three months, and he'd never invited her to the home he shared with his mother. It had been all dates about town and kisses on the front porch.

He never asked her to spend an evening at home with him. Never asked her to meet his mother. Alex had begun to wonder if his mother even existed. When they first met, he'd explained that he'd moved to Bellamy Bay to take care of his mother, who struggled with memory issues and could no longer live by herself. But this – now this was progress, wasn't it?

'Jack, I'd love to—' The front door jangled, and Celeste entered the shop. She was about five-foot-four, the same height as Alex, and they shared a similar fit, athletic build. But at twenty-three years old, she was four years younger.

A Brew for Chaos

Alex turned to Jack. 'Hold that thought.' She went to Celeste, who was unbuttoning her designer corduroy car coat, which was a soft camel color that brought out the gold in her light brown complexion and also matched her high-heeled leather camel boots.

'It's so warm and toasty in here . . .' She looked around the shop and inhaled deeply. 'And smells like apple pie. I love it.'

Celeste was a Magical like Alex. She descended from a charmed heritage beginning several generations back with a Polish soldier with Mer heritage who fought in Haiti during a Napoleonic campaign and had fallen in love and married a local woman descended from Mami Wata. Which made her half-Mer and half-water-witch, and related to the Sobieskis.

'Looking for anything in particular?' Alex glanced over at Jack, but he was keeping busy inspecting the stock.

'I can't get enough of your sweet potato pie candles.'

Alex grinned. 'They're a bestseller. So, how's work?'

Celeste, who graduated from Bellamy Bay College with an MBA earlier that year, was a junior executive at Wesley Inc, a local company with a diverse portfolio of businesses. She worked in their advanced weapons division.

'Great!' Her eyes lit up. 'We're taking to market a new non-lethal dart filled with venom from the Blue-Ringed Octopus. It silently stuns an assailant, immediately short-circuiting the nervous system, resulting in temporary paralysis.'

Alex laughed. 'That's good?'

'Yeah. Law enforcement can use the Octodart instead of bullets. Stops a criminal in their tracks. For about an hour.' Her hazel eyes framed by long dark lashes glimmered when they landed on Jack, and she lowered her voice. 'How are things going with lover boy?'

'Honestly, I don't know,' Alex murmured. 'He runs so hot and cold . . . but he just asked me to meet his mother.'

Celeste toyed with one of the long black curls that sprung around her face. 'That's progress, I suppose.' She eyed him critically. 'Still don't think he's right for you. You don't need a Mundane.'

In the Magical community, a Mundane was a human without magical heritage. And Jack, Alex thought with a grin, was the very definition of Mundane. By-the-book. No nonsense. Practical. But that's what she liked about him, his normalcy. With all that she was learning about herself and her family, he grounded her. And sometimes she needed a tether back to her old life. A life that reminded her of her father.

Celeste crossed her arms. 'If I were you, I wouldn't put up with his mess.'

Alex laughed. 'You mean like you did with your ex, Jasper?'

Celeste rolled her eyes. 'Do not mention that dragon's name.'

Alex gave her cousin a rueful grin. Then raised her voice. 'Candles are over there on that oak barrel. And we've got new s'mores bath bombs by the register . . . I'll be right back.' She hurried back to Jack, reaching for his hand and leading him to the back counter.

He glanced at Celeste, then looked at Alex, a playful grin on his lips. 'What were you two whispering about?'

'How I can't believe you want me to meet your mother.' She fixed him with a pointed stare. 'What changed?'

He had the decency to look embarrassed. 'The woman I hired to take care of her had to leave on a family emergency and I've had trouble finding a replacement on such short notice. You know with my work, sometimes I have to leave in the middle of the night, or without much notice . . .'

She took his hand and pulled him closer to her, noticing a new sleek black smart watch on his wrist. 'And you want me to . . . sit with your mom when you have to work?'

'Yeah . . . but only some evenings. She goes to a facility during the day, kind of daycare for dementia patients.'

'Sure.'

He sighed. 'It's a nice place. They bake, make crafts . . .' A look of misery washed over his face. 'I have to work, and I don't know what else to do with her. She's no trouble. But she just needs—'

'It's fine, Jack. I appreciate you asking. It means a lot to me that you'd even consider me.' Even though there were customers in the store, she sensed he needed a hug. She wrapped her arms around his waist and hugged him tight, feeling the tension in his body melting as she sent him waves of healing.

With Jack being a Mundane, she'd made a habit of never

A Brew for Chaos 13

practicing magic on or around him. Not reading his thoughts, nothing. She'd always had the sense it wouldn't go over well with him. And it was a secret she was determined to keep from him.

But this was different. He needed it and she could help him. She would do it just this once. She mentally pushed a large burst of wellness towards him.

His cologne of lemons and sea salt swirled around them, and Alex thought she felt the temperature drop just a smidge, but she could've been imagining things.

But Jack wasn't. He pulled back, a look of uneasiness in his eyes.

'What are you doing?'

She took a step back. 'What do you mean?' Alex tried to calm her features. Could he feel her healing him? Taking away his pain? She hoped not. How could she explain . . .

'I just felt . . .' He shot her a wary look. 'It just seemed like . . .'

She hated to gaslight him but . . . 'It was just a hug, Jack. Maybe you're so used to not giving and receiving affection that you don't know what it feels like.' Yikes, that was a bit harsh even if it was just the teeniest bit true. She turned away then, fiddling with a stack of apple cider scented bath bombs, then glanced at him out of the side of her eye.

His eyes crinkled at the corners, in the way they did when he restrained himself from showing emotion. Like he was squinting against the brightness of the sun. 'You must think I'm a real jerk,' he said, his voice soft with contrition.

Alex bit her bottom lip, feeling like the worst kind of heel.

'I'm sorry. Hugging you always feels amazing, and I probably don't do it enough. I spend a lot of time keeping myself at arm's length from most people – including you, the one person in this town I want to keep the closest.'

Alex blinked. It was the nearest Jack had ever come to sharing how he felt about her.

More people entered the shop, and he stepped away from her, glancing at his watch. 'I better go. I have a meeting at the station in twenty.'

Alex looked into his eyes and thought for just a moment she

saw the real him. Emotional. Sweet. Tender. And it softened her heart. 'Of course.' She walked him to the front door.

'Maybe you could come over tonight for dinner? Meet my mother.'

'I'd love to.'

He shot her a grateful smile. 'I'll text you the time and address.'

When he was gone, Celeste went to the register holding a basket full of candles. 'I don't know why you put up with him. He makes fun of the shop, and you know if he ever found out about Magicals, he'd be your worst nightmare.'

'God forbid,' Alex joked, then began ringing up the purchases. 'He's okay. You just don't know him like I do.'

Celeste crossed her arms. 'Since he's been in town, he's arrested your aunt . . . and me.'

'You gotta admit, you looked guilty as sin.' She told Celeste the purchase price.

Celeste lifted a shoulder. 'Even so.' And handed Alex her debit card. 'There's something off with him. Don't let his good looks fool you.'

'I know . . . I sense that too. But . . . I'm hiding a major secret from him. We both are. Maybe we're just . . . I don't know, projecting our own guilt onto him?'

'That's deep.' Celeste took her kraft bag by the twine handles. 'Maybe.' She took her receipt. 'I'll see you.'

By lunchtime, Aunt Lidia had arrived at the shop to give Alex her break. So, she headed to her second favorite place in town: Coffee O'Clock, located a block away from the shop but still in the historic district. It was housed in a brick-front building trimmed in bright teal, with two large picture windows decorated for the fall.

As she pushed open the bright red doors, heavenly scents of freshly baked bread, warmed butter and vanilla sugar danced around her. Alex inspected the display case of baked goodies: pecan and maple cookies, apple and salted caramel scones, both sweet potato and apple cake slices and sweet potato pie halves. Then made her purchase.

After she took her seat, Alex glanced at the clock on the wall. Pepper should be arriving soon. Just then the door flew open,

A Brew for Chaos   15

and Pepper hurried in, pencil stuck in her messy bun, brown freckles contrasting sharply against her pale skin and bright green eyes, which were dancing around the bakery, searching for Alex. She waved from the counter and completed her purchase.

'There you are,' she said with a triumphant grin as she shrugged out of her green leather overcoat and slid into their booth with her order. 'I have news.' Pepper leaned forward. 'Remember how I went to Atlanta to guest report at World News Network?'

Alex nodded as she sipped her coffee. 'How could I forget your photo dumps on Instagram? You on the set at WNN, you in the makeup chair. You in the—'

'Oh, stop.' She grinned. 'It's the biggest thing to ever happen to me. I had to document it.'

'Of course,' Alex said, taking a bite of her scone.

'I told them I'm co-writing an anniversary report on the Fisherman. And they said they'd be interested in having me back to discuss my report on air.'

'That's amazing news, Pepper. They'd be lucky to have you. So tell me about the case.'

Pepper laughed. 'He picked up young women on the beach, so it was like he was fishing for women. Get it?' She took a bite of her pie.

Alex's eyebrows shot up. 'Gross, but yeah, I get it.'

'This was back in the eighties, but the women were taken – poof! – just disappeared into thin air.'

'So, he was more a serial kidnapper?'

'The women were never found alive or otherwise. So the assumption was – is – that he killed them.'

Shaking her head, Alex glanced out the front window of the bakery, cataloguing the multi-colored historical store fronts, sidewalks lined with large planters filled with beautiful gold and orange mums and the banners atop lampposts that proclaimed *It's Fall Ya'll!* against a backdrop of red and yellow autumn leaves. It was difficult for Alex to reconcile the notion with the picturesque small town she'd come to call home. 'Was he ever caught? Did any victims ever get away?'

Pepper sipped her latte. 'That's the thing. He was never caught. He just stopped taking women – theories abound. He died. He

16   Esme Addison

was injured and couldn't act anymore. Or maybe he fell in love
with one of his victims . . .'

Alex screwed up her face.

'Ten women went missing, all presumed dead. It's the biggest
mystery to come out of Bellamy Bay. And that's where you come
in . . .'

'Me?'

'Yeah. If I can solve the mystery of who the Fisherman was,
the VP of Programming himself has promised me a job out of
their Atlanta or DC studio.'

'What does that have to do with me?'

'You've kind of made a name for yourself in town for solving
mysteries.'

Alex frowned. 'And?'

'And, with your experience and my talent for writing, well, I
thought you could help me figure out who the Fisherman was.'

'I'm done solving mysteries in this town,' she said, thinking
of how her interference upset Jack. 'It's causing problems with
my love life.'

'Oh.' Pepper's eyebrows shot up. 'Jack?'

'Yeah. Besides, if I was going to spend my time trying to
solve another mystery . . .' Her mouth dipped into a frown. 'I
should look into what happened to my mother.'

'What do you mean?' Pepper asked, pushing her empty plate
away.

Alex stared out the window, gazed unfocused. 'My mother
drowned in the bay. Her body was never recovered.' She returned
her gaze to Pepper. 'At least that's what I thought. But with you
telling me about this cold case . . . What if my mother was a
victim of this guy – this Fisherman?'

Pepper stopped smiling. 'I knew your mother had died, but
didn't know the details . . . When did she drown?' Pepper reached
into her tote and pulled out a leather journal filled with penciled-
in notes.

Even though Alex was seven when her mother died, the pain
still felt fresh, and she frowned at the memory. 'It would've been
twenty years ago. Early 2000s.'

Pepper cringed. 'I'm sorry. I know this is difficult . . .' She
paused. 'Just as I thought,' she said, flipping through the pages.

A Brew for Chaos   17

'The dates don't match. The Fisherman was active in the eighties – like forty years ago and for one chaotic summer.'

'Okay . . .' Alex said slowly. 'So, she just drowned. Like they said.' *Even though she was a strong swimmer. And a genetic mermaid.* Not that she could share that with Pepper. She had no idea Magicals existed and for the sake of their friendship, it had to stay that way.

Pepper reached across the table and rubbed her friend's hand.

Movement in her peripheral caused Alex to look over her shoulder. Montgomery Blue, the CEO of Leviathan Industries, a multinational company that worked in deep sea mining, defense and other areas. He stood at the counter waiting for his coffee. When he caught her glaring at him, he inclined his head in a gentlemanly nod.

Alex rolled her eyes, noting that per his usual, he was dressed elegantly in black leather loafers, gray wool slacks and a matching overcoat. With his dark eyes, olive complexion and thick dark hair full of gray streaks, he was a broodingly attractive man in his late fifties but made ugly by the fact that he was an immoral, cruel Magical.

Unlike most in their community who were descended from the Mer, he was descended from dragons, a legacy immortalized in the myth of the Wavel Dragon. The only tell-tale sign of a genetic marker that imparted certain abilities. Telepathy and compulsion, same as the Mer. But then they diverged with manipulation of fire and full-on mind control. But what really separated them from the Mer was their lack of morals. Compassion for others. They were cold-blooded, allowing their reptilian brain to completely drive their actions.

They had a willingness to do anything to anyone to get what they wanted.

Tall and strong-looking, Montgomery's wealth and ego wafted off him like the strong scent of an onion.

Pepper followed her gaze. 'Don't let him bother you.'

Alex suppressed a sharp retort. Pepper didn't know the truth about him. Didn't know about Magicals. Didn't know he was responsible for killing a friend of hers . . . 'It's hard. He's the reason Minka left the shop, and we're all worried about her working with him.'

'Minka's a big girl. She can take care of herself, right?' When Alex reluctantly nodded, Pepper continued. 'So, anyway, I'm going to look at the old case files. Review the suspect information and see what I can come up with.'

When Alex searched for Montgomery again, he was gone. Slithered out like the serpent he was. Slowly exhaling, she glanced at her journal with interest. 'Were there any legitimate suspects at the time?'

'A few, but nothing that really panned out. You know the owner of the Seaside B&B?'

'You mean grumpy old Mr MacInnes?'

'Yes, Carson MacInnes. The fuddy duddy sometimes known as Mac. Forty years ago he was in his early thirties and not so sweet. He lived on a houseboat in the bay. He did a stint in the Navy before that. Known to like his whiskey a bit too much.' She mimed drinking from a bottle. 'If you know what I mean.'

Alex recalled first meeting him when she'd looked into the death of a visiting artist, Neve, who'd stayed at Mac's B&B. And he was now also a customer. Which reminded her, she was due to drop by and refill his standing order of turmeric balm for body aches. 'He's such a nice man. I can't believe he had anything to do with hurting one woman, let alone ten.'

Pepper shrugged. 'Navy-issued shoe prints were found at several crime scenes.' She held up a sketch. 'Mac had the boots. And then there was Tobias Winston.'

Alex almost choked on her coffee. 'Aunt Lidia's attorney? That Tobias Winston?'

'Pretty silly, I know. But he did a stint in the Navy too, and apparently he dated one of the victims. He was cleared obviously.'

'Obviously. Any other suspects?'

'Yeah, and this one is a bit of a surprise.' Pepper laughed. 'It's my boss.'

TWO

Alex poured herself more coffee. 'Since you know him so well, does he give off serial killer vibes?'

Pepper hooted a laugh. 'Jonah? Not at all. But he *is* obsessed with the news, and knowing him, he probably mounted his own investigation and knew too much about the case for the authorities' liking. Hanging around crime scenes looking suspicious. I'm pretty sure I've done the same thing. In fact, I'm surprised your boyfriend hasn't considered me one of his suspects by now.'

Alex grimaced. 'God forbid someone else I care about be accused by Bellamy Bay's finest.'

Pepper mock gasped, bringing clasped hands to her chest in a dramatic swoon. 'You care about me?'

Laughing, Alex rolled her eyes. 'I suppose so.' She looked around the room, her gaze landing on a man in his late twenties.

He stood at the entrance, searching the tables.

Pepper waved at him, then gathered her things. 'And there's my next appointment.' She pointed to a wiry guy of medium height in jeans and a black Colonial Brewery & Tavern t-shirt. 'You know Zane Ballard?'

Alex shook her head.

'He's the guy who manages the tavern for Spencer. We're discussing logistics for the homebrew contest. He's a judge. See ya!'

Alex could admit to herself that she was nervous.

She was meeting her boyfriend's mother for the first time, and she wasn't sure how to fix her hair or what to wear. She'd finally decided on wearing her hair down, brushed until it shone like black silk, parted in the middle and hanging past her shoulder blades. It was early October and nights were getting chilly. So she'd decided on a sweater dress with a cowl neck in a pretty dark maroon and a large chocolatey brown belt cinched at the waist. Leather boots in the same shade of brown with a low heel completed the look.

She brought a gift bag filled with Jack's mother's favorite tea from the shop. Something pleasant to drink but not functional since Jack didn't want her giving his mother any of that so-called *witchcraft* her family sold.

When she first came to town, she didn't have a car because she'd lived in New York City since graduating from business school and what was the point? But six months later, after borrowing Minka's car and crashing it twice, she'd purchased in full a ten-year-old Audi Cabriolet, dark green – one of her favorite colors – with a tan leather interior.

As she drove away from the beach and towards the area of Bellamy Bay that was more farmland than coast, she marveled at the trees dripping with gold and orange and red leaves. Amazing that she could be this close to the beach and still see maple and oak leaves. When she passed a berry farm and a pumpkin patch, she slowed down to take in the glorious field of orange, filled with families plucking pumpkins from the soil.

She'd known where Jack lived but had never actually turned into the neighborhood, with its older ranch homes filled with retirees and young families. She pulled into the last house on the street, parking right beside Jack's truck, and walked up to his porch. It was full of burgundy and orange mums in navy-blue-colored planters, with several strategically placed pumpkins.

Had Jack decorated the house for his mother? Somehow she couldn't see him positioning pumpkins on the porch just so. He didn't seem the type. But now that their relationship had reached a new level, maybe she'd get to know more about her elusive boyfriend.

She knocked on the door. Moments later, a sweet-faced woman with her gray hair cut into a soft bob around a round face peered at Alex from behind the screen door. Her blue eyes were large and pale, her lashes long and white-blonde.

She smiled at Alex, who at once could see Jack in her features. The straight nose, the full pink lips. 'You must be Aleksandra. Please come in.'

'Thank you. I'm happy to be here.' She gave her the small

A Brew for Chaos

gift she carried, and the woman smiled when she saw the tufts of gold and burgundy tissue paper peeking out of the gift bag. 'How lovely. You shouldn't have.'

Alex wasn't sure what she expected, given the memory issues Jack said his mother was dealing with, but this woman seemed lucid and in control.

'I'm Maisie Frazier. Do come in.'

They sat in the living room, Maisie picking through the gift Alex had given her. Jack, his mother had explained, was taking a shower and would be down shortly.

'Jack says you like cookies, so I made shortbread, a family recipe. Would you like some?'

'Of course,' Alex said, then followed her into the kitchen to see if she could help. Alex stopped short when she entered the kitchen. It was covered in mermaid-themed décor. Whimsical mermaid paintings on the walls. There were coffee cups with mermaid fins for handles. A crochet mermaid mural hung on the wall. Hand towels with images of mermaids hung from the stove handle, and even a clock on the wall looked like a mermaid made of seashells. The décor was pretty but . . . surprising considering Jack's lack of interest in anything . . . whimsical. Okay, magical.

Maisie handed her a white dish covered in cutouts of pink mermaids, two pieces of shortbread set in the center. 'Would you like coffee? Or Earl Grey?'

Alex swallowed as she stared at the mermaid décor around her. 'Milk, actually. If you don't mind.'

'I love milk and cookies.' She pressed her hands together in a childlike manner before opening the refrigerator and showing Alex a bottle of organic milk from a local dairy. She poured the milk into a mermaid mug and handed it to Alex, who promptly dunked her cookie in the milk and ate it.

'These are delicious,' she said, smiling at the woman, who poured herself a cup of milk before joining her at the kitchen table, a small round affair covered in mermaid place mats.

They ate in silence, then Alex waved her hand around the room. 'Someone loves mermaids. I'm guessing it's not Jack,' she teased.

'Oh no,' she shook her head. 'Jack is not a fan. But I am. Most certainly.'

Alex nodded. 'I get it. Lots of people fall in love with mermaids when they move to the beach.'

'That's not it at all,' Maisie said, her face creasing in consternation. 'Yes, I enjoy living near the beach, but as you can see, I'm a good twenty minutes away from the coast even though I told Jack the sea air could be good for me.' She pursed her lips into a childlike pout. 'He doesn't think it's a good idea.'

Alex bit her bottom lip. 'Jack doesn't want you near the ocean? Why ever not? There are so many scientifically proven health benefits to living near and visiting the ocean. The salt air, the sound of the waves, the rhythmic motion of the water . . .'

'Don't I know it. I've given him all the reasons. Numerous times.' She waved her hand dismissively. 'He's just afraid I'll see another mermaid.'

THREE

Maisie's smile widened as she gazed around the room and took in all of the mermaid décor. 'That's why I have all of this. Because—'

'Mother,' Jack said, his voice heavy with warning. 'Are you boring Alex with your silly stories?'

Had Jack's mother just implied she'd seen a mermaid? Alex swiveled in her chair and saw Jack scowling at them both from the kitchen doorway. His lemony cologne filled the room as he stepped into the kitchen. 'When I told her you were coming, she insisted on baking.'

Alex's eyes widened. *Was he seriously going to ignore what his mother just said?*

'It was his father's favorite recipe,' Maisie shared with a grin. 'A random thing I can remember, but then again I do love to bake.' She shot Alex a conspiratorial look. 'Perhaps we can bake together sometime.'

'Definitely. And I hear Bellamy Bay has a bakeoff at Christmas time. You should enter your cookies,' Alex said, smiling at the woman before returning to Jack. His face was tight with worry. 'Come, let's return to the living room.'

After sitting together for a few moments, Alex thought Maisie seemed different with her son around. More tense. Alex wondered how much of her dementia was real and how much was . . . well, had Maisie really seen a mermaid?

Jack sat across from Alex on a couch and beside his mother. 'I'm glad you two are getting along well. Outside of the daycare facility she doesn't have many friends around here.' He stood and went to a window. 'She likes to work in the garden, right, Mother?'

She nodded.

'My Aunt Lidia has beautiful flower, vegetable and herb gardens in her backyard. Maybe I could bring her over for a visit sometime?' When Alex saw the doubtful expression on

24   Esme Addison

Jack's face, she sighed. 'Well, am I able to take her on a field
trip in town?'

He looked at her like the idea had never occurred to him. 'Like
where?'

Alex wanted to say to the bay so they could watch for
mermaids, but she knew that would only irk him. 'The aquarium.
The coffee shop. The history museum . . . There's plenty to show
her.' She turned to Maisie. 'Have you seen the sights since you've
been here?'

She shook her head, and Alex gave Jack a critical look. 'It
would do her good to get out, be around other people. I'll take
good care of her.'

'I know you will. Just don't talk to her about . . .' He looked
towards the kitchen. 'Mermaids. They stress her out.'

Alex bit her tongue. *No, mermaids seem to stress* you *out*, she
wanted to say. *They bring joy to your mother's life and light to
her eyes.* And how did he know that was precisely her next
question?

She regarded him, wondering how he'd react if she forced the
issue. Probably not good. And he'd definitely never invite her
back. No, she should bide her time and ask when the moment
seemed right.

'Sure,' she said. 'No mermaids.'

Alex looked around the house, noting for the first time there
were no family photographs anywhere. No little Jack in a Boy
Scout uniform – because surely Jack had been a Boy Scout. No
Jack at prom. No Jack anywhere.

'I thought I'd order a pizza from The Colonial Brewery &
Tavern? Half-veg, half-pepperoni okay for you?'

Alex nodded.

'And after my mother goes to bed – she's in pretty early – I
thought we could watch—' Jack's watch chimed with a brief
electronic sign, but he ignored it. Then his cell phone buzzed,
and he looked at the screen, swiping it a few times. Sighing, he
rose from the table. 'Believe it or not, I have to run out. And not
for pizza.'

His mother looked unbothered. 'Be careful, dear.'

But Alex went to him, trying to hide her disappointment. He
shoved the phone into his pocket. 'Everything okay?'

A Brew for Chaos

'Yeah.' He sighed. 'Just duty calling. This is just what I told you about. I'm on call and have to leave often at night. Usually, her caretaker stays in our guest room, and I can come and go as I need to. But until the service I use can send over someone suitable, I'm a bit stuck.'

She took his hands and wrapped them around her waist. Leaned in and kissed him on the cheek. Maybe some girlfriends would've considered this an inconvenience. But not Alex. She wanted to get to know her boyfriend better. She wanted to get to know his mother better. This seemed like the perfect opportunity for her to finally do both. She wanted him to know she was supportive of whatever he did, personally and professionally.

And just maybe she could find out what Jack was working on that was so top secret that even her cousin Kamila, a fellow policewoman, didn't know what it was.

She wasn't stupid. He was keeping something from her – she just wasn't sure what.

Alex smiled encouragingly. 'Go ahead. Your mother and I will . . .' She looked around the room, her gaze falling on a pack of cards. 'We'll play UNO and eat more shortbread.'

Jack gave her a peck on the cheek. 'I'll be back in a jiff.'

An hour had passed, with Alex and Maisie playing Uno. She set down a yellow card and waited for Maisie to cycle through her own cards. 'So, how are you enjoying your time in Bellamy Bay? Jack said you moved down here to be with a friend from college?'

She nodded. 'Yes, that's what he says.' She selected a yellow seven. 'Of course, with my memory issues I can no longer remember her. How's that for irony?'

Alex set down a green seven. 'Very sad. I'm sorry. You went to Bellamy Bay College then?'

She nodded. 'It was a long time ago. It's part of my memories that are all mixed up unfortunately.'

'What class were you in?'

Maisie shrugged. 'I can't remember.'

Wouldn't she have gone to college with Aunt Lidia? Alex wondered if her aunt would remember her, could help her recall some memories. They appeared to be around the same age. 'What year did you graduate?'

'I can't remember, dear.'

'What did you study?'

'I can't remember,' she said without remorse. Then smiled. 'Your turn.'

Alex frowned at her hand of cards. 'Are you seeing a doctor in town?' There were only a couple. Alex wondered if she could ask questions about her condition . . .

'No, my doctor is on the military base.'

'UNO,' Alex said automatically when she placed one card down. 'Were you in the military, Maisie?'

'Dear me, no. I'm a military dependent. Jack's in service. He didn't tell you?'

FOUR

Alex supposed Jack could be in the reserves – many in law enforcement were. He'd never mentioned it, but perhaps it had never come up. But then where were his service portraits? And what branch was he in? Was it something top secret? Is that why he was so hush hush about his background and his life?

'I'm going to lie down for a bit, dear. I'm afraid your visit has tired me out. You don't mind, do you?'

'Of course not,' Alex said, even though she wanted to ask her about her mermaid sighting despite Jack's warning. But if this visit went well, maybe he'd invite her back.

Maisie held out her arm. 'Would you help me up the stairs?'

Nodding, she walked Maisie to her room and watched as she lay on her bed, covering herself up with a soft fuzzy blanket covered in a mermaid print. Her room was likewise decorated. Alex softly closed the door, then stopped at another room furnished like a study with a desk, a large monitor and stacks of paper neatly set out. She stepped inside and touched the keyboard. The monitor woke up but was password protected. No photographs here either. Nothing personal. Nothing that told Alex one thing about who Jack really was.

She thought she heard the sound of an engine on the driveway. She rushed to the window, peeked out and saw Jack's truck idling down below. When he came in, he found her downstairs picking up the UNO cards.

He had a large greasy box of pizza in one hand. A sketch of a brick tavern decorated the top. A man in a soldier's outfit, holding a bayonet, slouched against a wall. 'Hungry?' He grinned.

'Famished,' Alex said, following him into the kitchen where he brought out plates and two frosty, amber-colored bottles.

'I hope my mother wasn't too much work?' He sat down across from her, sliding her a plate with a large cheesy slice covered in veg.

'She's a joy. I didn't even see signs of her dementia, just some general confusion about her time in college, the friend she came to see . . .'

Jack frowned. 'You were asking her questions about her past?'

Alex bit the inside of her cheek. 'Just trying to make conversation.'

'She had early onset dementia shortly after she graduated from college. It's rare, but it happens.'

'I'm so sorry, Jack. It must be so difficult for you to deal with this by yourself. Your father?'

'Left when I was a kid. I must've been three or four. No pictures of him. I can barely remember what he looks like. Honestly, I could walk past him on the street and have no idea who I was looking at. Just some tall guy, big shoulders, face like stone and cold blue eyes.'

She couldn't help but stare at him. Jack could've been describing himself, Alex realized even if he didn't.

'I guess her issues were too much for him. And after that, we moved in with my maternal grandparents and they took care of my mother and raised me until I graduated from high school. They both passed away when I was in college. I think I heard he may have died as well.'

Alex reached across the table and touched his hand. She almost sent him a wave of peace but knew it would be too much for him. She thought she might understand him just a bit more now. Why he was so prickly. Cold even. But it was just a façade. Underneath . . . he was sweet. Tender. A boy caring for his mother. Doing what he had to do.

She patted his hand reassuringly, her gaze dropping to his wrist. 'I meant to tell you, I like your new watch. Very fashionable. Is it an Apple?' She touched the band of the watch gently, but he moved his arm away, a look of irritation on his face.

'Don't do that.'

Alex sat up abruptly. 'Sorry, I—'

'No, it's me,' he said, embarrassment on his face. 'I'm just a little on edge right now.' He exhaled. 'Thanks. It's just one of those fancy fitness trackers.'

She stared at the watch, unable to read anything on its smoky black screen from her angle. Then looked at him. And sighed. Just when she thought they were making progress.

'Talking about my father upsets me. Please. Forgive me. Can we just eat?'

Pain pressed against Alex's chest. She liked Jack, and she wanted their relationship to work . . . But it was genuinely hard sometimes. On the other hand, he clearly didn't like talking about the father who'd abandoned him and his mother.

She nodded slowly. 'Okay, sure.'

FIVE

Next day at the shop, the front door jingled, and Pepper entered with Jonah trailing after her. He studied the items on the shelf as he made his way to the counter.

'I'm here for my hops,' he said loudly, then leaned over the counter, lowering his voice. 'And I'm also picking up the secret ingredient in one of my beer recipes. Lidia has been my source for years.'

Pepper beamed. 'I told Jonah he could trust you.' She gave him a long, admiring look. 'Right, Jonah?'

'That's correct. And once I reveal this to you,' he continued in somewhat dramatic fashion, 'you must promise not to tell a soul.'

Alex laughed at the theatrical way he spoke. But she wasn't sure he was kidding. 'Why so top secret?'

He rolled his eyes. 'Someone's in town who'd kill to have my award-winning beer recipe.'

Alex laughed. 'Really? Who?'

'Spencer Francis,' he spit out, then shook his head. 'She finagled her way onto the Oktoberfest planning committee just so she can get close to me.'

Alex cocked her head. 'Why would she do that?'

Jonah shrugged. 'I just wish she'd go back to partying and DJing in Dubai, or whatever she was doing before she inherited her family's business.' He sighed. 'Her manager, Zane, has been doing a perfectly good job running her businesses. She doesn't need to be here. And yet, for the last year, she's been asking me to sell her the recipe for my beer and I won't give it to her.'

Pepper scoffed. 'She's relentless. Or so I've heard.'

Alex raised an eyebrow. 'Are you concerned?'

'Nah, I can handle her. She's just persistent. It's more an annoyance than anything. She's offered me hundreds of thousands of dollars for the recipe. It's crazy.'

'How did she even discover you and your beer? No offense,' Alex added. 'Because you won a small-town beer contest?'

Jonah laughed. 'Word gets around, I guess.'

'But why would she do that?' Alex asked again, crossing her arms, and regarded the man with skepticism.

'I don't know.' He looked around the empty shop. 'But I know she'd do anything to find out my secret ingredient. Which brings me back to why I'm here. You promise not to tell anyone, right?'

Alex suppressed a laugh. 'Scout's honor.'

He planted both hands on the countertop and whispered, 'Seaweed.'

Alex looked surprised. 'Seaweed? Brewed into your beer? And that's what she's after?'

'Not exactly. She wants the precise recipe I use to make the beer.'

'Seaweed,' Alex repeated. 'That's certainly surprising.'

'Only to us Americans,' he assured her. 'In Scotland it's apparently a thing. There are a few brewers there working with sugar kelp and bladderwrack to create lager malts.'

'I think I've seen some in the back. Let me check on how much we have.' She began typing into their inventory dashboard. 'This is for the contest?' When he nodded, she said, 'I'm no expert, but I thought beer took time to create? Like age or whatever?'

'It can. But I can cold crash the beer before putting it into kegs and then use cylinders of CO_2 to carbonate it. I'll have finished bottles in a few days and well before our Oktoberfest.'

She looked up from the screen. 'We have fresh seaweed and dried. Do you have a preference?'

'I'll take one pound of both.'

'My aunt mentioned that she helped you with your brewing when you first came to town?'

His eyebrows dipped as he considered her. 'Before I was a journalist, I studied pharmaceutical science, so understanding how herbs combined together to make medicines intrigued me.'

'With that background, how did you become a reporter? If you don't mind me asking.'

He leaned against the counter, getting comfortable. 'I'd always enjoyed writing as a kid, but my father was a scientist and my

32 Esme Addison

mother a science teacher, so it was a family thing. And it was expected that I'd major in a science field in college, which I did. But by the time I graduated, I was burned out on the subject, and decided to go to journalism school so I could do what I really loved. Writing. And on the side? Craft brewing is a hobby that allows me to flex my alchemical muscles, shall we say.' He wiggled his fingers. 'But you don't want to hear about me, do you?' He laughed. 'I have many more interesting tales to share.'

'I wouldn't mind hearing more about the story you wrote on the serial killer years back. Don't you find it unnerving knowing he was never caught?'

'Well, I—' He shot her a rueful grin, then retrieved his cell phone from his pocket. 'Sorry, I have to take this.' He moved to the back of the shop for privacy, though Alex could still hear him.

'No, I won't do it. I won't be a party to your plans again.' There was silence while the caller spoke. And by the look on his face, Alex thought the response wasn't pleasant. Crossing her arms, she looked away and pretended not to listen.

'Yeah, well . . . you can try, but you can't make me.' He ended the call and shoved the phone into a pocket. He returned to the counter, face red and chest heaving.

'Everything okay?'

'It is now. Sometimes people find it hard to take no for an answer.' He forced a smile. 'That's when you have to stick to your guns and put your foot down . . .' A shadow crossed his face. 'No matter the consequences.' And then his face cleared. 'Sorry about that. Where were we?'

'Um . . . The Fisherman case?' Alex offered.

'Right. That. I wrote the most concise report to date. I did endless interviews, exhaustive research, talked to psychological profilers, all so I could figure out who this joker was.'

Alex stared at him, her fingers paused on his package. 'And did you?'

'There was somebody. He was perfect for the crime, but he had an alibi. Not the best one in my humble opinion, but good enough for the good town folk to get riled up . . .' He made a face as Alex rang up the purchase while Pepper roved around the shop picking up candles and sniffing their fragrance before

A Brew for Chaos

putting them down to test perfumes. 'I was sued for libel, but the case was resolved with a mediator and a pay-off.'

'Who did you think did it?'

'I can't even say the guy's name. Part of my settlement.' He lowered his voice. 'But he's an upstanding member of our community.'

'Carson MacInnes?' she guessed, recalling what Pepper had told her.

His eyebrows arched up. 'You didn't hear it from me.'

'And the local cops?' She thought of Jack. If he'd been the detective, there was no way he'd rest until the Fisherman had been caught.

Jonah chuckled, handing her payment. 'Those guys never had a chance of figuring out such a sophisticated crime. You know, I was going to name my beer the Fisherman's Brew, but then the serial killer happened and we – meaning the newspaper – decided to coin the killer with the same name.' His grin widened. 'I'm pretty good with names, right?'

'It was you? You coined him the Fisherman?' Alex counted out his change and handed it to him.

'Yeah. Some guy was abducting women, always by the beach. It just kind of fit.'

Alex frowned, slipping his receipt in his bag. 'Not disturbing at all.'

He nodded. 'Yeah. *The Fisherman.*' He flared his hands, staring into the distance. 'Looked great in the paper. Nice flashy title. Sold thousands of copies of the paper during his spree . . . Made all sorts of sales records.' He blinked, returning to the present. 'My brew has won the Oktoberfest award for best overall beer three years running. And it may win again.'

Alex opened her mouth to ask a question, but Jonah continued. 'I can't tell you how many people have asked for my secret recipe. Over my dead body, I say.' He laughed.

'But back to the Fisherman's case,' Pepper said, returning with several apple cider donut bath bombs with a pointed look at her boss.

Jonah smiled indulgently. 'We're writing the piece together, and if I get a Pulitzer, you'll get one too. That'll show your dad.'

Pepper's face was radiant. 'Jonah thinks the small-town police department's inexperience with serial killers and their delay in requesting assistance from the SBI and the FBI caused important clues to go missing – right, Jonah?'

Alex frowned slightly, never having seen her friend act quite so sycophantic before. Sure this guy was her boss, but he wasn't the god of journalism, was he? She bagged the bath bombs and rang up the purchase.

'I did more to put the case forward with my own research. Even though the detective in charge believed me, the chief and the other officers had a problem accepting my help; even went so far as to accuse me because I was being too helpful.'

Alex wondered what too helpful meant as she watched them leave the shop.

SIX

After work, Alex had one stop to make, to drop off Mac's monthly subscription of balm. Monthly auto-subscriptions had become big business for Botanika, with the majority of their orders being online and shipped out via the local post office. But since Mac was local, one of the Botanika staff dropped his order off on the way home. Like Alex was doing today – only she wanted to ask him a few questions since he'd been a suspect in the Fisherman case.

Carson MacInnes ran the Seaside Bed & Breakfast, a white Victorian house with a wide front porch. Alex walked down the brick path accented with antique lampposts, up the porch stairs and paused to admire the large brass pineapple decorating the door before entering. Homey scents of freshly baked cookies and coffee wafted on the air.

Mac stood when Alex entered and smiled. He'd been seated behind the counter, a large antique of wood and brass, reading the local paper. 'I was going to call your aunt tomorrow.'

'No need,' Alex said, handing him three tubes of *Get Up & Go!* balm for healthy joints. It was a cream made from high concentrations of turmeric, ginger and frankincense in a flax seed oil emulsion that helped with arthritis and other similar disorders. 'It's in our computers to make your delivery every thirty days.'

'Have some cookies?' he asked, pointing to a covered tray on a table down the hall.

'Maybe next time.' Alex patted her flat stomach. 'My aunt is baking, so I have to be careful.' She grinned. 'Lest I gain twenty pounds.'

He chuckled. 'Tell Lidia I said hello.'

'I will, if you'll answer a question or two for me?' She gave him a winning smile, which he returned with a suspicious glint.

'What is it?'

'The anniversary of the Fisherman's . . . activities are coming up and my friend Pepper is writing an article.'

'For the love of Pete,' he grumbled. 'You too?'

'Someone else has been by asking questions?'

'Sure. The editor of that paper. He came around a few days ago sniffing for information even though he knows better.'

'Jonah Fox.'

He jabbed a finger in the air. 'That's the one. Nosy feller. Had lots of questions.'

'What did you tell him?'

'I told him to get off my property before I got my shot gun and showed him what for,' he sputtered, his eyes flashing with anger. 'That's what. Twenty-five thousand dollars and an apology in the paper is what I got. But he was supposed to never ask me about that case again.'

'Why don't you calm down, Mac. It can't be good for your heart.'

His scowl relaxed, and he took a deep breath. 'I do have high blood pressure. But it just gets my goat. That case. The detective questioning me.' His features took a mournful turn. 'Jonah writing about me in the paper. My reputation was ruined during those days.' He waved an arm around the foyer. 'I went from military hero to murder suspect all in one fell swoop.'

'I'm sorry, Mac. I didn't mean to bring up old memories.'

His jaw hardened. 'We lost months of bookings here.' His eyes scanned the lobby. 'When it turned out he couldn't afford to pay us . . . We lost money due to him smearing my good name. I don't think my mother ever got over the scandal . . .' But then he looked at her kindly. 'It's not your fault. It's that editor. All his doing.'

'What exactly did he do?'

'As I recall back then, I was the number one suspect on his list – *his* list, like he was a cop or something. And all because I was in the Navy and still had my Navy boots with me. Ridiculous, like I was going to throw a perfectly good pair of boots out because I was no longer serving. But that Jonah? He thought it meant something, and he tried to convince the cops back then that I was their guy. He was convinced the killer wore a size-twelve boot. How many men wear a size-twelve boot? Like I was the only one in town that—'

The door jangled open, and an elderly gentleman in expensive

A Brew for Chaos 37

golfing clothes stepped inside. About the same height as Mac, he had proud, hawk-like features now covered in sagging sun-spotted skin. His face was lined with wrinkles and the area under his eyes were puffy with folds of skin. Alex would guess he was in his seventies – maybe eighties.

'I'm checking in,' he said, voice firm and authoritative but raspy with age. 'McDonald. Reservation for two.'

Mac rounded the counter. 'Of course, sir.' He took a harried breath, his voice shaky. 'Can I get your bags?'

'No,' he said, a practiced eye scanning the room. 'My grandson, Leith is bringing them in.'

Mac stood taller, his gaze following the man's scrutiny as he took in the antiques, floral wallpaper and vintage carpeting. He puffed out his chest. 'Is everything to your liking, sir?'

He glanced at the photographs on the wall behind the counter. A series of black and white photographs showed the original owner, a woman in her sixties, working on the property, and some with guests. 'Haven't done much to the place, have you?'

'Sir?' Mac's voice faltered. He frowned, looking around the space. 'It's supposed to be vintage, hearkening back to a nostalgic past in which—'

'Yes, I get it,' he said gruffly. 'But you could at least have upgraded the carpet.'

Alex turned to the man. 'You've been here before?'

He scowled at her, noticing her for the first time. 'No. I have not.'

But it seemed to Alex like he had. How else could he know that everything was original to the owner, Mac's mother, who'd left him the house when she passed?

His scowl deepened. 'Everything just looks . . . old.'

Alex looked around, surprised at his evaluation of the foyer. 'I love how it looks. Retro is in now.'

Just then the door swung open and a young man in his late twenties stepped inside. He had a suitcase in each hand and a pair of golf clubs on his shoulder. He was handsome with short reddish-blonde hair styled in a preppy cut with a precise side part, a rugged freckled face, and a brawny body like he played football in college. His bright blue gaze found Mac. 'I booked

38 Esme Addison

a two-week stay for myself and my grandfather? A suite with two bedrooms and a bathroom?'

Mac's gaze lingered on the knife-sharp crease of his slacks and the shininess of his shoes and nodded. 'Yes. Let's get you two checked in right away. You must be tired after your drive from . . . where did you say you're from?'

The older man frowned. 'I didn't. But we've driven up from Georgia.'

There was an awkward silence, and Alex thought to fill it with small talk. 'So, what do you both do in Georgia?'

The older man sighed, but his traveling partner took the opening. 'Granddad's retired, and I took over the family business.'

Alex shot him a look of gratitude. While Mac was still busy searching for their registration on his screen, Alex watched the two. The older man seemed grumpy with no patience for small talk, while his grandson was more relaxed, with a grin on his face and an interested eye on Alex.

She smiled back politely. 'You don't sound like you're from Georgia.'

The older man's cold glare landed on her. 'That's because we're not from there.'

'I've found your registration,' Mac interrupted. 'Two adults under the name Forbes McDonald.' He looked up with a grin. 'What clan are yee from?' he said with a thick Scottish brogue.

Forbes didn't smile, but his grandson laughed.

Mac chuckled back awkwardly. 'Just making a wee joke,' he said, still with the brogue. 'North Carolina had a large contingent of Scottish settlers beginning in the 1700s. Us MacInnesses were Highlanders, settling in the Cross Creek region. Now called Fayetteville? Where Ft Bragg is—'

'I know it,' Forbes spits out.

'I bet you do,' Mac said, a knowing look on his face. 'You served, did you not? It's all over you, sir. What branch if you don't mind me asking?'

Forbes bore hard blue eyes into Mac. 'Do you need this information to register me for your establishment?'

'No, sir. Of course not. I was just . . . I mean, I served, and I thought, well, it's always nice to—'

'Granddad isn't much for history,' Leith jumped in, and Alex

A Brew for Chaos

was grateful for his interruption. It was painful watching the interaction.

'Right, Gramps?'

'On the contrary, I don't mind history at all. I just don't suffer fools gladly.'

His grandson slapped his forehead in embarrassment. 'Granddad . . .'

Alex covered her mouth in surprise, her gaze sliding to the B&B owner.

'Now look here,' Mac began. 'I'm just trying to make pleasant small talk is all.'

Forbes gave his grandson a stiff smile, then turned to Mac. 'Our key.'

Mac plastered a smile on his face and handed the man his key, a real key made of metal – heavy, vintage and beautiful in its artistry.

Forbes looked at the key. 'Are you serious?' he grumbled. 'No key card? What is this, the 1940s?'

'It's quaint,' Leith said, taking the key from him. 'Forgive him. He's just turned seventy-two and is as ornery as a hornet. At this age it's like he has no filter.'

Mac relaxed a bit. 'Hopefully a few rounds of golf will lift his spirits.' He pointed to the bag of clubs with their luggage. 'Is that why you're here? A golf vacation?'

The grandson's smile thinned just a bit. 'You're nosy, aren't you?'

Alex felt the need to step in then. 'It's a southern thing. I'm new here and I noticed it when I first arrived. The locals are very friendly. If you're not used to it, it can feel intrusive. Overly familiar.'

'Like you're being right now?' Forbes observed, giving her a scathing once-over.

Alex stiffened, ready to say something much less polite when Mac laughed. A fake laugh, Alex could tell, but a laugh none-theless. 'The guest is always right at the Seaside Bed & Breakfast,' he said in a singsong way. 'If I'm being nosy, I apologize,' he said quite magnanimously. 'It's only so I can get to know you better and provide a better stay for you, customized to your interests.'

'I'll try and remember that,' Forbes said with a tad less rancor, then went to stand in front of the elevator a few yards away. He turned and looked at his grandson. 'Leith,' he barked out.

He shot Alex an apologetic grin. 'I better go.'

Mac frowned at the man's back as he faced the elevator. 'That's the type of customer who makes me want to sell this house and sail to the Caribbean.'

Leith smiled. 'Don't do that. The Seaside is really quite lovely. And my grandfather appreciates the ocean view.'

'I better go too,' Alex said. 'I'll see you around, Mac.'

Back in her car, Alex took a few breaths. The moment had already been contentious with Mac getting so upset about her questions on Jonah. But the arrival of the guest, that man Forbes, had really ratcheted up the tension. What an unpleasant man. And his poor grandson had to manage him.

SEVEN

Minka slammed down the phone and huffed in exasperation just as Alex was about to knock on her open office door a couple of days later.

She winced. 'Bad timing?'

Surprise lit up Minka's heart-shaped face and she waved her in. 'Not at all.'

At twenty-five years, Minka Sobieski was Aunt Lidia's youngest daughter and one of two cousins Alex had spent time with when she'd enjoyed summers in Bellamy Bay as a child.

Alex gestured towards the phone. 'You sure?'

Minka laughed. 'I was just trying to get information from the public affairs officer at Camp Malveaux, the US Marine Corps base about thirty minutes northeast of here.'

Alex nodded. 'I've heard of it.'

'Yes, well, the Marine that answered my phone call was polite but not very helpful. But enough of that. I'm so glad you're here.' Minka stood and closed the office door behind her. 'You're the first family member to come visit me at my new job.'

'I want to support you, no matter what. You know that.' She pointed at the sign on the door that read *Minka Sobieski, Director of Special Projects, Brave New World.*

Minka returned to her desk, looking uncharacteristically professional in a cotton-candy-pink pants suit and a frilly Edwardian-style white blouse. Her shoulder-length mane of brown curls was pulled off her face with a wide band of lace, which only accented her big blue eyes and baby-faced cuteness.

'Director . . . really?' Alex asked, lips in an impressed moue.

Minka was nonchalant. 'Sure. Why not?' Then she burst into giggles. 'It's amazing, I know. But it's not like I'm not *not* qualified. I've run operations and all marketing communications for the family shop since I completed graduate school. That's two years of operational experience.'

Alex couldn't hide the look of pride on her face. 'Though I'm

42   Esme Addison

unhappy you left the shop, and very concerned with you working
for Montgomery . . . I'm proud of you.'

Minka rushed to her cousin and pulled her into a tight hug.
'Thank you. That means everything to me.' She buried her face
in Alex's hair, her voice muffled. 'I know Mom and Kamila are
mad at me for leaving to go work for Montgomery's environmental non-profit, but I just . . .' She pulled back from Alex. 'I
just feel like my talents were being wasted at the shop.'

Alex's eyes widened. 'You can't mean that. You've helped so
many people . . . Well, what about me? I left my job in Manhattan
and now I'm making soaps. Happily.'

'I don't mean it like that. You've lived in New York City, you
were a risk analyst for a major company for crying out loud.
That sounds so important.'

Alex shook her head. 'I was good at my job, but I wasn't
happy.'

'Even so. I've been in Bellamy Bay all my life. I started
working at the shop when I was twelve. And before that I was
always in the shop anyway. I need a change. And I need a break
from Mom . . . She was not understanding at all when I told her
about this job.'

'That's because Brave New World is a division of Leviathan
Industries. And Leviathan is Montgomery's company.'

'Montgomery has been nothing but wonderful to me. He promised me I could travel with this position and do important work
for the environment.' Minka fiddled with a paperweight in the
shape of two dolphins curving to form a heart.

'Montgomery is being very accommodating. You know he has
offices at the Wesley building, but I didn't want to work in
Bellamy Bay's only glass high-rise building, so he found this
space in the aquarium for me. It's pretty, right? Open floor plan.
Close to the beach, the turtle hospital and hello.' She giggled.
'I'm literally swimming with the fishes.'

Alex looked around the office. 'Is it always this quiet?'

Minka followed her cousin's gaze as she looked around the
space. 'It's not normally this quiet, but with it being after hours
. . . I'm the only one here. Except for the security guard at the
front door.' She pursed her lips. 'And then there's the team of
guards for the basement.' She laughed. 'It's like Fort Knox

A Brew for Chaos

down there because of the chemicals they store for cleaning the facility.'

Alex settled into a leather chair, noting the framed photographs of sea creatures on the walls. Her eyes went to a vase of fresh sunflowers. 'Those are pretty.'

'I wondered if you noticed.' Minka giggled. 'They're from a guy.'

'Really?' Alex rose from her seat and searched for a card in the bouquet, but it had been removed. 'Do I know him?'

'Mum's the word for now. I've had so many false alarms I want to make sure this is real, but I will say he's very cute, smart and sincere. I talked his ear off about my dolphins, and he seemed genuinely interested.'

'What's his name?'

Minka shook her head, but her face lit up. 'If it gets serious, I'll let you know.' She glanced at the water level in the vase, which was low. She leaned over the flowers, murmuring to them. 'I need to top you up, don't I?' She held out her palm and wiggled her fingers in a cupping motion until a ball of water formed by the moisture in the air swirled before her. Then she floated her hand over the flowers and allowed the water to rain from her palms. A grin spread across her face. 'Much better.'

Alex watched the flowers as the petals perked up. Sometimes she forgot about her powers, like the ability to command moisture wherever it was found. She would've just taken the flowers to the faucet and added water.

'So, how's the move to corporate America? It's a big change from slinging herbs,' Alex joked.

'I'm happy.' Minka sank into her chair. 'Did you hire a part-timer yet?'

'Tanner's coming in a few hours a week after school.'

Her eyes widened. 'That poor kid . . . Maybe work plus school will keep his mind off what happened to his parents.'

'That's my hope as well. Still miss you being there though.'

'I miss being there too. But honestly, I don't miss being around Mom all the time. Now that I'm away, I realize how overbearing and domineering she can be.'

Alex frowned. 'Aunt Lidia loves you. This doesn't sound like you talking.'

'It's me . . . I just, I was talking to Montgomery about my life and he mentioned how influential she's been on me. He's really interested in me and our family and the shop, and—'

'You shouldn't tell Montgomery anything about us, Minka. Why do you trust him? You know his history.'

'He's been nothing but good to me. In fact, he's paying me so much that I can buy my own place if I want to. He suggested I consider it.'

'Why would he— But I just got here,' Alex pointed out. 'I've enjoyed being at the house with you and Aunt Lidia.'

Minka shrugged. 'Maybe we could get a place together. Or maybe I'll move in with Celeste. She's family, and she's got room and mentioned wanting a roommate.'

'You don't see that he's trying to separate you from your family?'

'He's not.' Her eyes widened. 'He's said multiple times that he has great respect for Mom. You too.'

'Me? Don't tell him anything about me, Minka. Or the rest of the family. You need to be careful. Maybe he's using his charm on you. Making you think things. Manipulating you.'

Minka bit her lip, the soft lines of her face sharpening into angry planes. 'You think I'm weak too. That's what he said, that you guys loved me but thought less of me. That I was the weakest link in the family. But he saw me differently. That with him I could grow strong and then you'd see me for who I truly was.'

Montgomery was a snake. That's all there was to it. First luring Minka away from the family business, poisoning her mind against the family and now she wanted to move . . . Maybe Minka was grown and it was time for her to get a career and her own place, but she couldn't help but think this was part of Montgomery's master plan. He had something in store for Bellamy Bay, and specifically her family. She just wasn't sure what . . . yet.

'Aren't you happy for me?'

'Of course I am.' Alex forced a smile, though her heart raced and anxiety swelled in her chest. She had to protect her youngest cousin, the baby in the family, from that monster. She just wasn't sure how to do it. Or what she was protecting her from exactly beyond his venomous influence.

A Brew for Chaos

'Anyway, I just wanted someone in the family to see what I was doing. Where I worked and the difference I'm making.' Minka's lips tugged downward. 'I have my own mind, you know.'

'I know,' Alex rushed. 'I just want you to be safe. How is it working for Montgomery?'

'It's really nice. We've only bumped heads on one issue. Other than that he's been truly supportive.'

'What's the issue?'

'It's the dolphins. Something's wrong with them.'

Alex twisted her lips in an attempt to not make a joke when she saw how serious Minka looked.

'Right now, I'm compiling data on the dolphins in the area. The estimated number in the bay. How many have been beached or injured . . . That number is really low fortunately. The aquarium has most in the bay tagged with GPS, so I can follow them. It's really cool work. I have this app, so I can track their movements on my phone.

'But I've discovered that the dolphin population in Bellamy Bay has suffered because of the nearby military base.' Her voice rose an octave. 'Who knows what they're dumping in our oceans, but it's clear from the data that our population has been impacted. They're behaving erratically. And when I told Montgomery about my concerns, he just dismissed them.'

'Start a petition or a letter-writing campaign,' Alex suggested.

'It won't help – at least, not fast enough.' She abruptly stood, pushing her chair back. 'The dolphins need our assistance now. Something is wrong with them.' She moved away from her desk, nervous energy wafting off her body in waves. She went to a large window that gave her a view of a pool for dolphin performances in the summer. And gazed at it. 'Their communication has stopped, and their swim patterns are off. Their trackers glitch and stop working and then we lose them for a time.'

'Calm down,' Alex began, rising from her own seat to join her.

'I can't hear them anymore,' Minka said, her voice trembling with emotion.

'You can't—' Alex stopped and stared at her. 'What do you mean you can't . . . *hear* them?'

She turned to her cousin, whose eyes were moist with tears.

'It's not a big deal . . . I can talk to animals. Obviously, sea creatures are the easiest.'

Alex's eyes widened. 'Wow . . . when were you going to share that with me?'

Minka sniffled, then wiped her eyes. 'You've learned a lot since you've come to live with us. I didn't want to overwhelm you.'

Alex couldn't find fault with that logic. She was still coming to terms with her new reality. But still . . . 'How do they communicate with you?'

'Same as us, through telepathy.'

'And what have they told you?' Alex tried not to focus on how weird that sounded and listened.

'That's it. That's the problem. They're not speaking to me. I used to hear them every time I went to the beach. Or at the aquarium when I go to work. I could hear their chatter. They're very high vibration. Always happy. Very free with their knowledge.'

Alex rubbed her temples. 'But what can dolphins possibly have to tell you?'

She shrugged, dipped her chin in embarrassment. 'Just silly stuff. Nothing important . . .'

Alex stared at her cousin, not sure if she could believe this latest revelation. Sure she was descended from a mermaid, but Minka could talk to animals like Dr Dolittle?

Minka sighed. 'Okay. I'll tell you, but you're going to think I've lost it. The dolphins would talk to me about their day, like where they were swimming, the foods they ate, cool things they saw in the water or on the ocean floor. Like stuff you'd expect from a dolphin.'

Alex burst into laughter. 'Are you serious?'

'Like I said, nothing important. But then it changed to them being upset and scared and worried – about what, I'm still not sure. They never said exactly. And then they were saying they weren't safe and could I help them?'

Her eyes flashed anxiously. 'So, something must've happened because now, I can't hear them. They've just gone silent. Like something's wrong.' She stared at the empty pool. 'And part of my work is to track their movements – many of the area's dolphins are

A Brew for Chaos 47

geotagged and we have years of historical data that show us where they travel, when and why. But in the last three months . . .' Minka's face flushed with color. 'Everything has gone all . . . haywire. It's not just that I can't communicate with them anymore, but they're constantly disappearing on my screen.'

Minka pointed to her landline. 'I've been on the phone with the military. I'm trying to get their accountability records for several projects they're collaborating on with Leviathan, and they're not being forthcoming. Like no transparency whatsoever, and that's literally part of my job. To track that.' A frown crossed her face. 'But Montgomery told me not to force the issue with the military, which makes me feel like they're hiding something.'

'Sounds like a delicate situation,' Alex finally said.

'It really is. But I'm going to try and do what Montgomery asks. Unless it's really clear the military is doing something . . . evil. Right now I just have a general dislike for their environmental practices, at least historically. But if I find something specific, something irrefutable, all bets are off and I'm going scorched earth on them. The news. Social media. The mayor. Our representatives and senators, the governor . . .' She laughed. 'I'm a force to be reckoned with.'

Alex grinned, happy to see her cousin so empowered. 'I see that. And I love it, I really do.'

Minka's smile lifted her rounded cheeks. 'Finally, somebody in my family gets it.'

As Alex left the aquarium parking lot, her phone rang. It was Pepper asking her to stop by the brewery and tavern to give her opinion on the Oktoberfest menu. Since it was on her way home, Alex reluctantly agreed.

She followed her GPS to the correct address, parked and entered the large brick building that looked like a colonial estate with black shutters and trim accented by black wrought iron and brass. The smell of roasted tomatoes, yeast and buttery garlic filled the air. The walls were brick, and the floors polished dark wood. The room was filled with long picnic-style tables paired with cushioned benches for family-style eating.

Pepper was watching TV with a few other customers, arms

48 Esme Addison

crossed at her chest and a look of skepticism on her face. She turned and waved when she saw Alex. 'You made it. Come on over.'

Alex passed several tables of customers enjoying pitchers of beers and large pizzas. Staff in black t-shirts and jeans moved around the space.

Pepper turned away from one of the widescreen televisions. 'Save me from this weird documentary about jellyfish that age in reverse.'

Alex glanced at the TV. 'The immortal jellyfish.'

Pepper made a face. 'How could you possibly know that?'

Alex laughed. 'Marine biology, freshman year of college.' She turned to look at a table covered in platters of German fare. 'Wow, that's a lot of food.'

'That's why I called you. Spencer was supposed to join us, but she was called away to deal with some inventory issue, so now it's just me and Jonah.' She waved a hand around the spread of food. 'We're to try everything out and decide what to put on the menu, but it's too much for me.' She pointed to Jonah, who was on the phone against a back wall in an animated conversation. 'Especially when he's too busy to help me.'

Alex looked around the room. 'I've never been here before.' She glanced up at the wooden beams that crisscrossed the ceiling. 'How old is this building?'

'One of the oldest in Bellamy Bay.' The tavern manager appeared at their table with a grin. 'Here since the colonial era and where your' – he glanced at Pepper – 'ancestor Captain Bellamy created the charter for the new town.'

Pepper grinned. 'That's right.' She turned to Alex. 'This is Zane, the guy I was telling you about. He keeps the beer flowing and the food delivered.'

Alex smiled at him, observing his thick, dark eyebrows over gray eyes and a bit of beard stubble on his cheeks and pointy chin. 'Nice to meet you. I've heard a lot about this place. I'm sure Spencer is grateful to have you.'

He chuckled. 'She's an entertaining boss.' He pushed black-rimmed glasses up the bridge of his thin nose. 'I've basically had carte blanche running the place. But with her back, it's . . . different.' His tone was wry. 'She's got lots of ideas.'

A Brew for Chaos   49

Alex couldn't tell by his tone if that was a good or bad thing. She turned her focus to the food. 'So, where do I begin?'

He considered the selection. 'Our pretzels are kind of amazing. The salt is from our very own Bellamy Bay and the butter is from a local farm.'

'Thanks.' Alex's hand hovered over the tray of pretzels. 'Don't mind if I do.'

He nodded. 'Let me know if you ladies need anything. And Alex, tell Minka I said hello.'

A smile crept across Alex's face, and she wondered if he'd sent the flowers to her cousin. 'Sure thing.' He moved to greet another table of customers, and Alex picked up a large, yeasty soft pretzel glossy with butter and flecked with glimmering sea salt. She took a bite, moaning her agreement. 'Obviously, the pretzel must be on the list.'

Pepper laughed. 'Obviously.' She dipped one in the accompanying mini-tub of spicy mustard and took a bite. 'So good.' She took another bite, this time dipping it in a small tub of beer cheese and then added the item to her list.

Potato cakes with sour cream or apple sauce. German brats and kraut. Breaded chicken with red cabbage and roasted potatoes. By the time Alex had tried everything, she thought she might explode – in the best possible way.

'This food is delicious,' Alex said, eyes on Jonah. 'Now, I could use a nap.'

Pepper laughed. 'My favorite is the schnitzel by far.' Her eyes followed Alex's point of interest. Jonah. 'Our menu is going to be amazing.' She waved at a waitress, who came over and began clearing dishes while another server brought out a tray of desserts.

Alex groaned. 'Seriously? I can't eat any more.'

'Take small bites,' Pepper joked, then frowned as they watched Jonah angrily stuff his phone into his pocket. 'I wonder what's going on with him. He's literally been arguing with someone for the past hour.'

He joined the table, tight smile on his face. 'Sorry about that. Putting out fires.'

'If it's not one thing, it's another,' Pepper commiserated. She looked at Jonah. 'Any news on the break-in at your house?'

'No. But fortunately, they didn't get inside.'

50 Esme Addison

'Well, you're back now and you can try the desserts. We're picking three.' Pepper picked up each card and read the German name with perfect pronunciation.

Alex looked impressed.

'I took German in high school,' Pepper said before continuing.

They tried moist German chocolate cupcakes. A cherry parfait called Kirschmichel with flaky buttery crust and tart filling. Bavarian apple fritters or Apfelkrapfen with warm spicy-sweet apples that melted in the mouth. Apfelstrudel or apple strudel frosted with a delicate vanilla topping and a red berry pudding called Rote Grütze that was full of tangy-sweet flavor.

'Only three?' Jonah complained.

'The planning committee has a budget,' Pepper reminded him with a smile. 'Which are your favorites? We need to have a consensus.'

Jonah tried each dessert again. 'I'm voting for the berry pudding, the cherry parfait and the apple strudel.'

Pepper turned to Alex. 'Your turn.'

'This is really, really hard, but I'm going to have to pick—'

A device chimed, and Jonah glanced at his phone and read a new text message, his good-natured face creasing. He took a step backwards. 'My God . . .' he muttered to himself, almost as if he was in disbelief. 'It can't be.'

Pepper reached for his arm. 'What's wrong?'

He wrenched his arm free of her grasp, shaking his head and muttering to himself. 'I have to go. There's some business I need to attend to . . . How in the world . . .' He trotted to the door, then took off running towards his car. He didn't look both ways as he crossed the parking lot, and one oncoming car skidded to a stop to avoid hitting him. Horns sounded, but he ignored them. With single purpose, he jumped into his car, movements hurried and jerky.

Pepper pressed her face against the plate glass of the front door. 'What's happening?' She whipped around to look at Alex. 'It can't be breaking news or he would've told me. He would've assigned me to the story, right? I mean, I'm his star reporter.'

Alex came up behind Pepper, looping an arm around her shoulder. 'Maybe it's a family emergency?'

They both watched as he sped off down the street.

'He doesn't have any family,' Pepper said almost to herself. 'He always said I was the daughter he never had.'

EIGHT

'She seems happy,' Alex said, after she shared her concerns about Minka working with Montgomery. She was standing side by side at the kitchen sink with her aunt, washing dishes. 'I'll admit, my ears began to bleed just a bit with all her talk of saving the dolphins.' Alex laughed. 'I felt like she was really trying to impress me with her desire to make a difference . . . At the end of the day, I think she just wants our support.'

'She already had that,' Lidia said, her anger rolling off her in waves and causing the cups and dishes in the nearby cabinets to rattle. 'But I can't support anything that man does,' Lidia huffed, putting away the last of the dinner dishes before turning to the coffee. 'He better not hurt my baby girl,' she added, her voice growing hard.

The water in the faucet suddenly sputtered out in a violent spray of hot water. Lidia took a deep breath. 'Sorry. I'm trying to control my anger. But Montgomery Blue gives me the creeps. Me! And I'm practically fearless.'

Alex gazed at her aunt, pride shining in her eyes. 'Yes, you are.' But she noticed her aunt's hands trembled with anger.

'You want some coffee with your pie?'

After taste-testing the food for Oktoberfest, Alex really didn't want pie. But her aunt was in a mood, so . . . 'Yes, please.'

Lidia set out plates and cups. 'Did Kamila say she was stopping by after her shift?'

'Yes, ma'am.' Alex settled into her seat and began slicing thick portions of sweet potato pie onto three saucers. 'You know, sweet potatoes are really growing on me,' she said to her aunt, but Lidia was still distracted.

Athena barked a moment before Kamila entered the front door with her key. 'Sorry I'm late, guys. There was an incident on the beach.'

Lidia and Alex exchanged glances. 'What kind of incident?'

A Brew for Chaos

Kamila washed her hands and slid into the seat with the largest piece of pie. 'Craziest thing. A woman was attacked and left for dead.' Her gaze circled the kitchen. 'No whipped cream, Mom?' Lidia popped up. 'I knew I was forgetting something.' She found a silver tray of freshly made whipped cream in the refrigerator and set it on the table.

'Thanks,' Kamila said as she ladled a whopping spoonful of cream onto her wedge of pie. 'She'll live. But she's at the hospital, apparently with no memory of what happened.'

'Do we know who she is?' Alex asked.

'Nope. She had no ID on her. And to thicken the plot, there was a body lying beside her.'

'A body? Someone died?' Alex said, frowning. 'Why didn't you lead with that? Man? Woman?'

'Man,' Kamila responded.

'And this man, do you know who he is?' Lidia asked. 'Out of towner? Local?'

'Oh yeah, easy to ID him. Everybody knows him in town. Jonah Fox? He runs the newspaper.' She tilted her head. 'I mean . . . *ran* the newspaper.'

NINE

Thirty minutes later, Kamila patted her six-pack. 'I hate to eat and run, but . . .' She took a final bite of her second slice of pie and stood. 'Jack wants me at the hospital to talk to the Jane Doe.'

Alex almost dropped her fork. 'Jack is there? I'll come.'

Kamila stopped at the front door. 'It's not a party, Alex. This is police business.'

Alex's phone chimed with a text. It was Pepper. Beside herself.

Lidia leaned forward. 'More bad news?'

'Pepper's driving to the hospital right now. She wondered if I could meet her there.' She gave her cousin a look. 'Come on. I'll be there for Pepper. Jonah was her boss, and I'm guessing she's taking this hard.'

'Didn't you promise Jack you'd stay out of his police business. Or else?'

Alex rolled her eyes. Unfortunately, it was true. Jack had given her an ultimatum about their relationship. Either she stopped interfering in his investigations or he'd break up with her. It was, he assured her, meant with her concern in mind, but it still annoyed her.

She nodded. 'Yes, I did promise Jack that and I mean it. I'm just coming along for . . . moral support. Pepper needs me. I'll stay out of your way, promise.'

Kamila rolled her eyes. 'Let's go.'

Pepper was pacing the halls outside of the female victim's room when Alex and Kamila arrived.

Alex gave Pepper a hug. 'You okay?'

'No.' She wailed, skin splotchy, and her eyes wet with tears. 'Jonah was my mentor. I was his Cubby.'

Kamila made an exasperated noise.

Alex shot her cousin a *be-nice* look, so Kamila, choosing *not* to be nice, stepped away and began scrolling her work phone.

A Brew for Chaos 55

'Not to take away from anything Jonah did for you, but your father owns the paper.'

'But that's it exactly. My father didn't want me to be a reporter. He didn't support my journalism degree and hoped it was just a phase. Jonah took a chance on me. He let me intern at the paper against my father's wishes. Nurtured my talent. Believed in me. Taught me what it was to be a real journalist. Gave me real world experience and went toe to toe with my father when he told him to fire me.'

'Oh,' Alex said, wondering what she could do or say to comfort her.

Kamila scoffed. 'She's a spoiled little rich girl with a family who owns most of the town. She's pretending to be a victim so you'll like her more.'

Pepper squeaked in protest. 'How dare you?'

'You're lucky Alex is nicer than me. I haven't forgotten how you had it out for our family. Digging for dirt on our history, hoping to write a tell-all in your paper.'

'Th-That's in the past,' Pepper stammered. 'I like Alex. And Minka . . .'

'Sure,' Kamila said with sarcasm.

Pepper exhaled loudly. 'Okay. I don't have to be nice either.' She looked through the window again at the woman. 'Well, did she do it?' She turned to Kamila. 'Don't just stand there looking at me with your cop face, find out what happened.' She pressed her face against the window glass and stared at the young woman. 'She was with him when he died. How is *she* not the murderer?'

'We're still investigating obviously, but as you can see, she's also an actual victim and there was no weapon found on her person. She had opportunity, yes. But no means. And no motive that we can discern.'

Means. Motive, Alex repeated in her mind . . . But no. She'd made a promise to Jack. She wouldn't get involved. Not if she cared about him and their relationship.

'I don't know . . . That blank look on her face. You're buying it?'

Kamila huffed in disbelief. 'She's got amnesia. She can't walk. She was left for dead . . .'

But Pepper shook her head, moved away from the door glaring

at Kamila. 'Why don't you go in there, talk to her and find out what her motive was.'

Kamila barked a laugh, then brushed past Pepper with her shoulder. Hard. And went into the room.

Pepper stumbled but caught herself, and Alex shot her a look. 'Easy, Pepper. Kamila is not the enemy here.'

And just that fast, Pepper's anger dissolved into tears. She wiped a cheek. 'I know. I'm sorry.' She rested her hands on her head. 'I'm just . . . on edge. Jonah was the only person in this town that really championed me.' Her hands fell, her shoulders slumped. 'But she's right, you know? Nobody likes me here. Besides you, Jonah was my only friend – and he was my boss. On my father's payroll. For all I know my father paid him to be nice to me.'

Alex wrapped an arm around Pepper's shoulders and gave her a reassuring squeeze. 'I know it doesn't seem like it now. But everything will be okay.'

'I just want to know what's going on and no one will tell me anything,' she said, her voice taking on a whining tone. 'Jack just left. He practically ignored me.'

'Go get yourself some coffee or something and I'll see what I can find out from Kamila and the doctor.'

Alex watched her friend walk down the hallway and pause at the elevator. Pepper jammed the button several times before grumbling in frustration and taking the fire escape.

Then the doctor exited the room. In his thirties, he was a light-skinned Black man, tall with a square jaw accented with a mustache that extended into a neat trim goatee, intelligent brown eyes and a shaved head. 'The officer said you can come in now, if you like.'

Alex glanced at the man. His photo ID read Dr Lennox Crow.

'Thank you, I appreciate that, doctor.'

Alex waited for him to leave, and then poked her head in. 'Hey, Kam. Can I come in?'

Kamila nodded.

The walls and floor were stark white, and a television was on, mounted on the wall, volume muted. A heart rate monitor beeped in the corner.

Alex stood beside Kamila and looked at the woman. 'How's it going?'

A Brew for Chaos

'Not well.' Kamila glanced down at her blank notebook, pen still in hand. 'She's not talking. I asked her if she knew who did this to her, and she just looked at me. Grimacing a bit like she was in pain.'

Alex stared at the woman who appeared to be in her mid-twenties with long dark hair like her own, that flowed over her shoulders and almost to her waist. Her skin was so pale as to be translucent and her eyes were large with round black pupils covering a grayish cornea.

She looked around the room, eyes wide and blinking. Sometimes fearful-looking, other times just curious.

'Okay, so she's not talking about the incident, but has she given a name?'

'No, you don't get it. She's not talking. Not speaking. Not making sounds with her mouth.'

'Hi there,' Alex said, her gaze going back to the woman. 'I'm Alex,' she said softly. 'Nice to meet you.'

The woman just looked at them.

'What did the doctor say?'

'There's only been a preliminary examination, but he thinks there's no physical basis for her not to speak, that she's experienced some sort of trauma – psychological.'

'Any other injuries?' Alex's gaze lingered on the bright blue veins that were evident underneath the skin on her arms. 'She looks pretty healthy.'

'She can't walk.' Kamila pointed to a wheelchair in a corner of the room. 'Can't or won't – he's not sure. She won't speak. Won't do anything but lie here.'

'Does she have an appetite?'

'No, though she's hooked up for IV feeding. The doctors did find two odd things when they examined her and did a tox screen. The first were marks around her wrists. The scars are old and healed, but they were deep and probably painful at some point.'

Alex leaned forward and looked at the woman's wrists. There were red marks – like old welt marks permanently embedded on her skin – encircling her wrists. 'And the second thing?'

'Remnants of an odd cocktail of chemicals in her body. Growth hormone. Immune system suppressants, like the kind they give patients who've had organ transplants. Odd animal proteins. Her urinalysis showed an extremely high concentration of iodine. The doctor said she had numerous puncture wounds along her spine too. Needle marks on her arms, like a junkie.'

'How horrible. What has she been through?'

'Probably nothing,' Kamila said as she snapped her notebook closed. 'She could be an addict filling her body with all sorts of weird drugs. It happens.'

'Do you think she had anything to do with Jonah's death?'

'Hard to say. Based on her bone density and body mass, I'd say she didn't have the strength to attack a six-foot-four man who appeared to be in good shape.'

Alex turned back to the woman. 'Do you need anything? Can I help you?'

The woman's expression was blank, and Alex turned to Kamila, lowering her voice. 'Maybe she doesn't speak English?'

'I thought of that. I tried Spanish. The doctor knows French and Italian. He tried that. Nothing.'

'Give her pen and paper. Surely she can write her name.'

Kamila shook her head. 'Doc said she has difficulty moving her fingers, and thought some of the drug needle marks around her wrist might indicate nerve damage in her hands.'

A look of horror crossed Alex's face, and she searched the Jane Doe's. 'That's horrible. Have you tried telepathing with her? Or searching her memories?'

'Absolutely not, Alex. This is my career we're talking about, and you know I don't practice magic for any reason on the job,' she hissed in a low voice.

'I know, but what if it's the only way to find out anything?'

'It's a cheat,' Kamila said. 'And I'm not using shortcuts to get my job done when no other cop is. What do you take me for?'

'Sorry,' Alex said. 'But *I'm* not a cop and I am practicing.'

'Alex, stop—' Kamila said. But it was too late. Alex was already focusing all of her energy on the young woman, probing her mind, searching for memories, bits of words, thoughts, anything that could help them figure out who she was and where she'd come from.

Alex hit a psychic wall. Nothing but darkness and silence. It was . . . not normal. The average human mind was loud, full of

A Brew for Chaos 59

random thoughts, mental chatter and words and sentences floating around in whole and half conversations.

She pulled out of her mind, feeling odd. Frowning, she turned to Kamila. 'Good thing you didn't bother. There was nothing there.'

Kamila stared at the woman. 'What do you mean nothing?'

Alex described the experience. 'It almost reminded me of what Minka said she's experienced with her dolphins.'

Kamila rolled her eyes. 'She's told you about her chatty dolphins, has she?'

'Well, yeah, and the lack of noise with the dolphins reminds me of her.' She looked at the woman with a frown. 'The human mind is loud and messy. Hers was dark and quiet.'

Kamila and Alex stared at the woman, who returned the gaze without expression.

Alex left Kamila alone with the woman and sat in the hallway.

Pepper returned holding two coffees. She pushed one towards Alex. 'I figure it's going to be a long night for both of us.'

'Thanks. That was sweet of you.'

'I'm sorry about earlier. I kind of went off . . .'

'I understand.'

'No, I don't think you do.' She smiled at Alex. 'You're new to town, and everyone already likes you. I wish I could do that.'

Alex glanced at Pepper. 'Maybe . . . just try being genuinely nice to others. Be compassionate. Caring. Kind.'

Pepper screwed up her face. 'I'm not all of those things now?'

Alex wasn't sure what to say. When she'd first arrived in town, Pepper had been mean and pushy. Since becoming friends, she'd mellowed a bit. 'Well . . .'

Pepper let it slide. 'I'm digging into Jonah's life, working my contacts, you know. And so far, nothing. They're not even sure how he died.'

'But he was on the beach, next to our . . . Jane Doe?'

Pepper nodded wearily. 'He'd expect me to figure this out. And I owe him. I was his star investigative reporter. What will I look like if I can't figure this out?' She let out a wail.

Alex shrugged, not sure how to help Pepper. Then she thought she saw Jack step out of the elevator, study his watch, scan the

60 Esme Addison

hallway, take a few steps and look down a corridor like he was searching for someone. But he only saw Pepper and Alex. He studied his watch screen with a confused look on his face.

Pepper touched Alex's shoulder. 'You'll help me, won't you?'

'I can't, Pepper. I'm sorry, but I can't get involved this time. I'm sure Jack is on top of things.'

Pepper's mouth fell open. 'You've figured out the last two crimes in this town. Not Jack.' She glanced up then and saw him coming up on them. She lowered her voice. 'How can you tell me no?'

'Ladies,' Jack said when he reached them. He gave his watch one more look then kissed Alex on the cheek. 'I didn't expect to see you here.' He gave her a knowing look.

'I was with Kamila when she got the call to come here. Problem with your new watch?'

'What? No, well, kind of. Signal interference. No big deal. Hospitals have all sorts of equipment sending out radio waves.'

Alex nodded. 'I'm just hanging out in the hallway as you can see.' She pretended to twiddle her thumbs. 'Minding my own business.'

'With our local investigative reporter?' he noted, then looked past them into the room. 'How is she?' He unwrapped a stick of gum from his pocket and popped it in his mouth. 'Still as talkative as a rock?'

Alex quickly gave him the rundown, and he looked disappointed.

'That was a trick question, Alex.'

Pepper laughed, covering her mouth with her hand when Jack glowered at her.

'You're not supposed to know anything.' His green eyes glinted, icy. 'You've talked to her then?'

Alex sighed. 'I just checked in on her with Kamila. She hasn't said one word.'

'She didn't speak to me either.' He glanced into the door window. 'I was hoping she'd be more comfortable with a female officer, but I don't think that's the issue here.'

'Any chance you can ID her?'

He shrugged. 'We've done all the things. Taken her fingerprints and entered them in our database. Uploaded her image to our

A Brew for Chaos 61

missing persons software search program. So far there are no matches. It's almost like she doesn't exit.'

'Send her picture to the media. I'm sure the news will pick it up and help spread the word.'

Jack shot Pepper an acerbic look. 'I've thought of that, but I want to keep this close to the vest at first. We also want to protect her. Someone tried to kill her. We don't want them to know they failed, lest they return. You'll get the scoop if that's what you're worried about.'

'Thanks, Jack. Look, Jonah was my boss, my mentor, and a friend. I'd really like to know what's going on with this investigation. I promise not to report this, but is there anything you can tell me?'

He paused, fixing Pepper with a hard look. 'Fox was electrocuted. His chest was swollen and red with burn marks radiating from the point of contact.'

She winced at the description. 'So, it wasn't our Jane Doe?' Pepper stared at the woman through the window.

'Not likely. She was passed out on the beach beside him when she was discovered. She had no means to electrocute him and appears to be a victim herself.'

'Was she electrocuted too?'

'Not sure. No physical signs, but if she were, it might account for why she's not speaking.'

'You're going on the assumption that a third party attacked them both but was only able to take Jonah out,' Alex said with certainty.

'Yes. And that's why I don't want to put her image on the news just yet. In fact, I'm going to ask you to report the story in a way that implies she didn't make it.'

Pepper's eyes widened. 'You want me to lie?'

'No. I want you to withhold important information on the case. If the murderer finds out she's still alive, they may come back for her.'

TEN

The next day after work, Alex drove to Pepper's townhouse, located a few blocks from Main Street.

It was a historic section of town where stately, ice-cream-colored townhouses in pastel shades of green, blue, purple, and pink populated a street lined with fragrant magnolia trees. She looked up and down the road, remembering the last time she'd been to Pepper's sherbet yellow house. It wasn't a good memory. But she pushed the thought aside, strode up the walkway and rang the doorbell.

'Thanks for coming over,' Pepper said as she welcomed Alex into her home. 'I think I know how to find who did this to Jonah.'

Alex stood in Pepper's home and felt slightly uncomfortable. The last time she'd been here, Pepper, while investigating Alex's family history, had found her ancestor's journal that mentioned Magicals, been kidnapped and had her memories wiped clean. Alex had found her in the trunk of her BMW.

The house had been ransacked and reeked of magic, the scent of ozone much like the fragrance that bloomed in the air before it rained hung thick in the air. But now, the house smelled of red sauce. Pepper had lured Alex over with the promise of pasta and wine.

She handed Alex a glass of Malbec first, and then a bowl of spaghetti. 'I'm not the best cook, but I promise it's not horrible. Okay?'

Alex kicked off her shoes and settled onto the couch beside Pepper, who had papers and notebooks and photographs spread on the coffee table before them.

'This is a working dinner,' Pepper said.

Alex took a bite of her pasta. The noodles could've been cooked longer, but the sauce was good. 'I gathered,' she said, pointing to the notes.

'I think Jonah finally figured out who the Fisherman was. And

A Brew for Chaos 63

he was killed before he could write the story – or give the information to me so I could write it.'

'You think you and I are going to solve a forty-year-old cold case? When others before us could not?'

Pepper drank her wine. 'Yes, that's exactly what I think is going to happen.'

'I promised Jack—'

'Jack is not looking into this – no one is – so what can he say? I'm doing this for Jonah, and you have to help me.'

Alex thought for a moment. 'I really don't want to look into this case. It's not my fight. Before I had to help my aunt. And then Celeste, but this . . . Like you pointed out, this was well before my time. I'm sorry those women were taken but . . .' She shook her head.

Pepper stared at her friend. 'Really? Wow. Do you know how many times I've been there for you, helping you figure things out?'

A wave of guilt washed over Alex. She was part of the reason Pepper had been thrown in a trunk with her memories wiped, the reason she'd had to see a court-ordered psychiatrist to talk about what happened to her. 'How about this: I'll listen to your theories, help you sound things out. But I'm not doing any legwork, okay? That's all you.'

Pepper tossed her wine back and set her glass down. 'Geesh. Sure, that's all I wanted anyway. What did Jack say to you to scare you off investigating?'

Alex looked away, embarrassed. 'Just that we were over if I got involved in any more of his investigations.'

Pepper stared at her friend. 'Wow . . . Let's keep your investigating in the armchair, shall we?'

Another glass of wine later, Pepper and Alex had gone through the existing list of previous suspects. Pepper held up a picture of Carson MacInnes, forty years younger, nice-looking with a head full of shiny hair and standing proudly beside his boat. 'He had a drinking problem. Was known to get handsy with women at the local bar when he had one too many. And he lived near the scene of the abductions.'

'Sure he sounds good for it, but he also had alibis for at least half of the cases.'

'Maybe I should question him,' Pepper said thoughtfully. 'The cops could've missed something. His alibis could be weak.'

'I spoke to him. He got really riled up.' Then Alex shared with Pepper everything Mac had told her.

'He actually sued Jonah? I never heard about this . . .' Pepper tossed her ponytail. 'He didn't sue me. I can ask him whatever I want and write whatever I want about him.'

Alex shot her an anxious look.

'What? I'm not afraid of him. You?'

Alex shrugged. 'No, not really. But if he is the Fisherman . . .'

'That was forty years ago. What can he do now? We could both take him, don't you think?'

Alex wanted to say that she didn't think Mac had done it. But what did she really know about the man? He was polite and bought products from the shop. Who knew what he was up to forty years ago. But still . . . 'I doubt it would come to that. What's gotten into you?'

'Someone killed my only friend in town. I have to find out who did it.'

Alex frowned. 'I'm your friend, Pepper.'

There was a knock at the door. They both stilled, then Pepper rose from her seat.

'Expecting company?'

'No,' she said as she peered through the peep hole. Then sighed. 'It's my dad. I told him I was fine and that he didn't need to check on me.' She opened the door. 'But here we are.' She smiled at the man who was both her father and the mayor of Bellamy Bay. 'Hi, Dad,' Pepper said wearily.

'How's my little peppercorn?' Oswald Bellamy, short, muscular and with fiery red hair like his daughter, embraced her in a bear hug that almost lifted her off the ground.

She pouted. 'I'm okay. Me and Alex were just . . .'

Raising bushy auburn eyebrows, he regarded Alex. His features were broad and flat, his skin covered in freckles, and his hair curly and coarse. Alex thought he looked like a bouncer in a nice suit. A little intimidating . . . but overwhelmingly pleasant in the way politicians always were. She smiled at him.

His nod was curt, but he didn't quite return her smile. And

A Brew for Chaos 65

Alex had the distinct feeling he thought she was getting his daughter into trouble.

He looked at the papers spread out around them. 'Doing a little sleuthing?'

Alex swallowed. He knew she'd solved two murders previously. He also knew his daughter had been attacked because of her involvement with her. Maybe she was projecting, but she felt guilty. 'Just trying to figure out who could've had motive to do this to Jonah,' Alex said. 'Pepper asked me to help her.'

'Twist your arm, did she?' Sighing, he sat down, making himself comfortable in a chair across from them. His lips twitched into a smile and Alex relaxed. 'I won't stay long. I was just worried about you. You didn't sound like yourself on the phone.'

'You know how I felt about Jonah. He was my champion at work.'

'I know. He was always pleading your case with me. And I listened. You're the senior writer, aren't you?'

'He believed in me when you didn't.' Pepper crossed her arms across her chest, not quite able to hide her accusatory tone.

He exhaled slowly. 'It wasn't a lack of faith in your abilities, and you know that, peppercorn. I was doing your mother's bidding. She had dreams of you marrying into an old money family. And making us grandparents.' He gave her a pointed look. 'What can I do to help?'

Alex looked at Pepper, her face pinched into a scowl. 'We could start with who would want to kill Jonah. As his employer, you had to know him well, right?'

He shrugged. 'Well enough. We weren't friends, but we did socialize together at events associated with the paper. Of course, I've known him for decades, going back to when he was having his troubles.'

Pepper sat up. 'What troubles?'

His eyebrows shot up, but then he regained his composure. 'I suppose it's okay now. He's gone . . . When he first came to town, he'd just been fired from his editing position at the *Paradise Beach* paper.'

'I never knew that. He was fired? Why?' Pepper asked.

'He had some financial debt from a . . . proclivity to gamble. To play cards. And it came out that he was taking money for articles. The town officials kept the story quiet because they didn't want it to impact tourism, but those in certain circles knew.'

'Sounds like possible motive for someone,' Alex theorized. 'For revenge maybe? Someone he wronged?'

Pepper turned to her father. 'What do you know about the trouble he was in?'

'As I recall, it was discovered he was on the payroll of someone at Camp Malveaux and he was writing articles that glossed over environmental issues many in the beach community there would have liked to have known about.'

'So he was fired when the true nature of his job was revealed,' Alex said. 'Not because he was actually corrupt.'

Pepper frowned at her words, but her father nodded. 'Pretty much.'

'How much debt are we talking?' Alex asked.

'About three hundred thousand is what I heard.'

Alex whistled. 'That's a lot of debt.' She thought for a moment. 'Wait. Mac sued him for twenty-five thousand dollars. How was he able to pay it?'

'He couldn't.' Oswald's tone was blunt. 'The paper had an insurance policy for just that situation. We paid it for him.'

Pepper's face had paled. 'If you knew he had this . . . troubled past, why did you even hire him?'

Oswald's cheeks tinged with pink. 'In this business, you do people favors, and they do you favors.'

Pepper's eyes widened. 'Daddy, what are you saying?'

He held out a palm. 'Now, now. I didn't do anything wrong. You know I live by a strong set of morals, all of us Bellamy's do. As I recall, someone working with Camp Malveaux told me if I just paid off his suit, no questions asked . . . and then hired him, they'd fund our town renovation projects for the next ten years.'

The tradeoff of good for bad sounded like someone she knew. Alex glanced at Pepper before turning to her father. 'Who offered to finance your projects if you hired him . . . sir?'

'Montgomery Blue. His company, Leviathan Industries, has long been a friend to the town.'

Alex bit back a retort. She knew first hand that whenever Montgomery did good, it was to hide something horrible.

A Brew for Chaos 67

Pepper shot her father a disappointed look. 'That doesn't sound moral, Daddy.'

His jawbone jutted out defensively. 'You liked Jonah just fine, didn't you?'

Pepper's mouth set in a thin hard line, and she locked eyes with him, looking like his mirror image.

Pepper's chin pushed forward. 'I didn't know all of this.'

'No disrespect,' Alex began, 'but how do you know he wasn't still working for the military while he ran your paper? Filling it with propaganda?'

Oswald snorted a laugh. 'We're just one small town. Our paper covers parades and the citizen of the year . . .' He shot her an amused look. 'I was told that he was done working for them, and this was his reward. A nice job in a nice town for his service to his country.'

Pepper rubbed her temples. 'Regardless of what anyone thinks, he did do a lot of good in the community. He made a point of profiling people in town that were doing good, he provided free publicity for new businesses and created that non-profit that provides toys to children in the hospital during Christmas. He even dressed up as Santa to hand them out.'

Oswald reached out and patted his daughter's hand. 'I think he tried to make up for anything bad he may have done in the past. Especially where you were concerned.'

'Me?'

'You have no idea how often he sang your praises to me and your mother. Explaining how hard you worked, how smart and tenacious you were. He wanted me to give you the paper to run one day – thought it would be a mistake to hire another editor-in-chief after him.'

'He said that?'

Her father nodded. 'He really believed in your talent. Once over drinks, he told me he wanted you to have the career he never had.'

Tears filled Pepper's eyes, and she wiped her cheek.

'And you are a good writer, I know that. Your mother knows it too.' His grin was rueful. 'She just has her own dreams for you.'

'And what do *you* want for me?'

'To be happy. That's it.' He slapped his thighs and stood.

'Are you going to hire someone to run the paper?'

Pepper's father shrugged. 'Not sure yet. We're not a big paper, you know that. In the meantime, you'll be the acting editor.'

Pepper's eyebrows shot up. 'Acting editor? Me?'

Her father nodded, and his expression firmed. 'So that means you'll be busy with the paper. No time to get yourself in trouble.'

'I'm working on an article about—'

'We have a competent police force, you know.'

Pepper nodded quickly. 'But what do you know about Carson MacInnes' lawsuit against Jonah?'

'Ugly business that. I'm afraid Jonah had it in his head that Mac was the serial killer, and he really had his heart set on proving it, even though Mac's mother gave him an alibi for several of the murders, her and her church lady friends.'

'I talked to Mac about the case, about Jonah, before this all happened . . .' Alex began. 'He felt Jonah used the newspaper to vilify him. He was very upset.'

Pepper exchanged looks with Alex. 'Upset enough to kill him?'

'I don't know,' Alex said.

'Maybe that's who Jonah was arguing with on the phone. Mac lured him to the beach, they had it out, and he killed him.'

'He was electrocuted. What could Mac have used?'

'I don't know. But there is a murder weapon. We just have to find it.'

Oswald looked from his daughter to Alex. 'Don't you two ladies have enough to do without trying to solve yet another crime? Pepper, with Jonah . . . gone, you're co-chairing Oktoberfest with Spencer, plus you have your acting editor duties now. That should keep you plenty busy.'

Pepper nodded quickly. 'Yeah, we know, Dad.' Then turned back to Alex. 'We just have to figure out Mac's link to Jane Doe – maybe she was just a witness, an innocent bystander, and Mac tried to take her out too.'

Oswald frowned. 'Okayyy,' he drawled. 'You girls need to find a hobby. Painting. Ceramics,' he suggested.

Pepper kissed her father on his cheek. 'We'll be fine. Remember, I'm an investigative journalist. I'm just . . . investigating.'

A Brew for Chaos   69

'I'll leave you two girls to your research then. Your mother wanted me to remind you about dinner this Sunday.' He nodded curtly towards Alex before he left.

Pepper walked him to his car, while Alex returned to the documents spread out around her. She focused on the folder filled with information on Carson MacInnes.

'Want to take a second look at Mac's alibis?' Alex asked when Pepper returned.

Sighing, Pepper flopped to her seat, picked up one of her memo pads and flipped through her notes. 'Those alibis my dad mentioned were airtight. He was at church, with his mother and other elders, when most of the kidnappings occurred. One of the parishioners gave a statement that Mac was an upstanding member of the congregation who'd answered the call of his country when he joined the Navy, then returned to serve as assistant youth minister, coordinating youth night every Wednesday.'

'I'm confused,' Alex said. 'Either he has a drinking problem and was capable of abducting women.' She arched an eyebrow. 'Or he's an angel doing the Lord's work.'

Pepper shrugged. 'I agree, but it really does look like Mac can't be our killer. It's a dead end.'

'You okay?' Alex asked.

Pepper exhaled slowly. 'I just discovered my journalistic hero and mentor was basically a criminal. And someone he did wrong probably found him and got the justice they deserved.' She shrugged again. 'I always wanted to run the paper one day. But I may be moving to Atlanta or DC . . . So, I don't know . . .' She stared disinterestedly at the research around her.

'Mac's mother could've lied for him. Seems to have been going around back then,' Alex said, choosing to ignore her behavior. When Pepper still didn't respond, Alex said: 'I get it, you're disappointed, but . . . what if we're looking at this all wrong?'

'What do you mean?'

'You said yourself that Jonah was a good person. That he spent his time in Bellamy Bay doing good things, highlighting the best of our citizens . . . What if he was killed because he was asked to do something immoral by someone in his past and he refused?'

Pepper stared at Alex, her eyes brightening by the second. 'Or what if he wanted to come clean about the bad things he did in the past and someone wanted to quiet him?'

'That does seem more likely given the way he's lived his life since he moved here, what, forty or so years ago?'

The fire returned to Pepper's eyes. 'You're right. This happened to him because he was trying to do the right thing. We have to find out who did this. We have to get him justice.'

Alex smiled. 'There she is.'

ELEVEN

When Alex arrived home, she found her aunt in the library and asked her if she thought her attorney, Tobias Winston, could be the Fisherman.

Lidia closed her book and stared at her. 'You can't be serious.'

Alex sank into an overstuffed chair across from her aunt. 'I know it sounds crazy, but . . . humor me.'

'I've known Tobias for many years. He's no criminal, and he had nothing to do with those women being abducted.'

'But he did date a woman who was taken?'

Sighing, Lidia rose from her chair and went to one of the wooden shelves that lined the walls. She pulled out a large scrapbook and gestured for Alex to join her at a nearby table. 'This is from the year those girls were taken.'

Lidia flipped through the pages, and Alex caught glimpses of old photographs of her aunt with a bobbed hairstyle, wearing mini dresses and with heavy winged black eyeliner over white eyeshadow. 'That's you?' Alex teased.

Lidia chuckled but nodded. She stopped at a page and pointed to Tobias. He was grinning with his arm around a pretty blonde with big round eyes. 'We weren't the best of friends, but she spent some time with our group. She was very popular, very involved on campus. Her name was Margaret . . .' She flipped the picture over. And read the name written there. 'Dunsmore. Margaret Dunsmore. She was a sweet girl.'

Alex stared at the image, noting her infectious grin. Her chin was tilted forward, like she had confidence to spare. 'What happened to her? She was taken, never to be seen or heard of again?'

'Not exactly. I believe she was with a girlfriend that was taken. Somehow Margaret got away, but she couldn't tell the police anything that was helpful. Or maybe she was friends with a young woman that was taken. Either way, she left town shortly after that – at least that's what the detective in charge of the case said. I haven't thought of her for many years.'

72 Esme Addison

Lidia tapped the photograph. 'I wonder what happened to her. She was always at the marina, a science major if I'm not mistaken.'

Something niggled at the back of Alex's brain. 'Do you mind if I keep this photograph for a while? I'll bring it back.'

'Of course.'

'Do you think Tobias would be okay answering a few questions about her?' Alex explained the research she was doing on Pepper's behalf.

'I doubt he'll mind. But tread carefully. He was pretty torn up when his girl left without saying goodbye.'

The next day after work, Pepper asked Alex to meet her at Jonah's house.

It was a row of three-story sun-bleached wooden buildings a few blocks from the beach with palm trees planted on the grounds. Pepper was waiting in her car in the parking lot when she arrived and jumped out as soon as Alex parked.

'You're late,' Pepper said as she led her to the apartment door.

Just then a woman ran past them and hopped into the passenger side of a Mercedes sedan. Alex whirled around and caught a glimpse of short blonde hair – it was Spencer. The engine roared to life and sped away.

'Was that Zane driving?' Alex mused aloud. They both stared down the street until they could no longer see the car.

'Yeah, it was.' Pepper frowned. 'Which is weird because he doesn't seem the type.'

'Type for what?'

'Driving a getaway car. What was that about?'

Pepper tried the doorknob. 'It's still locked, so she didn't get in . . . Reminds me of the alarm Jonah received the other night . . .' She looked thoughtful. 'He said no one had gotten in, though the police did find evidence that someone had tried to open the door.'

Alex recalled Spencer leaving early that night and told Pepper.

'Was she trying to get his recipe?' Pepper wondered aloud.

'And with Zane's help?' Alex shrugged. 'Are they working together?' Now Alex was really hoping Zane wasn't Minka's mystery guy.

A Brew for Chaos   73

Pepper punched a code onto a digital screen, which revealed another screen. She dragged her finger across the panel in a zigzag shape, the lock beeped, and she pushed through the door. She flipped on a switch, and they looked around the living room.

'Let's look for his home office. That's where I'd guess he'd have important documents.'

Alex stopped at a bookshelf, running her fingers along several thick book spines. 'Pharmaceutical Analysis, Pharmaceutical Biology.' There were at least three rows of worn college textbooks. 'He was serious about science at one point.'

Pepper shook her head. 'Writing was always his first love. Even if his parents didn't support that interest.' She glanced over her shoulder at Alex. 'Like mine. That's what we had in common . . . a desire to follow our passions no matter what. And why he was so adamant on helping me . . .' She walked down a hallway, opening doors and turning on lights until she found the right one. Pepper held out her arm. 'After you.'

Alex stepped inside, her gaze roving around the room. 'Um . . .'

'Ho-ly . . .' Pepper muttered to herself, eyes widening as she studied the area.

The walls were papered in old newspaper articles about the Fisherman case. Copies of police reports were taped to cork boards, and black and white photographs of the victims were pasted in rows.

'Jonah was obsessed.' Alex stepped closer to one wall and touched surveillance pictures of Mac around town.

'He had to have figured out who the killer was,' Pepper said as she picked up folder after folder on his desk and flipped through them. 'He's got everything ever written about the case right here.' She twirled around, one arm outstretched.

An hour later, Pepper rubbed her red-rimmed eyes. 'Have you found anything useful?'

Alex held up a folder. 'He seemed to really like Carson MacInnes for the killer.'

Alex opened a shoebox marked *MacInnes* and riffled through it. She held up a photograph of boots and additional images of footprints. 'These are Mac's shoes.'

Pepper stood and inspected the prints. 'They match.'

'And this?' Alex held up a sheaf of papers. 'Surveillance logs

74 Esme Addison

for Mac. Jonah was really trying to build a case against him. I guess I can see why he was so irate when I questioned him.'

'Or . . .' Pepper began, eyes narrowing on the documentation. 'Mac knows that you've solved two murder cases, and he's afraid you're about to solve another.'

Alex gave her friend a doubtful look before shuffling through more papers until she found one with a list of women's names on it. 'I think I found something. Twenty-five women's names with addresses from Bellamy Bay and the surrounding area. Their height, weight, hair and eye color. Notes about where they spent their time. Ten of them have a checkmark by their name.'

Pepper went to the photographs of the victims and stared at them. 'I've been so fixated on finding the killer I hadn't thought to look at the victims.' Pepper swallowed. 'They're so young-looking. Look at them, Alex.'

Alex stood beside Pepper. 'There's no type or look. Just attractive young women in their mid-twenties.' Women with short hair, long hair, heavy makeup and fresh scrubbed faces.

On a whim, Alex removed one photograph from the wall and turned it over. A name and age were scrawled on the back. Alex referenced the list and found the woman's name mid-way down the page with a checkmark by her name.

A twinge of something moved in the pit of her stomach. She removed another picture, and another and another, and cross-referenced the group of names. 'Pepper, Jonah had a list of the victims. Some have checkmarks by their name, which appears to indicate that they were taken. But there are fifteen other names. Not checked. Like they were meant to be taken but were somehow missed.'

Pepper looked at the paper. 'Let me look them up online. See if they're still around or if they're missing or dead . . .' A few minutes later, Pepper was done. 'I found them all on Peoplefinder.com, that website that compiles a dossier on people based on public records? They are all alive and accounted for.' She stopped. 'Wait. The Fisherman was working off a list?'

'And why did Jonah have it? I mean, how did he get his hands on it?'

Pepper stared at the wall of photos. 'I know exactly what

A Brew for Chaos   75

happened. Jonah found the killer. And this is proof. This is why Jonah was killed.'

Alex studied the document, reading off the victim's names. Matching the names with the faces. Ten in all. *Candace James. Beth Robinson. Caroline Bracy . . .*

She turned to Pepper, whose eyes had suddenly gone misty. 'What do these women all have in common? There has to be something.'

A tear rolled down Pepper's cheek. 'I don't know. But we have to get justice for these women. It's been forty years.' She wiped her face.

'Let's start packing all of this stuff up. I'm taking it to my office, and I'll keep it there while I continue my research.' Pepper stood. 'There's one more place we haven't looked.'

Alex followed Pepper down the dark stairway to Jonah's basement. The doughy scent of yeast billowed around them, and Pepper found a light switch.

'I guess you can have a basement at the beach?' Alex asked.

Pepper laughed. 'Yeah, there are a few here. I don't know all of the specifics, but there are construction companies that create them below the water table. Something about keeping the water in as you dig, not out.'

Alex shot her a look of disbelief. 'How do you know this?'

She shrugged. 'I wrote an article about it once. We had a big real estate developer out of Columbia as advertiser.'

They reached the basement level and looked around. One side had several large metallic tanks for brewing beer, one side held closed clear plastic containers about two feet tall and marked with ingredients, like hops, seaweed and sage. While the other two walls were lined with shelves covered in three different types of bottled beer. 'Wow, he was serious about beer-making, wasn't he?'

Pepper nodded. 'There must be over five thousand bottles down here.' She pointed to a row of bottles called *Beach Day*. Pepper read the label aloud. '*Drink one bottle and lie down . . . on the beach. Doctor's orders.* I love these cute directions.' But then she sighed. 'Jonah had a fun sense of humor.'

'I know he sold some to a few of the restaurants in town. Bread and Putter comes to mind.'

'Yeah,' Pepper agreed, coming to stand next to Alex, a bottle

76 Esme Addison

in her hand. She looked at the bottle's label. *Mermaid Magic.*
The label was designed in swirls of pink and purple, and showed
a beautiful mermaid with lavender skin and magenta hair holding
a frosty glass of beer to her glossy fuchsia lips. 'Cool label.'

Pepper inspected the bottle and laughed. *'Drink three bottles
daily with food, preferably fish and sea vegetables and wait for
the mermaid magic to begin.'* She set the bottle down, her lips
moving into a smile. 'I think these are like a gag or something.'
Her green eyes brightened. 'I bet he was going to sell these at
next summer's mermaid festival. Clever.'

'Maybe,' Alex agreed, staring at the bottle before moving away.

They explored the beer cellar to no avail.

Pepper blew a raspberry. 'A bust.'

But Alex wasn't so sure. She rifled through a cabinet and
found a stack of shipping labels pre-printed with Jonah's home
address as the shipper, and the aquarium as the recipient.

She held it up. 'What was Jonah shipping to the aquarium?'

Pepper looked around the room and shrugged. 'Beer?' And
laughed.

'Does the aquarium have a bar?'

'No, but they do have a small café where you can buy drinks
and chips. Maybe that's why the mermaid-themed beer?'

'Maybe,' Alex agreed, returning the labels to their place, then
went to the large plastic containers of ingredients. She lifted each
one in turn, looking inside and finally underneath. When she
reached the last jar containing seaweed . . . she found
something.

A manila envelope was taped to the bottom. Alex pulled it
off, set the container down and opened it. There were flimsy
shiny sheets inside, with dark squares on them. She held one up
to the dim light of the basement. 'What is this?'

Pepper laughed, a confused look on her face. 'I'm not that
much older than you, Alex. And I only know this because the
newspaper still uses this for archival purposes, but it's
microfiche.'

'Which is what?'

'It's like a paper made of film. And each of those little squares
are a document minimized to like a 1/25 of its original size. Lots
of universities and government agencies and newspapers used

A Brew for Chaos

this to store information before the internet. Again, I know this because the paper has a huge room full of this stuff waiting to be digitized and placed in our cloud storage.' She rolled her eyes. 'I'm exhausted just thinking about who is going to actually complete that project.'

'But what's on it? Don't you think it's important? Why else would he hide it?'

Pepper gently took the film and held it up to the light. 'I have no idea. It could be about the Fisherman case or maybe it's the secret recipe for his award-winning beer.'

'How do we read this?' Alex asked, gently pushing the film back into the envelope.

'A microfiche reader.' Pepper began walking upstairs, turning off the light as they went. 'We have one at the paper, but it hasn't been in use for years, so I don't know if it works. The library may have one collecting dust in a closet.'

They left the house and Pepper locked it up. 'I wish I could be more excited about the microfiche, but honestly I feel like it's probably his tedious notes on the beer-making process, and his eccentric use of microfiche was his way of kind of encrypting the material.'

'I'll hold on to the microfiche,' Alex said. 'And you let me know if the reader at your office works. I'll check around town.'

TWELVE

The next morning, Alex was making a coffee run for herself and her aunt. After nine, the morning rush had come and gone. And while the tables were full of customers, Coffee O'Clock thankfully had no line, save for the one man paying for his purchase at the counter.

Coming to stand behind him at the counter, she was silent until Dylan Wesley sensed her presence and turned around.

His grin was slow and easy. 'Well, well, well . . .'

She couldn't help but smile back. 'Morning, Dylan.'

Six-foot-two and exuding confidence from his frequent karate and boxing sessions, Dylan Wesley possessed the chiseled physique of a male model. His dark hair, longer on top and cropped on the sides, was swept back from a high forehead. Thick dark eyebrows and intense brown eyes paired with a perennially tanned complexion, making him one of Bellamy Bay's most sought-after bachelors.

Yet, Dylan's allure extended beyond his striking appearance. As the CFO of Wesley Inc, his immense family wealth added another layer to his charm. But Alex had known Dylan long before he'd grown into the man before her. When she'd come to town as a little girl, she'd played with him in her aunt's gardens. Not knowing his name or anything about him. Just that he directed his limo driver to stop at her house when he saw her in the yard on the way to his piano lessons.

When she'd returned to Bellamy Bay six months earlier, they'd rekindled a friendship that despite an irresistible attraction to each other was . . . fraught with challenges. Namely his family. Montgomery Blue was his uncle. His sister Bryn was a murderer – one that Alex had brought to justice. And his mother Tegan and her aunt hated each other.

Complicated only began to describe their relationship.

'Buy you a coffee?'

Alex knew that he'd purchase the coffee shop for her if she asked, but she only shook her head. 'No, thanks.'

A Brew for Chaos   79

The barista handed him his drink, and he raised an eyebrow at her. 'See you around?'

'Not if I see you first.' She smirked.

Grinning, he shook his head. 'So cold and yet so beautiful.'

After he left, Alex ordered a caramel apple latte for herself and a maple bacon-bourbon latte for her aunt. Lidia wasn't a fan of seasonal coffees, but Alex was sure the lure of bourbon-flavored maple syrup and bacon would change her mind.

Refusing to give Dylan another thought, she focused on Jonah. Why was he so sure Mac was the Fisherman? And there was his gambling debts and shady connection to Montgomery. She wondered if—

'It's true what they say about small towns,' said a voice behind her.

Alex turned around and saw Leith. He was dressed for a day of golfing. 'How are you?'

'I'm great. Just getting a large black coffee for ol' Gramps.'

Alex moved to the pickup area, watching Leith as he paid for his coffee. 'And playing golf?' she teased.

'Actually took a break from the green.' He grinned. 'I wasn't sure there'd be much to do here in off-season besides golf,' he began. 'But this morning, I've visited the history museum and the aquarium. Got the VIP tour and everything. Your Minka showed me around.'

'You met my cousin?'

His eyes twinkled. 'She's a doll.'

'She doesn't normally give tours, how'd that happen?'

'Montgomery Blue set it up for me.' He moved to join her in the pickup area. 'Do you know him?'

'How do you know him? If you don't mind me asking.'

Leith grabbed some napkins and placed them in his pocket before answering. 'I don't know him well,' he admitted. 'Montgomery arranged it at my grandfather's request. Apparently they go way back, like the cart and buggy.'

'That is way back.' Alex laughed, warming to his personality.

'He set up the tour for me when I expressed an interest in visiting. Said he's on the board of directors.'

Alex eyed him speculatively. 'And what's your interest in the aquarium?'

He shrugged, amused at her interest. 'I can't like sea creatures?' He chuckled when her mouth dropped open.

'I'm sorry. Of course you can. It's not you . . . Montgomery is just . . . an interesting person.'

He grunted. 'The way you say that sounds like *interesting* is not a good thing to be.'

She sighed. 'It's not, I'm just trying to be polite. How'd your grandfather meet him?'

He rocked back on his heels. 'They've worked together in the past. My grandfather is long retired, but the friendship remains.'

The barista placed the first of Alex's two beverages on the counter. She picked it up and sniffed. It was hers. The scent of buttery sweet caramel floated around her. She took a sip.

Leith watched her. 'Good?'

'Very good. And surprisingly not too sweet. How are you finding the town?'

'My mother would love it here. In fact, I should stop by your store and buy her a gift. Montgomery told me about your apothecary.'

'Oh yeah?' Alex said, her voice razor sharp and hackles raised. 'What else did he tell you?'

A confused look crossed his face. 'That's it. Just that your family had been in town for generations and your shop was an important part of the local history.'

'Really,' Alex said, doubt dragging out her word.

The barista set Alex's second drink down and turned to begin on Leith's.

'Obviously, there's bad blood between you and Montgomery. Not that it's any of my business.'

'There is. And I'm sorry I'm sharing that with you. I'm glad you like the town. Most do.' She scrambled to change the subject, embarrassed that she'd not been polite. 'What are you doing besides playing golf? Or is that it?'

He laughed. 'Isn't that enough? Your country club has one of the best courses on the East Coast.'

'Wow. So, you've been playing golf every day?'

'Every single day.' His grin widened. 'And I'm loving it. I need the break.'

'High-stress job?'

A Brew for Chaos 81

'The highest.'

The barista set down Leith's two orders in a carry-out tray.

'That's me. It was nice seeing you again.'

'Same. And do stop by the store. I'll be happy to help you find your mother a gift.'

Alex had been back at the shop for a few hours and was sweeping the hardwood floors when the front door swung open. She looked up to see Spencer step inside.

Spencer unbelted her trench coat, removed her sunglasses and pushed them onto the top of her head.

Alex propped her broom in a corner, wiped her hands on her apron and approached the woman. 'Can I help you?'

'Possibly.' She moved to a shelf and inspected several types of dried basil. 'I was wondering if you were Jonah Fox's supplier.'

'Of?'

The woman laughed. 'Whatever he might need.' She walked across the shop floor, this time lifting jars of four types of lavender.

Alex stared at her. 'Are you really going to act like I didn't see you outside of Jonah's house? Skulking about?'

Spencer laughed. 'You have no proof it was me.' She handed Alex a business card. 'I'll pay handsomely for his ingredient list.'

Alex scrutinized the card. Then looked at her. 'Why?'

A blonde eyebrow arched. 'I beg your pardon?'

'He's no longer with us. Why are you still trying to find out what he put in his beer? Why is it so important to you?'

Spencer gave Alex a once-over, from her ponytail to her purple store smock, worn jeans and dusty tennis shoes, and wrinkled her nose. 'You know, don't you?'

Alex stared at her.

'His secret ingredient? Or is it *ingredients*?'

'I'm afraid I can't help you, Spencer.'

'I know he bought his ingredients from this store.' She narrowed her eyes. 'And I will find out what they are. I always get what I want. No matter how long it takes.' She stalked towards the glass door and pushed it open with a violence that caused the bell hanging from it to crash to the floor.

* * *

82   Esme Addison

Later in the day, Kamila stopped by Botanika. It was one of her rare days off from the local police force, so she was out of uniform and dressed in sleek black workout gear that accentuated her lean muscle.

'Mom, do you have a minute?'

Lidia looked up from the pumpkins she was arranging on a table in the back of the space and took in her daughter's appearance. 'It's your day off. You don't have to wear your hair in a bun, you know.'

Kamila laughed, touching her blonde locks. 'Function over fashion, Mom. You know that's my motto.'

An inch or two taller than Alex, Kamila, who was twenty-seven, had a fresh-faced girl-next-door beauty that she downplayed by rarely wearing makeup.

'What is it, dear? I'm kind of busy.' Lidia pointed to the pumpkins. 'Up to my eyeballs in seasonal gourds.'

Kamila's blue eyes narrowed as she surveyed the table. 'Nice.'

'Thanks,' Alex said, coming out of the backroom with a crate of bath bombs that looked like apple cider donuts. She set them on the counter and began arranging them on a decorative wicker basket filled with red and white gingham cloth.

'Dr Crow is ready to discharge Jane Doe. Only she has nowhere to go. I thought maybe she could stay with you for a few days until she either gets her memory back or we can find a place for her to go?'

Lidia gave her daughter an appraising look. 'That's very thoughtful of you, Kamila. But I'm not sure our home is the best place for her.'

Kamila rolled her eyes. 'You're better than a doctor, Mom. And if anyone can figure out what's wrong with her. Or get her talking. Or bring her memories back . . . it's you.'

Lidia thought about it. 'I don't see why not. I have the room. And I am a healer . . . But short term only and you need to make sure the chief or Jack – whoever's in charge – is okay with this.'

'I've already got approval from the chief.'

'All right. We'll set her up in the guest room overlooking the gardens.'

'She's in a wheelchair – so she'll need to be on the first floor,' Kamila said.

A Brew for Chaos

She scanned the area around her. 'I'll move the day bed from the first-floor guest room into the library. We'll set her up in there.' She turned to Alex. 'Any objections, dear? It's your home too.'

'Of course not. I'll be glad to see her again. Hopefully we can help her. Heal her.'

Kamila's cell phone rang, and she stepped into the hall to take the call. A few minutes later she returned. 'Sorry about that. That was the owner of the surf bar on the beach.'

'It's your day off,' Lidia reminded her. 'You could've let it go to voicemail.'

'Justice never sleeps.' Her eldest daughter grinned. 'Besides, he's concerned. Someone broke into his bar, which is closed for the season, but didn't steal anything. Really strange. He was hoping we could find the intruder.'

'Security footage get anything?' Alex asked.

'Nah. Bad angle. Just a blurry figure breaking a window to gain entry, then searching the bar.'

The next morning, Alex was surprised to see her first customer of the day was Leith.

'Shopping for your mother?'

His smile was wide for her. 'You remembered.'

Alex rounded the counter to stand by his side. 'What does she like?'

His eyes sparkled with mischief. 'Mermaids.' He looked around the shop. 'And I hear this town is known for them.' He moved to a table stacked high with fragrant soaps and selected a thick slice of translucent blue studded with white pearls that were actually bath beads, large grains of sea salt threaded with seaweed, and read the title. '*Queen of the Sea*. I'll take it.' He turned to Alex. 'Anything else?'

'You should come back in the summer. That's really when we have our mermaid merch out. Right now, it's all about the fall.' She held up a sweet potato pie candle. 'How about this? Made it myself.'

'No, thank you. But my mother . . .' He narrowed his eyes, searching the tables and shelves, until he landed on a display of decorative canisters holding pre-packaged herbal blends. 'Enjoys tea. She'd like something robust and spicy.'

84 Esme Addison

Alex moved to the dried herb canisters. 'Sure, I have just the thing.' She grabbed a brown kraft bag and began scooping malty black tea leaves mixed with licorice, ginger, black peppercorn and cardamom. She handed him his purchase. 'I think she'll like this.'

He opened the bag and sniffed deeply. 'Smells good. Thank you.'

'Maybe next time you can bring your mother.'

He chuckled. 'With two murder victims recently found on the beach? Not likely.'

Alex opened her mouth to correct him. But then she recalled Jack's insistence on keeping Jane's survival a secret and realized Pepper must've reported her death. She smiled tightly instead. 'Of course.'

He watched her as she rang up the tea. 'Has my grandfather been by to see you?'

She laughed. 'Why would he? I don't know him. And the one time I did see him at the B&B he was hardly nice.'

He shrugged. 'I don't know. Maybe he's doing a little shopping like me.'

Alex held up the soap he'd looked at earlier. 'Still want this?'

He glanced at it. 'Sure.'

When he left, Alex decided to do a little internet research while the store was empty. She wanted to learn more about the projects Leviathan Industries had funded when Mayor Bellamy agreed to hire Jonah to run the paper. Her hope was that she'd find out more about Jonah in the process.

She settled behind the counter with her laptop and opened her internet browser. On the town's website of public projects, she searched for anything funded by Leviathan during the time period Jonah was hired. She found details about a plan to repair roads leading to the Maritime Forest, a renovation at the aquarium and an effort to rebuild a portion of the beach's sand dunes. The town was getting a lot from Montgomery's company for simply hiring one man. The question was, what was Jonah doing for Montgomery in return?

Alex then logged into the newspaper's online archives and searched the papers published during the time the town was benefitting from Montgomery's generosity. First she searched for Montgomery's name. She found a handful of articles covering

A Brew for Chaos   85

Leviathan Industries that created a positive, optimistic image of the company's philanthropic endeavors.

She searched online and saw that many of the articles had been picked up by national media. Alex closed the tab. Clearly, Montgomery had used Jonah to counter bad press. What else had he used Jonah for?

She went back to the newspaper archives and searched for news during the time the Fisherman was active. The headlines were all about the case. It was the summer of chaos, the large font screamed to the reader.

Images of the victims were plastered beside photographs of a young Mac with numerous articles proclaiming his guilt. The coverage was more tabloid than Alex had expected. And Jonah clearly believed the worst of Mac. No wonder he disliked Jonah; his words were accusatory and stinging. Anyone reading these articles would think Mac was indeed the killer.

She looked up from the screen, disturbed. Mac probably thought he had every right to harm Jonah. Sure, he'd taken him to court and won. But had that been enough for him?

Later that morning, Alex and Tanner were at the shop counter when something occurred to Alex. She turned to the teenager. 'You still go to church in town? You're a part of their youth group?'

'Sure. Every Wednesday night at the big brick Baptist church on Main and Front.'

Was it possible that the youth group was the same Mac has taught? There weren't that many churches in town . . . 'The name of your church?'

Tanner told her. It *was* the same church that Mac had gone to on the nights six of the ten women had been taken. 'Tell me about the group. What kinds of things do you do?' Alex wasn't sure what she was looking for, but she felt like she was on to something.

'Are you interested in joining the church?'

'Not sure. I grew up going to a Presbyterian church with my dad. But once I moved away for college and then work, I stopped going . . . Would you be able to do me a favor?'

Tanner shrugged. 'I guess.'

*   *   *

Later in the day and after giving it much thought, Alex decided to call Dylan. She needed his help.

'It's nice to hear your voice, Alex. I haven't heard much from you since our last private talk. And of course, the coffee shop.'

There was an awkward silence, and Alex wondered if he was regretting telling her the truth about his Magical heritage. Most Magicals assumed he was Mer like the majority of the community, but he'd confided in her and told her that while his late father had been Mer, his mother was a dragon descent, making him a Magical hybrid.

It was true she wasn't sure what to say around him. But she was also terribly attracted to him, though whether it was organic or part of his natural dragon magnetism that suppressed a person's freewill, she was never sure. But she was with Jack and tried to keep her distance from Dylan as much as possible. Until now.

'I have a list of names I'd like you to run through your various databases.' Because of his position at Wesley Inc, Dylan had top-secret government contracts, and access to information that compiled both open source and classified information – genetics, biometrics and much more. 'I can send you a picture now, if you don't mind.'

'I don't mind, but are you going to tell me what I'm getting involved with?'

'I'd rather not. Safer that way.'

'Safer for whom?'

Alex sighed into the phone. 'Don't be difficult.'

He chuckled. 'Send it to me.'

When Tanner returned from his break, he had a bag in his hand. He brought it to the counter and set it in front of Alex. She was just finishing up a social media post, an ASMR video of her slicing into several cakes of soap. Grinning to herself, she could only hope the viewers of the Botanika Instagram feed found it as relaxing and satisfying as she did to make it.

'What have you got there?' Alex eyed the bag. It was one of theirs, with a store sticker sealing the bag shut.

'It was in the trashcan on the corner. Like someone bought it, and then tossed it. Who would do that?'

Alex tore the sticker of the bag that sealed it up and looked

A Brew for Chaos 87

inside. 'That's strange.' She looked towards the glass door as if she could still see Leith standing there. 'I packed this for a customer this morning. He was shopping for his mother . . . Or so he said.' Tanner reached into the bag and pulled out the tea and soap. 'It's paid for, right? Can I have it? I'll give it to my grandmother.'

'Of course,' Alex said distractedly. 'Take it.' She closed the store laptop, mind on Leith. Why had he stopped by, pretended to buy something and then left? He'd clearly wanted information from her, but on what?

She replayed the conversation, finally coming to stop on what Leith had really wanted to know.

Has my grandfather been by to see you?

That's what he'd really wanted to know. But why? She didn't know that man from Adam.

Around lunch, Jack called Alex. 'How about we grab something to eat?'

'The museum's café has just opened,' she suggested. 'Why don't we go there?'

He agreed, and she told him she'd meet him there in thirty minutes.

Alex removed her smock and told Tanner she'd be gone for about an hour.

It was a chilly fall day, but the air was crisp and the sun filled the sky. It was the perfect day to get bundled up and walk a few blocks. With her scarf around her neck and her jacket tightly buttoned, Alex began the short walk to the museum.

While crossing the street with a group of walkers, she bumped into someone she hadn't seen in a while. She regarded his bronzed complexion, close-cropped Afro-curly black hair and handsome features. 'Harrison?'

He grinned, his dark brown eyes creasing at the corners. 'Miss Daniels, it's nice to see you again.'

The last time she'd seen him, he was working behind the front desk at Wesley Inc, dressed in a blazer with the letter W for Wesley Inc monogrammed to the breast pocket.

Alex rubbed her palms together against a chill in the air. 'Oh, stop with the Miss. We're close enough in age . . .'

He laughed. 'It's that military training. Hard to chuck, ma'am.'

'There you go again. Just Alex.'

'All right, *Just Alex.*'

She regarded his attire. Obviously on his way from work, he was dressed in an expensive suit that was clearly tailored for his tall, muscular frame. Not bulky, showy muscle, but you could tell he spent a lot of time in the gym and probably ate baked chicken and brown rice for every meal.

'Where have you been? I know I haven't visited Wesley in a while, but I haven't even seen you around town. Small as this place is, I should've bumped into you at least ten times by now.'

He wasn't wearing an overcoat, but he did have a thick silk scarf around his throat. He pulled it tight as the breeze picked up, rustling golden leaves around them. 'My work takes me on assignment, occasionally. But not to worry, we'll be seeing each other again. I hear you're helping plan Oktoberfest?'

She laughed. 'Pepper Bellamy volunteered me. Why, are you—'

He nodded. 'Yeah, I'm entering the beer competition.'

'Didn't have you pegged for a homebrewer.'

Harrison chuckled. 'Don't judge a book by its cover, and all that.'

'I've been learning all sorts of fascinating things about beer this fall.' Alex paused as the wind whipped up a cloud of gold leaves nearby. 'That it can be used as medicine. What the various types taste like . . . What kind of beer are you entering?'

'It's a molasses porter. An old family recipe going back to North Carolina's colonial days.'

'Sounds interesting.' Alex grinned. 'So, the recipe was just passed down through the generations?'

'Kept in a brewer's cookbook, I guess you could call it. And even though brewing was historically a woman's occupation, most of my male ancestors made beer and added to the family cookbook.'

'You included?'

He pushed his hands into his pockets, 'I'm carrying on the Willoughby family tradition.'

'Your family's from Bellamy Bay?'

A Brew for Chaos   89

'No. I relocated here by myself. My family's from a small town near New Bern. Robbinsville.'

Alex thought of the few North Carolina cities she was familiar with. Raleigh. Charlotte. Wilmington . . . She shook her head. 'Never heard of it.'

'No reason you should. It's smaller than the Bay. And nothing there but a bunch of history museums.' He retrieved a gold time-piece from his pocket secured by a chain attached to his belt loop and checked the time.

Alex saw an ornate letter 'W' etched across the top. 'Fancy.'

'Another family heirloom.' He grinned at her. 'It was nice seeing you again, but I have an appointment. Stop by Wesley sometime. I'm sure Dylan would be happy to see you.'

Alex arrived at the history museum and cut through the main exhibit hall to get to the café in the garden. She had good and bad memories of this place. A good friend had died in one of their offices. But she'd gotten her justice.

She stopped in front of a new exhibit that highlighted the local indigenous tribe, the Shashanoke, awed by beautiful images of their ancestral lands in the Maritime Forest. And then another collection that showed photographs of local tunnels that began at the beach's sea caves and ran under the town proper. When she had more time, she'd have to come back and learn more about the tribe's history.

Once Jack had arrived, the waiter took their order. Minutes later they were enjoying sandwiches, a basket of house-made sweet potato chips and a mug of hot gingerbread tea for Alex and a soda for Jack when she received a text.

She read it, then sighed in disappointment.

'Bad news?'

'I'm looking for a microfiche reader. Been putting in calls all over town and so far, no dice.'

He laughed. 'You'd probably have better luck looking for a VCR. What's the need for such an old piece of equipment?'

She shrugged. 'I have microfiche and no way to read it.'

His eyebrows dipped. 'What's on it?'

She caught herself before she divulged that she was in fact investigating the Jonah Fox case. 'You know I'm helping Pepper

90 Esme Addison

with Oktoberfest?' He nodded, eyes narrowing in suspicion. 'We think Jonah left his beer recipes on some microfiche we found in his basement.'

His shoulders relaxed and he smiled at her. 'Good luck with that.' He finished his drink then sat back in his chair. 'My mother really enjoyed your visit. Thanks for being so good with her.'

'I was happy to do it.'

He took a bite of his sandwich and chewed. 'She wondered if you could come over tonight.'

'Your mother wondered, or you wondered?' Alex teased.

'Maybe both,' he admitted with a grin that showed a dimple on his chin.

They ate in silence until Alex conjured the strength to ask what was really on her mind. 'Why didn't you tell me you were in the military?'

Jack froze as he held a potato chip to his lips. And then a slow grin appeared across his face. 'My mother?'

'It came up.'

He ate the chip, then wiped his fingers on a napkin. 'Army reserves. I went to college on an ROTC scholarship – Reserve Officers' Training Corps. It's part of the tradeoff.'

'Were you ever on active duty?'

'Sure. A couple of years.'

Alex watched him. He didn't appear to be hiding anything, but nor did he seem reticent to share the information with her. Perhaps it was a nonissue. Just as he said. She'd drop it.

'So, can you come over tonight? I hopefully won't have to run out. My mother can spend some time with you. And then you and I can spend some time together as well.'

'I'd like that.'

He grinned at her. 'Perfect. It's a date.'

Minka sat on Alex's canopied bed, watching her get ready for her evening with Jack. Alex held up two tops to her chest and looked at her cousin.

'Wear the purple sweater,' Minka suggested. 'The deep plum is pretty with your dark hair and green eyes.'

Alex nodded. 'Good choice.' She shrugged out of her shop t-shirt and put the sweater on.

A Brew for Chaos

'You guys are spending a lot of time together. Getting serious?'

Alex stepped into a pair of dark brown boots, tucking her dark denim inside. 'I think so. I feel like Jack has finally come around. He's letting me in. And the more I get to know him, the more I like him . . .' She paused.

'What is it?' Minka asked.

'I just can't help but feel like he's still hiding something though. Maybe work-related.'

Minka shrugged. 'He's a cop. Kamila doesn't tell us everything she's working on. Why should he?'

'You're right. Of course.' Alex sat beside Minka on her bed. 'Would you braid my hair? One long French braid down on the side?'

'Absolutely.' She squealed. 'Remember when we used to play beauty shop when we were kids?'

Alex handed Minka a brush and turned around to face the mirror across the room on the bureau. 'If I recall, you wanted to put glitter on my and Kamila's hair no matter the style.'

Beginning to brush Alex's hair, Minka giggled. 'Every girl can use a dash of glitter in her life.' Her phone, which lay on the bed beside her, chimed a notification. She picked it up, swiped the screen and read the message. A smile played on her lips as she typed a response. She set the phone down and blushed when she met Alex's eyes.

'Your new guy?'

'What can I say, he's dreamy.' Minka picked up a spray bottle and spritzed Alex's hair with rosewater infused with jasmine. 'But mum's the word.'

'Come on. I won't tell Aunt Lidia or Kamila, if that's your concern.'

Minka laughed, then divided her hair into three sections and began braiding. 'Not yet. Don't want to jinx it.'

'Is it Leith Forbes?' Alex persisted. 'He said you gave him a tour of the aquarium.'

Her cheeks turned pink. 'I did.'

'And Zane from the brewery told me to tell you hello. Is it him?'

Minka's cheeks were practically burning now. She giggled. 'He's a sweetheart. Always gives me a free app when I come in.'

'Really?' she asked, thinking of him driving Spencer away. 'He's not a troublemaker?'

Minka made a silly face. 'Not at all. He's a law-abiding beer geek as far as I know. Does a podcast and everything.'

'So, who is it?'

'Well,' Minka tilted her head coyly. 'Whomever he is, we've been texting almost every night.'

'Really, how did I miss that?'

'Too busy looking for the Fisherman with Pepper, I've heard.' Minka laughed. 'Cracked the case yet?'

'Not even close.' Alex could see her cousin's reflection as she worked on her hair.

An inquisitive glint brightened Minka's blue eyes. 'Why *are* you looking into that old case?'

'Honestly? At first it was about helping Pepper research her article. But then Jonah was killed, and he was clearly important to her . . . I think they're related.'

Minka finished the braid and searched a drawer for a hair tie. 'So, if you find out who the Fisherman is, you think you'll discover Jonah's killer?'

'Yeah . . .' Alex half-smiled half-grimaced. 'Don't tell Jack, though. Or that will be the end of us.'

Laughing, Minka rolled her eyes at the mention of Jack's name. Then held up a dark blue ribbon to match Alex's jeans. 'Found it.'

'Not a ribbon.' Alex mock groaned. 'What am I, twelve?' But she allowed Minka to tie it to the end of the braid that landed near her elbow. 'So, how's work going? I want to stop by this week.'

'I'm still really bothered by the dolphins' lack of communication. Something is still wrong. Something is preventing them from talking to me. And their movements are off for the season. But I'll figure it out.'

'No more calls to the military base?'

'We'll see. I'm just glad Montgomery is supportive of my research in general, even if he's not when it comes to this.'

'You know Montgomery is only working with you to hide something horrible he's doing for the environment. That's his MO. Cover up his bad work with good – only we don't know what the bad is yet.'

Minka sighed. 'Does it matter if I can effect positive change?' Alex caught her cousin's eye in the mirror. 'Of course it does. Montgomery is not a good person. No matter how much money he throws at the environment. You remember what happened to Neve. Montgomery was involved in her murder, even if he didn't get punished for it.'

'I can take care of myself.' She wiggled her fingers. 'One cross move, and I'll zap him.' She pointed a finger at a bottle of lotion on Alex's dresser and knocked it over with a beam of energy. 'Just imagine that bottle is Montgomery's head.' She laughed.

But Alex didn't return the humor, remembering Leith's assessment of her. 'We know he's a dragon. They play by different rules. Or no rules at all.'

'Don't worry, *Mother*,' Minka said with an arched eyebrow. 'I'm being careful.'

'Speaking of your mother.' Alex fixed her with a look. 'When are you going to make up?'

Minka laughed. 'When she apologizes.'

Alex sighed, knowing that wasn't likely to happen, barring a miracle.

'Anyway . . . I'm using my time wisely. I'm drilling down on the GPS data. I think it's key to figuring out what's happened to the dolphins' ability to communicate.'

'Maybe Montgomery's underwater mining operations are doing something to the dolphins. Have you considered that?'

Minka sighed.

'I'm serious, Minka. What's Montgomery working on? Do you know? He's been pretty quiet these past few months.'

'Not sure. I mean, they do more than deep sea mining, what with all of their research and development contracts with the Department of Defense . . .' She hesitated. 'He's got a good heart.'

'He's a full-blooded dragon descent responsible for the death of someone we both knew,' Alex reminded her cousin.

Minka pursed her lips but didn't speak. And Alex decided to change the subject, lest Minka be on the outs with another member of her family. 'Okay. How are things with you otherwise?'

Minka relaxed the muscles in her face. 'I'm pretty focused on my work, especially with my office not being with the rest of Leviathan, but I do sit in on the weekly meetings with the other department heads.' Her smile returned. 'Can you imagine, me director of Brave New World in a suit and giving the rundown on my latest finds with the rest of the bigwigs.'

Alex smiled. 'You're a Sobieski. Of course I can.'

Minka found a handheld mirror and gave it to Alex. 'What do you think?'

Alex looked at her hair. 'It's perfect. Thank you.' She touched her cheek, eyeing her complexion. 'Maybe some blush?'

Minka stood beside her and handed her a compact. 'Montgomery's working on a big government contract. Something super top secret and worth billions of dollars.'

'Wow,' Alex said as she swept a baby pink color onto her cheekbones. 'I wonder what the specifics are.' She returned the compact to Minka, then inspected her reflection.

'I'm not privy to those conversations, but I do know they're working to advance the capabilities of our armed forces. Everyone is super proud to be working on the project whatever it is.'

Alex picked up an eyeliner pencil and lined her eyes with black kohl. Then brushed a few coats of mascara over her lashes while Minka inspected her collection of lip glosses. 'That's unexpected. Montgomery's company focuses on ocean mining. I wonder how that could be related to the military or a defense contract.'

She also wondered what Montgomery had been working on during that summer of chaos. Seemed like she needed to pay him a visit. But honestly, if she could avoid talking to him, she would.

Minka leaned forward, uncapped a mauve-colored gloss and lined her lips. 'Their portfolio is very diversified. I'm not surprised at all. But I do know they're partnering with Wesley Inc's new defense division on this project – whatever it is.'

Alex stood and gave her reflection a final look. Of course Dylan would be involved.

THIRTEEN

When Jack opened the door to his home and invited Alex in, she took one step inside and stopped.

The lights were dim, with candles lit and placed strategically around the living room. Jazz played softly in the background and Jack had a bouquet of sunflowers in his hand.

'For you,' he said, his grin lopsided with affection.

Alex took the flowers. 'This is . . .' She wanted to say uncharacteristically romantic, but that might seem rude. 'Thank you. They're beautiful.'

He chuckled, then helped her take her jacket off. 'I just wanted to show you how much I appreciate you. My mother can't stop talking about you, and that means a lot to me. She likes you. And so do I.'

She took in the room again. 'You've been planning this for a while?'

He only smiled in response.

Alex set the sunflowers on a table, then sat on the couch. Jack brought her a glass of red wine. 'Chicken Marsala's almost ready. I hope you're hungry?'

'You made Chicken Marsala?'

'It's the one dish I can cook well. I hope it's okay?'

'It smells wonderful. And I'm famished.' Alex looked around the house. 'Where is your mother?'

'She's resting. She worked in the yard all day and now she's all tuckered out. Hard to have a romantic evening with your girlfriend when your mom lives with you, I know.' He chuckled. 'But I'm trying.'

Something tugged at her heart, and she smiled at him. 'I appreciate the effort.'

Minutes passed and they were quiet as they ate. Alex tried to find a tactful way to bring up a delicate subject that wouldn't ruin the romantic mood Jack had so thoughtfully created.

'You seem a little distracted tonight. Is everything okay?'

She glanced up surprised – then not surprised that he'd noticed. She had been trying to get up the nerve to admit something to him all evening when he leaned forward.

'I can't take it any longer.' He laughed. 'What is it?'

'How'd you—' She laughed too and drank the rest of her wine for courage. 'Never mind . . . You know how you asked me not to investigate any more crimes, right?'

A guarded look crossed his eyes, and he leaned back in his chair. The Hollywood actor was gone, back was the stone-faced cop. 'Yeah.'

'It's not that exactly. But in full transparency, I wanted to share something with you. You're making an effort – I can see that, so . . .'

His jaw hardened. 'You're trying to figure out who killed Jonah Fox. I knew this couldn't last.' He sighed. 'Look, Alex, I told—'

'No,' she said quickly. 'It's not that.'

'No?' he repeated, his shoulders relaxing slightly. 'What then?'

'Pepper's writing a story about the serial killer, the Fisherman?'

He nodded. 'Yeah?'

'I'm helping her with her research. That's all. And I wanted you to know.'

He gazed at her. 'Okay.'

'Okay?' she squeaked in surprise. 'No *We're over. I'm out of here* . . . Just okay?'

'I'm done with the ultimatums. Besides, it's not an active case. I'm certainly not investigating it. I know you and Pepper are friends, she's a journalist and you have a . . . nose for information.' He grinned.

Nosiness again. She winced. 'That's a diplomatic way of putting it, I suppose.'

'Like I said, I'm trying. I get it. The anniversary of the first abduction is coming up and it was a big deal when it happened. When I first joined the force, I was given all of the cold-case files, just as a need-to-know thing for the new detective. It was pretty interesting reading.'

Alex finished her dinner and pushed the plate aside. 'Anything stand out to you as strange? I'd love to be able to give Pepper some new information.'

A Brew for Chaos 97

He shook his head. 'The main thing I noticed was that the case was poorly investigated. Information was left out – basic stuff like addresses of witnesses. Last names omitted and the suspects were barely looked at, even though there were some interesting witness accounts of the abductions. Not nearly enough follow-through.'

'Who was in charge of the investigation back then?'

'Former naval officer out of Maryland. He'd just retired from service and taken over the position when the activity began.'

'Tough luck for a rookie detective, huh?'

'I wouldn't say rookie exactly. He was former naval intelligence, so he was probably up for the job . . . but those reports.' He laughed. 'They were a mess. Can't explain it.' He stood, gathering their empty plates. 'Room for dessert? I know how much you like the pie at Bread and Putter, so I picked up two slices for us.'

'I'm pretty full, but maybe a bite or two of yours?'

'One slice of pie and two forks it is.'

'Can I help?'

His gaze softened when he looked at her, and butterflies filled Alex's stomach. 'Nope, you stay right there.'

Alex's thoughts returned to the former detective. 'Pepper said the case suffered because they waited too long to call in the SBI.'

He set a plate on the table between them and handed her a fork. 'Sounds about right.'

Alex took a bite of the pie. 'Pepper thinks that Jonah uncovered the identity of the Fisherman and that's why he was killed. He had a lot of information about the case in his home office.'

'And you know this how?'

'Helping Pepper. Remember?'

'Ri-i-i-ght.' He gave her a knowing look.

Alex didn't ask him about the Jonah Fox case, and he didn't share anything. But of course, she wondered what progress was being made in finding the killer.

After dinner, they moved to the couch and were a half hour into a Danish mystery when Jack's watch and phone simultaneously chimed. He actually groaned. 'Just one night. One night alone with my girl is all I ask.' He stood, ignored his watch but checked his phone.

98   Esme Addison

His girl? A ticklish feeling bubbled in the pit of Alex's stomach, and she watched him pace as he read his text.

'Isn't there someone else they can call?' she asked. 'Is it about the Jonah Fox case?'

'No, it's . . . it's something else,' he said, his voice vague, eyes averted.

Alex's throat tightened. He was keeping something from her, she was sure of it. But what could it be? *Another woman?* She scoffed. He didn't seem the cheating type, but you never knew . . .

'I have other cases.' He glanced upstairs. Then looked at his watch. 'It's late and she's probably in for the night . . . But—'

'Go.' She stared at him, trying to find signs of deception on his face. 'I'll stay. I don't mind.'

He looked at his phone again. 'I really do need to check this out.'

'Jack,' Maisie called from the second floor. 'Are you down there?' Her voice sounded faint and fearful.

He set his phone on the table. 'I'm going to check on her, let her know you're here and then I'll run. Okay?'

Alex went to him, hugged him tight despite her mental warning bells sounding off. 'Tonight was amazing and I'm happy to stay.'

He leaned towards her and kissed her on the mouth. 'Thank you.' Then sprinted upstairs.

Where was he going? What was this case he was working on that wasn't Jonah's?

When Alex heard Maisie's door open, she turned to look at his phone. The contact was anonymous. The message brief. A string of numbers Alex recognized as map coordinates. And a directive. **Confirm magical activity and subjects involved.**

What the . . .? Her breath caught in her throat, and she felt as if she'd been slapped in the face. Her gaze bounced to the staircase. *Magical?* That couldn't possibly mean what she thought it meant. She returned to the phone, certain she'd read it wrong. But the words were still there.

And Jack's response was equally brief. **Copy that.**

What did that mean? What did he mean? Her heart beat uncomfortably against her chest, causing a dull ache against her breastbone. She got out her phone and quickly took a photo of the coordinates.

A Brew for Chaos

Alex pretended to watch a school of goldfish float by in an aquarium when Jack returned.

'She's good. I told her you were here, and she wondered if you could make her a cup of tea?'

She forced her features into what she hoped was a normal expression. 'No problem.'

When he was gone, Alex set the tea kettle to boil and then went to the image she'd sent herself. She found the longitude and latitude points and plugged them into a website that translated them into addresses.

She looked at the residence. It was familiar. *Why was it so . . .* She plugged the address into her map app then clicked on the link to see an image of the building located there.

The tea kettle shrieked. And she jumped.

He was going to Celeste's house.

FOURTEEN

Alex dialed Celeste's phone number.

It went straight to voicemail, so she sent a text. What are you doing right now???

When she didn't respond immediately, she sent another text. Whatever you're doing, stop it. Right now. Someone is watching you.

She poured the steaming water into a mermaid cup, then placed a bag of *Spring Garden* – a Jack-approved blend – inside and waited for it to steep.

'Is my tea ready?'

Startled, Alex looked up and saw Maisie standing in the kitchen doorway in a light blue night gown and blue slippers. She rubbed her eyes sleepily but smiled when she saw Alex.

Alex jumped up. 'Yes. I'm sorry, I got . . . I was just about to bring it to you.' She removed the tea bag from the cup, set it on a saucer and placed it on the table. 'Why don't you join me? I'll have a cup as well.'

A moment later, Alex and Maisie were sharing a cup of tea.

'Jack will be home soon,' Alex assured the woman.

But she waved a hand. 'He's always running off in the middle of the night doing his *important work*,' she said with a titter. 'Top-secret work that's going to make the world a better, safer place, he tells me.' Maisie sipped her tea thoughtfully. 'He's been at it for a while. I hope he achieves his goal. He's always been so driven, you know.'

'I can see that,' Alex said. 'I'm glad he found meaningful work after he left the Army. That doesn't always happen for our veterans.'

'Hmm?' Maisie's forehead moved into a deep V. 'No, he's still in the Army. I'm just not supposed to tell anyone.' Her eyes widened. 'I was not supposed to say that. Oh dear. You won't say anything, will you?'

Alex shook her head, stunned at the news. 'So, Jack isn't really a detective?'

A Brew for Chaos

Maisie's hand trembled slightly as she brought her mermaid cup to her lips. 'I suppose it's okay if I tell you. You're his girlfriend.'

'That's right.' Alex's heart beat faster. 'I'll keep his secrets . . .'

'My Jack is an officer in the US Army. He's just pretending to be a detective for his job. His mission is what he calls it. It's his cover, you see,' she said proudly. 'So no one will know what he's really doing in town.'

FIFTEEN

After Alex had washed the dishes and Maisie returned to bed, Celeste video-called Alex.

'Hey, I just saw your missed call and texts. *Someone's watching me?*' She laughed. 'So dramatic. Like who?'

But Alex didn't laugh, her hand gripped her phone. 'What were you doing when I sent that text?'

'I don't understand why—'

'Just answer the question. Please. And then I'll explain.'

Celeste paused. 'Promise you won't laugh?'

'Of course not.'

'It's just odd that you'd ask about that specific time. I hadn't planned on telling anyone about this – this new venture of mine. At least not yet.'

Alex glanced upstairs, hoping Maisie wouldn't choose this moment to leave her room. 'Celeste, what were you doing?'

'Just practicing a little light magic.' Her bottom lip poked out into a pout. 'Okay?'

Alex took a deep breath, then explained where she was, who she'd been with and what came across his phone.

'Someone sent Jack to my house to confirm magical activity? He's the last person I want knowing,' she moaned.

'Why would he care?' Alex mused aloud. 'You're not breaking any laws . . . are you?'

'Of course not.'

'Then why would he—'

'How could he know?' Celeste asked, emotion lifting her voice. 'Just a tiny little bit of good luck magic for a customer.'

'A customer?'

'Yeah, I may or may not have a YouTube channel where I enchant subliminals for a fee.'

'Subliminals?'

'Yeah, like I record words and messages that only your subconscious can hear set to music or nature sounds . . . for weight

A Brew for Chaos   103

loss, more confidence. Subliminals are scientifically proven to work, only I boost mine with a bit of enchantment. I'm using my powers for good. Don't worry. But I'm officially creeped out by your boyfriend.'

Me too, Alex wanted to say. *Me too* . . .

'Is Jack working for the Council now?'

Alex frowned. The Council was the legal governing body of the Magical community. They enforced the rules that Magicals lived by, including limiting the use of black magic to an agreed upon percentage. They also judged and punished Magicals when they committed crimes. There was no way he was a Council enforcement agent.

Celeste laughed, then stopped cold. *'Wait,* he doesn't know about Magicals. *Ohmigod.* He *knows* about Magicals.'

A heavy silence hung between them.

'Someone sent him a message to drive to your address and confirm who you were and what you were doing.' Alex scrubbed her eyes with the palms of her hands. 'Is this what he's been up to when he's had to run off for some special case?'

Celeste swallowed. 'There has to be a logical explanation . . . Right?'

'Right . . .' And it was probably in Jack's study. As quietly as possible, she walked up the stairs, pausing at every creak, holding her breath and feeling very much like a cartoon character trying to be sneaky. When she finally made it to the study, she quietly closed the door behind her and breathed a sigh of relief. Alex glanced over her shoulder at Jack's desk before darting to it and setting the phone down, and pulling open one drawer and then another, running her hand over ink pens and other office supplies.

Celeste's mouth dropped open as she watched her from the phone screen. 'Ohmigod. You're going through his things?'

'I'm not proud of what I'm doing, but like you said, there has to be . . .' Her voice trailed off. 'I think I found something.' She picked up a small pamphlet that featured a diagram of the smart watch Jack wore. The one he didn't want her touching.

Only it wasn't a watch.

She showed the illustration to Celeste, who leaned forward. 'The QES3050.' She frowned. 'That sounds familiar . . . I just can't remember why . . . . What does it say?'

'Um . . . It's a quantum energy sensor?'

'Why would Jack have that?' Celeste mused. 'Sounds like something we'd produce at Wesley.'

Frowning, Alex turned the paper over, reviewing the device's description. Her throat constricted as she realized what she was reading. 'Oh my God.'

Celeste leaned forward. 'What is it?'

Alex began reading aloud, not sure she could believe her eyes. *'The QES3050 is designed to detect the particle-like behavior of magic in the quantum realm called "magical quanta", the smallest unit of identifiable magical energy.'* She slowly looked up from the paper and met Celeste's shocked expression.

Swallowing, she dropped her gaze and continued reading. *'Your device is calibrated to capture only powerful magical events or spells above a certain threshold, leaving weaker magic undetected. This threshold is used because actions like prayer, meditation and New Age acts of reality manifestation can at times appear as magical activity.'*

The paper dropped from Alex's hand onto the floor and the women stared at each other.

Celeste finally spoke. 'What are you going to do?'

Just then, Alex saw the lights from Jack's truck wash over the front window. Panic gripped her chest. 'I have to go.' She quickly returned everything as she found it.

By the time Jack arrived at the front door, Alex had her purse on her shoulder, ready to leave. She didn't think she could face him and any more of his lies right now. And she definitely didn't want him to look in her eyes and see that she was hiding something from him.

'How was my mom?' he asked when he entered the house, his gaze floating to the second floor.

'She was fine.' She cleared her throat, hoping she didn't sound strange. 'She had her tea, we chatted for a bit, and she went back to bed.'

He touched her chin and brought her face into the light and towards his. 'What's wrong?'

She hated that he always knew when she was lying or withholding something. Best to be as honest as possible. 'I got a bit of bad news while you were out, and I just want to go home.'

Jack is not really a policeman. He's not who he says he is. He's lied to you from day one, Alex thought to herself. *He's lied to everyone in town.*

She forced a smile. 'That's all.' She averted her eyes, really not wanting to look into his beautiful baby blues. Not tonight. Then a thought occurred to her. 'Did you find what you were looking for?'

He paused, forehead wrinkling. 'Yes. I did. Thanks for asking.'

Great, Alex thought. *What did that mean for Celeste?*

He hesitated, then walked her to her car. 'Get a good night's rest. And I'll call you tomorrow.'

Even though Alex did not make eye contact with him from the time she got in her car and backed out of his driveway, she knew his eyes were on her as she drove away.

SIXTEEN

The next morning, Alex spent a few minutes staring out her bedroom window as the sun rose.

She always found comfort with the mermaid fountain in their backyard. Fashioned from silver metal blue undertones, it was a life-size statue of a beautiful mermaid kneeling in a large shell filled with water. She held a small fish that trickled water out of its open mouth into the shell below. The mermaid's hair, a long tangled mass of waves, covered her bare chest, and her fish tail curved seductively around her.

But this morning it wasn't working. Alex put on her robe and fuzzy socks, and headed downstairs to the kitchen for breakfast. She hadn't slept well worrying about her so-called boyfriend. What was Jack up to? He wasn't really a police detective? He had a device that tracked magical activity, and someone else was dispatching him to check on the Magicals in town? She'd tossed and turned, waking up several times.

Her dreams had been nightmarish – not that she could remember them. She'd just woken up with a vague sense of dismay. Why was he dating her? Was their relationship part of the cover-up? Or did he really care for her? And who could she tell?

Her phone rang. It was him. She stopped in mid-descent and stared at the screen. Taking a deep breath, she sent the call to voicemail.

When she entered the kitchen, she stopped short. Lidia and Minka were seated at the kitchen table. But they also had a guest. It was the Jane Doe from the hospital, sitting in a wheelchair beside her aunt.

'Good morning, dear,' her aunt greeted her, rather formally.

She blinked, trying to push away the cobwebs of sleep. And then she remembered her aunt mentioning the woman would be staying with them for a while. 'Morning,' she mumbled, feeling as if she was a million miles under the sea. She needed caffeine

A Brew for Chaos   107

and fast. Alex acknowledged the woman, who stared back at her blankly.

How was dinner with Jack? Minka telepathed with a knowing grin.

Alex sighed, sliding into her chair. She paused, wondering if she should respond with her magic but remembered telepathing wouldn't register on the device. *Fine, I guess*, she telepathed in return, feeling a mixture of depression and dread.

Minka frowned at her. *What happened? You seem upset.*

Alex shrugged, taking in the breakfast spread. It looked delicious as usual, but she didn't have an appetite. *He surprised me with a romantic dinner.*

But that's great, Minka telepathed, her enthusiasm evident even without speaking.

Lidia turned a concerned eye towards Alex when she joined her, Minka and their guest at the table. 'Are you okay?'

'I'm fine. Just didn't sleep well. I'll be okay.' She reached for coffee, hoping the caffeine would lift the sense of dread that cloaked her like a wet wool blanket. 'As soon as I have this.' She poured the dark brew into her mug.

Minka frowned at her. *What did Jack do?* she telepathed to her cousin.

Alex glanced at their silent young guest. 'We can talk later.'

Jane Doe looked at Minka and then back to Alex.

'Girls,' Lidia said in her schoolteacher's voice. *Don't be rude.* 'We have a guest.'

The woman turned to look at Lidia.

Alex observed her. Her long hair had been pulled back into a high ponytail, giving her an appearance slightly younger than her twenty-some years.

'I'm Alex. I stopped by the hospital?'

The woman just looked at her.

Alex turned to her aunt. 'Are we sure she can't understand us? Has her hearing been checked?'

Lidia eyed the woman. 'Dr Crow called this morning to see how she was getting settled in . . . He also shared some results of an examination he did.' She inclined her head slightly. 'She doesn't have a larynx or vocal chords.'

108 Esme Addison

Alex's mouth dropped open. 'What? But how?' She locked eyes with Minka who'd brought a hand to her mouth.

'He thought perhaps she had throat cancer when she was younger, and they were removed.'

Aunt Lidia's voice was steady, but Alex could see how disturbed she was.

'But that's not the worst of it . . .' She took a breath before she continued. 'They found some sort of device implanted at the base of her neck.'

Minka stifled a gasp.

Lidia glanced at her daughter before continuing. 'Further tests will be needed to figure out what it is.'

Alex turned to the woman. 'Can you hear us? Understand us?'

The woman looked at her plate.

'I can't imagine what she's gone through,' Alex said. 'What's Dr Crow's next step for her?'

'More tests, and then he'll let me know when I need to bring her in for her next examination. But right now my main concern is feeding her. She's not eating,' Lidia said. 'I've made pancakes. Scrambled eggs. Potatoes. I don't know what to give her. She's already so tiny. She needs to eat.'

Alex glanced at the woman. She wore one of Minka's tank tops and pink and purple plaid flannel pajama bottoms. Her shoulders were broad – swimmer's shoulders – and her arms were thin but very toned. 'We have to give her a name. We can't keep calling her Jane Doe.' She turned to the woman. 'What's your name?'

The woman blinked.

Alex pointed to herself. 'I'm Alex Daniels.' She pointed to her cousin. 'She's Minka, and that's Lidia. What's your name?'

When the woman didn't respond or even change her expression, Lidia spoke. 'It's settled.' She rose from the table. 'Jane it is.'

That night before Alex went to bed, she thought of Spencer Francis' visit to the shop. Why did she need Jonah's recipe? Did she have anything to do with his death? What had Jonah said – that he'd give up the recipe over his dead body?

She turned off her light, snuggled under her comforter then picked up her phone and began searching for information on the

A Brew for Chaos 109

woman. There were tons of articles. Society pages. Old gossip items. Business coverage of her family's company. Historical profiles on the tavern. Product releases and content discussing their newest beers.

There was nothing that was out of the norm or appeared as a red flag to Alex. The last article she read before she put her phone down was a notification that the beverage division of Spencer's company had merged with a European pharmaceutical company a year ago. After their merger, they kept the beverage-centric name but added new divisions that focused on over-the-counter drugs and herbal supplements.

Eyes heavy with fatigue, Alex set her phone on her nightstand and fell asleep.

The next morning after breakfast when Alex returned to her room, she saw texts from Pepper and Dylan on her phone. She followed up with Pepper first, who asked her to meet at the tavern for lunch, and said she'd be there. Then she texted Dylan.

We need to talk about that list you sent me, he replied.

After agreeing to meet him at the park, Alex dressed for a jog with her hair in a ponytail, leashed up Athena and took off running. She'd stopped to catch her breath when she saw Leith at the entrance of the park buying a cup of something hot from a beverage cart.

She followed him at a distance for a few minutes until he stopped in front of the large mermaid fountain that anchored the park. She and Athena walked up alongside him.

'She's a beauty,' he said without turning to look at her. Then he shifted to face her with a grin. 'Clocked you watching me five minutes ago.'

There was something about him she found unsettling. Too aware, always assessing . . . Alex couldn't put her finger on it exactly. He was nice, but . . . it wasn't arrogance. Too smooth? No. She pushed the thought aside. 'You must be mistaken. I'm meeting a friend here. If anything, I was looking for him.'

He rocked back on his heels, shoving his hands into his pockets. 'I see.' He pointed to the fountain. 'The town's mermaid theme is very unique. I'm glad they've leaned into it.'

'Speaking of mermaids . . .' She narrowed her eyes at him.

'I guess the products you bought at our shop weren't good enough for your *mother*.'

His grin was slow. Easy. 'Ah. You've caught me.' He leaned down to pat Athena on her head, but she jerked backward with a low rumbling growl, and he rose with an awkward grin. 'Animals don't always love me. Not sure why.' He fixed a direct gaze on Alex and sighed. 'Where to begin?'

'Oh, I don't know. The fake mother? The fake shopping?'

He chuckled. 'I'm going to come clean with you, but you can't tell anyone.'

She tapped her foot impatiently. 'What are you trying to hide?'

'It's my grandfather.'

'What do you mean?'

'I'm worried about him. He's . . . not well and in his dotage has gone a little senile. It's the real reason I'm here. I knew he was planning a trip, and he wanted to come here alone. But with the behaviors I've seen from him?' He whistled. 'I knew I had to come with him. So I took leave from work and accompanied him here.'

The wind flowed around them, causing a cloud of orange and burgundy leaves to dance in the air before falling back to the ground.

'What's he doing that's so concerning?'

'He was making phone calls, then couldn't tell me who he was talking to. He'd leave his home without telling anyone – me – where he was going and then wasn't able to tell me where he'd been.'

Alex supposed those were the actions of a man dealing with senility. That or he just wanted privacy from an overzealous grandson.

'He's very sick and wants to . . . find peace. Before . . .' His voice faltered, and a wave of empathy washed over Alex.

She reached out and touched his arm. 'I'm sorry, I know it can't be easy.'

He took a long breath and regained his composure. 'I'm very, very worried about him. He's behaving in ways that are out of character for him. And I know it's because . . .' He cleared his throat. 'I found a list of names and places in his luggage. I guess they're places he wanted to see on this trip and people he wanted to talk to.'

A Brew for Chaos
111

'When was he last in Bellamy Bay? What's his connection to this town?'

'Honestly, I don't know. He only talked about golfing here, so I assume he had fond memories of the area.'

'Mac said he was in the military. Was he ever stationed at Camp Malveaux?'

'I'm not sure. That was way before my time, but it's possible.'

'Was I on the list?'

'No, but your shop was.' He shrugged. 'No idea why, and he can't or won't tell me when I bring it up. And I'm certainly not going to ask him about the list since I'm not supposed to know about its existence.'

Alex stared at Leith. The muscles of his face were relaxed, and his eyes clear, if not tinged with concern for his grandfather. The face of someone telling the truth. 'My apologies.'

He grinned. 'Accepted. And I get it.'

'You didn't have to throw the soap and tea away, though.' Her tone was teasing. 'I worked hard on those.'

'Noted. And if you happen to see my grandfather wandering around alone . . . let me know?'

'Of course. I'll leave a message for you at the Seaside.' She watched him walk away, then turned to find Dylan.

He was sitting on a bench in front of a large mural that featured mythological gods and mermaids. A few yards away, she stopped at the dog water fountain for Athena, and Dylan approached them. He was dressed casually for a Saturday morning stroll in the park.

He reached out and let Athena sniff his hand before rubbing her head. 'Hey, girl. You have a good run?' He turned to Alex. 'Thanks for meeting me. And how was your run?'

His scent of something dark and spicy drifted her way. Frankincense, maybe sandalwood? It was good. 'I needed to clear my head,' she said, thinking of Jack's deception. She needed to tell her family about him, but first she needed more information before she sounded the alarm.

Dylan headed for the bench, and they sat down. Exhausted after their run, Athena plopped down at Alex's feet.

'Where did you find that list of names?' he asked without preamble, his expression graver than she'd ever seen it.

She was almost afraid to answer him. 'Why?'

'Because it contains information that the general public is not cleared for.'

'*Cleared* for?'

'The way the people on that list are connected is top secret.'

'I don't understand. I got that list from a member of the media.'

'Don't play, Alex,' Dylan insisted. 'Just tell me why you asked me to look those particular names up.'

Alex's heart tripled time. 'It's a list of victims from the Fisherman. The names that were checked off were taken. The ones that weren't checked, well, I guess he never got around to grabbing them.'

Dylan closed his eyes and rubbed his temples. 'That can't be.'

'I've never seen you this upset. What's wrong? What do *you* think it's a list of?'

He ran a hand through his hair and closed his eyes before turning to Alex. 'I ran each and every one of those names through a series of databases. And every name on that list has a family member with the mermaid gene. Which means every woman on that list is – was – a genetic mermaid.'

SEVENTEEN

'That can't be a coincidence,' Alex said, gazing at the large mermaid fountain in the distance. 'So, the Fisherman was abducting women with the mermaid gene.' She shook her head slowly, unable to wrap her mind around this latest information.

Dylan shot her a strange look before turning his shoulders away from her. 'It's actually the reason my father started Wesley Inc.'

She stared at him, almost afraid to learn more. 'Please tell me Montgomery doesn't have anything to do with this? Minka said Leviathan was partnering with Wesley on a new defense contract.'

He stood up and began to pace in front of their bench. 'One thing at a time. This list . . . Where did you find it?'

'Jonah Fox had it, along with a lot of information about the Fisherman. Pepper thinks he was researching the case and knew his identity. And that's why he was killed – he was about to tell the world who the Fisherman was.' Alex swallowed slowly. 'And if I can figure out who the Fisherman is, I'll know who killed Jonah.'

'I checked and double checked. That list of names hasn't been published in relation to the mermaid gene. But I told you – Neve told you, before she died – that there were people compiling a list of everyone with that gene.'

'But to what end?'

'How can I contain this?' he murmured to himself. 'I'm trying to protect our people. Trying to fix what my grandfather started—'

'Dylan, calm down,' Alex said, grabbing his arm. 'How is your grandfather involved in this?'

He glanced down at her hand on his arm then back into her eyes. Something sizzled between them.

She snatched her arm away, unsure of what she was feeling.

He took a deep breath, and the moment was gone. 'I don't want to talk about this here. Now. Out in the open. Why don't you come by the house later?'

'And the list?'

'I pray I'm wrong, but I think I know why those women were taken. I'm going to have Harrison contact the other families on that list, make sure they know to take precautions in case someone is still looking for other family members.'

'Harrison? But he's—'

'Discreet.'

Alex nodded, thinking she had no clue what Harrison actually did at Wesley. 'But the Fisherman is no longer active. No one has been abducted for decades. There's no danger, right?'

He gave her a guarded look. 'Come by the house tonight at seven. We'll talk then.'

EIGHTEEN

'Mom is trying to figure out how to help Jane,' Minka said when Alex returned from her jog.

Minka trailed her into the kitchen while she refilled her water bottle.

'You're talking now?' Alex asked over her shoulder.

'We're civil. We have company. Besides, I'm not the one with the problem. It's her.'

'By *her* you mean your mother?' Alex turned to look at her cousin. 'Sounds like you're holding a grudge too.'

Minka flicked her hand. 'I'm not a child and she can't tell me what to do anymore.'

Alex cocked her head but didn't respond.

'So anyway,' Minka rushed to change the subject. 'She completed a body and aura scan and said Jane appears to be healthy, at least physically. Though there is something hinky with her bones and joints.'

Deciding to let the matter rest, Alex refilled Athena's water bowl too. 'Okay. So that's why she can't walk. Is it because of the attack?'

Lidia entered the room, ignoring Minka completely. 'That was the initial thought, but no. Turns out the muscles simply aren't strong enough to hold her weight up. And the bone density in her legs is lower than it should be.' She selected a mug from a stand, then opened the refrigerator.

Alex glanced at Minka, who was glaring defiantly at her mother's back as if daring her to speak to her. When Lidia retrieved a jug of tea and closed the door, she kept her gaze on Alex.

'Her low bone density in her legs, paired with the healed scars on her wrists, leave me to believe that she was held against her will for a time. Perhaps she was tied to a bed or just unable to exercise.' She poured amber liquid smelling of cinnamon and nutmeg in her mug, then returned the jug to the refrigerator.

'So, the police should be looking for whoever held her captive,' Alex said, forgetting about Minka for the moment. 'Do you think she escaped from someone, and Jonah tried to intervene – to protect her – and was killed and she was left for . . .' Alex shook her head. 'None of the pieces of this case are fitting together.' Then she thought, she should call Jack. But no, he wasn't a real cop. And she'd successfully dodged his calls. No way she would initiate a conversation with him. 'We should tell Kamila.'

Growing uneasy with her mother's cold shoulder, Minka crossed her arms tightly across her chest, a frown growing on her face.

'I've already called her,' Aunt Lidia said, turning to face Alex and block out Minka's angry body language. 'She's coming by tonight to try and speak with her again. And I've called Daphne and Celeste to come over too. We're going to perform a healing over Jane and hopefully we can help her walk again. And hear. And talk. You come too. The more people, the stronger the healing.'

Finally, Minka couldn't take it anymore. 'You're healing our guest but won't heal the rift between you and me?' Her cheeks flushed pink with anger. 'You're just going to pretend like you didn't say all those mean things to me? Never going to apologize?'

'Mean things?' Lidia thundered. 'And apologize for what? I was only reminding you that you were a Sobieski, and you have no business working with that dragon. He only means you harm.'

Minka's eyes filled with tears. 'You just don't respect me or my decisions.'

'That's not true.' Lidia set her cup down on the table with a clink. 'I don't trust Montgomery.' Her eyes flashed. 'Neve worked with him, and we saw what happened to her.'

'I can take care of myself.' Minka moved around the room, grabbing her purse and keys. 'Montgomery was right. You still see me as a child, and I'll never be fully independent until I completely break from you.'

Alex stared at her aunt then glanced at her cousin, unsure what to say to deescalate the moment. 'Guys . . .'

'Is that why you quit your job?' Lidia interjected. 'Because you were trying to get away from me?'

'In part, yes.' Minka's chin jutted out. 'But I've also just decided . . .' Panic washed across her face and her eyes roved around the kitchen. 'I'm moving out.'

Lidia flung her arm, and the faucet turned on with explosive force. 'This is that monster's doing. He's gotten into your head, making you think things.'

Wincing, Alex moved to the faucet and turned it off.

Minka turned to Alex, pointing a finger at her mother. 'See what I mean. She thinks I'm weak. Easily manipulated . . .'

'Minka,' Alex exclaimed. 'You don't mean that.'

Minka nodded, tears splashing down her cheeks. She took a moment to calm herself with a steadying breath. 'I've finally figured out why the dolphins aren't communicating.' She wiped the tears from her eyes. 'Once I send my report to Montgomery, hopefully he'll do something about it. I want to get it to him tonight, before our Monday morning team meeting.'

'And then?' Alex prompted, sneaking a glance at her aunt.

'Then I'll let you know where I land.'

NINETEEN

Minka fled the house.

Lidia refused to talk about the argument with Alex, so Alex drove to the tavern a few minutes before noon and searched the dining room for Pepper. But she stopped short when she saw Montgomery having a drink at the bar. Minka's words floated through her brain. *Montgomery was right. You still see me as a child, and I'll never be fully independent until I completely break from you.*

Anger pushed her towards him without a second thought.

By the time she'd reached his side, she'd taken several breaths and looked, she hoped, composed.

He looked up and smiled when he saw her. 'Hello, Miss Daniels.'

She gritted her teeth. 'Montgomery.'

'Can I buy the lady a drink?' He pushed a laminated menu towards her, but Alex shook her head.

'Thank you, but no. I'm actually here because of Minka.'

His grin widened at her name. 'You must be so proud of her. She's done a lovely job thus far with our ocean-based initiatives.'

'Is trying to separate her from her family a part of *your* initiative?'

He took a long draw from his beer mug. 'Whatever do you mean? I've always been a strong advocate for family.' His dark eyes glinted. 'It's why I've stayed in town. My sister is here.' He raised a suggestive eyebrow. 'And my nephew.'

Alex ignored the look. 'Minka has mentioned several times that you think she'd be better off without her family, or that she should move out.'

'She's such a delicate flower who hasn't been allowed to bloom under the shadow of her mother.' He tilted his head. 'You can't deny that your aunt has a strong presence that might stilt growth in her children.'

'Kamila is fine.'

A Brew for Chaos

119

'Kamila is very different from her sister. More importantly, she doesn't practice. She wishes she were a Mundane.' His nostrils flared as if the very idea was repugnant to him.

Alex tamped down a wave of panic. Minka had shared too much with this man.

'But Minka embraces her identity and has expressed a desire to test the limits of her abilities in ways her mother would never allow.'

Something hot and stinging flowed through Alex's body, and she leaned forward, her voice a murmur. 'Leave. Minka. Alone.'

He moved even closer, so that Alex could feel the heat of his breath on her cheek. 'Or what?'

She pulled back and saw he was grinning.

He finished his drink and stood, throwing a few dollars on the bar top. 'You're fun, Alex.'

Body trembling with anger, she watched him snake his way through tables and exit the building. And then Leith was at her side, a calming hand on her arm. 'You okay?'

She took a breath. 'Where'd you come from?'

He jerked his head towards a nearby table. 'Saw you getting into it with Montgomery, and thought I'd play referee if needed.' He raised an eyebrow. 'But you stood your ground.'

Her laugh was weak. 'Is that why I'm shaking?' She held up a hand so he could see her trembling fingers.

He looked towards his table. 'You're welcome to join me and my boys.'

Alex looked at his *boys*. Four rough-looking men with strong athletic builds. Two had beards, one was shaved bald and the other had a buzz cut. 'Golfing buddies?'

He laughed. 'No. Old military pals.'

She smiled. 'You served like your grandfather.'

Leith nodded. 'We get together whenever I come up from Georgia. Two live in Wilmington, another in Morehead City and one's in Myrtle Beach.'

She gave them a second look, taking in their heavily tattooed arms. One of them raised his beer glass to her and she couldn't help but notice the ugly pink burn scar on his forearm. He winked at her. Her cue to stop staring. 'And what do you do when you get together? If not golf.'

He bopped her nose like a father might do his child. 'There goes that nosiness again.' He grinned when she took a step back, then laughed at his cheek. 'Water sports mostly. Skiing, jet skis, snorkeling . . . beach stuff.'

'I'll let you get back to your friends. Thank you for checking on me.' She stood in the middle of the busy tavern, watching him weave his way through tables, when Pepper caught her eye, waving with a wild arm.

When Alex reached her, Pepper swatted her shoulder playfully. 'What were you doing? Chatting up Montgomery and that cutie pie.' Her mouth dropped open. 'Who is that?'

'Leith McDonald. He's in town for a golf weekend.'

Pepper eyed him with interest. 'Was he asking you out?'

Alex followed her gaze, watching him thoughtfully. 'No, he was just being one of your southern gentlemen. Seeing if I needed to be rescued.'

'I've been trying to catch your attention for the longest.' She waved a hand towards the table. 'Ta da.'

Alex noticed several flights of beer. A slow grin crossed her face. 'What are we doing?'

Pepper held up a shot glass of amber liquid. 'Taste-testing the beers for Oktoberfest.' She looked towards the tavern's opening door. 'With her.'

Spencer advanced upon them in tight jeans, high-heeled boots and a mustard-colored sweater. 'I'm here. Let's get the party started.'

Alex sighed, resigned to her duty. Not that she was complaining. After the tense moments with her aunt, Minka and Montgomery, she could use a beer.

Spencer shrugged. 'I told her we could use my brewery's beers, already approved by me, but she wants to support local beer-makers.' She fanned her hand around the flights. 'Here we are.' She pushed a flight forward. 'We're going to try five different types of beer in the German style. They are all brewed by North Carolina breweries, including my own.

'The first beer flight is brewed in the Märzen style. Look for a variety of colors and a robust maltiness that develops into a rich caramel and finishes with a crispness.' She pointed at the

A Brew for Chaos

flight of four glasses. 'They are from Chapel Hill, Asheville, New Bern and, of course, my brewery.'

Alex and Pepper selected a glass and took sips.

Spencer leaned forward. 'What do you think?'

Pepper tapped the one that was golden brown. 'Medium body. I pick this one.'

Alex tried it again. 'It's good, but I like this one.' She held up a copper-gold beer and sniffed. 'Smells like buttered toast. With jam?'

Spencer nodded encouragingly. 'You have a good nose.'

Alex didn't share that enhanced sense of smell was just another superpower she had courtesy of her mermaid DNA. 'Thanks.' She took another sip. 'Yeasty, like freshly baked bread. Maybe with a hint of cardamom?'

Pepper rolled her eyes. 'Seriously? Cardamom?' She laughed. 'Show off. Let me try.' She picked up the glass and tossed it back. 'Okay, sure it's good. I get the dinner roll taste but no jam. Definitely no spice.'

'This one is my pick.' Alex held up her glass.

A smug grin spread across Spencer's face. 'Wonderful. That's mine. We partnered with a brewery in Bavaria to make that one.' She pushed another flight towards them, four glasses of gleaming gold ale. 'Next one is Helles.'

Alex swayed a bit. 'I think the beer just hit my brain,' she whispered to Pepper.

Spencer laughed. 'I heard that. Lightweights,' she scoffed. 'Märzen has one of the highest ABV, alcohol by volumes, at 6.3 per cent. And we're just getting started.' She snapped her fingers at the bartender. 'Bring us a charcuterie board.'

Alex saw Zane behind the counter and excused herself. Spencer didn't provide an explanation for her behavior the other night, but Zane might. Minka vouched for him after all. She reached the counter and waved her fingers at him.

'Hey.'

He raised an eyebrow. 'Hey. Help you with something?'

'You gonna give me a free app like you do Minka?'

His eyes widened. 'She told you that?'

'Yeah. You like her, right?'

He grinned. 'What's not to like? She's beautiful, smart and passionate about her work.'

'That's what I thought.' She eyed him critically. 'So, now I'm concerned, since I saw you driving Spencer's getaway car.'

He paled, beads of sweat covering his forehead. His eyes darted to Spencer before he spoke. 'I don't know what that was about.'

'Really?' Alex couldn't hide her skepticism. 'I would've thought you drove for NASCAR the way you pealed away from me and Pepper.'

'That *was* embarrassing.' He chuckled. 'She jumped in the car and said punch it. So, I punched it.'

Alex looked over her shoulder at Spencer. 'No questions asked?'

'No questions asked,' he agreed. 'You learn that real quick working for her. She's a good businesswoman but really brings the drama, if you know what I mean.'

'Did she tell you why she went to Jonah's?'

'No.' His tone rose in indignation. 'That's the thing. We were supposed to be going on a supply run – paper napkins, light bulbs, that kinda thing? We were on our way back from the big box store in Wilmington when she told me to stop at an address. I did. Did some research for my next podcast while she did whatever it was she was doing. And next thing I know, she's jumping in the car like she's in *The Dukes of Hazzard*.'

Alex searched his face for signs of deception, but only found sincerity. If he was a liar, he was a good one. 'Okay, I choose to believe you.'

He sputtered in bemusement. 'But I didn't—'

'If you take Minka out, I'll be watching.' She jokingly punched his shoulder. 'Treat her like the princess she is.'

His eyebrows dipped slightly, but then he smiled. 'Of course.'

Alex returned to the table. After an hour had passed, they had selected all of the beers for the festival, and both Pepper and Alex were sucking down glasses of water, though a plate of cheese and pepperoni helped to soak up some of the alcohol.

The bartender was bussing their area when Spencer looked at the pair. 'It's a shame Jonah couldn't be here to help us plan, huh?'

A Brew for Chaos

Wary, Pepper nodded. 'He loved Oktoberfest.'

'And too bad we don't have any of his beer to include in the event . . .' She eyed Pepper shrewdly. 'We don't, do we? Because I'd love a sample.'

Pepper glanced at Alex, who frowned. 'Why? So you can reverse engineer his award-winning beer?'

Spencer laughed, tossing her bangs out of her face. 'You really think this is about winning a state fair competition?' She rolled her eyes. 'You yokels . . .' She stood, pushing back from the bar. 'He's dead, you know. Why are you still protecting him and his property?'

Pepper also stood, anger slanting her features. 'Because he clearly didn't want you to have it.' Annoyance stiffened her movements as she picked up her purse. 'You're only involved in this event because you paid your way in. It doesn't mean you're leaving with his secret recipe.'

'Doesn't it?' She cackled, seeming to enjoy the interaction. 'It has to be here, in this town. And I will find it.'

Pepper stepped closer to the woman, her face flushed red. 'Did you kill him?' Her voice rose. 'Did you kill him when he wouldn't give you what you wanted?'

The bartender stopped wiping down the bar and looked over. Several customers turned to stare, and Alex grabbed Pepper's arm and pulled her back. 'Let's get out of here. We've all had a bit to drink, you're emotional and she clearly likes to push buttons.'

Pepper allowed Alex to drag her out of the tavern. But when they were on the sidewalk, she squealed in frustration. 'We have to find out who did this to Jonah. And right now, my money is on her.'

TWENTY

Later that evening, Alex called a taxi to take her to Dylan's house.

After her beer taste-testing, even though she felt okay, Alex thought it was better to let someone else drive. She'd pick up her car in the morning.

Alex gazed out of her window as the taxi drove her out of town and crossed the bridge that connected the mainland with a sliver of land called The Peninsula. The exclusive area was home to large estates on even larger plots of land, most of which backed up to the bay.

Pepper came to mind as she descended the bridge and made her way down a long winding road that ran parallel with the ocean. She agreed with her friend that Spencer seemed suspicious. She'd have to do a little digging.

And then she was upon the Wesley estate, and riding through the tall, black wrought iron gates that protected Dylan's ten acres. The taxi circled the driveway in front of his family home, a massive thing of gray stone and black spires, topped with a dramatic pitched roof and bolstered by epic pillars, when she received a text from Minka.

Almost done with my work. A friend is stopping by for coffee and a chat, and then I'll be on my way. Despite my argument with Mom, I want to help Jane.

Alex typed a response. Are you okay?

I'm fine. Don't worry about me.

Alex hesitated, responded with a thumbs up, paid for the ride with a phone app, thanked the driver then stepped out of her car.

Alfred, the butler, brought her into the foyer. 'Miss Aleksandra, it's been several months. Nice to see you.'

'Thank you, Alfred.' Alex followed him into the library, where Dylan was waiting for her in front of a roaring fire. He'd changed into Italian leather loafers, olive-green slacks and a merlot cashmere sweater. He waited for Alfred to close the door before speaking.

A Brew for Chaos   125

'Thank you for coming, Alex. Alfred will bring in wine and appetizers shortly in case you're in need of refreshment.'

Alex saw that his hair was still damp from the shower. She allowed him to air kiss her cheeks on both sides and breathed in his spicy-sweet scent when he was close to her. 'Were you able to contact the families?'

'Harrison is working on it as we speak.'

'You mentioned that. You know, when I first moved here and met him at the front desk at Wesley, I thought he was a receptionist.'

'Harrison is a former Recon Marine who heads up my security operations. One of his guys had a family emergency, so he filled in at the front. Our receptionist is actually an armed guard.' He paused when he saw Alex's face. 'We deal in top-secret government contracts. Corporate espionage is a concern.'

'Okay,' Alex said.

'So, Harrison has no problem handling the front desk if one of his team calls in.'

She regarded him. He appeared to be relaxed, but he sounded on edge. She needed to tell him about Jack, but maybe after he'd had a glass of wine. 'You wanted to tell me about the origins of Wesley?'

He stared into the fire, the muscles of his back tense. 'My grandfather established Wesley Inc in the early fifties. Mythological weapons had just begun to surface, and he got his hands on several weapons mentioned in the Ramayana.'

'The Indian epic?'

He nodded. 'Weapons with unimaginable power, that were previously thought to be figments of an overactive author's imagination, were real. And the wrong types of people were grabbing them. He sent a team out to get them first, keep them in the hands of the good guys—'

'Like you did with the Mermaid of Warsaw's shield.'

He nodded. 'My grandfather was able to save many weapons. But then he wanted to reverse engineer them, mass produce them and sell them to the military. He thought it would give us the edge we needed over Russia. World War II had just ended, and many feared for the next war. He created a company . . .' He paused. 'With the help of Uncle Montgomery and his

126 Esme Addison

connections, he hired some scientists from Operation Paperclip—'

Alex stared at the rows of old books around them. The first time she'd been in this room she'd had a run-in with Dylan's sister. This time was much more pleasant. 'Of course your uncle would know the Nazis scientists brought over to the US after the war.' She crossed her arms. 'They were here in Bellamy Bay?'

'Not here. Paradise Beach and Camp Malveaux. So yes, my grandfather is responsible for bringing Montgomery to our town. At least initially.' He gritted his teeth. 'Uncle Montgomery used his connections to help the American government. And my grandfather pitched his ideas to the Department of Defense,' Dylan continued.

She regarded him for a moment, until a note of something familiar floated under her nostrils. She sniffed the air, then rose from her seat, moving to get a closer look at the books while Dylan tracked her movements with his eyes. She trailed her fingers over the volumes, glancing at him over her shoulder. *Could he smell it too?*

He followed her, a quizzical look on his face but didn't ask her what she was searching for. 'He was given a budget, support from Camp Malveaux, and Wesley Inc was off. Several new weapons were created based on the technology he had, in particular surface-to-air missiles. But once those contracts were over, they wanted more from him. More advanced technology.'

She sniffed the air again . . . and smelled . . . magic mixed with the tangy scent of old books. Probably not an oddity in the Wesley home, but it was particularly strong in the library. She followed the scent to a shelf, and selected a red leather journal before looking at Dylan. 'And?'

Dylan's jaw was set in a hard line. 'And . . . This was when he made a calculated decision to tell someone – his contact in the DOD – about Magicals.' His gaze fell to the book in her hand. 'As far as I know, this was the first time they were made aware of . . . us.'

She flipped through the pages of the book, skimming the lists of names on the yellowing paper. 'What did he tell them exactly?'

Dylan shook his head as if he were embarrassed. 'You're looking at it.' He gestured towards the book in her hands. 'For

A Brew for Chaos

starters, he gave them a list of families prominent in the Magical community. Just the heads of the families. But with that information . . .' He trailed off.

'They could track family members through the generations,' Alex finished for him. Her stomach flip-flopped. 'Is my family in here?' When he nodded slightly, she closed the book abruptly and returned it to its place on the shelf. 'So they know who we are.'

'Not precisely. They have people they suspect of Magical heritage. But they can't know definitively unless they test their genetics or see their abilities being used.'

'Or read that book?' She pointed at it. 'That's dangerous knowledge. Why do you keep it?'

'As you smelled, it's protected by magic. So it is safe. Only another Magical can read it.'

'But—'

'The pages appear blank to a Mundane. But . . . My father kept a list of every name he gave to the military. Thought maybe one day we'd need it.'

'I can't believe the government has knowledge of Magicals and just lets us . . . I don't know, run around being magical.'

'They don't. That's one of the reasons the Council was created. Once the proverbial cat was out of the bag, knowledge about Magicals was designated an unacknowledged Special Access Program within the government. Most of the normal reporting requirements were waived and only given in oral reports to the heads of certain senate committees. However, one mandate the government insisted upon was a checks and balance system for our community.'

'The Council,' Alex said.

'Yeah. Fortunately they allowed us to police ourselves. Not that they could really control us if they wanted to, but most of us want to be law-abiding citizens and appreciate the oversight. As you know, there's always one apple to spoil the rest . . .'

He made a face, and Alex knew he was thinking of his sister.

Dylan began to pace, a nervous habit Alex noted he had lately. 'Wesley got the contracts to develop the policing tools the Council needed.' He shrugged. 'A new clearance had to be created. The establishment of the program, the regulations, the budget, it was rolled into the Atomic Energy Act of 1954.'

'But why a nuclear program?'

'Silly, right?' He laughed. 'For one thing it was considered the most protected type of information at the time, and they wanted the program established with rigorous security procedures already in place. But on the other hand, technically magic is a type of energy . . . quantum, not nuclear, but still the powers that be at the time thought it was the right place for the program.'

'It's really fascinating how the history of Magicals is so intertwined with the US government, the military . . .'

'All because of my grandfather. And it went well for a while. He got rich, and the government had powerful weapons that helped position them as a world power. But as time went on, and more people received M-Class clearance and learned about the Magical community, the more information they wanted about our people. Our abilities. At first my grandfather didn't want to share more information, he really wanted to protect the community, but they offered him more money and just kept raising the offers. I'm talking millions and millions of dollars for information. And like us all, he had a price.'

'Your family's wealth comes from . . .'

Dylan's expression turned bitter. 'My grandfather was a good man. A patriot. He wanted to help his country . . . so, he told them about his Mer heritage, and about his abilities. He thought he could contain the information to just him, so he offered himself up as a test subject with the idea that a DNA-modifying serum could be created from his DNA that could be injected in our armed forces, giving them things like enhanced swimming abilities, improved agility, internal GPS, echolocation, the ability to stay underwater longer, in cold temperatures, deeper depths . . .

'I'm not sure why, but the idea of a serum fell out of favor when he told them there were other men and women with the gene.' He shook his head, a look of disgust on his face. 'Everyday people. Regular people who didn't even know they had Magical genetics. They wanted him to bring these people in as test subjects. When he refused, they took all of his research which was proprietary to the DOD and said they'd continue their work without him.'

'That's horrible, Dylan.'

'He completely lost control of the project. He spent his last days writing names in that book. From memory. And when he died, he felt he was a failure, that he'd betrayed his people, and he made his son – my father – promise to spend the rest of his life cleaning up his mess. And my father did until he died of a heart attack in his forties. I think the stress . . .' He sighed. 'So, I've spent a lot of resources diversifying our portfolio so that our money is one: not tied up in military contracts related to what my grandfather started, but two: buying up the private companies that inherited his research through past and current government contracts so I can help contain it.'

'So the Fisherman's list . . . Those women. You think they were abducted and tested on, then killed?'

'I cross-referenced the Fisherman's list against the one my father made. Each woman was connected to a family in the book. My father's legacy,' he said, his voice barely a whisper. 'My legacy . . .'

'That would make the US government, the DOD, the military all complicit in ten women's deaths.'

'I know.' His shoulders slumped. 'It was called the *Anomalous Trait Genome Evaluation Program.* Something so innocuous sounding.' He ran a hand through his hair. 'I don't know how I can bear this, Alex. The weight of what my grandfather has done. What my father was not able to accomplish . . . This is what ruined my parents' marriage. Turned my mother and sister into what they are today. This is what killed my father. And now . . . now it's my burden.'

Alex went to him, wrapped her arms around him and flooded him with healing and tranquility and light. She gave him everything she had, hoping to wash him in peace, drown him in love and . . .

He pulled back slightly and gazed into her eyes. 'My God, Alex, you're powerful. The strength of your healing . . .' He closed his eyes until a smile appeared on his face. 'Thank you. I needed that.'

She took his hand, overwhelmed by the amount of pain she'd wicked from his body. She'd momentarily felt it as it passed through her body and disappeared around them and into the ether, chilling the air and lowering the temperature in the room by at least five degrees.

He fell into a leather chair. 'I never think to heal myself.'

'Me either. But the compulsion to heal others sometimes is overwhelming. I hope you don't mind,' she said, remembering how Jack had responded. *Did he know what magic felt like? Did he suspect her?* She pushed the thought away.

He laughed. 'Who in their right mind would be annoyed by that?' He shook his head. 'My mind is clear, and I can think properly. I'm afraid the news of that list hit me hard. It confirmed my worst fears, that the government is continuing their research into the Mer gene based on the information my grandfather gave them. Really knocked me for a loop.'

'So, the Fisherman wasn't some psycho who hated women. He was probably a government operative. Which means the Fisherman himself probably killed Jonah.'

'Definitely suspicious,' he agreed. 'Sounds like there was a secret operation happening that summer. Then the Fisherman returns forty years later to clean up the mess.'

'Maybe he found out Jonah was on to him?' Alex suggested, then told him her theory about the police detective who'd investigated the cases. 'Could it be that the detective was a plant from the government working with the Fisherman?'

'Who knows?'

Alex sighed. 'I wonder what happened to those women.'

'They were probably tested on at some secret military facility and then their bodies were disposed of . . . like throwing trash into the ocean.'

Closing her eyes, Alex covered her mouth with a hand. 'Camp Malveaux?'

'No. That's not secret. It would have to be a location that is on no one's radar. No senatorial oversight. No media watchdogs. No concerned citizens. A completely black site for inhumane testing on humans.'

'Sounds like something out of World War II. And why women? Why not test men too?'

'I know the answer to that. As is the case with female and male sharks, studies showed that Mer women's abilities are stronger then Mer men by about 30 per cent. A substantial difference in a testing environment.' Dylan's shoulders slumped further. 'I'm running out of ideas to contain this situation.'

A Brew for Chaos 131

'I'll tell you what we have to do. We have to find out what happened to those women. And in order to do that, I have to know once and for all who the Fisherman was. He killed Jonah . . . he's the key to everything.'

And then the door opened, and Alfred entered with a bottle of red wine, two glasses and a tray of fresh bread, cheese, dried olives and prosciutto.

Alex put a few items on her plate, while Dylan poured them both a glass of wine. And after Alex watched him take a few sips, she set her plate down.

'There's something I have to tell you, about Jack.'

TWENTY-ONE

'You're just in time,' Lidia said, when Alex returned to the house.

Alex watched her aunt, checking for signs of the earlier anger she'd felt . . . but she seemed fine. Alex relaxed her shoulders, and after she greeted Athena, she took off her coat and hung it up on the nearby coatrack and kicked off her boots.

Dylan's confession rang in her ears. Jack's duplicity made her chest ache. She needed to tell everyone about Jack, but it never seemed like the right time. Dylan hadn't responded well, and she knew her family wouldn't either. But right now she needed to focus on helping Jane.

'Glad to hear it. I want to help where I can,' she told her aunt. She went into the living room and saw Celeste. She was standing beside her mother, Daphne, who was also Lidia's cousin and best friend since high school. With a coloring similar to her daughter's, she was a petite, full-figured woman who wore her naturally textured hair back in a French twist. They were already kneeling on the floor in a semi-circle around Jane, who sat in her wheelchair. Athena went to a corner and curled into a comfortable position.

Alex would've been worried that Jack would pick up on the magical activity they were about to begin, but she knew her aunt had a protective spell over the house and shop decades old that hid their magic from witch hunters. It would prevent Jack's watch from sensing their magic as well.

'I've explained to her what we're going to do, what we hope to accomplish, and asked her to let us know if she wanted us to proceed,' Lidia said.

'She just looked at us, so let's hope that's her giving us consent,' Celeste said with an optimistic smile.

Alex looked around the room. 'Where's Minka? She's supposed to be joining us.'

A Brew for Chaos

133

'I guess she's still at work.' Lidia stiffened. 'But perhaps she's changed her mind and gone elsewhere.'

Alex looked at the wall clock. 'It's almost nine.'

Lidia pursed her lips. 'You heard what she said . . . Maybe she's staying with a friend.'

Celeste glanced at them both curiously. 'What's going on?'

'Nothing,' Alex rushed. 'Minka's burning the midnight oil.'

Celeste shrugged. 'Welcome to corporate America. I've been at the Wesley offices until midnight sometimes when I have a project to complete.'

'She wanted us to wait for her,' Alex hedged.

'Speaking of work.' Celeste wrapped an arm around Alex and moved her out of earshot of Lidia and her mother. 'I knew that watch Jack had looked familiar. It's a Wesley Inc product. Before my time, but apparently Bryn headed that project.'

Alex rolled her eyes. Bryn was a vicious businesswoman who'd literally killed to close a business deal. 'How did it get in Jack's hands?'

'It was made for the Council – you know how they track the practice of black magic in the Magical community. Well, according to the documents I read, she tweaked it and sold it to the government to track down decent hardworking Magicals practicing good magic.' She wrinkled her nose. 'Like myself.'

Alex puffed out a breath. 'Anything to make a buck.'

'We've waited long enough.' Lidia interrupted their conversation. 'I gave Jane a tonic to enhance our efforts to heal her and strengthen her immune system.' She reached out her hand to Alex. 'Join us.'

Alex glanced at the door, hoping Minka would burst through, but ultimately joined the circle, with them all sinking to a kneeling position, heads bowed. Athena stood to join Alex on the floor, but she shook her head. 'Place, Athena.' And she returned to her spot, though her big brown eyes watched the group with interest.

Alex. Lidia's voice telepathed to her. *I know this is your first time doing this in a group. It's the same as when you heal someone by yourself. Just gather the energy of healing within you and allow it to merge with everyone else's energy. Together it will grow in strength and power, and then as a group we will direct it to Jane's body.*

Okay, Alex sent back in response.

Lidia's voice rang loud and clear in everyone's mind. *Our intent is to heal Jane's voice and ears and legs, and any other trauma she may have that is manifested in the spiritual, emotional, physical body.*

Alex closed her eyes and visualized healing energy that coursed latently through her body. She could feel her face covering with perspiration with the effort, as a vague ethereal body of something accumulated over her head. Sweat began to drip down her forehead as the temperature in the room rose. It was the exact opposite of what she'd done with Jack and Dylan. She wasn't taking their pain, dissipating it and replacing it with healing. She was amassing the power to heal first so they could collectively blast Jane with a good health bomb.

The heat in the room was almost unbearable, and Alex looked up and saw a cloud of vapor – like the kind that comes out of your mouth on a cold day – hovering over them, only it was flecked with silver glitter-like elements.

Alex glanced at Athena, who'd risen from her supine position and sat at attention, her ears alert.

Now, she heard Lidia say. *Send it to Jane.*

Athena whined softly.

A *whoosh* of wind whipped around the room, and the cloud of health floated over Jane. For a moment she was covered in silver flecks as they flitted over her like light snow and then they evaporated into her skin. She lit up within like a light bulb shimmering with silver incandescence. The light lifted around her in a beautiful shiny halo, and an instant later it evaporated into the ether.

Athena cocked her head as she watched.

Before Alex could process the beauty of the moment, a chill came over her as the sweat on her skin turned icy. A wave of exhaustion caused her to fall to her side and she lay her head on the carpet for a moment, unable to move. When she was able to turn her head, she glanced up and saw everyone looked tired, with sunken eyes, dark smudges underneath, and wet hair.

Athena barked, and Alex waved her over. She trotted over to stand next to her, nuzzling her thigh while Alex rubbed her fur.

It takes a lot out of you, Alex heard Daphne telepath as she slowly got on her feet.

A Brew for Chaos

'There's tea in the kitchen for us to drink,' Lidia said aloud. 'It will help us recover quickly.'

A moment later, they were all standing.

Alex looked at Jane. 'How do you feel?'

In contrast to the rest of the women in the room, Jane looked like the picture of health. She opened her mouth, like she wanted to speak, worked it a few times . . . then closed it.

'I think she's trying to talk,' Lidia said. 'But without a larynx and vocal cords, she'll never be able to. And there's no magic to bring back body parts, I'm afraid.'

That's okay. I can speak without words like all of you.

Celeste looked around. 'Who said that?'

I did.

They all turned to look at Jane. She was telepathic like them.

TWENTY-TWO

A lex stared at Jane. 'Is that possible?'

Lidia regarded the young woman. 'Healing her wouldn't give her something she never had. But it would restore something she's lost. You can hear us, yes?'

Jane nodded. *Loud and clear.*

Why haven't you tried to telepath with us before now? Lidia asked.

Jane screwed up her face in thought. She shook her head slowly. *I've been trying to send you thoughts ever since I got here.*

Daphne headed to the kitchen. 'I'm going to get everyone some tea. I know I could use some.'

Lidia followed her. 'And I'm going to call Kamila. I'm sure she'll have questions.'

Do you remember anything? Do you have your memories back? Alex asked.

Jane shook her head. *I can't remember anything before I was found on the beach.*

Celeste leaned forward. *Do you know why you were there? Why you were found beside a man named Jonah Fox?*

A look of pain flickered over her face. *I can't remember. But I sense that I was afraid of him.*

A thought ran through Alex's mind. *Was he the Fisherman?* But no, he was just a journalist obsessed with finding out the identity of a serial killer. Pepper would've sensed something, surely.

Daphne returned with a pitcher of tea and a tray filled with glasses of ice with Lidia behind her.

'Kamila's on her way,' Lidia announced before helping to serve the tea. 'Drink up, everyone. When we do this kind of work, our sympathetic nervous system is overloaded. So, I've created a blend to help us recover.'

'Like Gatorade for Magicals,' Celeste offered with a grin.

A Brew for Chaos   137

Lidia chuckled. 'Sure.'

Daphne rolled her eyes good-naturedly.

Like Gatorade for Magicals. Alex began to smile but stopped herself. *Or Mermaid Magic. Take it three times a day with food until the magic happens.*

'This is Rhodiola,' Lidia continued, glancing at Alex. 'For the mental and physical strain on the body. Sage for mental stress and fatigue. And holy basil to strengthen the immune system. All sweetened with lemon balm honey and chilled with lavender ice.'

And you? Lidia turned to Jane. *How do you feel?*

I feel strong. Full of energy. She wiggled her fingers. Then looked down hesitantly at her legs.

What is it? Celeste asked, concern in her voice.

I'm not sure. I have pins and needles in my legs. And they feel really itchy. Almost as if . . . She rested both of her hands on the arms of her wheelchair, braced herself and rose to her feet. Her legs wobbled briefly, and then she took a step. And another. And another.

I . . . I can walk. She looked up, a triumphant expression transforming her features.

Lidia stared at her, a memory of something coming to her. And then she gasped.

Alex turned to her aunt. 'What is it?'

She took a moment to compose herself before she spoke. 'I just realized where I recognize her from.'

TWENTY-THREE

'She smiled,' Lidia said. 'And it came to me. She hasn't smiled before and the gesture really changed her face. At least it reminded me of . . . I mean, I could be wrong.' Lidia stood and began anxiously moving around the room, touching knick-knacks. Moving vases. Rearranging flowers.

Alex watched her nervously. 'Aunt Lidia, you're stressing me out. Would you sit down?'

But Lidia acted as if she didn't hear her niece. 'Her hair is different. And her eyes look . . . changed.' Her voice wavered. 'But I think it's her.'

Daphne went to her cousin and placed a calming arm on her. 'Lidia, take a deep breath.'

There was a sound at the door, and Athena barked once, then went to greet Kamila when she came in.

'Hey, guys.' She took a moment to ruffle Athena's fur. Then looked around. 'What's wrong?'

Lidia pointed at Jane, frown lines creasing her forehead. 'I know who she is.'

'Great. Tell me, so we can call it in.'

Lidia turned to Alex. 'Would you bring your laptop down? There's something I need to show you.'

Alex returned with her laptop, and Lidia directed her to go to the *Bellamy Bay Bugler* news archives.

'Okay,' Alex said. 'I'm there. What am I looking for?'

Lidia told her.

Alex's fingers stayed on the keys. She looked at her aunt. 'Why am I . . .'

Kamila crossed her arms over her chest and shot her mother a strange look.

Alex keyed in the search terms. An image of ten photographs in two rows of five appeared. They were the ten victims of the Fisherman.

A Brew for Chaos

'Mom? I hate to state the obvious here, but they've been missing for over forty years, considered dead,' Kamila said.

Lidia leaned forward, inspecting each face. She stopped on the second row, third image from the left. 'That one,' she said confidently. 'That's her. That's Jane.'

Everyone in the room leaned forward and stared at the image. Alex pointed to one of the women. 'It says her name is Caroline Bracy.' She glanced at Jane and then her aunt. She was right about one thing. The young woman in the photograph *did* look like their Jane Doe. They shared the same facial shape and bone structure. There were only a few differences. Jane's – Caroline's – hair was long, hanging to her waist. The woman in the image had a short pixie cut, cute and boyish, cropped on the sides with long bangs in the front. And her eyes were light brown, almost hazel, while their Caroline had pale, watery blue-gray eyes.

Lidia looked indignant. 'I see it. Clearly. You all don't see it?'

Kamila cleared her throat. 'We all see the similarities, right?' She looked around the room and everyone nodded. She glanced at Jane before continuing. 'But this photo would've been taken at least forty years ago, making Caroline Bracy sixty if not older.'

Celeste noticed Jane looking unsteady as she tried to walk and grabbed her arm, guiding her to a chair. 'Enough standing for one day. Baby steps. Literally. Okay?'

Jane nodded and sat, while Lidia stared at the photograph, hands on hips. 'I understand what you're saying, that it's not possible for her not to have aged, and yet my intuition tells me that the woman in this photograph is in fact our Jane Doe.'

They all turned to Jane, who stared at the image on the screen. Her forehead moved into a line of wrinkles as she studied the image.

'Do you recognize her?' Lidia said aloud.

I . . . I don't know, she said.

'That makes her a genetic mermaid, like us,' Alex said. 'Because that's who the Fisherman was abducting.'

'What?' Lidia asked sharply.

Alex took a deep breath and told everyone about the list she and Pepper had found in Jonah's papers. And then what Dylan had told her about his father's work.

The room was heavy with silence.

'My God,' Daphne finally said.

Lidia frowned and exchanged a dark look with her. 'So, the scars around Caroline's wrists, the debilitated state of her legs, her inability to talk . . .' Her mouth twisted with distaste. 'The scar on the back of her neck . . . all a result of the monstrous testing done on her.'

'What could they have possibly done to them?' Celeste asked, her voice cracking with emotion.

Kamila stared at their guest. 'I have the same questions you all do. But we're ignoring the obvious. Why hasn't she aged? I mean, is this another of our abilities? Being able to resist the physical signs of aging? Because honestly, we don't know if she's internally still in her twenties, right? She could be a senior citizen inside for all we know.'

'Maybe they figured out how to reverse aging?' Daphne offered. 'As part of the testing.'

'I've heard,' Lidia began quietly, 'that before we lost the ability to shift into our Mer form, we would maintain our appearance for as long as we were in the ocean . . . Could be true for genetic mermaids as well.'

'What if staying in the water for extended periods of time is what unlocks our ability to convert back to our Mer form?' Celeste asked, jumping up with excitement. 'Maybe we can all still actually be mermaids. We just have to—'

'What? Stay in the ocean for forty years?' Kamila said bluntly. Then laughed. 'Sure, go ahead and do that. Let me know how it works out in four decades.'

Celeste threw herself back on the couch. 'I was just asking a hypothetical.'

Kamila grinned. 'I know. I'm just busting your chops like I do with Minka when she needs her head yanked out of the clouds. Speaking of which . . .' She looked at her watch and frowned.

Lidia eyed Jane thoughtfully. 'We can't stay underwater indefinitely. Yes, our capacity to hold our breath is much more than the average Mundane, but eventually we'd have to come up for air.'

Annoyance flickered across Kamila's face. 'Where is Minka?'

'Work,' the entire room chorused together.

A Brew for Chaos

She sighed. 'I just don't want her spending more time with Montgomery than necessary.'

'If you'd taken the time to visit her at work like I have,' Alex began, tone light, 'you'd know her office is at the aquarium and not at Wesley Towers with the rest of the Leviathan team.'

Kamila glared at her without comment, and Alex went to Jane, kneeling beside her. 'Are you *sure* you can't remember anything about your time before you were found on the beach?'

She shook her head, a simple smile on her face. *It's all a jumble of images. Blurry images that I can't make out.*

Alex stood, a strange feeling swirling in the pit of her stomach. She glanced at Kamila to catch her eye, see if she sensed anything . . . off kilter. But she was checking her phone. Alex smiled at the woman, hoping she didn't sense the skepticism she felt. Jane seemed unbothered by her lack of memory. It reminded her of something . . . Like Jack's mother, Maisie.

'We still don't know how or why Jonah was found beside Caroline.' Lidia paused and looked at the woman. 'May we call you Caroline? I feel strongly that's your name.'

Jane – Caroline – shrugged, looked around the room, then nodded. *It's a pretty name*, she telepathed to the group.

'Jonah was investigating the Fisherman case,' Alex said. 'Pepper thinks he figured out who it was and that person killed him. I think so too. It's the reason I'm determined to find out who the Fisherman is.'

'How does Caroline fit in?' Celeste asked.

Alex watched Caroline for a moment. 'She escaped from wherever she'd been held for forty years.'

'So you must have theories,' Celeste urged. 'What are you thinking?'

Alex looked at the group. 'Well . . . maybe she was meeting with Jonah to tell him about her experience when the Fisherman came upon them, he took Jonah out and maybe he thought he'd done the same with Caroline, only she survived.' She thought for a moment. 'Or maybe, Jonah found out where the Fisherman was keeping his victims and he was able to take Caroline with him. The Fisherman caught up with them and fought with Jonah?'

'You have quite the imagination,' Lidia observed.

142   Esme Addison

'I want to help you solve this case,' Celeste said, eyes bright with interest. 'What else have you got?'

Daphne gave her daughter an amused look, but didn't comment.

'I think Jonah was with me and Pepper when he was called to the beach.' She swallowed hard. 'And met his end. He'd been arguing with someone, and then flew out of the tavern.'

Kamila put her phone away and looked up. 'Why am I only hearing about this now?'

'The police checked his phone, didn't they?'

'I don't know.' Kamila huffed in frustration. 'It's Jack's investigation. I'll follow up and see what they found. Maybe whoever called him is the same person who killed him and attacked . . . our guest.'

'The Fisherman called Jonah, invited him to the beach then killed him and probably tried to harm Caroline . . .' Celeste's lips moved into a frown. 'He would have to be at least in his sixties, right? Maybe even older?' She looked around the room.

Kamila nodded. 'Now that that's settled . . . So, we're officially going with the idea that Caroline is a genetic mermaid who has been trapped in the ocean for the past forty years, which prevented her from aging?' Her eyebrows rose as she gazed at her family.

No one disagreed.

'This case is bonkers.' She sighed. 'I'll make that call now and check on the evidence.' She strode down the hallway with Athena close on her heels.

'I'll go through Jonah's papers again with Pepper. Maybe I missed something, something that would tell me where Caroline was held all this time.' Alex glanced at Caroline again to see if anything she was saying had an effect.

It didn't.

Lidia noticed too. 'What is it, Alex?'

Alex watched Caroline for another moment, taking in her almost childlike innocence and sunny disposition. 'I don't know . . . Maybe it's a characteristic of memory loss, but Caroline doesn't appear to have suffered any trauma at all. I should ask Dr Crow. Jack's mother has dementia, and she couldn't care less about her loss of memory. I mean, she's struggled with the condition for . . . I don't know, almost thirty – no, forty – years, so maybe she's had time to come to terms with it at the age of sixty-one.'

A Brew for Chaos 143

Lidia made a face. 'Thirty or forty years? That would mean she was in her, what, twenties when she was first diagnosed? The poor thing.'

Alex nodded. 'It's a sad story, and she's such a sweet lady. I'd like to bring her by sometime. Jack is so cautious with her he keeps her locked away in that house . . .' She paused, remembering that Maisie had gone to Bellamy Bay College during the same time as Lidia. 'Did you know her? She went to the college around the same time as you.'

'What's her name?' Lidia asked.

'Maisie. Maisie Frazier.'

'Doesn't ring a bell, but Frazier would be her married name, wouldn't it?' Lidia said. 'And Maisie, if I'm not mistaken, is a nickname. For what, I'm not sure. Nonetheless.' She glanced at Daphne. 'We'll need to contact the Council and let them know about Caroline. Maybe they'll have ways to confirm her Magical status.'

Daphne nodded. 'Agreed.'

Kamila returned, a look of mystification on her face.

'What is it?' Daphne asked.

'The DOD commandeered all of Jonah's effects, including his phone. There's no way for me to know who called him to his death.'

'Why on earth . . .' Alex stopped. Then told them what she'd learned from the mayor about Jonah's past.

Lidia crossed her arms. 'Sounds like Jonah Fox was still on the government's dime.'

'If I didn't know better, I'd think they were protecting someone. Well, that's that,' Kamila said, voice bitter. 'So now, I need to go check on my little sister. I've reached out to her a few times telepathically like we do. And she hasn't responded. She always responds, even if it's just to say, *hey I'm on a date leave me alone.*'

'Wait,' Alex said. 'Let's all try to reach out to her.' She looked at Kamila. 'Maybe the problem is you somehow,' she said, hope raising the timbre of her voice. 'Maybe your telepathy is off? You said you had a headache.'

'It doesn't work like that.'

'Or she could be ignoring you. You've been upset with her since she started working with Montgomery.'

Kamila glowered. 'What the actual . . .'

Alex looked at her aunt. 'You too. Respectfully, Ciociu, neither of you have been very supportive of her choices . . .'

Lidia narrowed her eyes as she considered her niece's words, and Kamila shook her head, her features hardening into her cop face.

'Let's all try.' Alex looked around the room.

The group of women nodded and were silent. One minute passed. Then two. Then three . . . One by one each shook their heads, a sense of dread filling the room.

'See?' Kamila said, her voice hard. 'I told you. And,' she said, scowling at Alex, 'we're wasting time.'

Alex grimaced. 'Sorry,' she murmured, not liking being on the other side of Kamila's anger.

'What can we do?' Lidia said.

'Nothing yet. I'm going to ask a patrol officer to ride by the aquarium and see if her car is still there. If it is, I'll have their security guard do his rounds and check on her and see if she's in her office. Who knows, maybe she just fell asleep at her desk or something.'

'All right. It's very late.' Lidia turned to their guest. 'Caroline, why don't you go to bed and get some rest?'

Caroline rose with shaky legs. *I am tired*, she telepathed to the women. *I hope you find Minka.*

'Daphne and Celeste, you guys head home. I'm going to make coffee and stay up with Kamila.'

'And me,' Alex said. 'I'm not going to bed until I know Minka's okay.'

Daphne huffed. 'Lidia, please. We're all family here and ain't nobody going home until we know Minka has arrived home safely.' She stood, heading for the kitchen. 'Let's get that coffee percolating. The stronger the better.'

A few minutes later, everyone was recharged with cups of coffee and slices of thick, moist sweet potato bread. Kamila was on her radio with a police officer while he drove around the aquarium parking lot.

'Her car is there,' she told everyone with relief in her voice. Then called the security guard on duty, who agreed to go to

Minka's office to check on her. 'He's knocking on her office door,' she informed them. 'Right now.'

There was no answer.

'Use your keys and open the door,' Kamila directed in her cop voice.

A moment later, the door was open. Kamila's knuckles turned white as she gripped the phone. 'Where is she?' she said into the phone, her voice tense. 'You've got security footage, right?' She glanced around the room, face tight with concern. 'Pull it. Everything you've got from the time she arrived onsite until now. I'll be there in five minutes.'

She disconnected the call and turned to her family. 'You heard that, right?'

Lidia wrapped her arms around her chest. 'Where's my baby girl?'

'I don't know, Mom.' Kamila was already running for the front door, and Alex and Celeste stood up to go with her. 'But I'm going to find out.'

Ten minutes later, frustrated, Kamila stormed out of the aquarium's security guard's office. 'How could he not see anything?' She turned to Alex and Celeste. 'He's got a bank of security monitors in his face. He saw her go into the bathroom, but she never came back out.' Gritting her teeth, she strode towards the ladies' room.

They approached the hallway, and Kamila pulled her gun out of her holster and outstretched a hand. 'You guys stay here,' she whispered. 'Just in case.'

She pushed the door open, gun in front of her, clearing every corner of the large bathroom. She looked under the six stalls, then kicked each door open. The space was empty. 'It's clear. Come in,' she called. They entered and she directed them not to touch anything, but to just look and let her know if they saw anything suspicious.

Kamila called the police station, asking them to send a forensics team. She closed her eyes, trying to reach out to Minka again.

'Nothing. I can't believe it.' Her voice rose in pitch, echoing off the bathroom's tiled walls. 'I can't hear her, sense her, feel her . . . nothing. It's almost like she's . . .'

'Don't say that,' Alex said harshly. 'She's fine. We just have to find her.'

'Who would take her? And why?' Celeste began nervously braiding her hair, her voice trembling with worry.

Kamila's hard gaze swept the room. 'There's no windows. How did she leave?'

TWENTY-FOUR

The forensics team arrived.

Fingerprints were taken, and the security guard interviewed several times.

Jack clapped Kamila on the back. 'We've checked for DNA. Searched the premises.' He held up his phone, with blueprints of the aquarium on the screen. 'No sign of her anywhere. Why don't you head home and get some rest? Take tomorrow off and let us work this case.'

'Absolutely not. Let me stay.'

'Tomorrow,' he repeated with a bit more emphasis.

Kamila took a breath. 'Okay, I'll be in tomorrow first thing to help with the search. But look, I don't need sleep. I can keep going, I can—'

Jack's eyes softened. 'Go home. Get some rest and return to the station bright and early. We'll be working around the clock on this. You can rejoin the search then. But right now you're no good to us tired.' His gaze went to Alex, who stood several feet away against the wall. 'Alex, you okay?'

Alex stared at him, half of her grateful he was here to take charge, while the other half was fearful of his real agenda. Would he do his pretend job? Would he really work his hardest to find her cousin? Did this explain why she'd been able to find two past killers before him? Because he wasn't really looking?

When she didn't move, he searched her face, brow furrowed.

Kamila moved to stand next to her cousin and wrapped an arm around her waist. *You good?* she telepathed to Alex.

Alex took a deep breath, relaxed her hands and tried to smile but felt it probably came out more like a grimace. *I just want him to do his job, that's all*, she responded, then bit her bottom lip to keep from suddenly crying as the magnitude of the situation hit her like a wall of bricks. 'So it's official? Minka's missing?'

'Yeah.' He frowned. 'I'm sorry to say it, but this is now a missing persons case.'

TWENTY-FIVE

'We'll find her, Ciociu. Don't worry,' Alex said to her aunt, arm tight around her shoulder.

She'd been back home for about an hour, having had the daunting task of explaining the situation. She hadn't been alone; Kamila was there briefly. But she'd left, hopefully to get some sleep but most likely to make more calls to her contacts in law enforcement. Caroline was asleep, and Celeste and her mother had gone home with promises to return first thing in the morning.

But Alex's explanations didn't calm Lidia. 'My last words to her were harsh. Why didn't I choose love over anger when I spoke to her?' She rose from her seat and stalked across the living room. 'What could've happened to her? Where is she? And why isn't she responding to our telepathy? I've never been out of communication with my children.'

'The police are doing everything they can,' Alex said, not sure she believed her own sentiments. Alex stared at her aunt, unsure of how to help her. And then overwhelmed by her own anxiety, she went to the tea tray on the coffee table and poured more Calm Down tea for herself and her aunt. She tapped her aunt on the shoulder and handed her the cup. 'Drink.'

She took the cup from Alex's hand. 'Thank you.' She drank. Took a deep breath and drank some more. Then finished it. 'I'm going crazy right now. My baby is out there somewhere,' Lidia continued. 'Someone took her. Is she okay? Is she hurt?'

Alex tried not to let a tear slide down her cheek. 'I don't know. Who would harm her? She's the sweetest person I know.'

Lidia ran a hand over her hair, composing herself. 'I knew something bad would happen when she went to work for Montgomery Blue. That dragon . . . He has to be involved.' She searched for the clock on the wall. It was three am. 'I should go over to his house and pull out every ounce of moisture in his body, desiccate him like a dried mushroom until he tells me what he knows,' she seethed.

A Brew for Chaos   149

Alex had to talk her aunt off the ledge. What she didn't need to do was confront Montgomery in her current state.

She had no doubt she would try to hurt him – would attempt to pry whatever information he had from him – but she knew first hand that battling a dragon descent was no picnic. It had taken her along with Minka, Celeste and Daphne to fight another dragon. And none of them had left that fight unscathed. 'Let's think about this,' she said tentatively, not wanting to upset her aunt. 'Montgomery is a dragon.'

'And *I'm* a mermaid. What of it?' she said, her voice rising. 'Being a mermaid doesn't mean I'm the kinder, gentler option.'

The walls were vibrating with her aunt's anger. Mermaids were fierce and fiery, not always sugar and spice.

Except for Minka . . . She was excited about the dolphins, the information she'd found. And then tonight she'd been working on a report about the dolphins, was going to send it to Montgomery.

Had she sent the report? Was there something in the report that had put her in danger? But it was just dolphins, right? What could the danger be in that? She needed to take a look at her work computer. Kamila would know if the police had it.

'I'll go see Montgomery in the morning. Ask a few questions. He may be more likely to answer if it's just me – alone.'

Lidia thought for a moment. 'Perhaps you're right. If I see his smug face, I might do something that would get your boyfriend on my case again.'

Alex sighed. Now was not the time to drop the bomb on her aunt and Kamila about Jack. But as soon as they found Minka, she'd spill the beans. Until then she and Dylan would try to figure out what he's up to and what to do.

The next morning – only a few hours after Alex had gone to sleep – she was showered, dressed and ready – she hoped – to face Montgomery. When she came downstairs and entered the kitchen, Celeste and Daphne were setting the table.

'We brought food,' Celeste said, lifting up a basket of biscuits.

'Lidia doesn't need to cook this morning,' Daphne added, placing serving spoons in large ceramic platters of hot buttered grits, hash browns, scrambled eggs with fried onions and a tray of bacon.

Lidia stood in a corner, a carafe of coffee in hand. There were dark smudges under her eyes, and she looked slightly dazed.

'Good morning, Ciociu,' Alex said as she went to her aunt and hugged her. 'How did you sleep?'

'I didn't.' She blinked. 'Or if I did, I can't recall it.'

Everyone exchanged silent glances, then Daphne pulled out a chair. 'Sit, Lidia.' She took the carafe from her hands and set it on the table. 'Let's eat breakfast. Get some caffeine in you.'

The sound of clinking utensils filled the room, while Alex stole looks at her aunt. She'd never seen her so . . . defeated. Her complexion was paler than usual, and she looked overwhelmed.

'Operation Save Minka begins now,' Celeste declared with forced cheer. 'Let's talk strategy.'

'Absolutely,' Alex continued, trying to change the vibe in the room. Trying to lift her aunt out of her depression. 'I'm going to talk to Montgomery this morning, and then I'm going to take a look at Minka's computer to see if I can find out what she was working on before she went missing. I wonder if Kamila can access her text messages too,' Alex continued. 'Minka talked about a new guy in her life. Maybe, whoever he is, he has information we can use.'

Lidia perked up. 'I haven't heard about a new man.'

Celeste raised her eyebrows. 'She mentioned him to me too. She was very coy though. I think they met for drinks this week.'

'She received flowers from someone,' Alex began. 'Can the police check with the florist in town to see who ordered them?'

'I'll call Kamila and find out,' Celeste volunteered.

'If we find out why someone might want her out of the way, we'll have a better idea who kidnapped her,' Alex reminded the group. 'I think starting with her research is the best way to go. We'll find her.' Alex drained her cup, then stood, placing her dishes in the dishwasher. 'I'm going to see Montgomery now.'

TWENTY-SIX

Alex stepped off the elevator and onto the twelfth floor of the Wesley Inc building. A young woman greeted her and began walking her briskly through the hallway.

Alex took in her surroundings. The name of Montgomery's company, Leviathan Industries, stood out on the walls in large three-dimensional silver letters. Images of sea creatures, squid, octopus, advancing to creatures that looked like swimming dinosaurs were painted on the oceanic-blue wall.

The woman stopped at a door with a shiny silver name plate announcing Montgomery's title as CEO. She knocked, while Alex gazed at one drawing of a massive whale curled into battle with a shark.

'That's the original Leviathan of the Bible,' Montgomery said in greeting.

Startled, Alex looked up as the assistant walked off.

Montgomery gestured to the drawing. 'Fifty feet from head to tail and weighed as much as fifty tons.'

'Hello, Montgomery.'

'Hello.' He grinned in his slick, oily way, and Alex felt like taking a step back.

'An apex predator from the Miocene epoch. Lovely, isn't it?'

Lovely wasn't the word Alex would use. Nor did she want to talk about sea creatures, but apparently he did.

He continued to gaze at the large whale. 'This monster inspired my company, the concept, my attitude . . .' His eyes trailed to Alex and his lips quirked up. 'Always be the predator. Never the prey.'

Alex rolled her eyes. 'That's your company's mission statement?'

'Of course not.' He grinned. 'But it is mine. That attitude has served me well, young lady.' He touched the painting reverently. 'Neve did these sketches for me. Before she died.'

'Before you had her killed, you mean,' she hissed in a low

voice. Unbelievable that he'd still use her drawings. And then gloat about it.

'I wanted a mural, her specialty as you know, but we were only left with her sketches. I had another artist work off her illustrations. Not as interesting as a mural, but this way you really focus on the beauty of each sea creature, eh?'

'Minka is missing,' she said bluntly.

His eyes flickered. Something . . . Alex wasn't sure, and his demeanor changed. More compassionate. Turned on like a switch.

'Of course. This way.' He outstretched his hand, and Alex followed him into his office.

Alex ignored his offers of tea or coffee as she settled into a leather chair and sat across from him at his desk, a large monstrosity of gleaming wood. 'What do you know about Minka's abduction?' The word fell off her tongue, awkward and clunky, and she didn't like saying it. It made the situation real, and she didn't want to believe it.

'Same as you.' He spread his hands out. 'She went to her office at the aquarium and never left.' His forehead creased with worry. 'Perhaps if she'd taken my first offer to work here with the rest of the Leviathan team, this wouldn't have happened. Security is tight here.'

'Did she send you the report she was working on last night?'

He inclined his head to the right. 'Report?' He rubbed his chin thoughtfully. 'Doesn't sound familiar.'

'No?' Alex sat forward in her chair. 'She went to work on a Saturday to complete a report for you, but you don't know anything about it?'

'I have over four hundred employees spread over three continents. Multiple layers of management in between. How do you expect me—'

Alex's hands gripped the arms of her chair. 'I don't want to hear about your millions of employees. I only care about Minka. What was she working on?'

'So fiery.' He chuckled as he reached for a small stone statuette on his desk. 'Like your ciocia.' His tone was almost condescending. 'Mermaids are deceptively sweet in appearance. Under all that purple hair and shimmering skin lies a passionate heart.'

A Brew for Chaos   153

Alex stood. 'Don't stonewall me, Montgomery. Tell me what you know.'

He took his sweet time in responding as he turned the small figurine in his hand. A man with a long curly beard and a peaked cap on his head, wearing a ceremonial robe. 'I care for her too, you know. Like a daughter. Her and Bryn, and of course you know what happened to her . . .'

Alex shook her head to negate his words.

He held up the statue. 'Enki, the Sumerian god of water, wisdom and creation.' He set the statue on the desk before him with a clink. 'Much like he felt fatherly to his subjects in ancient Mesopotamia, Minka brings out the paternal in me.'

Alex wanted to gag. This psychopath was not capable of emotion, certainly not paternal feelings.

'You know she cares very much about the environment. I placed her on a project where she could have the greatest impact. I don't know about any specific report, but she may have been compiling data from the app she managed for the non-profit.'

'The one that tracked dolphins,' Alex prompted.

An eyebrow shot up. 'Why yes. She discussed her work with you then?'

His tone was casual, but Alex sensed an undercurrent of concern. But maybe she only imagined it.

'The basics.'

'Ah.' He steepled his hands together. 'We have a weekly meeting on Mondays. She probably wanted to share what she knew with me then.'

Alex sighed. He wasn't telling her anything she didn't already know. 'If she's working for Brave New World, your non-profit, why would she report her findings to Leviathan?'

He tilted his head as he watched her, looking almost impressed. 'Her work paralleled a project we were working on at Leviathan. We often find ways to create solutions that are both profitable *and* charitable.'

Alex processed that for a moment, wondering what type of project they were working on. 'She said she knew where the dolphins were going.'

'Did she?' He looked amused. 'My goodness. She was quite the achiever then. That question had vexed our team for a while.

They've been literally swimming in circles trying to figure it out, and Minka comes in and solves the problem in just a few weeks.'

He did sound impressed; however, there was something else underlining his words. And that something caused the muscles over her chest to tighten. But she had to continue, had to push, otherwise how would she find out what she needed to know?

She took a breath. 'And I think that information is the reason she was taken. *Someone*, for *some reason* I can't quite suss out, didn't want that information shared.' She was reaching, but she had nothing else. Montgomery's response would let her know if she was barking up the wrong tree or not.

His face hardened then, and then he reclined against his chair. 'Why would anyone care about dolphins and where they were going enough to take our Minka? Assuming she did know that information.'

'Minka does not belong to you.'

'*Our. Mine,*' he said with emphasis. 'That's how I always refer to my employees. We're a family. Using that type of language fosters familiarity. Comfort in the workplace, or so some consultant assured me.'

Alex gritted her teeth. 'You're a government contractor, so I know everything you do is related to some project or other with military oversight. Who is managing the project Minka is on? I know what she's doing isn't just some "save the environment" crap you made up.'

His laugh filled the room. 'Quite right you are.' Then his lips thinned into a smile. 'That's top secret, dear.'

Alex crossed her arms over her chest and stared at him. 'If you don't tell me, I'll just figure it out on my own.'

His smile widened. 'I like you, Alex. I really do.' He rose from his seat, and Alex also stood. 'In fact, I like all of you Sobieskis, despite what you might think. You're a lovely family of women. Powerful, royal lineage. Did you know?'

No, she didn't know. Alex took a step back, feeling the opposite of powerful. Montgomery scared her. Intimidated her. Not that she would show it. But the fact that she knew he had dragon DNA in his body, that he'd orchestrated a murder of someone she'd known and cared for, was frightening to her. And she knew

A Brew for Chaos   155

that for some reason he had it out for her family, no matter what he said to her now.

'I'm going to bring all my power to bear to help you find Minka because I don't want anything bad to happen to her.'

Despite her fear, anger flared. 'Something bad has already happened to her,' she said, her voice raising an octave. 'She's missing.'

A look of kindness softened his face. 'True,' he agreed. 'But there are worse things than just being taken.'

Alex swallowed.

'Maybe she's . . .' He paused to look thoughtfully at the ceiling, then back at her. 'Just out of the way. Being kept safe. And that's all that will happen to her.' He stepped closer to her until she stumbled backwards and was pressed against the door.

She was shaking. Absolutely shaking. She wasn't sure what to do. *How to fight a dragon.* Jasper had almost beat her with his fiery bag of tricks and she sensed, no, she knew that Montgomery was infinitely more powerful, more dangerous. It almost made her not want to fight him at all. Could she even hurt him?

She blinked, realizing he was working her. He was in her head, causing her to doubt herself, spinning up her fear and anger. She shuttered her mind, and the self-defeating thoughts stopped immediately.

She stared at him. He'd slipped in her mind and manipulated what he found there for his own benefit. Could Dylan do that too? Of course he could. Maybe he already had. It's why she didn't trust the way she felt around him.

Montgomery grinned, unbothered. Smug. 'If I had to guess,' he began in a ponderous tone, 'I'd think that Minka accidentally stumbled upon information she wasn't cleared for.' He nodded as if he was working it out as he spoke. 'And in her eagerness to help those poor, poor dolphins, she inadvertently put herself in harm's way. Purely innocent.' He looked at her. 'How am I doing? Sound plausible?'

'What kind of information?' Alex spit out. 'She said she knew where the dolphins were going. What's so dangerous about that? It's the ocean. Where could they be going? A cave. An abyss . . .'

His eyes danced with light as she spoke. 'Perhaps when this is all over, she'll be returned. Unscathed.'

'Is that a promise?'

'Sure,' he said, pleasantly. Grandly. 'As long as you and your nosy family don't interfere.'

Interfere in what? 'Right. Like I can trust you. You're a *dragon*.'

'I am, aren't I?' he said, barely able to hide the pride in his voice. His chest puffed out, and he hissed at her, an ugly, low vibratory sound. And then his pupils dilated vertically, momentarily appearing as dark, dead-looking slits.

Alex recoiled, her face twisting in revulsion. She wondered if Dylan could do this as well. God, she hoped not.

She coughed. Once. Twice. Her throat tightened and it was hard to catch her breath. The scent of sulfur swirled around her. 'You're disgusting.'

'No, I think the word you're looking for is . . . intimidating.' He leaned forward, invading her space.

Alex's breath caught in her throat as the smell of sulfur grew, filling her nose and mouth. She felt as if she were choking. Was she choking? Was he choking her? She scanned the room, her eyes falling on a crystal decanter of whiskey. Hands outstretched, she willed the liquid inside – for she could command anything as long as it had moisture in it – towards her.

The whiskey and the heavy carafe danced towards Alex, hovering in the air behind Montgomery. She flicked her hand, and the receptacle rushed towards his head.

He waved the carafe away with a finger, and it fell to the thickly carpeted floor with a thud. But the choking sensation cleared, and Alex gasped for air.

He chuckled. 'Cute. But ineffective.' He walked away, rounded his desk and settled back into his chair. His gaze fell to the whiskey seeping out of the carafe and into his carpet, the smell of it permeating the office. 'But you see your initial assessment was correct. It is futile to challenge me, to impede me in any way. Do you understand?'

Alex nodded as if she understood.

He smiled, mistaking her gesture for agreement. 'Someone like you or Minka wouldn't stand a chance against a dragon.' He dipped his head gallantly. 'Repulsive as we are.'

But that wasn't what Alex understood. She wasn't agreeing to stand down, to stand aside while he did as he pleased in her town and with her family members. With Minka.

No. What she understood was that one day she'd have to take him down herself.

TWENTY-SEVEN

'He did what?'

Alex stood in Dylan's office. He paced the floor, listening to her explain for the second time how her encounter with his uncle went.

'Why did you bait him?'

'I didn't.'

Dylan turned to look at her, pain etched across his face. 'What did he say exactly?'

Alex's fists clenched at her sides. 'That Minka was probably taken because she learned something about the dolphins.'

'Did he admit to having her taken?'

'Of course not.' Her tone was acidic. 'But my impression was he knows *exactly* who has her. Apparently, she'll be returned safely to us if we don't get in his way, but forgive me if I don't trust a single word that man says.'

He returned to his desk. 'Do we know where her work computer is?'

'That's what I want to know. I'll call Kamila.' A few minutes later, Alex was off the phone. 'There was no computer in Minka's office, and all of her paper files were taken.'

'That confirms your hypothesis that this is related to her work, doesn't it?'

Alex nodded, her expression grim.

'Was she working on anything else?'

Alex shook her head. 'I wonder what she could've possibly discovered about the travel patterns of dolphins that was so dangerous to—'

'Say that again.'

'I— what? What did I say?'

'The travel patterns of dolphins.' His forehead creased. 'That's what she was tracking?'

Alex nodded. 'Why? Does it mean something to you?'

'Yeah.' He winced. 'The military has used dolphins for years.'

A Brew for Chaos 159

'In what ways?'

'Mine clearing, force protection, recovery missions, military base and nuclear weapon cache security. And that's just for public consumption.'

Alex laughed. 'We're still talking about dolphins?'

'Yeah. And sea lions. And whales. And not just us. Russia. And possibly Israel, China and North Korea. Yeah, and Minka was tracking the dolphins in the bay.' He frowned, swallowing hard.

Alex noticed his discomfort. 'You know something?'

'The Navy has a top-secret program based out of Camp Malveaux that's training dolphins. Been going on for years. Decades. Uncle Montgomery has most of the contracts.'

'Minka said she found out *where* they were going.'

Dylan rubbed his temples. 'She must've discovered a secure location for black ops testing.'

'And we think the Fisherman was taking women to a secure location for testing . . . It can't not be related. Two top-secret military tests related to the ocean, same town, same bay,' Alex exclaimed. 'Montgomery might have told Minka that her work was about saving dolphins, but he obviously lied. Somehow, she's gotten herself caught up in the Fisherman case.' A wave of anxiety almost made her swoon. Did Montgomery know who the Fisherman was? Was he working for him? Or did he just not care? It didn't matter either way. All Alex knew for sure was that Montgomery had promised Minka would be returned safely if she didn't interfere in their business – and she didn't believe him. 'I have to find this Fisherman. He spent an entire summer terrorizing our town, and now he's back doing it again. Killing Jonah. Hurting Caroline and now this. He's taken Minka.'

Dylan placed a hand on Alex's. 'Take a breath. Calm down.'

She looked at him, surprised as a tranquil energy eased from his palm into her body, slipping and sliding around her like a cool breeze. She closed her eyes as her breathing eased. 'Thank you.'

His gaze was intent. 'Just returning the favor.' Dylan went to a beverage cart in a corner and poured her a glass of water. He handed it to her, and murmuring her thanks, she drank it.

160 Esme Addison

She set her glass down. 'Were there any underwater research facilities or testing sites in use during your grandfather's time?'

'I don't think so . . . Actually, I don't know.'

'Let's say there is a military black site,' Alex posed. 'How would the dolphins be involved?'

'Security,' Dylan said without delay. 'For our troops, a ship or an underwater military base. But the US doesn't have a history of hosting black sites on their own soil.'

'So Minka found out the dolphins were swimming to a black site, and she must've sent the report to Montgomery ahead of their meeting on Monday. Obviously, she didn't know it was a secret. So Montgomery shared the report with whoever he's working with on the contract – and someone took her.'

Dylan looked up from his computer. 'I got it.'

'Got what?' Alex moved to his side.

'While we were talking, I was thinking. We really need Minka's computer.' He grinned. Pointed to his screen. 'But we've got it right here. Minka works for Uncle's non-profit, which is associated with Leviathan. Which is now housed in the Wesley building, meaning they use Wesley servers.'

'Minka's work should be saved in Wesley's cloud,' Alex said, finally allowing herself to smile. 'This could be the break we need.'

Dylan was already calling his IT department. When he got off the call, with a confident expression on his face, Alex allowed herself to breathe.

'I'll get a call when her information has been accessed and then it will be sent to me in a zip file.' He stood. 'While we wait, why don't I order us some food?'

Twenty minutes later, hot dogs and fries from Dylan's favorite dive diner arrived. They were almost done eating when Dylan got the call. A minute later he set the phone down.

Alex noticed his grim expression. 'What is it?'

'Someone in the Wesley building deleted the entire server that housed Minka's information.'

Alex watched Dylan as he cleaned up the food wrappers and bags and tossed them in the trash. 'Now what?'

* * *

By the time Alex returned home, Kamila was in the living room briefing her aunt. Daphne had just left, and Celeste had finally gone into work.

The fireplace was roaring, giving the room a warm, toasty feeling. And the house smelled like orange, cinnamon and clove. It should've been a cozy, comforting scene, and it would've been if Kamila wasn't standing in the center of the room in her police uniform, heavy black boots, bullet-proof vest and what Alex thought was more guns than usual strapped to her person.

Despite the fact that Kamila's eyes were red and puffy like she'd been crying, she was ready to rescue her sister.

Alex shrugged out of her coat, and Athena trotted to her side for a welcome rub. 'Any sign of Minka?'

'No,' Lidia said, staring into the dancing orange flames.

'What about the flowers?'

'They paid with cash.'

Alex watched her aunt with concern. She hadn't looked up when she entered the room. 'Kamila, how are you holding up?'

Kamila grunted a response, and Alex's heart broke for her. She knew this was tough on her no matter how hard she tried to act. Athena went to Kamila and sat at her feet, nuzzling her head on her thigh.

Alex cleared her throat. 'I think I know why she was taken.'

The expression on Kamila's face cleared, and for the first time since Minka's abduction, she looked hopeful.

Alex went on to explain what Montgomery had said – along with his threat that if they interfered, they'd never see Minka again.

Lidia covered her face with her hands. 'So if we confront him, she's dead? But if we don't confront him, she'll be dead anyway.'

'Mom,' Kamila said, 'don't give up hope. We'll find her. We just have to run down all the leads.'

'I keep reaching out to her and nothing.' Her eyes looked wild as she gazed at her daughter and niece. 'It's like she's already . . .'

'Don't say it, Mom,' Kamila warned, voice hard. She shook her head. 'She's strong.'

'I know that. And that's what worries me. Minka is a formidable fighter. What must they have done to subdue her? I'll tell you what I'm going to do. I'm going to round up some members of the Council and we're going to use our magic to search for her and—'

Alex bit her lip. Her aunt couldn't practice magic outside of her home or shop. Not yet. Not now. Not until they were confident Jack couldn't track the use of magic. Because even though the house and shop shielded the family's use of magic, Alex was sure Aunt Lidia would go to war wherever she needed to. And when she did, Jack would know she was a Magical.

She couldn't wait any longer to tell everyone the truth about Jack. She looked around the room. 'There's something you should know.'

TWENTY-EIGHT

'You can't be serious.'

Kamila jumped up from her chair. 'Jack is not a secret agent for-for the enemy,' she sputtered, her face turning red with anger.

Alex looked at her aunt, who was surprisingly calm.

'It's not the first time a witch hunter has been sent after our kind and it won't be the last,' Lidia said, her features composed. 'But federal witch hunters certainly takes the cake.'

'He's not a witch hunter,' Alex said, hating the way the words sounded. 'Because we're not witches.' It was almost absurd as to be laughable. Not her – a Magical dating a Magical hunter.

'To them,' Lidia continued, 'we're all witches. The name is meant to be dismissive. The origins of our abilities doesn't matter or whether we're good or bad. Magicals are seen as a threat.' She stared past Alex at the wall, lost in thought. 'I'll have to tell the Council.'

Alex nodded. 'I understand.'

'I have to work with him,' Kamila said, almost accusatory. 'I have to pretend like I don't know.' She looked towards the kitchen door. 'Any Calm Down tea in there, Mom?' She was moving towards the door before Lidia could answer.

'In the fridge. Behind the cider and apple fritters.'

Alex ran after her, catching her arm. 'I didn't want to say anything, at least not yet. But he's tracking magic. Trying to find us.'

'Not practicing magic looks really convenient right now. Doesn't it?' Kamila pulled her arm away from Alex and pushed the kitchen door open with a heavy hand.

Alex watched the door swing closed then turned to face her aunt.

Lidia sighed. 'She's angry. Not at you but about everything. Don't take it personal.'

'I'm trying not to.'

'And Alex,' Lidia said, looking in her eyes.

'Yes, Ciociu?'

'For the record, I never liked Jack.'

Alex went to the shop, but her heart and mind were not there. The mystery of who and what Caroline was still remained unsolved. Minka was missing. Jack was a liar – a witch hunter. And despite her desire to break up with him and never see him again, Dylan and everyone in her family insisted she stay with him, continue the charade so she could keep an eye on him until the Council could figure out what to do with him.

And she'd reluctantly agreed. Now, she stood behind the counter staring into the distance, trying to process it all. Too much was happening. Too much needed to be figured out. And it seemed like it all fell on her shoulders. Or at least she felt great pressure to solve everything herself.

Jack had called her three times, each time leaving a voicemail. Each time asking her if she was okay.

'Hello. Hello.'

Alex heard a laugh, and blinked, bringing her vision into focus on the person standing before her.

Pepper snapped her fingers in Alex's face. 'Earth to Alex.'

'Sorry, I . . . I have a lot on my mind.'

'I know. That's why I'm here. Checking on you. You okay?'

'No, not really.'

Pepper shifted uncomfortably in her high-heel boots. 'I'm not here as a journalist. So feel free to talk to me. Like, you know, a friend?'

Alex nodded. 'Yeah, of course. Thank you.'

'Do you have any leads? You're helping me with Jonah, so I want to help you.'

'This isn't about Minka, but I did want to go through Jonah's papers again. You know the Jane Doe is staying with us? Well, she's been identified as Caroline Bracy, one of the Fisherman's victims and the only one to get away. And I think—'

'Wait.' Pepper's eyes lit up with excitement. 'I've seen that Jane Doe and she's not old enough to be a victim from the eighties.'

'The immortal jellyfish,' Alex blurted out, the idea suddenly coming to her.

A Brew for Chaos

Pepper frowned in concentration. 'I think I heard . . . oh, right, it was on that documentary airing on TV at the restaurant when we were trying out the Oktoberfest food. The jellyfish doesn't age?'

Alex nodded. 'It's part of the testing. The military has created a serum from the immortal jellyfish, and she was injected with it . . .' She looked at Pepper, wondering if she'd buy the story.

'They've found the fountain of youth? In a jellyfish?'

'It's for soldiers,' Alex added for good measure, wincing at the lie.

Pepper gazed into the distance, trying to work it out, but finally gave up when her one college-level chemistry class failed to confirm or refute the idea that a government scientist could create such a serum. 'This is an amazing story. Like unbelievable and impossible and yet somehow possible. If we can put a man on a moon, and create AI to do God knows what . . . They've found a way to stop soldiers from aging? This is major. Ohmigosh – I have to be the one to write this story. You know that, right?'

Alex placed a hand on her arm. 'Don't get too excited. And there's no need to take notes. This is all top-secret stuff, the kind that never comes to light, and definitely is not written about in the papers.'

Pepper frowned, excitement dissipating as fast as it had appeared. 'I hate those types of stories. But you think she's suspicious, right?'

Alex nodded slightly, trying to identify what it was about Caroline that caused her to doubt her story. So many holes in her story, and then there was just a feeling that she couldn't shake. 'I think she knows more than she's telling.'

Pepper's eyes stretched wide. 'Right? I knew it. I knew there was something off about her.'

'Yeah . . .' She glanced at her phone, checking to see if there was news about Minka. There wasn't.

'Has she remembered something?'

'No. I'm just connecting dots, and I hope there's something I missed in Jonah's research.'

'Come by the newspaper after work, and we'll go through it again. And bring provisions. We're going to need it.'

After Pepper left, Alex scanned the shop. Today was the first time she didn't want to be there. The sparkling scents of lemongrass and clementine didn't uplift her spirits. She'd even brewed herself a blend of tea for clarity, but it hadn't quite lifted the brain fog. She'd tried to enchant it for a boost, but she just felt off. Unmoored. The same way she felt when her mother died when she was seven. And when her father died nine months earlier.

Fortunately, the shop was slow and the few people who'd come in were only browsing, saving her from having to interact with anyone. Another hour passed, and Alex had moved from the counter, dusting shelves and making sure all of the products were in the right sections, when the doorbell jangled and Tanner came breezing in.

'Hey, Alex. What's shaking?'

She held up her phone. 'Hoping there's news about Minka.'

'Anything I can do to help?'

'Maybe. I have a question for you. About your blog?'

'Shoot.'

'Do government whistleblowers ever send you tips about militarized dolphins?'

Tanner's eyebrows lifted.

'Or . . . black sites used for testing on . . .' She lowered her voice, though they were alone in the shop. 'Magicals.'

'Wow. When you ask a question, you ask a question.'

'Is that a no?'

'Nope,' he said, shrugging out of his backpack. 'I remember my dad mentioning them, before he . . . well, you know. But since I took the blog over, nothing like that.' He hopped on a stool at the back bar and took his laptop out. 'Let's see what I can find.'

TWENTY-NINE

An hour later, Tanner went to Alex. 'Your question,' he began, 'about the dolphins and black sites – I found something.'

Alex checked the time before returning to Tanner. Almost time to close up. She tapped a few buttons on the cash register's screen to begin running end-of-day reports. When she was done, she looked up. 'What did you find?'

'Just one blind item, and not much to go on.' He pulled up the page on his laptop and showed Alex the email. 'Someone claiming to be in the Navy, said they worked on a program that had a public-facing explanation of training dolphins to clear mines, but it was a lie.'

'A lie that they're training them to clear mines or that they're using dolphins?'

Tanner laughed. 'Versus what?'

She moved to the front door to flip the 'open' sign to 'closed' and engaged the lock. 'I don't know, sea lions? Whales? What else did they say?'

'Just that they felt the DOD was crossing a line with the program and they hoped somebody would be able to stop it before it got further along.'

'Seems like Minka was right to be concerned about the dolphins.'

'What else can I do to help?'

Alex returned to the counter and peered at his screen. 'Nothing in there about black sites?'

'Not really. That's top secret and maybe unethical, but it's not bizarre, you know?' Alex nodded. 'It's not Area 51 bizarre. But I'll put some feelers out and see if I can find out anything from my Navy, Marine and Coast Guard contacts. Okay?'

'Sure.' She handed him a smock and pointed him to an empty shelf in the back of the store. 'The new cinnamon spice shampoo and conditioner sets need to be put out.'

He closed his laptop. 'I'm on it.' Tanner reached for the smock and placed it over his t-shirt. 'By the way, I did just like you suggested with the church. Told them I was writing an article for the school paper, and they gave me what I needed.' He reached into his bag and handed her a folder. 'Now are you going to tell me what this is about?'

Alex took the folder and began shuffling through it. 'I'm helping Pepper research her article on the Fisherman. One of the suspects was the youth leader at the time, and he used the church as his alibi.' Alex stopped and looked at a roster of youths in Mac's group during the time the Fisherman had been at work. 'Most of the older members of the church have died, the ones that actually gave him an alibi. But when I heard about the youth group, well, the members would be younger and hopefully I could find someone to ask.' She skimmed through the names.

Tanner leaned forward, trying to read the paper upside down. 'See anyone you recognize?'

Alex shook her head as she made her way down the list. And then she stopped, blinked and read it again. She pointed to the paper, tapping the line. 'I know this one. So she was in Mac's group . . .' She glanced at the clock on the wall. 'I'm supposed to meet Pepper in an hour, but I really need to check up on this.' She was already skirting the counter and grabbing her coat and purse. 'Would you mind finishing close-up for me? You can leave an hour early on your next shift.'

Tanner grinned. 'Go.'

Alex sat on the couch, sipping hot apple and cinnamon tea. 'Thank you,' she said when Daphne handed her a small plate of cookies.

Daphne settled across from her on her couch. 'No word on Minka?'

Alex shook her head.

She nodded. 'I'm sorry to hear that, but I was pleasantly surprised to hear from you, Alex. You said on the phone you wanted to talk about my time at Cypress Baptist?'

'Yes. How long have you been a member?'

'Since I was a child. My mother was Catholic, but my father was Baptist, and it was his family church. I went often as a child.

A Brew for Chaos 169

The hope, I think, was to keep me out of trouble.' She chuckled, then sipped her tea.

'Carson MacInnes was your group leader?'

Daphne stilled, her dark brown eyes narrowing as she placed her teacup down. 'He was.'

'And Mac was a good leader?'

'He was fine. Why? What is this about?'

Alex swallowed, sensing an unexplainable emotion from Daphne. She explained her research with Pepper and saw Celeste's mother relax a bit. 'So, he was there every Wednesday night.' She glanced at the paper. 'Five pm to eight pm?'

Daphne paused. 'Well . . .'

Alex sat up. *Well?*

'I wasn't completely honest with the police back then,' Daphne said slowly. 'I may have told a little white lie.' She cleared her throat. 'Lies.'

'About what?'

'Back then, Mac and I . . . well, we dated.'

'*You* dated Mac?'

Daphne nodded, crossing her legs. 'He cut quite the figure back then, returning from the Navy in his dress uniform. Tall, athletic and very worldly.'

'And you were eighteen? Your name was redacted from the documents?'

She nodded. 'My father requested that to protect me from the media.'

'So no one ever knew you were one of his alibis?'

She shook her head. 'No. My interaction with the police department was very limited. My father had a friend on the force. He came to the house, took my statement and that was it.'

If the Fisherman was taking women with the mermaid gene, she wondered why Daphne wasn't on the list. Maybe too young at the time? Or was it because she was only half-Mer? The other being water witch of the Mami Wata variety. For that matter, why hadn't her mother or Aunt Lidia been targeted . . .

'What is it?' Daphne prompted.

'The Fisherman was abducting women with the mermaid gene. Why not you? Or Aunt Lidia? This was happening all around you. Did you ever see anything?'

170   Esme Addison

Daphne's brow wrinkled. 'It was a crazy time. It was a hot summer, one of the hottest on record. Packed with tourists as always and the mayor and the town board really wanted to keep things quiet, but the paper kept screaming headlines about women being taken.' She stopped to sip her tea. 'Caused a lot of friction, at least I remember my parents talking about it . . . I was a kid, aware that something was not quite right but still wanting to have fun, you know? I think my parents thought if I went to church three times a week . . .' She laughed. 'I was a bit boy-crazy in my day.'

Alex grinned. So Celeste got it honest. 'Were you in love with him?'

'No. No . . . I don't think so. I was crushing on a new guy every other week. Though I liked Mac, I really did. He was smart, a real deep thinker. And kind.' Her smile was wan. 'I remember him telling me he'd keep me safe back then. During all the chaos? That's what the papers were calling it – the Summer of Chaos. Think the movie *Jaws*, except women were being snatched on land. But that's why I wasn't really worried. I must've expressed my concern to him at some point, because I remember him telling me he wouldn't let anything happen to me.'

'How could he guarantee that?' Alex asked. *Unless he was the Fisherman and just wasn't going to take her.* 'Was it serious?'

'I suppose I thought it was at the time, but all we ever did was hold hands under the moonlight.' Her expression became wistful then cleared. 'It was all above board, and he a perfect gentleman.' She pressed her lips together. 'Sometimes we'd leave during the youth group sessions and Mac would let his assistant take over the group. It didn't seem like a big deal. It was when everyone was reading or watching a movie. He wasn't needed or missed, and he said it was the only time we could be together.'

He left the church? Alex studied Daphne, trying to see the giggly, pretty teen she must've been. 'Where would you go?'

'Usually a walk on the beach. Holding hands. An occasional kiss on my cheek or forehead.' She frowned. 'He was almost brotherly, now that I think of it.'

Alex screwed up her face, trying to understand. 'So you were Mac's alibi, and the police knew it?'

She cleared her throat.

'What is it?'

'I was one of several, yes. Everyone at the church rallied around him, not believing he could be part of the crimes. But I'm afraid that I was young, infatuated and impressionable.'

'What are you saying?'

She lowered her head. 'It was me that convinced the others to vouch for him, but . . .' She swallowed.

'What is it?' Alex pressed.

'There were several times when Mac left me on the beach to tend to some sort of business nearby.'

Alex's eyes widened. 'The women at church alibied him based on what you said, which was a lie.'

'I thought it was true.' Daphne frowned. 'I didn't believe he did anything wrong.'

So, Mac really didn't have an alibi.

'Why didn't I see your report in the police file? Even a redacted version?'

Daphne blushed. 'Like I said, my father had friends on the force. He donated to a police charity, and my statement disappeared after the case was officially closed. He didn't want me associated with the crime in any way.'

'What happened on those nights?'

'He'd leave me on the beach. And I was fine to sit on a blanket and gaze at the ocean or count the stars, while he talked business with men he'd meet on the boardwalk. Occasionally a woman.'

'What did they talk about?'

'I don't know. It was so long ago, and I'm not sure I even cared to ask.' She shrugged. 'I was eighteen after all. He said they were old friends from his time in service. Men he sometimes played cards with.'

'But why so cloak and dagger? Leaving church to meet on the beach during the time women were being abducted . . .' She looked at Daphne. 'Doesn't that seem suspicious to you?'

'When you put it that way . . . You know, I haven't thought about that summer or Mac for years. It was a long time ago.' She settled in her seat, and looked at Alex, her features pinched with unease. 'I remember something else.'

'What?'

'The last time I saw Mac alone, on the beach . . . He'd gone

172   Esme Addison

off to do whatever it was he was doing. I was sitting on a blanket listening to a little transistor radio he'd bring for me. It was a magical time. Pitch dark on the beach, only the stars to light the sky and the sounds of the ocean . . . A woman came alongside me. Said she was a friend of Mac's and wanted to know if she could sit with me.' She shifted uncomfortably. 'I said sure. A friend of Mac was a friend of mine, you know?'

Alex nodded, though the muscles in her stomach had tightened with anticipation. 'Did you recognize her?'

'No. I could barely see her. It was dark, and the lights from the boardwalk were a football field away. It was a really dark area that I was in. I guess you could say I was hidden . . . She just stayed with me, and we talked about school, and my family, regular stuff. After a while I asked her why she was on this part of the beach at this time. I was friendly but not stupid.'

Alex wondered who the woman could be. 'What did she say?'

'She said Mac wanted her to keep me company until he returned.'

'And did she?'

Daphne nodded. 'Only the weird thing is, when he returned and saw her . . . he got really upset. Wanted to know why she was there with me.'

'Maybe she was an old girlfriend being stalkerish,' Alex offered.

'That's exactly what I thought. I knew a jealous girl when I saw one. There was a weird tension between them. She said to him, *so this is your girlfriend, your little secret, huh?* I remember her words exactly and getting really indignant about it. One, I wasn't his girlfriend, and two, I was no one's dirty little secret. I was getting riled up then and wanted to know what she meant by that. But by then Mac had packed up our stuff, put his arm around me and was taking me back to his car. I remember looking over my shoulder and seeing the silhouette of her just watching us walk away. I'd forgotten about that night. And that woman.'

'You never saw her again?'

Daphne shook her head, a disturbed expression on her face.

'Bellamy Bay isn't that big. Do you and Mac still talk?'

'No. I lost interest in him after that night. It was a weird summer, and I didn't need the drama. I told my mother I wanted to start going to the Catholic church in Wilmington instead, which

A Brew for Chaos   173

she was overjoyed to hear. And then I went to college in town that fall, and our paths just never crossed. Of course, I met my husband my senior year of college and only had eyes for him.'

'So you've never seen Mac in town?'

'I've seen him, but it was so long ago. I don't speak or wave . . . it's like we agreed to pretend like we don't know each other and that's just what we've done.'

After she finished her tea and cookies, Alex gave Daphne a hug and thanked her for her time and candor. She needed to see Mac again. But she wondered if he would be so forthcoming with his answers as Daphne had.

On the way to Pepper's, Alex grabbed a carafe of coffee from Coffee O'Clock, sandwiches and scones. She'd checked all of her messages and texts and scrolled through the local news for word on Minka. There was nothing.

It was so frustrating Alex wanted to scream. She felt useless, though she hoped that if she could just figure out what Minka was working on, it would lead to the person or people who had taken her.

The *Bellamy Bay Bugler* was located two blocks away from Botanika in a historic two-story brick building that used to be a general store back in the 1920s. Alex put her phone away when the building was in sight.

The sun had set, and streetlights came on, glowing amber in the chilly October night. Alex hunched lower into her jacket as she waited for Pepper to let her into the locked building.

Pepper appeared and opened the glass door. 'Hey, girl. Come on in. Everyone's gone for the day, so it's just us.'

Alex followed her up the wooden stairs, balancing their provisions as she went, filling Pepper in on the latest with Mac. 'I think there's more to his story than we know.'

'Okay, let's schedule some time to talk to him.' Pepper looked up and down the stairs. She continued walking to the top floor, pushed open another door and they entered a small open space with nine cubicles. Pepper pointed to one in the back, slightly larger than the others. 'That's my space.'

Alex passed Jonah's office, and she pointed at the door. 'I'm surprised you haven't moved in yet.'

174   Esme Addison

'Doesn't feel right. Besides, I may not stay. Remember?'

Alex sat in a chair across from Pepper's desk, which held a desktop computer, stacks of papers, books and notepads. A set of locked cabinets rested under the desktop.

Pepper reached for the coffee and poured some into a mug on her desk. 'Thank you. I needed this,' she said before taking a long sip, then set her mug down. 'Okay.' She leaned down, opened a cabinet with a small key and pulled out the shoeboxes of information they'd originally found in Jonah's apartment.

'What are we looking for?'

'I'm not sure . . .'

They spent an hour combing through documents, media clippings and written notes on yellow legal pad paper.

Pepper picked up a stack of letters and began filtering through them. Her mouth dropped open, and she looked at Alex. 'You need to see this.' She held out several business letters, and Alex skimmed them before meeting her gaze.

'These are all from Spencer Francis.' She frowned down at the pages. 'Offers to buy his recipe for her company. This one is quarter of a million.' She flipped to another page. 'This is half a million.' She handed the letter to Pepper. 'And this one is a million dollars, plus a position on their board of directors.'

Pepper frowned. 'What's so special about his beer?'

'I have no idea.'

Pepper held up another letter, this one handwritten on lined paper, also from Spencer. 'It's a threat.' She began reading.

> *Jonah,*
>
> *I've done everything possible to create an attractive offer for your recipe. I've offered you the moon and stars and still you refuse me. I kept your secrets since college. Take our offer and give me the recipe or I'll tell what I know, and still figure out how to get it without you.*
>
> *Spencer*

'What secrets did she keep?' Pepper asked, shaking her head. 'I feel like I didn't know the real Jonah.' Her bottom lip poked out. 'Was it all lies?'

A Brew for Chaos 175

Alex sighed. 'I'm sorry. I know this is difficult . . . They clearly had a history together. What do we know about her?'

Pepper logged into her computer and began typing. 'She's got a Wiki page.' She began reading. 'Spencer went to Bellamy Bay College for undergrad.' She typed some more. 'That's interesting . . . She was a senior during the time the Fisherman was active. Jonah was here, so maybe they were friends.'

Alex wondered if Spencer was the woman Daphne met on the beach. 'Sounds like she felt Jonah owed her something.'

Pepper laughed. 'But a beer recipe?'

'The beer industry is a multi-billion-dollar industry. They clearly think Jonah's recipe is the next big thing.' Alex shrugged. 'But she could be a suspect in his case. Spencer knew Jonah, she had motive to harm him, and she was in town during the murder. I wonder if she's on Jack's radar.' *If he's actually investigating, that is*, she thought sourly.

'If she's not, she's definitely on ours,' Pepper said, voice hard.

Alex stared at the Wiki page until her vision blurred. She blinked. 'I should pay her a visit. Try and get her to talk.'

THIRTY

The next morning, Alex slept in while Lidia opened the shop.

She'd asked Alex to stay with Caroline all day in case she needed anything or wanted to leave. Since she'd been reported deceased for her own safety, it was important she stay inside and away from prying eyes until the killer was found.

When she came downstairs, coffee had been made, and there were platters of apple cinnamon biscuits, hickory smoked bacon and fried potatoes with onions warming on the stove. Caroline was at the table drinking a cup of tea.

She'd just finished off a large plate of sardines, which they'd discovered was a favorite of Caroline's. Athena sat at her feet, hoping for a dropped morsel.

'Good morning,' Alex said when she joined her at the table with a mug of coffee and only a biscuit. She didn't have much of an appetite. Especially after she'd texted Kamila for news and found there was none.

Morning.

Alex remembered Caroline could only telepath her thoughts and switched to the same manner of communication. *Since I have the day off, I thought we could spend some time getting to know each other better.*

I'd like that. Caroline licked her fingers and pushed her plate away.

Do you have any family we should try and contact?

She shook her head. *They were older parents when I was young. Remember, I should be in my sixties. I found their obituaries online.*

I'm sorry. Alex set her cup down.

It's okay. And I was an only child, so . . . Anyway, how would I explain my disappearance or the fact that I haven't aged? It's for the best that anyone I would've cared about is long gone.

How much do you remember now? Alex asked.

A Brew for Chaos 177

I remember everything – my entire life up until the time I was taken. The last forty years have been a blur and then I was on the beach. She shrugged. *I remember everything after that too.*

You're a genetic mermaid like me and the rest of the family. You're a Magical. Did you know that growing up?

A smile appeared on Caroline's face but quickly disappeared. *I'd never heard the term Magical growing up. I just knew I was . . . different.*

Tell me about your time at Bellamy Bay College. Maybe there's a clue in your past that could help us find Minka. We think that she was taken to the same place the Fisherman took you.

She expected this information to upset Caroline, but she only nodded, a vague look of contentment on her face. As if her time in captivity had been a pleasant memory.

I enjoyed my time in college. I had a best friend, a roommate—

Do you remember her name?

She nodded. *Margaret. Margaret Dunsmore.*

Alex stared at her. Margaret Dunsmore was Tobias' girlfriend. The one everyone thought had been taken by the Fisherman, only to return and abruptly leave school. Never to be heard from again.

By lunchtime, Alex was getting restless. She knew she needed to stay with Caroline, but she was eager to find Minka.

She'd showered and dressed and was doing dishes when her cell phone rang. It was Dr Crow.

'Just checking on my patient,' he said with a smile in his voice.

'She's doing well.'

'I'm happy to hear that. I received the results for the device we removed from her neck.'

'Is it related to a throat surgery like you theorized?' Alex asked.

'I wish.' He hesitated. 'It's a tracking device.'

Alex gasped. 'My God. They put a tracking device in her neck? How cruel. Wait – is it still active?'

'It doesn't appear to be. That was my concern as well.'

'That poor woman. Thanks for letting me know.'

'There's more . . . The device held a type of electrode that possibly interfaced with her nervous system . . . to shock her.'

Alex gasped again. 'Someone would've had a remote and the ability to . . . punish her, I suppose.'

Silence filled the air.

'Ugly stuff we're dealing with,' he finally said.

'Thank you, doctor.' Alex ended the call just as Kamila arrived. She felt sick to her stomach.

Kamila looked around the kitchen. 'Where's the newest member of the Magical community?'

'Caroline is in the library reading.'

Kamila leaned against the counter and picked up a biscuit. 'Has she shared any other abilities I should know about, besides possibly being immortal?'

Alex forced herself to smile. 'Ha. Ha. Very funny. And no.'

'The analysis of the security feed from the aquarium came in this morning. An empty hallway was swapped for the footage that must've shown Minka leaving the bathroom and someone snatching her. Whoever altered it had professional skills. The editing was almost flawless, though we were able to detect the film was changed.'

'That's unfortunate,' Alex said as she turned the dishwasher on. Then she told her about Caroline's tracker.

'What the . . .' She shook her head. 'Weird. Creepy. Inhumane. I'd love to get my hands on these monsters.'

'I uncovered some information about Mac . . . He didn't have an alibi for the Fisherman abductions like we thought.'

'Mac?' She scoffed. 'Even so. Doesn't seem the serial killer type.'

'I know, and I agree. But he does have both means and opportunity to be both the Fisherman and Jonah's killer. I'm concerned, to be honest.'

'Jonah's killer is Jack's department . . .' She sighed. 'But we don't know if he's really investigating, do we?'

'No. We don't. Would you find out if he has an alibi for the time of Jonah's attack? And I'll keep digging on the Fisherman case.'

'Yeah, I'll—' Kamila's dispatch sounded and she listened. 'I have to go. Fender bender by the beach. But Alex . . .' She paused as she headed to the front door.

'Yeah?'

A Brew for Chaos 179

'Sorry about the other day. I'm not mad at you. With both me and Mom upset with Minka, I'm glad she still had your support. And the thing with Jack?' She shook her head. 'I really liked him. Looked up to him even, professionally speaking.'

'I'm kind of crushed too. I thought I was falling in love with him . . . And with him finally inviting me to spend time with his mother, I thought he felt it too. It didn't feel perfect, but it did feel good.'

'Lately he's been trying to convince me to take the detective exam. I thought it was because he saw something in me, talent. But now, I'm guessing it's because he'll be leaving as soon as his secret agent case is over.'

Alex blinked, trying to school her features into a non-expression. She wasn't sure how she felt about Jack leaving. She thought she might love him. She was pretty sure she hated him. But did she want him to leave town?

Kamila opened the front door. 'I'll be back around later.'

After Kamila left, Alex and Caroline parked on the couch.

Covered in cozy blankets and fluffy pillows, they watched a romance about a woman who inherited her grandfather's apple cider business in the Virginia mountains only to be targeted by a big city soda company who wanted her grandfather's age-old family recipe. It reminded her of how Spencer had been badgering Jonah for his beer recipe.

When a commercial for Tobias Winston's attorney practice came on the television, Caroline leaned forward.

I remember him, she telepathed, her sense of urgency reverberating through Alex's brain.

He was always with Margaret. She and I planned on traveling the world together, making amazing marine biology discoveries in places like the Great Barrier Reef in Australia and Thailand. But then she went missing, and then . . . I guess so did I . . .

Wait. You don't know, do you? Alex leaned forward. *No, how could you . . . Aunt Lidia said that Margaret did go missing, but she was returned with no memory of what happened. It must've happened after you were taken.*

Tobias said the college sent a letter out stating they thought she'd been a victim of the Fisherman, but a couple days later

180   Esme Addison

she was found – and her father unenrolled her from school and took her home. Then—

Caroline stood, her legs shaking under her weight. *Margaret didn't have a father. He died in World War II.*

So, some guy just came to school and took her? What happened to her? Alex found her phone on a nearby table and began dialing. *I'll call Kamila and see if she can email me the case file. There has to be a logical explanation for this.*

Finally an emotion from Caroline. A tear slid down her face.

Alex's fingers stilled on her phone. *Are you all right?*

Caroline shook her head. *Margaret was my best friend. I wasn't close to my parents. At the time, they wanted me to marry and start a family. But I wanted to go to school and have a career.*

It created a real rift between us that was unfortunately never healed. Margaret was like a sister to me. I went home with her on school breaks, met her mother and her aunt – they were all like family to me. More than my own.

And I owe it to her to find out what happened to her.

Even if it ends in me finding her obituary online.

THIRTY-ONE

'No news,' Kamila said as soon as she stepped inside the house, carrying a folder in one hand.

'Come on in. You look exhausted.' Kamila followed Alex into the living room. 'Did you talk to Leith?'

'I left a message, but he's been golfing all day.'

'What about Zane Ballard, from the brewery? I think he has a crush on her. Maybe he sent the flowers.'

Kamila covered her mouth as she yawned. 'I'll look into it.'

'Never mind. You've got enough on your plate. I'll talk to him.'

'Suit yourself.' Kamila sank into a couch and threw her head back against a pillow. 'So, I was going to go home, take a shower and get some shuteye, but I started reading the missing persons case file for Margaret Dunsmore,' Kamila said. 'Pretty interesting stuff.' She opened the folder. 'So the first thing I thought weird is that the same day Margaret was returned, Caroline here' – she pointed to their guest – 'was taken.'

Caroline's expression crumpled. *It's almost like they made a mistake, like they meant to get me first, returned her and then took me.*

'That's what I thought.' Kamila regarded her suspiciously.

'Margaret's name is not on the list of victims Jonah had,' Alex noted. 'So maybe it was a mistake. She didn't have the gene. And when they realized . . .'

It's my fault my best friend was taken. Caroline leaned over her lap, hands covering her face. Her shoulders suddenly heaving with emotion.

Kamila watched her uncomfortably before she returned to the folder. 'The other weird thing is that Jonah Fox is the one who found Margaret on the beach back in the eighties and brought her into the police department.'

'Jonah again.' Alex sighed. 'He was investigated as a suspect for a time. Why was he eventually disqualified from the list of suspects?' She gave Caroline a sideways glance. 'Because it's looking more and more like he was involved in the Fisherman case in ways not related to him being a journalist.'

'I'll have to check the files when I return to the station.' She handed Alex the folder. 'It's a copy. You can keep it. Read it. Maybe I missed something.' Kamila suddenly swayed on her feet. 'Okay, I gotta take a nap. I'm dead on my feet.'

'Come back in a couple of hours. I'm making dinner.'

'You?'

Alex laughed. 'I'm gonna try. Want to do something nice for Ciocia.'

'All right. I'll be back.'

A large pot of chili bubbled on the stove, sending up a mélange of onion and green peppers. Alex set up her laptop on the kitchen table while her corn muffins were baking. The sweet scents of butter, cream and roasted corn wafted in the area, and Alex had to admit it smelled really good. Maybe she should cook more often. It was calming, like making candles or soap.

She typed in *Detective Gordon Clarke*, the man who'd been in charge of investigating the missing women, and the search terms *police detective*, *Bellamy Bay*, *North Carolina* and *the Fisherman case* for good measure. Several articles came up but nothing with the detective's name, not even an article from the *Bugler* quoting him about the case. It was weird, like he was a ghost. A spook.

It was almost as if the internet had been scrubbed of his name. But surely the local paper had something in their archives on the man who'd served as Bellamy Bay's detective for two years?

She quickly did a search for Jack's name and found over twenty hits, and he'd been in town less than a year. But nothing about him before he relocated. Was Jack Frazier even his real name?

She rose from the table and sent Pepper a text asking her to check the paper archives for any articles referencing Detective Clarke. A thought occurred to her, and she sent a follow-up message requesting one more thing: Anything of interest on Jonah.

When Pepper asked why, Alex shared Jack's reservations about the detective. She responded immediately saying she'd check ASAP.

Alex looked at the clock on the kitchen wall. Her aunt should be home soon, so she began setting the table. A few moments later, her phone, sitting on the counter, was buzzing with an incoming text. She ran to it, hoping it was Kamila with news of Minka. Or Pepper, eager to see what she'd found on the man. Her instincts told her there was something fishy about him.

It was Pepper. And she read the text. Once. Twice. Unbelievably, there was nothing in the news archives about Detective Clarke.

Disappointed, she responded with her thanks, but then she had a thought. Clarke was a law enforcement officer. He had to have had a work portrait done, right? But would it still be there?

She called Kamila. 'Sorry if I woke you?'

'Nope, you're good.'

'I have a favor to ask.'

'Dinner almost ready?'

'Yes.'

'Tell me what you need.'

After talking with Kamila, Alex saw she had another message. She tapped on the notification and saw Pepper had sent it. She swiped the screen, and her messaging app opened.

An image appeared. Black and white, with text written under it. She studied the image taken from the *Bellamy Bay Bugler*. It showed a much younger Jonah dressed in a tux, wide grin on his face, and arm wrapped around an elegant woman in a strapless black dress that skimmed her knees. *Bugler editor-in-chief, Jonah Fox, and his girlfriend, local socialite Spencer Francis.*

Spencer Francis had been his girlfriend? Why hadn't he mentioned that? For that matter, why hadn't she?

'You've really outdone yourself,' Lidia said as she entered the kitchen. 'Dinner looks lovely. New England Chili you said?'

Alex's cheeks warmed as she looked at the set table. 'It's not much, but it's what my dad and I often made in the winter.'

Athena barked and trotted to the door to greet Kamila with a wagging tail.

'He-e-ey, girl.' Kamila rubbed her neck and back, then went

into the kitchen and washed her hands. 'Smells good in here.' She gave her mom a side-eyed glance. 'Alex told you?'

Aunt Lidia nodded.

'No news is good news. Let's hope for the best.' Kamila handed Alex a manila envelope as she sat down.

Alex took it from her, noting the dark circles under her eyes.

Kamila placed two muffins on her plate while Alex unsealed the envelope. She spooned chili into her bowl. 'Where's the salt?' Kamila looked around the table.

'I'll get it.' Alex jumped up, wanting the first meal she'd made for the family to be perfect. She set the envelope on the table, the black and white photo half spilled out. 'Do you like spicy?' Alex asked over her shoulder. 'If so, you might want a splash of hot sauce in yours.'

Kamila tasted the chili. 'Nah, I'm good. It's got just the right amount of kick.'

Lidia leaned over to look at the photo peeking out of the envelope. 'What have you got there?'

Kamila munched on a muffin. 'The service portrait of Detective Gordon Clarke, who was in charge of the Fisherman case.'

Alex sighed, head in the cabinets. 'What happened to the sea salt?'

Sorry, I took it, Caroline said. *I've been adding it to my seaweed tea. I'll get it. It's in my room.*

'Don't worry about it.' Kamila waved a hand. 'It's fine. I'll eat it as is.'

Lidia held the portrait up for a better look. 'I remember this man. Very handsome with a commanding presence. But a little cold in his demeanor.'

'Sit down, Alex.' Kamila waved a hand towards her chair. 'Finish your food before it gets cold.'

Alex returned, ate a few bits of her chili then picked up the photo with her left hand. She inspected the image, taking in the hard eyes, long nose, narrow face and slicked-back hair with a side part.

Her spoon fell to the floor with a loud clatter.

Kamila glanced at her. 'What's wrong?'

'I've seen this man before. He's much older now, but I'd recognize him anywhere, especially his eyes.'

Her fingers shook as she set the photograph down.

If she wasn't mistaken, the man in the photo was the cantankerous elderly gentleman staying at the Seaside B&B . . . Forbes McDonald.

THIRTY-TWO

Lidia pursed her lips. 'It can't be a coincidence that Forbes McDonald shows up at the same time Jonah Fox was killed.'
'His grandson, Leith, said he was here to golf,' Alex replied.

Kamila made a face. 'Does Leith know his grandfather worked here under an assumed name? And what's *that* about? I need to research his real name and see what I can find . . . if Forbes McDonald *is* his real name, that is.'

'I'm going to talk to him,' Alex said.

Lidia looked worried. 'Please be careful. You too, Kamila.' Lidia stared into her bowl. 'I want to make sure you girls are using your time wisely. How will investigating this man help you find Minka?'

Alex took a breath. 'We think that the Fisherman was abducting women for the government for military testing. And the fact that Caroline was missing for forty years leads us to believe they kept these women somewhere, at least some of them at a military black site in the ocean.'

'If we can prove Forbes is involved in the case, maybe he'll come forward with more information to save his own hide, like where Minka is being held.'

Lidia looked at Alex. 'You know what you have to do.'

Alex gulped. 'I do?'

'Call your boyfriend.' She rolled her eyes. 'The *witch hunter*.'

Alex groaned.

'No.' Lidia held up a hand. 'Hear me out. He's still pretending to be your boyfriend.'

Alex winced.

'And still pretending to be this town's detective. So if you tell him what you've told me, he'll have no recourse but to investigate, and then hopefully do what he does best. Arrest people.'

Kamila shrugged. 'She's not wrong.'

* * *

A Brew for Chaos

187

After dinner, Alex prolonged the inevitable by taking an extra-long shower, folding her laundry and rearranging her closet before she sat cross-legged on her bed and called Jack.

He answered on the first ring. 'Hey you,' he said, his voice warm and sweet. 'I thought you were dodging my calls.'

Alex smiled weakly. 'I just took the day off to veg out.'

'My mother's been asking about you.'

Alex could hear a teasing smile in his voice. 'How is she?'

'She's fine, and wanting to spend time with you again. I told her I'd ask you the next time we spoke. Maybe it will distract you from . . . things?'

'Of course. That would be nice. I actually called you to see if you wanted to get breakfast tomorrow. There's something I want to discuss.'

'That sounds ominous.'

'Nothing is ominous over biscuits at Coffee O'Clock.' She forced herself to laugh. 'How's nine?'

'It's a date.'

She ended the call, then dialed the brewery. She needed to find out if Zane had sent Minka the flowers. Loud chatter filled her ear, and a staff member answered the phone.

'May I speak to Zane?' She raised her voice over the sound of customers talking and drinking and eating.

'I'm the assistant manager, can I help you?'

Alex paused. 'No, I need to speak to Zane, specifically.'

'You're out of luck. He's on vacation for a few days.'

A sick feeling rumbled in Alex's belly. 'I'm a friend,' she lied. 'Do you know where I can find him?'

'It's not a secret. Big beer podcast event in Asheville.'

Alex hung up the phone, wondering if Zane leaving town the same time Minka went missing was a coincidence.

The next morning, Jack stared at her in surprise. 'You want me to arrest somebody.'

'Uh huh.' Alex sipped her coffee. Then explained all the reasons why.

Jack picked up his bagel – six months in the south and he was still not a fan of flaky, buttery biscuits. However, Alex was coming around. He stared at the toasted ring of bread, lost in thought. 'It's certainly odd, him working here under an assumed name.'

'Why do you think he'd do that?' She eyed him innocently. 'Come to town pretending to be someone he's not, deceiving everyone that he comes into contact with?'

Jack's forehead wrinkled as he considered his bagel. Plain with no cream cheese.

Alex used to think that order represented Jack. Simple, down to earth, without pretentions. Just like his favorite coffee drink. Black with two sugars. But it was probably just an act. He probably really loved an Everything Bagel with onion and chive cream cheese with a fancy coffee drink and that order was just part of his cover.

She smothered a sigh. Had she ever really known him? When she looked up, he was staring at her with interest.

'You want my bagel.' He grinned. 'You were staring mighty hard at it.'

She blinked. Smiled. 'Nope. Just . . . my mind wandered for a moment.'

'You feeling okay? It's only been two days since the . . .' He shrugged like it pained him to bring it up.

But did it? Alex wondered. Did he really care about her? 'You didn't answer my question.' She smiled. *You deflected by asking me about your stupid bagel.*

'If Forbes McDonald was here under an assumed name,' he began carefully, 'he was probably here at the behest of a government agency. Doing something he was assigned to do: his job.'

'And his job was to botch the investigation so that no one was ever charged,' she suggested.

'Which he did. And now it makes sense why a decorated serviceman would complete such sloppy work with the witness interviews and reports.'

'Which would follow that he was somehow working in cahoots with the Fisherman.' Alex swallowed. So Forbes was undoubtedly working for the same government agency doing the testing on Magicals. Was that the same agency Jack worked for?

'This guy,' he continued, as he tore pieces of his bagel off, 'I'm sure he considers himself a patriot and is – was – doing his duty for his country.'

Alex wondered if he was talking about himself now, too.

'The question is what did the government want with these women?'

Did he seriously not know about the testing on Magicals? Was it an act? Did they know each other? Was he pretending now? 'And why is he back forty years later?'

'Logic would follow that he's been sent here to tie up loose ends,' Jack said.

'By killing Jonah Fox?'

'Possibly.'

'That would mean that Jonah knew the identity of the Fisherman all this time.' She thought of Leith then. He was concerned about his grandfather. Had he really come to town for golf?

'And we still haven't answered the question of Jane Doe's identity or why she was found beside his body.' He eyed her curiously. 'Has the woman remembered anything?'

Alex shook her head. She wasn't sharing anything with him. Not this liar. 'No.'

His eyes narrowed as he considered her, and Alex tried not to squirm under his gaze.

'It's certainly suspicious. All of it. And you want me to arrest him why?'

'He might know where Minka is being held.'

'Sounds like arresting him could be complicated.'

Seriously? *Now* he was reluctant to arrest someone? Not quick-to-arrest-anyone Jack taking it slow for the first time ever.

'This is definitely out of my jurisdiction, but I have some friends who work in the government who may be able to help . . .'

I'll bet you do, Alex thought uncharitably.

'I'll look into it for you. Okay?'

'That would be wonderful. Thank you, Jack.' She paused. 'There's one more thing.'

He sat back in his chair, arms crossed. 'What is it?'

'Carson MacInnes.'

'What about him?'

'He was the main suspect in the Fisherman case, and I've recently discovered that some of his alibis that summer weren't as strong as we thought.'

'I read the files. Detective Clarke brought him in numerous times for questioning.'

'And Jonah—'

'And Jonah was sued for defamation by Mac . . . I suppose you want to know where he was when Jonah was attacked?'

Alex nodded, eager to say more but biting her tongue.

'At home. Alone. Watching television.'

'This is me not butting into your investigation.'

'But you want to know if he's on my list, right?'

Alex nodded, and he sighed.

She leaned forward.

'He's on my list of suspects. At the very top.'

'So there are others?' she asked in a leading tone. 'You said suspects with an "s" at the end.'

'Only because you've been trying not to interfere and I appreciate it, I'll tell you who I'm looking at, but then we change the subject. Deal?'

Alex nodded.

'The Jane Doe is suspicious to me. There's no evidence against her – yet. I'm keeping an eye on her. Your pal Pepper keeps buzzing in my ear about how suspicious she is of her. She's a victim, but she's also a person of interest.' He thought for a moment. 'With no memory of what happened. Horrible for her, or extremely convenient.'

'Who else?'

'Then there's Mac with his lawsuit, his history in the Navy with Jonah – they served at the same time and in the same unit, did you know that?'

'No, I didn't.'

'And his lack of alibi . . . not looking good for him.' He studied her expression. 'You're dying to say something, aren't you?'

Alex pressed her lips together and shook her head.

He almost laughed. 'Go ahead, tell me.'

'It's just that my research into the Fisherman case with Pepper may have some overlap with your investigation into Jonah's case.'

He leaned forward, steepling his hands on the table. 'Such as?'

She hesitated. 'Spencer Francis.'

'Pepper also mentioned her to me.' He couldn't hide his

skepticism. 'She explained her reasons, but I can't believe she'd kill over a recipe. It's ridiculous actually . . .' He shrugged. 'What about her?'

'She's a former girlfriend who sent Jonah threatening letters. So there's motive.'

Jack regarded her. 'But no means or opportunity, and what could she have used to electrocute Jonah? And why assault the Jane Doe?'

'It's a mystery . . .' Alex trailed. 'One that *I* am not investigating but *you* could.'

'If I look into Spencer, will you do something for me?'

'Of course. Name it.'

'This morning when I told my mother I was coming to meet you, she wanted me to ask if she could have a little outing with you.' A dimple appeared when he smiled. 'And I don't see a problem with that.'

Alex toyed with a napkin, trying to hide her excitement. Yes. Another opportunity to search his house and find out what he's really up to in Bellamy Bay. 'I'd love to. I have to work today and then I have a delivery to make.' Alex thought for a moment. 'How about tomorrow afternoon? Tanner will be managing the shop then.'

THIRTY-THREE

Later in the day, Alex was stocking shelves when Tanner entered the shop.

'Any news on the search?'

She shook her head. 'They're still looking, but if they don't find another sign of her soon . . .' She sighed and shook her head. 'I don't want to think about it.'

'I may have found something.'

'What is it?'

'Project Oannes.'

'Oannes. The Sumerian fish god, right?' Alex laughed. 'Don't ask me how I know that.'

'Right, one of the seven sages from the Sumerian creation myths that taught ancient Mesopotamians farming, writing, mathematics and astronomy. Supposedly he was like a man in a fish suit – I'm paraphrasing. Anyway, the Navy started a program in the sixties that evolved from one of their submarine development programs.'

'Which was?'

'Creating a security force for submarines. See, subs are equipped with torpedoes and missiles for attacking enemy vessels. And the crews usually have guns in case they're boarded by enemies, but I'm guessing they want more strategic self-defense, so they're trying to create an elite force of soldiers that can stay underwater longer, swim longer, faster. And fight and defend the ship if necessary.'

'Sounds like what Dylan's father was trying to help the DOD with, a serum that could be injected into their soldiers for a kind of upgrade. Only once they heard about Magicals . . .' She swallowed. 'What else did you learn?'

'Initially, they were trying to train dolphins to provide security because they could already swim fast and stay underwater longer, but according to my source they needed more strategic proactive thinking than the dolphins could provide.'

A Brew for Chaos 193

'So, they're back to creating a serum based on Magical DNA to inject into existing soldiers?'

'Not exactly. My source said they're training actual Magicals to be security forces.'

'I suppose that's okay if it's done ethically and the Magicals have volunteered for the program. Do we know anything about their location?'

'Not yet. It's literally a state secret. But I'm keeping my ear to the ground.'

Alex turned to Celeste, who sat in the passenger seat of her car. 'I really appreciate you agreeing to come with me.'

'I've got your back, cuz. You know that.'

'So, we're just going to be very low key and have a chat with Mac. I've talked to him once, but I feel like he's still holding back.' She parked and turned off the car.

'Let's get our Nancy Drew on.' Celeste flashed a grin, then bounced out of the car.

When they entered the B&B, Mac looked up from his newspaper. 'I don't have anything else to say to you, Miss Daniels.'

But Alex planted her feet on the ground and studied him. 'When Forbes checked in, you recognized him, didn't you?' she asked, her voice low.

Mac lay his paper down. 'No. No, I didn't.'

'I know,' Alex said. 'I know who he really is.'

Mac seemed to deflate. He nodded. 'I recognized him, yeah. Those mean eyes of his haven't changed even if the rest of him has. He was the cop that tried to make me take the fall for that Fisherman business.'

'Why do you say that?'

'Because he was trying to frame me. Him and that newspaper man what got himself killed. He'd write stuff in the paper that made it sound like I was the killer, and that detective would bring me in each time and ask me if I was ready to confess.'

'You think they were working together?' Celeste asked.

Mac turned to look at her. 'I know they were. Seen 'em with their heads together all the time.' He laughed. 'How else do you think Jonah paid all his gambling debts all of a sudden and became an upstanding citizen? He was a dirty journalist on the make.'

'You knew about his debts?'

'Sure, I did. We played cards together.' He raised an eyebrow. 'I also know how they got paid.'

'Why haven't you said anything to anyone?' Alex asked. 'Told Jack?'

'If the cops and the newspaper are against you, what chance do you have? For all I know Jack and the paper is still on the take. Nope, I'd rather run my mother's house and keep my head down.'

'Who did you play cards with? Do you remember?'

He tapped his forehead. 'Mind like a steel trap. My joints on the other hand . . .' He chuckled. 'Now, let's see. There was me. Jonah. The policeman – Detective Gordon Clarke. And—' His expression changed. Mouth snapped shut.

Alex wondered about the woman who'd approached Daphne. 'There wasn't a fourth? Maybe a woman?'

His face completely shuttered. 'I don't know what you're talking about.'

He is clearly lying, Alex thought to herself. No way Daphne made that woman up. But why lie about her?

'They were your friends, right?' Alex cocked her head. 'Why did they turn on you like that? Why did Jonah go so hard for you in the paper?'

'Jonah was just paying the piper.' He gave her a pointed look, his features twisting with scorn. 'Nothing personal. That's what he told me.'

A chill ran down her spine. He was referring to Montgomery, she knew it. He'd paid Jonah's debts, got him a job then told him to make Mac look guilty. But why?

'This group,' she began, her eyes on his. 'Is this the same group you'd meet on the beach when you'd leave the teens' Bible study meetings?'

A hard look crossed his face, and his chest stilled like he'd stopped breathing. His eyes darted to Celeste, and then his face softened. 'You know?'

'I know.'

He was quiet. 'Yes, the same people.'

'What were you meeting about?'

'I can't say.'

'You were out of the military, weren't you?'

He shrugged, a closed look on his face. 'It was classified business.'

'And even now you can't talk about it?'

'Correct.'

'And the girl?' She tried not to look at Celeste, who watched them both with interest.

He swallowed, his Adam's apple moving up and down at a slow pace. 'I cared for her. I kept her safe. Kept her close. It was a dangerous summer.'

'You cared for her,' Alex said, realizing the truth in his eyes. 'You loved her.'

He inhaled slowly. 'I did. But it wasn't meant to be.'

Celeste made an exasperated noise. 'Are you guys going to stop talking in code and tell me what's going on?'

But Alex could only stare at Mac, wondering if she was looking at the Fisherman. 'Did you do it?'

He blinked. 'No.'

'But you were involved?' His face went icy, and she nodded. 'And you can't or won't discuss it.'

'All I'll say on the subject is that summer I hung with a crowd which was into some really shady business. Contracted out top-secret shady business that I was a part of for a time, and then I realized . . . well, I determined that I no longer wanted to be a part of what was happening. Didn't want their money, didn't want that on my conscience. So I declined to continue working with them . . . and they, well, they tried to frame me.'

'What were they into?' Alex asked, tone urgent. 'You can tell me. Please.'

Mac's eyes skittered around the lobby like he was being watched. 'Top secret is top secret. There's no expiration date unless information has been declassified and I'm pretty sure this will never be declassified.'

'Not even through a Freedom of Information Act request?' Celeste asked.

'Not even then.' He stared at her. 'You know you look just like your mama did when she was young.'

Celeste made a face. 'You knew my mother?'

He chuckled. 'Did I know your mother?' He paused, then

rubbed his chin. 'Seen her around town.' Then he sobered, turning back to Alex. His nod was curt, and Alex realized she'd have to figure it out without his help. Her stomach did a flip-flop. Was it possible the Fisherman had been in Bellamy Bay all this time? And she'd delivered joint cream to him.

'The detective, you don't wonder why he's back with a different name?'

'Looks like he came back to kill Jonah.' He picked up the newspaper, the air between them clearing. 'Back then those two were thick as thieves. Nothing lasts forever.' He shrugged and began reading again.

A thought occurred to Alex. If Mac had been protecting Daphne from the Fisherman that summer, was it because he knew of Magicals, that she was half-Mer? Or was he just acting as any guy would about a young woman – okay, teenager – that he cared about?

'One more question?' she asked, eyebrows lifting.

'Sure,' he dragged out. 'If it will get you out of here.'

'Did you both have an M-Level security clearance?' *Did he know about Magicals? Did he know about her and her family? Like Jack*, she realized. He must have the clearance too.

His expression blanked, but a muscle on his jaw twitched. 'M-Level?' He paused, then rubbed his chin. 'Can't say I ever heard of it.'

Alex's eyes narrowed. He'd done the same thing when he'd lied about knowing Celeste's mother. Repeated the question. Paused. Rubbed his chin. It was his tell. The things he did unconsciously when he was lying. So, he was lying now.

They drove in silence for a few moments, then Alex slowed when she heard a police siren behind her. She pulled over onto the side of the road and waited for a pickup truck with a siren placed on top to wail by. That, she thought with a start, looked like Jack's.

Was there another murder? She eased back onto the road.

Alex began to drive alongside the edge of the Maritime Forest that led up to the coastline. They saw several police cars and two fire trucks in the public parking lot of one of the beach public entrances. She slowed down when she saw Jack's truck

A Brew for Chaos   197

and then Kamila jumping out of her cruiser and running towards
the beach. 'What's going on?' she wondered aloud.

'Park,' Celeste suggested. 'Let's see.'

Alex turned into the parking lot and parked her car. They
bounced out of the car and began walking towards the beach
when they approached a fireman standing beside his truck.
'What's happening?'

He turned towards the beach, gaze hopeful. 'It's good news,'
he began. 'The missing woman was found.'

Alex's eyes widened. 'Which woman?'

'Minka Sobieski. She's on the beach.'

THIRTY-FOUR

Alex and Celeste began running on the uneven ground covered in roots and moss. Towering trees on either side of them. A quarter of a mile later, out of breath and hearts racing, they reached a flight of steps that took them to the beach.

It was a cold, blustery day, and the ocean was gray, the sounds of the waves loud and crashing against the surf.

Police officers were on the beach with a portion secured by bright orange safety cones and more officers. Alex saw Jack talking to a passerby with his notepad and pen out. They stopped short when Kamila called Alex's name. 'Over here.'

Alex saw Kamila standing at the open back of an emergency vehicle. Upon closer inspection, they saw Minka sitting on the tailgate, an emergency blanket wrapped around her shoulders. She trembled in the cool autumn air but had a smile on her face. An EMS technician was checking her vitals.

'Minka!' Alex shouted as she ran towards her with Celeste a few steps behind. She reached her and wrapped her in a tight hug.

'Mom's meeting us at the hospital,' Kamila said, her voice terse. 'Best for her not to see all of the chaos out here.'

'What happened?' Celeste asked. 'And why is she wet?'

'She doesn't know,' Kamila said before her sister could respond.

The EMS tech put his tools back in his satchel. 'She seems okay, Officer Sobieski. Her pulse is normal. Her blood pressure is a little low but within acceptable range. She complained of dizziness and symptoms of vertigo, but they've appeared to pass with time. I'd recommend taking her to the hospital for further examinations and then maybe a psychologist to address any trauma she's experienced.'

The EMS cleared his throat and lowered his voice. 'Like I said, she seems okay but not *okay* if you know what I mean.'

He gestured towards the smile on her face. 'Her expression, her insistence that all is well could be a sign of shock.'

Kamila nodded, the muscles of her face tight with concern. 'Strap her in and let's take her to the hospital.'

The EMS worker gestured for the driver to join him, and they pulled the gurney out. They indicated that Minka should get on the stretcher and lie down, which she did.

Alex reached for her hand when she was comfortable with another blanket tucked around her. 'Minka, you all right?'

Minka nodded, her features composed in a pleasant expression. 'I'm fine, why?'

An EMS worker gave Kamila a pointed look before locking her straps in place.

Kamila huffed in exasperation, eyes on Alex. 'She's been like this ever since she was found. With this stupid smile on her face.'

Alex put a hand on Kamila's arm. 'Just calm—'

Kamila shook her hand away. 'I can't calm down. I want to know who did this so I can bring them to justice. But she's got no actionable intel for me.'

Alex turned to Minka. 'Tell us what you remember.'

'I was at work, remember? I had a report.' Minka looked up from the gurney, her eyes large. Alex nodded. 'The lights went out in my office, and I went to investigate. When I stood up, I thought I heard a noise, so I turned around . . .' She closed her eyes, trying to recall. 'There was a bright light, like a flash, and then . . . Well, I'm here.'

'A flash?' Celeste repeated.

A look of desperation crossed Kamila's face. She leaned forward, placing her hands on Minka's shoulders. She touched her forehead to Minka's and closed her eyes. 'Remember when we used to do this as kids,' she whispered.

Minka nodded. She closed her eyes and they stayed in that position for a long minute. When Kamila stood, a tear ran down one cheek. 'They've completely wiped her memories. They've done something to her,' Kamila said, anger returning. 'Something that messes with your memories. It confuses you and puts you in a trance that makes you so happy you don't know something bad has happened to you.'

200   Esme Addison

She stepped back while the techs lifted the gurney and placed
Minka inside the truck.

'Wait. What did you say?' Celeste said to Kamila.

Kamila shrugged. 'What? I don't know . . . Something that
messes with your memories?'

'And puts you in a trance,' Celeste said, her expression
thoughtful.

Kamila shot Celeste a questioning look before turning to
Minka. 'I'll be right behind in my car. Go ahead and lie down.'

Minka lay down and Kamila secured the straps, making sure
they weren't too tight around her sister. 'I'll meet you at the
hospital. And Mom should be there by now.' She closed the doors
of the ambulance and slapped it twice.

The siren was turned on, and the vehicle moved away. Kamila
trotted to her car, and Alex saw Jack approaching them with a
fast stride.

'Hey,' he greeted her, then nodded to Celeste, who busied
herself with her phone.

She forced a smile. 'Hey.'

'I was hoping to catch you before you left. I'm sure you want
to get to the hospital.' He jerked a thumb towards the beach. 'I
was getting witness statements while Kamila handled Minka.
Wow, right?'

Alex wondered if he really cared that Minka had been found.
Minka was a Magical after all. But did he even know about
Minka and the rest of her family? About her? 'Yes, wow is right.'

He looked concerned. 'You don't seem as happy as I thought
you would be.'

'No. I'm happy. So happy she's back. And relieved . . . But I
guess I'm also feeling shock. Shock that she was taken and shock
now that she's returned.' She mustered some enthusiasm. 'Get
anything good from the bystanders?'

'There were a few eye witnesses, and they all say the same
thing. She just appeared on the beach.' He pointed to an area
where the water met a rocky embankment covered in foliage.
'One moment she wasn't there and then she was.'

Alex gazed towards the stony outcropping, trying to imagine
the scene. 'But where did she come from?'

Jack squinted at the ridge. 'Apparently there's a small sea cave

A Brew for Chaos 201

there? With tunnels . . . She walked out of it and collapsed. Someone called 911, and another covered her with their coat because she was trembling from the cold. She stayed with her until the first EMS team arrived.'

'That's weird. I've never heard of a cave on the beach before.'

'Me either. But we're both new here. I'll bet your aunt knows something. But more importantly, she's alive.' He looked apprehensive. 'I know you probably want to spend time with your family tonight. You want to reschedule for later this week?'

Alex didn't answer. Harder to say no to his face. She didn't want to see him, and yet she was supposed to pretend like everything was fine. Jack the witch hunter. Her throat tightened. She wasn't sure she could do this.

Jack stepped closer to Alex, his eyes turning a stormy blue. 'This is not the best time for this, but I still feel like you've been avoiding me.' He lowered his voice. 'Have I done something to upset you?'

Alex didn't respond, not sure what to say.

He searched her face for answers. 'My mother was looking forward to seeing you tonight.'

She needed to keep him close. Needed to question his mother. Alex found her voice. 'I need to be with my family tonight. I'm sure you understand.'

He looked relieved, leaned forward and planted a kiss on her cheek. 'Of course I do.'

'Rain check then? Tomorrow?'

'Absolutely.' He cleared his throat. 'Now, I better get back to the station.'

'Dump him already.' Celeste huffed loudly when he was out of earshot.

'I can't do that. Not yet, at least.'

'I didn't think he'd ever leave. I need to talk to you. I have an idea what could've wiped Minka's memories.'

THIRTY-FIVE

Alex sat with Celeste in her office while she searched for information on her computer.

'Do you remember when I told you my current project consisted of boring catalog work?'

'Yes, you said you were organizing files related to old caches of weapons.'

Celeste looked up from her computer screen and gestured for Alex to join her on the other side of her desk. 'Look.'

Alex read the entry. '. . . *A handheld electroshock weapon used to incapacitate people by first disorienting them with a flash grenade.*'

'That's the flash Minka saw.' Celeste interrupted. 'The military typically calls them flashbangs.'

Alex continued reading, trying not to imagine the weapon being used on her baby cousin. '*The device then hijacks their musculature and nervous systems. The shock renders them in an almost catatonic or zombie state in which they are susceptible to any and all suggestion. Additional shocks or increased voltage will cause temporary confusion in which serotonin, dopamine, oxytocin and endorphins are released, creating a happy, positive state of contentment for the subject, which renders them not only susceptible to suggestion but agreeable and complicit in their own capture and containment.*'

Celeste turned to Alex. 'It has a technical name, but everyone in the industry calls it the Zombie Maker or ZIM from the initials ZM.'

Alex pointed to the screen. 'Look.' She began reading the next paragraph. '*Originally developed from data sourced from a top-secret naval program that focused on militarizing marine life, one government contractor was able to secure the bid to create weapons based off the project's research for special force operators.*'

Celeste read the last sentence. '*The ZIM is manufactured by a division of Leviathan Industries.*'

'You think the ZIM was used on Minka?' Dylan said, suddenly appearing in the doorway of Celeste's office. Harrison was beside him.

Celeste nodded, her lips pressed into a grim line.

Dylan turned to Harrison. 'Any way to track who has access to these ZIMs?'

'Difficult. But not impossible. We could guess the SEALS, the Green Berets. But none of them would be operating here in Bellamy Bay.'

'So . . .' Celeste prompted, giving Harrison an interested look.

'So, I'll look into it. I have contacts in the intelligence world.'

'You do?' Celeste added, her gaze going up and down Harrison's body. 'I thought you were just the director of security for the Wesley building. Like making sure the doors were locked, guests were signed in . . .' Harrison tilted his head, an amused smile on his lips, and Celeste's cheeks colored. 'I don't mean *just*. Because that is important, obviously. I meant—'

Dylan chuckled.

'I know what you meant.' Harrison crossed his arms. 'I provide security for Wesley as a whole, not just the building. Physical security of this campus is just one basic element of my job.'

Alex gave her cousin a sideways glance. *I wonder if he knows he's talking about Magical weapons and not just advanced technology.*

No way, he's giving Boy Scout vibes, Celeste telepathed back.

'Of course, we don't know for sure that's what was used on Minka.' Harrison glanced at Alex. 'We'd need visual confirmation.'

Alex's phone vibrated with an incoming text. 'It's Kamila.' She swiped the screen and inspected it before showing a photograph of a pencil sketch to Dylan and Harrison. 'Did it look like this?'

Dylan and Harrison examined the image.

Harrison nodded. 'That's it.'

'If Minka's dolphin research is involved with the Fisherman case, doesn't that confirm Montgomery is too?'

Harrison rubbed his smooth-shaven jaw. 'If anyone has the capabilities . . .'

Dylan sighed. 'I know.'

'I think the testing is called Project Oannes,' Alex said.

'Oannes,' Dylan repeated. 'Clever.'

But Harrison looked concerned. 'I've heard of that from when I was a Marine. It's a joint operation between the Army, Navy, and Marines operating out of Camp Malveaux, with the Army overseeing operations and strategy.'

'Dylan mentioned the project was about militarizing dolphins, but I learned from Tanner they were weaponizing . . .' She glanced at Harrison and stopped. 'Certain people, possibly against their will.'

Harrison shot Dylan an amused glance.

'How can we find information on such a protected program?' Alex continued.

'How about a paper trail,' Celeste suggested. 'Since the US Army is lead on the project, their contracting department would have an RFP, a request for proposal.'

Dylan laughed.

'What?' Celeste asked. 'Anything we can find could help. Even the smallest detail. Besides, it's the government. Layers upon layers of bureaucracy. They still have their paperwork, right? Do we know anyone with connections to the US Army?'

'Most of our contracts are with the Navy and Marines, but I could probably find someone,' Dylan volunteered.

Alex looked at him. 'I think I know someone. The problem,' she began, 'is how to explain why we need to learn' – she glanced at Harrison – 'about this weapon and program.'

Harrison's forehead wrinkled and he looked at Dylan.

Dylan grimaced. 'Why would you want to ask *him* for help?'

Even though Alex hated Jack's deception, a part of her still wanted to believe he was a good guy. 'To see if he'll help. To see whose side he's on.'

Dylan shrugged off his annoyance. 'We just tell the truth. The truth is: I know from my work that this Zombie Maker was used on Minka, and it is advanced military-grade weaponry connected to a top-secret military testing program. We don't have to mention the use of . . .' He glanced at Harrison, who nodded. 'Magicals.'

Celeste gasped, her eyes flying to Harrison.

Alex frowned, her eyes sliding to the only Mundane in the room.

A Brew for Chaos

Harrison's lips quirked up. 'I couldn't do my job properly without knowing,' he said, his voice dry. 'I have M-Level security clearance as many non-Magicals working with Magicals do. Your secrets' – he looked at both Celeste and Alex – 'are safe with me.'

He knows? Celeste stared at Harrison as if she'd never seen him before. *Why have I never noticed how hot he is?* she telepathed to Alex. Then she slapped a palm over her mouth. 'You can't read minds, can you?'

'No.' He shot Dylan an amused glance. 'The government has developed a neural implant that can replicate that Magical ability, but I've declined it for now.'

Celeste exhaled in relief, and Alex suppressed a grin and chuckle.

'Celeste,' Dylan said. 'May I use your computer?'

'Of course.' Celeste jumped up, offering her boss the chair. 'But what are you—'

He held up a finger. 'One sec. I just want to check our databases for something.' He began typing, logging into several classified databases. 'Now that we know the name of the weapon . . .' He kept typing. Reading and typing. Finally his fingers stayed, and he looked up. 'There is some good news.'

'Counter weapon?' Harrison asked.

Dylan nodded. 'Part of my father's strategy to contain the damage his father created by partnering with the government was to develop technologies that would counter weapons made by the government against his wishes but based on Magical abilities.'

Hope fluttered in Alex's chest. 'What is it? Where is it?'

'It's a tool that adapts our ability to heal. It's similar to transcranial magnetic stimulation that doctors use now.'

'I always thought our healing power was one of our coolest gifts and so unique. Now anyone can be a telepath or heal. Wait.' Knowing gleamed in Celeste's eyes. 'It's not on the market, is it?'

'No,' Dylan said. 'We tried to bring large-scale models for hospitals as a first rollout, but other companies – industry lobbies for big pharma – advocated against it. No money in being healthy. But I hope one day . . .' He shrugged. 'Until then it's sitting on a proverbial shelf collecting dust.'

Alex thought of her father. If she'd only known about her ability to heal or this advanced technology, maybe she could've saved him.

Dylan caught Alex's eye. 'But I will get our handheld prototype for you.' *You okay?* he telepathed.

Yes. And then her thoughts returned to the present. 'Don't forget Caroline. It might help her too.'

Dylan nodded at Harrison, who looked antsy, ready to leave.

'Contact me if you need me, boss,' Harrison said as he headed to the door. 'I've got work to do.' He winked at Celeste. 'Ladies.'

Celeste tried not to swoon.

THIRTY-SIX

Minka was wrapped in a fluffy pink robe with her favorite pink elephant bedroom slippers.

A marathon of fall-themed movies played all day on the television and Lidia had baked her youngest daughter's favorite treat: wuzetka, chocolate sponge cake filled with whipped cream and a thin layer of orange marmalade, then decadently topped with chocolate icing and a dollop of cream.

And there were pitchers of tea, restorative blends to fix whatever was wrong, and a very special spend of Cozy & Calm, lavender, ginseng, dark chocolate and dried strawberries to increase dopamine and serotonin levels, then enchanted to make the drinker feel wrapped up in their happiest memories like a warm blanket.

Lidia fluttered around Minka like a nervous hen, while Kamila, Alex, Daphne and Celeste watched.

'I've apologized to her a million times,' Lidia began, eyebrows knitted together. 'For not being supportive and loving, and showing her grace . . . And it still doesn't feel like enough.'

Minka tried to shoo her away. 'I'm fine, Mom. And I accept your apology. I love you. You love me. And I'm not moving out, at least not for a while.' She held a saucer of cake on her lap, fork poised at her mouth. 'This cake is fabulous by the way.' She looked at her sister. 'Kam, try some.'

Kamila's face twisted into a sour expression. 'I can't eat right now.' She looked pained. 'You know how much I love to eat, but the sight of food makes me nauseous. It happened when you went missing, and now . . . well, I need to find out who did this before my appetite comes back.'

Alex frowned. 'Heal yourself.'

'No,' she said, her voice sharp. 'I want to feel the pain. The nerves. The anxiety. It's a reminder that I have stuff to do. So, go through it again,' Kamila said, voice like a razor. 'Tell me what happened. Everything you remember, starting at your office.'

An aggrieved expression crossed Minka's face. 'I've told you three times already.'

'Leave her be.' Lidia shot her eldest daughter a dark look, then sat down beside Minka, reaching for a cup of tea. 'I don't understand why I can't bring her memories back.' She glanced at Daphne. 'I've tried everything, right?'

'Yes, you have,' Daphne said in a weary voice.

'It's like I said,' Alex began. 'There's this weapon . . .' She quickly told Kamila what Celeste had shared with her about the Zombie Maker, and Dylan's suspicions that it had been used on Minka.

Minka's eyes were on the television screen that was playing a movie with muted sound. She giggled. 'I hope he realizes she really loves him in time for the pie-baking contest. I don't want them to compete against each other.'

They all turned to stare at the television screen. Then Minka. Then at each other.

'A happy zombie,' Kamila amended. 'That's some weapon.' Kamila stood, her expression tense. 'I can't take this sitting around, eating cake, drinking tea and doing nothing to solve this case.' She turned to her sister. 'I'm really, really glad you're back.' She forced a smile. 'But I'm going back to the station to see what I can do. And then I'm going to the gym to beat the crap out of a punching bag.'

Athena trotted after her to the door, and Kamila stopped and rubbed her ears.

Alex followed her to the door, and her cousin lowered her voice. 'I'm worried about Minka.' She tapped her temple. 'She doesn't seem all there.'

'It's just the effects of the weapon. She'll be okay.'

A look of skepticism crossed Kamila's face. 'She may have had it used on her multiple times. Who's to say what happens to the mind in those conditions? How does it affect the mind after multiple uses? How long do those effects last?'

Alex looked over her shoulder at Minka, whose pleasant smile seemed all the more odd considering the context. She was worried too, but she didn't want Kamila to know that. Even Aunt Lidia wasn't herself. At least one of them had to be strong for the others. 'Dylan has something to counter the effects. He just has to retrieve it from some secure location. But then she'll be back to normal soon.'

'I hope so.' Kamila abruptly wrapped her arms around Alex and hugged her. 'I'm really glad you're here, Alex. With my sister bonkers and Mom barely holding it together . . .' She broke the embrace, looking embarrassed. 'Well, you know.'

She left, and Alex closed the door behind her, hoping beyond hope that Minka returned to health as quickly as possible.

THIRTY-SEVEN

The next morning, Alex had just sat up in bed and rubbed her eyes when Pepper called. 'Hey, girl, can you talk?'

Alex glanced at the clock on her nightstand. 'Sure. What's up?'

'First, how's Minka?'

Alex explained her condition, hoping Pepper didn't want to interview her for the paper.

'I'm glad she's back. Send her my well wishes?'

'Of course.' Alex held her breath, preparing to argue with Pepper about talking to Minka.

'So, I dug up a little dirt on Spencer.'

And Alex exhaled. She placed the phone on speaker and began making up her bed. 'And?'

'Her company's not doing well.'

'Dish.' Alex yawned, trying to blink away her morning grogginess.

'Control of the company started by her mother's family transferred to her two years ago when her father passed away. Her mother died several years before that . . . A year after that, with a local manager of the brewery and an acting CEO at the head of the beverage business, stocks plummeted, and they were hit with several lawsuits. And her father left her a ton of debt.'

Alex placed her pillows and shams in a row. 'This is all about the time she started making offers to Jonah.'

'She sounds desperate for money.'

'But I remember reading that she merged Colonial Beverage with some company based in the EU.' She picked up her cell phone and took it off speaker mode. 'Belgium or Denmark. Could she really make money with Jonah's beer recipe? I mean, it's just beer.'

'And did she kill Jonah when he wouldn't give it to her?'

Alex stood at her window and pulled back the curtain. Streams of pale yellow light shone into her bedroom, and she turned her face up to the warmth. 'What do we know about the company that purchased her business?'

'Checking now.'

Alex could hear the sound of Pepper's keyboard clicking as she gazed out of her window, marveling at the beauty of the fall foliage that blanketed their yard in orange and gold leaves. Yellow goldenrods and burgundy mums lined the walkway to the house's front porch, creating a palette of jewel tones against the green grass.

'Uhm . . . Alex?'

Alex stepped away from the window. 'What did you find?'

'The company is called Chandeuz . . . Based in France with offices in Belgium.' More clicking. 'Widely known for their organic supplements and plant-based pharmaceuticals.'

'Why would they want a beer company? It doesn't—'

'You're not going to believe this.'

'What is it?'

'Leviathan Industries purchased Chandeuz two years ago.'

After the phone call and a shower, Alex was blow drying her hair when her phone lit up with another early morning call. It was Jack. She put her phone on speaker and began brushing her hair into a ponytail.

'I know we were supposed to meet later in the day,' Jack said, 'but I actually have some errands to run now.'

By errands, Alex thought to herself, *did he mean check up on some unsuspecting member of the Magical community?*

'Would you be able to come by and spend a few hours with my mother?'

'If I can take her out as promised,' Alex said.

'Sure,' he said hurriedly. 'I have something rather urgent to attend to this morning, so if you could come over—'

Alex glanced down at the towel wrapped around her. 'I'm still getting dressed, Jack.'

'As soon as you can then?'

She wondered what was so urgent. What witch-hunting task was so important that it couldn't wait until she had at least two cups of coffee? 'Can you at least put some coffee on?'

212   Esme Addison

'I'll do you one better. How about a complete breakfast?'
'I'll leave in fifteen.'

When Alex arrived at Jack's house, he was slipping into a dark
blue blazer with a piece of bacon dangling from his mouth.

'What's the hurry?' Alex asked, pulling off her scarf.

He shoved the bacon into his mouth and finished chewing it.
'I have to drive to Paradise Beach this morning. It's next town
over, and I need to speak to a witness about a case I'm working
on.'

'Minka's?'

He wiped his hands on a nearby towel, then glanced at his
watch. 'Something different.'

'And Spencer? Did you find out if she has an alibi?'

'I did.' He studied her. 'She has a house on The Peninsula and
said she was there alone when Jonah was killed. But I was able
to access the security camera of the house across the street from
hers and her car wasn't there.' He shrugged. 'So, now we know
she's got motive and opportunity.'

And I need to talk to her, Alex mused to herself.

Maisie entered the room, holding a pitcher of orange juice.
'More juice, dear?'

Jack pecked his mother on her cheek. 'I have to run. Alex is
going to spend the morning with you.'

A grin spread across Maisie's face. 'Wonderful. Do you like
apple muffins?'

After Jack left, Alex told Maisie she'd left an earring in Jack's
room, and would she mind if she searched for it? The implication
of the lie made Alex blush, but Maisie only giggled like a teenager and said she'd make more coffee while she looked.

Alex made her way up the stairs, past Jack's bedroom, and
entered his study again. It looked the same. Neat, organized and
smelling faintly of his cologne. She wasn't sure what she was
looking for, but she'd darn near know it when she saw it.

She went to his desk and began pulling open drawers, slowly
and methodically going through papers, file folders and envelopes
until she found a large red binder stamped with the words: *CIA,
M-Class Only* and *Top Secret*. Inside was a thick black and white

document: *Anomalous Trait Genome Evaluation Program: Genetic Research into Anomalous Mental Cognition Capacities.* It was dated 1948.

She paused staring at the title. Why did that sound familiar to her? And then a wave of nausea settled over her as she realized . . . It was the name of the government testing program Dylan told her about. But why did Jack have it?

Alex flipped through the pages, not really reading any of it but understanding the CIA had created a study of people like her after World War II. She looked into the case and saw another binder similar to the first in its marking.

Heart thumping against her chest, she reached for it and turned to the first page and read aloud. *'Joint Taskforce Anomalous Cognitive Practitioner National Security Threat Assessment.' Threat assessment?*

'Alex, breakfast is ready,' she heard Maisie call.

Snapping out of her confusion, she returned the binders as she found them. She hurried to the kitchen and sat at the table covered in platters of food. 'There's enough here for five people,' Alex declared.

'Cooking brings me joy,' Maisie said as she settled into her seat and spooned scrambled eggs onto her plate. 'Help yourself. You're practically family.'

Alex froze, glancing at the woman. She hated to disappoint Jack's mother. She was so sweet, but eventually she'd have to know that Alex was leaving her son. They ate in silence while Alex tried to figure out how to broach the topic of mermaids without upsetting her – per Jack's request.

She gazed around the room, finally landing on a set of mermaid-themed oven mitts. 'Those are cute. Did Jack get those for you?'

'Oh no,' she said. 'He hates my fascination with mermaids. I ordered those online.'

Alex picked at her food. 'And why does Jack dislike your interest in mermaids? I mean, it's harmless, right?'

Maisie nodded, a look of helplessness on her face.

Alex turned to the table, picking up dishes. 'Let's get this cleaned up. And then we're going on a field trip.'

* * *

First, Alex took Maisie to a clothing boutique on Main Street, and they shopped for hats to keep out the autumn chill.

'It's so nice to finally get out of the house,' Maisie declared as she held up a yellow bucket hat. 'This is pretty.'

Alex smiled her agreement, wondering about her medicines, wondering why Jack kept her locked away in her house. 'Maybe I can come by and take you out more.'

Maisie's lips quirked downward. 'I doubt it. Jack thinks it's dangerous for me to go out.'

'Why, if you're with someone?' She watched as Maisie tried the hat on and stood in front of a mirror.

Maisie looked at Alex's reflection and smiled. 'I don't remember.'

A frisson of irritation ran through Alex then. It didn't make sense that Maisie should suffer such debilitating memory loss like this. Surely, there was something she could do for her. Jack had said no to healing teas, but Alex had the ability to heal. She had to at least try. What if she could improve Maisie's quality of life? What if she could help her remember something? Anything would be better than the nothing she could recall now.

And what would it hurt if Maisie did remember something? She strode toward Maisie and put a hand on her arm.

Startled, Maisie glanced at her in the reflection of the mirror. 'What are you— Oh,' she smiled as healing energy suffused her body. 'That feels nice.' She giggled then sighed in contentment.

Eyes closed, Alex conjured healing, soothing, restorative energy and allowed it to seep from her hand into Maisie's arm where it would diffuse through her body, hopefully healing all that ailed her.

She removed her hand and stepped back, eyeing the woman. 'Maisie, how do you feel?'

Hat still on her head, she wiggled her fingers. 'I don't know . . . I feel like I've got a bit of pep in my step.' She glanced at her reflection, at the rakish set of the hat. 'I think I'll take it.'

As they continued walking, the hair on the back of Alex's neck bristled. And she looked around. *Was someone watching her? Them?* She scanned the streets but didn't see anyone.

Next they stopped by a gift shop, and Maisie picked up several mermaid Christmas tree decorations. 'These are beautiful.' She looked over her shoulder at Alex. 'Aren't they?'

'They are.'

'Christmas will be here before you know it.' Maisie put several in her basket, and then moved to a table displaying woven beach bags. Maisie's fingers trailed the totes, touching the magenta and teal material as she passed.

'Do you remember anything?' Alex asked her.

Maisie thought for a moment. Then smiled. 'Not especially.'

Disappointed, Alex helped Maisie make her purchases, wondering if the severity of Maisie's condition surpassed her healing abilities. They left the store, walking to their car parked on the street a block below the shop. A cart on the street selling hot apple cider and sweet potato donuts caught Maisie's eye.

She pressed her hands together. 'Let's get donuts. I love donuts.'

They walked to the cart and stood in line while the scent of warm butter, sugar, cinnamon, nutmeg and yeast wrapped around them. Alex ordered the donuts, and the cashier told her the amount due.

'I'll get that,' came a voice from behind them.

Alex turned around and saw Forbes McDonald standing there. 'That's not—'

He shook his head, handing the money over their heads to the cashier. 'Consider it my good deed for the day.'

'Okay . . .' Alex took the brown bag of donuts and handed Maisie one as they moved out of the line. Alex watched Forbes as he purchased a cup of apple cider and then joined them.

'You don't mind if I stand with you, do you?' His words were for Alex, but his eyes were on Maisie, who smiled at him, her blue eyes brightening. The wind increased, causing her hair to lift and settle on her scarf.

'Thank you. That was so sweet of you.'

He inclined his head. 'It was nothing.'

Alex shifted awkwardly, trying to ignore the strange feeling in the pit of her stomach. Forbes had masqueraded as a detective under a fake name and failed to solve the Fisherman case. She pulled her coat tighter around her. 'How are you finding the golf here?'

216 Esme Addison

He turned to her as he sipped his cider. 'It's been fine. A bit chilly, but I don't mind the elements.' His face softened as he looked at Maisie. 'Who is your friend?'

Alex cleared her throat, made herself smile. 'Her name is Maisie Frazier,' she said. 'My boyfriend's mom.'

A muscle on his jaw moved. 'Your boyfriend . . .' He turned to Maisie. 'You have a son?'

'I do. Handsome. Smart. I couldn't be prouder.'

He nodded again. 'Here, in town?'

Alex's scowl deepened. She suddenly felt protective of Jack. Was this man looking for him? Here to harm him? Maybe he thought he was on his trail? 'He's the police detective here.' The words came out stronger than she meant, and one of his eyebrows lifted when she spoke.

But then his face relaxed, and he sipped his cider, the spicy steam curling around his face. 'I just wanted to stop and say hello to you ladies. I won't keep you a moment longer.' He strode away and was soon lost in the crowd.

Alex stared after him. 'That was weird.'

'Was it, dear?' She smiled. 'He seemed nice enough.'

'Let's head back to the car. It's getting windy out here.'

They returned to Alex's car, and as she started her ignition, Minka called.

'Can you come by the house? I've remembered something.'

Alex turned to look at Maisie. 'I have Jack's mother with me. What about Aunt Lidia or Kamila?'

'Mom's out and Kamila is too intense right now. She needs to be at the station doing something. Please?'

'I suppose it couldn't hurt, bringing Maisie along.' Though Jack might mind . . .

'Bring her,' Minka said. 'It's important. And I don't think it can wait.'

'All right, we're on our way.'

When Alex arrived home, she found a romcom on TV for Maisie, poured her a cup of milky coffee and went into the kitchen to speak to Minka privately.

'You feeling better?' Alex asked, noting Minka's eyes had lost that dazed quality.

A Brew for Chaos 217

She nodded. 'Yeah. It's kind of like coming out of a fog, like being really sleepy and not being able to wake up. But also not wanting to wake up because sleeping feels so good.'

Alex sat at the table and gestured for Minka to do the same. 'I know Aunt Lidia is trying to heal you. Any luck?' she asked, thinking of her failed attempts with Maisie.

Minka shook her head. 'She said she can feel the power of whatever is suppressing my memories – it's strong and unlike anything she's encountered before.'

Alex told Minka what she'd done to Maisie. 'I didn't feel any resistance. But it also didn't work.'

'Well, she's got a medical condition, while I've been assaulted by a weapon adapted from Magical abilities.' Minka tried for a lighthearted tone, but it didn't quite work. 'I'm just grateful my brain isn't fried.'

'Okay. But you said you remembered something, right?'

'Nothing about being abducted, I'm afraid. But I know I was taken because of what I discovered. My research.'

'We already thought of that, Mink. Dylan checked and the servers have been wiped clean.'

'I figured,' she said excitedly. 'But I thought about it. And my analysis, my conclusions, my reports, they're all gone. But the raw data is still there. I just have to comb through it again and figure it all out one more time.'

'That data's not on Wesley servers?'

Her eyes lit up. 'No. It's on the apps cloud server. And they're owned by a company out of Australia. I checked. Our NGO uses the app, but they don't own it. They license usage.'

'Assuming it hasn't been wiped either.'

'It hasn't. I called the rep that serviced our account, and he assured me it's all there.'

'How long do you think it will take for you to come to the same conclusions as before?'

'Before it took me a couple of months, but this time I can be more targeted in my data mining. It has to be about the location of where the dolphins were going when their GPS locaters glitched. So maybe a few days if that's the focus.'

'You'd need to be somewhere private and secure – could you cloak your work so whomever abducted you the last time and whomever he was working for' – Minka gave her a sharp look but didn't say anything – 'can't find you either.'

'This is not Montgomery's doing. He's very kind to me. He wouldn't have any part of this. I know it.'

'Coffee?' Alex asked, to avoid responding to Minka's comment.

Minka exhaled loudly. 'Look, Alex, we—'

But before she could finish, she was interrupted by a scream and the sound of fracturing glass.

They both turned to look towards the kitchen door.

THIRTY-EIGHT

Alex and Minka rushed into the living room.

Maisie had dropped her coffee cup on the hardwood floor, her mouth falling open and her eyes wide, like she'd seen a ghost.

Caroline had entered the living room from the hallway and smiled apologetically to Alex and Minka. *I think I startled her.*

Minka shot Maisie a comforting look. 'I'll get the broom and a towel. No problem.' She returned to the kitchen, while Alex went to Maisie and guided her to the couch with an arm around her shoulder. Perhaps she was easily excitable. The healing hadn't helped her; it had overwhelmed her. Maisie's body trembled, and Alex wondered if the outing and questions had been too much for her. A wave of guilt washed over her.

Jack might be a liar, but he did care for his mother. He'd asked her not to tax his mother because it was the best thing for her. That much was obvious. Perhaps she needed her medicine after all.

Caroline's long hair was pulled off her face in a ponytail. Her face was freshly scrubbed, and she looked healthy with just a bit of sun, unlike weeks past when her skin had been pale, with hollow cheeks and dark rings under her eyes. Perhaps the healing treatments and restorative teas Lidia plied her with daily were helping.

With bright eyes and pink cheeks, she looked like the college-aged student she'd been when she was abducted. She was dressed in a pair of Minka's fuzzy light blue pants and a blue tank top covered with white hearts.

Her arms, which had been downright bony, had a little meat on them now. *Probably from all those sardines*, Alex thought with amusement. She smiled warmly at Jack's mother before making herself comfortable on the couch. Alex could feel Maisie continuing to tremble and she patted her thin leg beneath her floral dress. 'Are you okay, Maisie?'

She shook her head, a quavering finger pointing towards Caroline. 'Caroline?'

Caroline sat on the edge of her seat, staring at Maisie.

Frowning, Alex turned to Maisie. 'You know her? You're . . . remembering something?' She swallowed the lump in her throat. Maybe her healing had worked after all. Just delayed?

Maisie blinked once. Then twice as if trying to clear her mind of cobwebs. 'It's all so . . . foggy, but . . . yes. I know her.' Her hand fell to her lap. 'But it can't be.'

It can't be. Those words floated into Alex's consciousness. It was the same thing Jonah had said to her and Pepper before he'd hurried out of the restaurant . . . to his death.

Maisie closed her eyes tightly and shook her head. Then opened them slowly as if she was afraid to see again. 'She's Caroline. Caroline Bracy. My friend from college . . .'

THIRTY-NINE

A slow grin spread across Caroline's face, her eyes brightening with recognition.

She stood, her legs steady, and crossed the floor. She held out her hand and Maisie stood, reaching for it. 'Margaret, is it really you?'

Margaret? Alex gasped, turning to the elderly woman. 'Maisie, what's your maiden name?'

Eyes never leaving Caroline, she said, 'Dunsmore. I used to be called Margaret Dunsmore long before I was Maisie Frazier.' A little laugh erupted from her trembling lips. 'Maisie is short for Margaret.'

Alex's hand went to her mouth, a cold feeling prickling the backs of her arms. *No. Wait, it couldn't be* . . . Jack's mother was Margaret Dunsmore, the college student who mysteriously disappeared only to reappear days later?

Minka appeared, broom in hand. 'What did I miss?'

Alex stared at Minka. Then Maisie. Like Minka, Maisie had gone missing – maybe been abducted? Then reappeared . . . possibly with memory loss? Confusion? No. She had a medical condition . . . But none of it made sense.

'I-I don't understand,' Alex said, her voice suddenly dry. And did Jack know? A breath caught in her chest. What did Jack know about his mother's past?

Caroline pulled Maisie to her in a hug. 'I can't believe it's you. You've . . .' She searched her face, taking in the graying blonde hair, the softly lined face, the wrinkles around her eyes and mouth. 'You've changed,' she said finally.

'But you haven't! How?' A tear slid down Maisie's cheek. 'Where have you been? What happened to you?' She frowned and rubbed her temples. 'Sometimes when I begin to remember things, my head hurts . . .'

Alex winced, knowing she was the cause of that pain.

But Maisie shook the pain away, trying to push through the

222   Esme Addison

haze of confusion. A determined look on her face. She wanted to remember, Alex realized. The silly look of contentment was gone from her face.

Minka stepped closer to Alex, touched her arm. 'What's going on?'

Alex filled her in, and Minka almost dropped the broom but caught it before it slid to the floor. She set it against the wall and returned to Alex's side.

Alex froze in place, then turned to Caroline, incredulous. '*Wait*. You're talking. You can talk?'

Caroline's eyes widened. She grabbed her neck, cleared her throat and worked her jaw. She bit her bottom lip as a look of joy spread across her face. 'Your aunt has been trying different teas and healing techniques on me.' Her voice was low and husky with a lulling quality. 'One must've finally worked.'

'But you don't have a larynx,' Minka pointed out. 'How is that possible?'

Caroline leveled them both with an amused stare. 'I'm not like you.'

'*Oh*,' was all Alex could say.

Caroline's grip tightened on Maisie's hand. 'What do you remember?'

'I don't know . . . Um . . . I remember being a young girl and riding horses on my family farm . . . Then, there's a lot of gaps . . . I remember my mother driving me to North Carolina to begin college.'

'I wonder why her memory loss is so severe,' Alex mused aloud.

Maisie rubbed her eyes. 'And I remember you,' she said to Caroline suddenly. 'Being at the beach . . . and meeting you for the first time.'

Caroline nodded encouragingly. 'What else?'

'You wanted to go to school with me.' Her eyes lit up at the memory. She stared off in the distance. 'And then . . . It all gets blurry again. Wait . . . We were roommates.' A look of nostalgia softened Caroline's face. 'We told each other every-thing, didn't we?' Tears flowed down Maisie's cheeks. 'No secrets between—'

'Best friends.' Caroline finished the sentence.

A Brew for Chaos   223

Caroline gazed at her, her eyes roving her face and body, then gave her hands another squeeze. 'It's so good to see you again, Margaret.' She looked around, her legs beginning to shake. 'I think I need to go to my room. This has been a lot.' She coughed, massaged the front of her neck. 'And my throat hurts. It's dry from talking. Maybe I need a humidifier? Tea?'

Alex regarded Caroline with interest. *There was more to their guest than met the eye*, she thought to herself. *I'm not like you*, she'd said. Her tone a bit snippy. But they were both genetic mermaids. What had she meant by that?

'Aunt Lidia will be gratified to know her healing has helped you . . . find your voice. And I think we have a humidifier in the attic. I'll find it later and bring it down.'

'I'll get you some tea. The restorative blend,' Minka added, giving Caroline a reassuring smile as she headed to the kitchen.

On the drive home, Alex was quiet as Maisie chatted about her best friend from college. 'She was just so different from the other girls,' she was saying. 'I was intrigued by her at first, but then we became so close.'

'What do you know about her past? Her family?' Alex glanced at her as she switched on her turn signal and wheeled her Audi to the right.

'My memory is still so hazy, but I don't recall her having any, which is why we hit it off so well.'

Caroline had told her she'd found her parents' obituaries. That they had died while she was gone. A simple mix-up or a straight-up lie? And if so, why lie?

'My father had died, so it was just me and my mother, and she was a bit aloof. Like Caroline, I guess. But we had a lot in common.'

'Like?'

'We both loved marine science – that was my area of study,' she said with excitement. 'I remember.'

'Maybe that's where your love of mermaids comes from?'

Maisie frowned. 'Maybe. But Caroline loved them too. She wanted to enroll in the same program I was in, but there was some . . .' She squinted, trying to remember. 'Trouble. I can't recall what though.' She stared out the window like she was

224   Esme Addison

seeing the pumpkin patches and stacks of hay for the first time. And perhaps she was.

'Do you remember going missing? And then returning? What happened to you?'

Maisie bowed her head and rubbed her temples. 'My God the pain is intense.' She looked up, blinking.

'I'm sorry, I'm asking too many questions.'

'No, it's okay. I want to remember. I feel like I'm waking up from a great sleep.' She stared out the window. 'I went to the beach,' she said finally.

'You were dating Tobias Winston at the time. Do you recall?'

She gasped. 'Toby. I haven't thought of him in decades. Sweet, studious Toby. He was talking marriage the last time . . .' She frowned. 'I went to the beach.' She turned to Alex. 'To meet someone . . .' A shadow crossed her face, and she went silent.

Alex pulled into Jack's driveway – his truck was there – and she turned to Maisie. But before she could say anything, the front door opened, and Jack stepped onto the front porch. Features pinched with worry, he glanced at his watch.

Had they been gone too long? Alex's stomach clenched into a knot, and she turned to look at Maisie. How could she keep all of this from Jack? The sudden memories. Meeting Caroline . . . She couldn't ask Maisie to pretend like she hadn't remembered anything. This was news. Major news. Surely she would want to share this with her son.

She got out of the car, and Jack approached the passenger side, opening the door for his mother. He leaned down and kissed her cheek before taking her hand and leading her out.

He examined her face, noting the lively expression and bright eyes. He almost smiled but ended up only looking confused. 'Have a fun outing, mother?'

Her voice was soft. 'Yes, dear.'

He glanced questioningly at Alex, who returned it with her own innocent smile. 'As you can see, I've returned her safely.'

He returned to his mother. 'Anything interesting happen?'

'A nice man bought us donuts on the street.'

He turned to Alex, his expression of concern turned into a scowl.

But his mother smiled. 'And I bought a hat, dear. It's in the back. Would you get it?

'I better take my pills,' Maisie was murmuring to herself as she shuffled up her porch steps.

Once Maisie was settled inside, Jack walked Alex to her car.

'I was hoping we could at least have lunch together.' Jack gave her a rueful look then took her hand. 'I also wanted to thank you for taking such good care of my mother. It means the world to me.'

Alex glanced at their joined hands and forced a smile. 'You're welcome.'

'A stranger is buying my girl donuts?' he asked, his voice only half-teasing.

'He really bought your mother donuts. And he was older. A man I've met before . . . He's a tourist in town for golf.'

'Okay. So, lunch?'

'I really wish I could, but I have errands to run and then I have to get back to the shop.'

He pulled her close and nuzzled his nose into her hair. 'When can I see you again? You tell me.'

She pulled away as gently as possible. 'I'm not sure. I'm really busy right now. Can I call you? And I do need your help.'

A smile warmed his face. 'Tell me.'

'Can you find out who has the contract for a particular military project for me? And any other details about the project you can dig up. I need someone connected to the Army to look into it.'

His gaze lingered on her, a curious glint in his eyes. 'I'm just a small-town detective. What connections do you imagine I have?'

'But your military background . . . Please, Jack. You must know somebody . . . It's important to figuring out who took Minka.' She held her breath, waiting for his response. Wondering if he'd bail on her, or care enough to help her.

'Let's say I do know somebody . . . What am I looking for?'

'It's called Project Oannes.'

'I have heard of it.' Jack's gaze hardened. 'How do you even—'
He shook his head.

And she took a breath. Maybe he really did care. Maybe, just maybe, it wasn't all an act.

226 Esme Addison

'I'll see what I can find out. Anything to help.' He looked at her like he wanted to say more, but he only patted her car. 'Drive carefully.'

As she drove out of Jack's neighborhood, she called Pepper. 'Do you have an in at Bellamy Bay College? I need some information about a former student.'

Pepper laughed into the phone. 'Are you kidding me right now? My great-great grandfather founded the college, donated the land. What do you need?'

'I need to find information on Caroline Bracy.'

There was a pause. 'Why does that name sound familiar? Wait a minute . . . That's a . . . She's one of the Fisherman's victims.'

Alex sighed. She couldn't keep anything from her.

'Is there something I should know? Alex, we're supposed to be friends. You can't—'

'You can come with me,' Alex said, hoping this would stop her rant. And it did.

'I can?'

'Yes. Do you know someone who has access to student records?'

Pepper smiled. 'Yeah. Me. What do you need?'

'For starters, I guess we could look through yearbooks and determine when she was a student? And then dig up whatever we can about her time at school with Margaret Dunsmore.'

'I'll make some calls.'

'That would be perfect. I'm heading back to the shop. I'll close up a little early so we can get to the admin offices before they close.'

An hour later, Alex glanced at the wall clock. She was looking forward to digging into the college's records. Her intuition told her there was more to Caroline Bracy's story.

Time passed, and she'd waited on a few customers, posted on the shop's social media – Minka's old job – and restocked the apple cider donut bath bombs when the doorbell jingled. Alex looked up to greet the customer, but the words stuck to her tongue.

Forbes McDonald stood in the doorway, blocking the light that should have streamed in from the street. A shadow cast over

A Brew for Chaos

his tall lanky body, and Alex held her breath. Did he know she'd been asking about him? Why was he here?

'Hello,' she called out, pretending like all was normal. 'Welcome to Botanika.'

And he grinned.

She frowned. Why was he grinning at her?

'Thank you.' He stepped inside. 'I've been meaning to stop by. Heard a lot about this place.'

'Oh?' Alex looked around the shop, wondering when another customer would come in. She glanced outside. It was half past five and the sun was already beginning to set. 'What can I help you with?'

He moved around the shelves, picking up items and reading labels. 'Regrets, for starters.' He chuckled, his shoulders moving with the joke.

Alex watched him with suspicious eyes. 'Regrets about what?'

He picked up a glass jar filled with a glittering pink liquid full of rose petals and jasmine buds, held it up to the light and inspected it. 'Choices made. Commitments kept.' He placed the jar back on the shelf and turned to look at her.

His eyes weren't mean and hard as Alex remembered them from the bed and breakfast. Instead, his blue eyes were soft. Sad. And red-rimmed. Upon closer inspection she saw dark hollows under his eyes and his skin had taken on a yellow tinge, the texture papery and thin.

'Perhaps something for sorrow, while you're at it?'

He wasn't well, she realized.

She watched him move to a row of perfumes, and then love potions. A smile crept across his thin lips.

'Why are you sad?' Alex asked, arms crossed, not wanting to like him or feel bad for him, but she did. She could see a vague shimmer of purple and green outlining his body. A purplish-black cloud hovered near the upper right portion of his torso, a trail of green morphing into an almost translucent yellow dissipating behind him. She realized with a start that, like her aunt, she could see auras.

Swirls of black laced through his auric field. His energy was weak, his life force leaking from him as he walked. She blinked and the appearance of his aura was gone.

228   Esme Addison

'It's been a long time since I've been to this charming little town,' he began, while she grabbed a linen tea pouch and went to the rows of glass canisters filled with dried herbs. She scooped out a heaping dose of licorice, ginger and garlic, and then added milk thistle and ginseng.

She returned to the counter where he waited for her. 'This is what you need. I'm guessing you have liver issues, and this will help with some of the more severe symptoms. Make a tea with it, drink it often.'

'I don't want to be healed.' He chuckled though the sound fell flat. 'And to be honest, I'm not sure I deserve it.'

'You're clearly in need, and the healer in me desires to heal . . . even you.'

One eyebrow rose. 'Even me?'

And she thought she saw a spark of the man he used to be. 'I know who you are.'

A slow grin. 'Really?'

She rang up the tea. Told him the price. 'Yes, you're the man who came to town pretending to be a police detective. Only you didn't solve the Fisherman case, you botched it. Hoping that no one would ever be able to figure it out.'

His features relaxed. 'Ah. I see . . . Well.' He counted out bills and paid for the tea. 'I guess you got me, young lady.' He held up the bag of tea. 'You're good. It is my liver.' He sighed. 'This trip is my last hurrah. I'm here . . . not to make things right, because there's just no way to do that. I guess I wanted to return to the place of my greatest sorrow one more time before I . . .'

Die, she knew he was going to say. 'How much time?' Alex asked, her anger lifting.

'A few weeks. Maybe a month. I talked often about returning here to make amends if I could. Leith wanted to come with me. I thought it would be a fitting place to go before I return home . . . and to hospice.'

'I'm sorry to hear that.'

His nod was slight. He lifted the bag to his nose and sniffed. 'I was a healer once.'

'Seriously?' Alex asked, unable to hide the skepticism in her voice.

A Brew for Chaos   229

Forbes laughed. 'Yes. Took the Hippocratic Oath and every-thing.'

'Then why were you selected to fake being a police detective?'

'I was military police, an MP for a time before the Navy put me through medical college.'

'Why did you do it?'

'Decide to be a doctor?'

'No,' Alex said, her voice rising. 'Pretend to investigate the Fisherman case. Barely fill out the case reports. Not follow up on clues. *That.*'

He stared at her, his face hardening with righteousness. 'Because it was my job. Because it was the right thing to do.'

'But how . . .' Alex couldn't get the words out. 'Those women. They needed justice. They—'

'You can't understand what patriots do for their country, how we protect the citizens. The sacrifices we make. The hard choices, the dilemmas we have to push through. The horrible, unspeakable things we must do to ensure the safety of the greater good.'

She shook her head slowly. 'You sound like my boyfriend. Jack. You'd think he was Captain America himself . . .' But he wasn't. He was a liar. A deceiver. Just like this man.

Alex looked up and saw that Forbes had tears in his eyes, his fingers grasped tightly around the tea bag. 'We must all make sacrifices to protect the ones we love.'

Frowning, she watched him go. And then realized it was time to lock up the shop and meet Pepper.

As Pepper and Alex walked down the halls of Bellamy Bay College, one of several red brick buildings spread across eighty acres of land centered around a lake, Pepper pointed to the wide glass doors accented with brass leading to the library. 'As former editor of the yearbook and newspaper, it was fairly easy for me to get access to them from the time Caroline was a student.'

'Pretty sure you being a Bellamy had something to do with it too.'

Pepper waved to the librarian seated at her desk, then led Alex through tall stacks of books and long wooden tables. Students

230 Esme Addison

dotted the large room in various stages of reading and research, dressed in sweats and jeans.

Pepper entered a private study room and Alex followed. Her mouth dropped open when she saw the stacks of yearbooks and crates filled with newspapers waiting for them.

'I guess they haven't been digitized.'

Pepper slid into a chair, and Alex followed suit. She pushed a stack of five books her way. 'I'll take the first half of the eighties, and you get the latter.'

Nodding, Alex reached for the first leatherbound book.

Thirty minutes later, Alex rubbed her eyes. 'She's not in any of my years. Have you found her?'

Pepper shook her head as she turned the pages of the last yearbook in her stack. 'I'm hoping she's in this one. I mean, she has to be, right?'

Alex sat back in her chair, waiting for Pepper to finish her search. Watched as she slowly closed the book and met Alex's interested gaze.

'She's not listed.'

Alex stretched her arms and shoulders. 'The newspaper articles said she was a student, right?'

'Yeah.' Pepper reached for her phone. 'I'm calling the registrar's office. There's a little old lady that's worked there since I was a student, and she loves me like I'm her granddaughter.' Pepper grinned. 'It's possible she missed picture day. Maybe she can at least confirm Caroline was a student and tell us what year.'

'Ask her about Margaret too,' Alex reminded her.

A minute later, after talking to the registrar's office, Pepper placed the phone on the table.

'Well.' Alex leaned forward. 'What did she say?'

Pepper's brow furrowed. 'She said Caroline was never enrolled as a student, but that they did have a file on her because she did apply.'

Alex crossed her arms. 'Applied?'

'Yeah. I told her I'm trying to solve the Fisherman case, and she wants to help, so she's going to email me the records of Caroline and Margaret with any personal information redacted.'

A few minutes later Pepper received an email notification, and Alex moved to peer over her shoulder to read the file.

Alex skimmed it. 'It says Caroline Bracy applied for admission but was denied due to lack of records.'

Pepper pointed to a note. 'Says she was homeschooled and didn't have health or academic records. And no character or academic references.'

'I suppose that's plausible . . .' Alex said as Pepper moved to the next page.

They both read.

'Margaret Dunsmore volunteered to vouch for her.' Pepper frowned. 'Another student can't do that . . .' She read a note from the registrar. '*Based on Margaret's exemplary academic record, character and personal integrity, we will allow Caroline to audit one class.*'

'Caroline was never a student here. Why did she lie? And why would they take Margaret's word as reference?'

'Here's why.' Pepper flipped the screen to Margaret's file. 'Class president. Honor student. Maintained a 4.0. Was president of the marine biology club, and a founding member of the Environmental club. She was awesome.'

'Does it say who took her from school?'

Pepper bumped her shoulder. 'Remember, some family member unenrolled her.'

'Yeah. It was a man. Only, her father had passed away and she didn't have uncles.'

Pepper flipped through the papers. Her eyebrows shot up and she showed Alex the screen. 'Her husband. Alasdair Frazier.'

'Her husband?' Alex exclaimed. 'But . . . but she was dating Tobias Winston during college. That's a lie—'

'Jack's last name is Frazier,' Pepper pointed out.

Alex tried to remember what Jack had said about his father. It had only been one conversation, but she thought he'd said his father had left when he was young. She'd have to ask Jack about him, and Maisie too if she remembered.

'Is there any additional information about Alasdair Frazier?' Alex asked, leaning forward.

'There's a copy of his driver's license, but it's so blurry you can't make out the image.' She pointed to the screen.

232 Esme Addison

Alex thought for a moment. 'Did no one question her leaving in that manner?' She thought of Tobias.

Pepper stared at one of the stacks of yearbooks, thinking. 'It's a long shot, but let me call the campus police and see if they have anything they can send us.'

A minute later she was off and drumming her fingers. 'When I told the officer I was in the library conference room, she said she could send it to the printer.'

They both looked in a corner where a large industrial printer stood.

'Apparently,' Pepper continued, 'there was an investigation of some sort.'

Suddenly, the printer cranked up and Alex volunteered to get it. It was several pages, and she quickly skimmed through them before reading aloud. 'Let's see . . . A student, Toby Winston, filed a complaint with the campus police and requested information on who removed Margaret from the campus. Poor Tobias,' Alex murmured.

'What did they find?' Pepper asked, leaning forward to get a glance at the papers.

'There was one witness statement. A custodian said he saw a man help her pack, then left campus with her. He described him as a tall white man.' She looked at Pepper. 'She appeared to go with him willingly.'

'That's it?' Pepper asked.

Alex nodded.

'That was a surprise,' Pepper said as they walked down Main Street towards Tobias' law office.

'I think the question is becoming who the heck is Jack's father?' Alex said, a deep frown on her face.

They walked in silence for a block, then a bright red cart came into view, and Alex pointed against the chilly breeze. 'Let's grab something warm before we get to his office.'

They stopped and ordered two apple cider donuts and two hot apple ciders to go. When their orders were ready, they crossed the street.

'I hope Tobias can shed some light on Margaret's last day at school,' Alex said as she sipped the spicy warm beverage.

'And won't he be surprised,' Pepper said around a bite of donut. 'If he was in love with her like you said.'

They stopped at Tobias' office, a small brick building with yellow mums in large black planters on either side of the glass door. Alex pushed it open, and a flood of warm air rushed over them.

Pepper greeted the receptionist and asked to see Tobias.

Once they were settled in his office, Alex leaned forward and cleared her throat. 'I had a few questions about Margaret Dunsmore, if you don't mind?'

His expression grew thoughtful, but he agreed.

Pepper pulled out her pad and pencil. 'I hope you don't mind if I take notes?'

His brows knitted together. 'Nothing on record, if you please, Ms Bellamy.'

'I'm not here as a journalist. I mean, I am if there's something good, but really I'm here to help Alex.'

He leaned over his desk, hands clasped. 'Alex?'

'You said you dated Margaret Dunsmore during college. Did she have other male friends? Maybe guys she dated before you?' she asked delicately.

He shifted in his leather seat. 'You're asking if the love of my life was cheating on me?'

'Yes,' Pepper replied, pencil poised over her pad.

Alex shot her a startled look. 'Sorry, Tobias . . .'

'No. Margaret was sweet, innocent, loyal . . . She would've never.' He shook his head firmly. 'Why do you ask?'

Alex hesitated. 'Because her academic records show that her husband is the man who picked her up from school after she was returned and disenrolled. That's how he identified himself.'

He rubbed a hand over his face. 'The campus police told me the same thing when I asked . . . But I didn't believe it. And when I insisted they find out what happened to her, they thought I was being jealous and couldn't accept that she'd found some-body else. But she was dating me. There was no other man.'

'Did she say goodbye?'

'No. One day she was here, then she went missing, and everyone thought the Fisherman took her. Then she was back. And then she left. Permanently.'

Tobias' phone rang, and he excused himself to take the call.

Pepper leaned towards Alex. 'Should we tell him his college sweetheart is back in town?'

'I don't think so, not until Jack knows who she really is. And Maisie herself might not want to publicize her stay here. After all, the Fisherman is still on the loose. What if he finds out Maisie is alive and wants to include her in his tying up of loose ends? I'd never forgive myself if I put that sweet woman's life in danger.'

Pepper put her notepad away. 'If she decides she wants to go public, you know who gets the exclusive.'

FORTY

As Alex and Pepper walked back to their car, Pepper received an email notification.

She slid into the passenger side, reading the message. Alex glanced at her as she backed out of her parking spot. 'About the case?'

'Not exactly. I had a friend at a beverage industry magazine research the lawsuits against Spencer's company, just trying to find anything that could be helpful.'

Alex turned out of the college parking lot. 'And?'

'A spokesperson for Spencer's company said it was corporate espionage, and purposely done to drive down the profits of the company and ruin their reputation.'

Alex stopped at a crosswalk to let students stroll by. She looked at Pepper. 'Who would do that?'

'A competitor?' Pepper suggested, returning her phone to her purse.

'Or . . .' Alex pressed the gas. 'Someone purposely ruining the company so they could buy it for cheap.'

After Alex dropped off Pepper, she stopped by the coffee shop. As she approached the front door, she saw Spencer leaving the yoga studio and juice bar next door. She carried a mat under one arm and a large smoothie to go in the other. She was glancing at her smart watch and walking with purpose to her car parked on the street but slowed when she saw Alex.

'You got a minute?' Alex called out when they met on the sidewalk.

'What do you want?' The woman's voice was imperious, with the expression to match.

'You're interested in Jonah's recipe, why?'

Spencer's frown deepened. 'Why would I tell you anything?'

Alex jutted her hip out. 'Because maybe I have it.'

The blonde's expression changed then, and a look of cunning

glinted in her eyes. 'I'll pay you for it. Whatever you want. Money's no issue.'

Alex maintained her look of indifference but inside her adrenaline was pumping. *She was on to something, she just knew it.* 'You don't have somewhere to be?'

'It can wait,' Spencer said, eagerness increasing her gait.

A few minutes later, they were seated at a table.

'So,' Spencer began after Alex finished pouring cream and sugar into her coffee. 'Where'd you find it?'

Alex sipped her drink. 'Why don't you tell me why you need it so bad.'

Spencer narrowed her eyes, then leaned forward. 'My father ran my mother's family's company into the ground. I'd never had any interest in the business until I found out he'd passed away and left it in shambles. So I stopped my life of luxury – I did have a business degree after all – and tried to save the company.'

'By getting it healthy enough for another company to buy it?'

Her eyebrows lifted. 'That's right. A pharmaceutical company offered to purchase the company contingent on me delivering one thing.'

'Jonah's prize-winning beer recipe,' Alex said with a smirk. 'Why?'

'The *why* is not important. But what is, is the timeline. They've taken over the management of the firm and are making it successful – they've saved the company. But I won't get my portion of the sale, which is considerable, unless I deliver what I promised. Which is the only reason they agreed to buy my company along with all its debts, lawsuits and poor publicity.' A pout formed on her lips. 'I've been living off my trust fund for the last few years. I will eventually need the money from the sale of the company.'

'This all hinges on a recipe?'

'Yes.' Spencer's eyes were hopeful. 'If you help me, I'm willing to be very generous.' Her smile widened. 'You wouldn't have to work like a peasant in your family herb shop.'

Smiling, Alex played along with her, wondering what else she could find out. 'I'm still thinking . . . but generous sounds nice.' Alex knew people like this, people that thought anyone would

A Brew for Chaos   237

do anything for money. She'd known trust fund babies like her in New York City. 'I read you believe corporate espionage is the reason you've been having problems?'

'You've done your research.' She nodded. 'Yeah, looks like a hit job when you really analyze what has happened.'

'And when did Montgomery Blue offer to buy your company?'

'You know about that too?' She studied Alex with suspicion. 'When I refused to settle out of court. We weren't at fault no matter what the evidence showed.'

'And it never occurred to you that maybe Leviathan was behind the hit?'

Spencer sat up. 'No, never. If anything, he's been my savior. Even offered me the use of his company's attorneys . . .' She frowned. 'He's been nothing but helpful.'

'So, he's the one that wants the recipe?'

'Yes, and I want to get it for him. I'm grateful. He saved my family's company. Our legacy remains intact.'

'Where have you looked?'

'Jonah once let it slip that he'd hidden a copy of the recipe in an archive. I've searched the newspaper archives. In old books in the library . . .'

'How long did you date?'

'You know that too? What are you, a stalker?' When Alex didn't respond, Spencer flipped her bangs out of her eyes. 'Just a fun summer. And then I got bored.'

'One more question. Where were you the night Jonah was killed? You weren't at your house.'

Her eyes turned cold. 'You're the reason that cop questioned me. I didn't have anything to do with Jonah dying. How does that help me – if I still don't have the recipe?'

Alex shrugged. 'Maybe you got angry.'

Spencer abruptly stood up and threw her half-full cup to the ground. Orange smoothie splattered over the table and Alex's face and jacket. 'Like this?' She knocked the napkin holder over, while Alex grabbed several napkins off the floor and mopped smoothie off her face. She licked her lips. Tasted like sweet potato.

She watched the woman storm out of the shop.

So, Spencer had a temper.

*   *   *

238   Esme Addison

While Alex drove home, she called Kamila and asked her to see if Spencer had a history of violence. When she arrived home, her aunt's car was gone and so was Minka's. She opened the door and was greeted by Athena. She took a moment to pet her dog and plant a kiss on her forehead.

Afterwards, Alex pushed open the kitchen door and was startled to see Caroline in there, leaning against the counter with a cup of something hot in her hands. The makings of seaweed tea and a grinder of sea salt behind her.

'Hey, Caroline. I thought you were resting.'

'I'm feeling better.'

Alex shook her head. 'Still weird to hear your voice after all this time.' She opened a cabinet and reached for a can of salmon and popped the top. 'That's so crazy that your old friend from college is my boyfriend's mother.'

She sipped her tea. 'Small world, yes?'

'You're beginning to remember your time at Bellamy Bay College?'

'A little.'

Alex retrieved a container of rice and fresh diced carrots from the refrigerator, wondering what kind of testing they'd done on her. Poor thing.

Caroline set down her cup and picked up the sea salt shaker and shook the crystals directly into her mouth.

Alex watched, slightly disturbed as she licked her lips then returned the shaker to the counter. 'What do you remember about your time at college?'

'Just going to classes with Margaret.'

Classes. Something sparked inside Alex. 'Which classes? Do you remember?' She set the bowl on the floor by a wall where Athena had been patiently waiting.

'The sciences mostly,' Caroline was saying. 'Psychology, marine biology, human anatomy. Classes you'd need for a marine biology major – that was Margaret's area of study.'

'And yours too?'

'Yes. That's how we met. We discovered we had many classes in common.' She smiled. 'I guess it was fate.'

Alex returned her smile. 'Yes, it must've been fate.' But inside,

A Brew for Chaos   239

her stomach clenched. *She is lying*, Alex realized as she watched Athena wolf down her food. *But why?*

'Could you do me a favor?' Caroline grabbed a memo pad and pen from a counter and began writing. 'I'm out of the ingredients needed to make my tea.' She looked up from a list of herbs she was writing and smiled at Alex. 'Lidia said I could get them from the shop as needed.'

Alex nodded, watching as she finished her list. Caroline handed it to her, and she read the list off. 'Astragalus, olive leaf, horsetail, ginger, turmeric, citrus bergamot, milk thistle and echinacea. This is what you've been drinking?'

She nodded. 'Yes. A mix of herbs designed to strengthen and heal me. With a healthy dose of sea salt to boost absorption.'

So that explained her obsession with salt, Alex thought to herself. She thought it was supporting her healing.

Alex folded the paper up and slid it into a pocket, wondering at the depth of knowledge her aunt had to create such a remedy. 'Absolutely. Next time I'm at the shop.'

When Athena was done eating, Alex went into her room, with Athena trotting after her. She closed the door, set up her laptop and began searching for information on Caroline Bracy. She'd been looking for five minutes and had only found articles that simply listed her as one of the victims of the Fisherman. But she finally found an article published by the *Wilmington Star-News* that profiled each victim and consulted with a police profiler who tried to find commonality between the victims.

Alex read each profile with interest, wondering what these women had in common beyond their mermaid DNA, which the writer couldn't possibly know about. And it was as she thought. Their profiles were all over the place. Some were local, some were not. Some came from two-parent families while others did not. Each victim had a quote from a loved one, a parent, a boyfriend or best friend. Caroline had nothing.

Alex read her profile again, which had been compiled from the statements of several students at Bellamy Bay College. They were all under the impression she was enrolled there and talked about how friendly and outgoing she was, involved with extracurricular activities and very social – always at the parties.

A small note in italics stated the author of the article was not able to provide a quote from a family member for her because both her parents had died and she had no siblings.

Alex looked up. How sad, Caroline was essentially an orphan with no one left to even notice she'd been taken. The writer claimed Caroline had always told everyone she was a military brat and didn't claim one particular area as home. One student was quoted as saying Caroline had told him her father had been an officer in the Navy and they'd lived in Maryland for a time, but the reporter was not able to confirm this information.

Alex's cell phone rang. It was Jack. She hesitated before answering.

'We need to talk,' he said before she could even fake a greeting.

'Okay.' Her stomach turned. Had his mother told him everything that has transpired? Did he know she'd been asking her questions? She swallowed. 'Everything all right?'

'I think I found what you're looking for, what you asked me to check on?'

He sounded a bit cagey, and she realized he didn't want to share the information on the phone.

'Right. That's great,' she said, playing along. 'I was hoping you could find your mother's family shortbread recipe.'

A pause. 'Yeah, my father's favorite . . . Would you like to come over tomorrow morning and get the recipe?'

'Sure. See you then.' The phone call ended. Alex exhaled.

FORTY-ONE

The next morning at her aunt's request, Alex drove Minka to Dr Crow's office.

It was close enough to walk, but Aunt Lidia was worried about Minka and thought the drive would be best. As Alex drove down the street, she stopped at the traffic light that put her right in front of the coffee shop.

Spencer was standing on the sidewalk talking to Leith. Or rather, Spencer had her finger in his face, while he appeared to be responding to her in a calm manner. Alex didn't want to gawk, but she wondered what that was about. Kamila had texted her and told her she'd found a charge of domestic assault against Spencer from a former boyfriend when she'd been in college. But the charge had been dropped. And she was known to aggressively push the paparazzi away when they tried to photograph her on vacation.

'It's green,' Minka reminded her.

She gave the couple one more look and saw Spencer push past him and stalk down the sidewalk.

A minute later they were parking in front of the doctor's office.

'I don't know why I need to have this checkup,' Minka complained. 'I feel fine.'

'We have no idea what you went through, Minka. It's for the best.'

Minka shrugged and stared out the window, a complacent look on her face.

At least that dazed quality she'd had for the first few hours after she'd returned was gone, Alex noted, but she still wasn't quite herself. She wondered if Dylan had procured the counter weapon yet.

They went directly into the doctor's office. He sat at a desk with a stack of papers in front of him, while Minka and Alex sat across from him in high-back leather chairs.

Dr Crow shuffled the papers. 'How are you feeling, Minka?'

242   Esme Addison

'Fine, as I keep telling everyone who asks.'

'I received your test results back and except for one anomaly, everything else looks fine.'

She leaned forward. 'What was the anomaly?'

'Your brain scan.'

'Oh,' Minka said, sitting back in her seat. 'Am I okay?' She hesitated. 'I feel okay.'

'Your scan was consistent with someone who's had low dosages of ECT – electroconvulsive therapy.'

Alex's eyes widened. He was referring to the effects of the Zombie weapon, but it still upset her. 'You're talking old-school shock therapy? These psychos shocked her into the state we found her?'

'Essentially yes. Your electrocardiogram was normal, fortunately. Headaches, feeling nauseated, or having general aches and pains is typical after this type of procedure – if this is indeed what you had. It's also possible to experience some memory loss. You still can't remember what happened, correct?'

Minka nodded slowly, a look of fear on her face.

'I'm still recommending rest and hydration. I'm sure your mother is keeping you refreshed with healing herbal tea blends, which along with plain ol' water is what you need right now. Plus potassium pills, which you can get over the counter.'

'Will I get back to normal?' she said, her voice soft and vulnerable.

'Over time, yes. Though speaking with a counselor could be helpful. You might be dealing with feelings around being violated or experiencing PTSD. Whatever the case, it would be good for you to talk through what you're experiencing.'

Minka's gaze fell to a ceramic bowl on the doctor's desk. She picked up the trinket inside of it and began fingering it. 'I'm not opposed to talking to someone.'

'I can recommend a colleague.' He found a pen and wrote a name and number on it. He slid the paper across the desk, but Minka's eyes were on the device.

'What is this?' she said, holding her palm out to him.

'A GPS tracker. It was embedded in the recent Jane Doe's neck. I wasn't sure what to do with it, so I just placed it here.'

She immediately dropped the tracker back into the decorative

A Brew for Chaos   243

bowl with a clunk. 'How horrible. I'm sorry, I didn't know.' She stared at the device. It was metallic and inscribed with a serial number. She stared at the numbers etched on it, and something like recognition flickered in her eyes. And then was gone as quickly as it appeared. 'Poor woman. I hope she can find peace as well.'

The doctor stood. 'We're done for today. I mostly wanted to speak with you, get a nice visual inspection and answer any questions you may have.'

'Thank you.'

'If your memory loss doesn't improve and the symptoms of dizziness, vertigo or lightheadedness return, alert my office, and we'll have a full examination next time.'

When they stood outside of the closed office, Minka smiled. 'That wasn't awful.'

When Alex greeted Jack on the porch, he didn't hug her or kiss her, which on one level relieved her because she didn't want to be touched by him. But on the other hand, she was worried that he knew what she'd been up to with his mother, or worse yet he'd figured out she was one of the Magicals he was tracking and now she was coming to his house.

'How's your mother?' she asked as she followed him into his home.

'She's fine,' he said, his voice tight. 'In her room watching that channel you introduced her to.' He glanced at her over his shoulder. 'When she was at your house?'

Alex swallowed. So he knew about the visit. 'She wasn't there long. I had to make a stop.'

She watched him nervously as he gestured to the couch.

'Have a seat.'

The tightness of his features and the position of his shoulders alarmed her. She'd never seen him quite so . . . She wasn't sure. Not angry exactly. Anxious maybe? She sat down while he paced across from her. 'What's wrong, Jack?'

He stopped pacing and looked at her. 'I looked into your ask. About Project Oannes.'

'And?'

'I couldn't find much about that particular project, or who

244   Esme Addison

owned the contracts. But I did find several auxiliary projects that were connected.' He went to a drawer and retrieved a folder filled with several sheets. 'Here's what I found.'

She took the folder from him but didn't open it yet, still focused on his agitated state. 'Are you okay?'

He ignored her look of concern and nodded. 'They were all tests sponsored by the Navy in the 1980s, all in North Carolina and measuring various types of underwater activities.' He ran a hand through his hair. His eyes looked tired when he returned Alex's gaze. 'You know, don't you?'

She cocked her head. 'Know what?'

His scowl deepened. 'Why I'm really here. In Bellamy Bay, I mean.'

Alex stared at him, the folder almost slipping from her hand.

He swallowed. 'I need to come clean.'

Alex's stomach flip-flopped. 'About?'

'I don't know how to say this except to just say it . . .' He sat down beside her and stared straight ahead. 'I'm not really a cop.'

FORTY-TWO

Alex's breath caught in her throat.

'You're not?' *What was going on? He was going to tell her the truth?*

'I'm working a case for the US Army jointly with the DOD and CIA.' He gave her a sideways glance, his jaw muscle twitching. 'I wondered if you'd found out somehow. You've been acting strangely.'

The old human lie detector was at it again, she thought wryly. She wanted to smile at the thought, but it didn't seem appropriate. 'What kind of case?'

'You figured it out, didn't you?' he persisted, his eyes intense as he watched her.

She took a deep breath. 'Yes, I knew something was off, that you might not be who you said you were.'

He didn't look angry. Relieved actually. 'I didn't like lying to you, but I had a cover to protect and a mission to complete. Now that you know, I trust you'll keep my secret?'

Alex pressed her lips together to keep from speaking the truth, that she'd already told a few people about him. She nodded, hoping he couldn't tell she was lying from such a simple gesture.

He took a breath then slowly exhaled. 'What I'm going to tell you is going to . . . well, it's going to sound . . . for lack of a better word . . . *bananas.*'

Alex bit her bottom lip. *Was he going to tell her about Magicals?*

'There are people – people that look like you and me' – disgust flickered across his face – 'that for whatever reason have advanced capabilities. The ability to hear our thoughts, to harm, to kill . . .'

To heal, Alex wanted to say. *To help.* But the look on his face . . . She kept quiet.

'These people are dangerous, a menace to society, and I've made it my life's work to help find them and contain them so we can keep our world safe.'

246 Esme Addison

Alex was trying to understand the derogatory way he spoke about her and her people as he continued.

'I'm not sure how they came to *be*, but the government is aware of them, is studying them, trying to figure it all out.' He looked at her then. 'So these studies you wanted me to look into, they are related . . . and they're a good thing. They're helping us figure out how these people tick, so we can better defend ourselves from them.'

She couldn't help herself, she moved away from him. 'You knew about the government testing on these people?'

'I was aware there were various studies, but no specifics. Our missions are compartmentalized, so I don't always know what other agents are doing. And I don't know about anything that may have happened here related to the Fisherman. But we do get intel from the studies when it's relevant.' He reached for her hand, and she reluctantly gave it to him. 'When you asked me to look into Project Oannes, I thought you knew what I was up to and it was your polite way of letting me know and giving me time to tell you myself.'

Alex closed her eyes as the pressure built at her temples. It didn't sound like he knew about her or her family. But maybe he did, and he was just playing her. If he didn't know, how long would it be before he did? This all suddenly felt very dangerous.

A feeling of tightness expanded in Alex's chest. Almost a pain. Had she been found out? Her family? If he knew so much, why didn't he know about her? She could barely breathe, as fear, tight and cold, curled around her. Was him calling her here a trap? Was her family right now in this moment being detained?

'How are you finding these people? How do you know who is who?' she ventured, hoping her voice sounded normal but knowing it did not.

And he noticed. 'Don't worry. I'll keep you safe.'

His words reminded her of what Mac had said to Daphne as a teenager.

'It's scary, right, knowing this – that's why it's classified and then compartmentalized. It's like realizing that superhero movies are real, except we have the villains and no Batman to save the day.'

She thought sweat was forming on her hairline, threatening to

A Brew for Chaos 247

fall down her forehead, alerting Jack that something was wrong. Everyone knew sweating could be a sign of lying, of nervousness. She tried to smile, but thought her lips trembled just a bit. 'You fancy yourself Batman, do you?'

He chuckled. Finally, his face was brightening. 'Superman, if I had to pick. Batman is a bit too mysterious for my taste. Superman is a good guy and everyone knows it.'

She swallowed back bile rising in her throat. *He thought he was the good guy?* Alex thought she might vomit.

'To answer your question, it's complicated. It takes a bit of good old-fashioned intuition plus some work tools.' He tapped his watch. 'Like this device. It's paratech – technology based off the PACs' paranormal abilities. When someone practices magic, if it meets the energetic frequency threshold, it will show up on a radar at our command center, and I'll see it here.'

Command center? Alex's throat tightened.

He moved forward to show her.

She hesitated. 'Last time when I tried to touch it, you almost bit my head off.'

Jack blushed. 'I know. I'm sorry. This device costs more than this house. I'm afraid I'm going to damage it, but I have to wear it, and then obviously I didn't want you to see it wasn't a real watch.'

Alex leaned in for a closer look.

'It provides analysis about each Paranormal Fluctuation.'

Alex gave him a sideways glance. It was all so technical. Strange to hear him talk about what she'd come to know as her magical heritage like it was a science experiment.

'And a dispatcher at a base I can't mention gets notified and he or she sends me the location. I check it out – it's why I'm always running out of here.' His laugh turned into an exhausted sigh. 'And it's never-ending. This area, small as it is, is a *hotbed* of paranormal activity.'

'You have a list of locals then?' *Look him directly in his eyes*, she told herself, remembering what her father had told her. *These are gestures of an honest person. Steady your voice. Still your movements. Slow down.* She was doing all of these things now, hoping Jack couldn't see the truth on her face.

'I have a few people of interest but nothing solid. I haven't

248   Esme Addison

caught anyone red-handed and that's what I need before I can send their name up the chain for action.'

For action? What the heck did that mean?

'Celeste is on that list,' he admitted, his voice careful. 'There are frequent bursts of activity around her house. Combined with the fact that I . . .' He almost laughed. 'I found a doll stuck with pins on her person and witness accounts of odd behavior.' He shrugged. 'But I haven't caught her in the act.'

'She's just playing around. You know that.'

'If you knew what I knew, you'd know that witches are real but not in the way TV and film present them. No pointy black hats and green skin. They're normal-looking humans with genetic mutations that result in paranormal capabilities.'

Alex couldn't hide her concern, since at least one family member was clearly on his hit list. 'Celeste is family.'

'And we've found that these abilities are genetic,' he said, his voice low and steady. 'You said she was your cousin. That worried me – at first.'

Alex couldn't help it. She held her breath.

'But a little research showed that her abilities, if she truly has them, come from her maternal descendants in Haiti, generations back. Haiti is full of paranormal activity as well. Not that they even try to hide their voodoo worship.'

'Celeste doesn't practice voodoo,' Alex said, tone indignant. *It was something else . . . He hadn't made the connection between the Sobieskis and the Mermaid of Warsaw*, Alex thought with relief. But how long before he did?

'And my immediate family?' she said lightly. She hoped it was light. 'When I moved here six months ago, one of the first things I heard was that they were a group of witches selling herbs and spells in their shop. And now I'm one of them, working at the apothecary.' She couldn't help it. Anger and fear were pushing her now. 'If Celeste is a witch, what does that make me? My aunt. Minka. Kamila – an officer on your force, I might add.'

His eyebrows floated up in concern. 'Calm down. I *was* suspicious of your aunt at first. Especially after she was charged with poisoning Randy Bennett. But I also thought, if she was one of the people I was investigating, she could've used her abilities to kill him, not poison him like a human would.'

A Brew for Chaos   249

She clenched her jaw. His use of *human* bothered her. She and her family were humans too. 'That, combined with the fact that there's been no magical activity around your shop or house . . .'

Alex hoped she'd hidden her surprise. All the magic her family did? That was . . . well, a revelation. She wondered why, then remembered the shield of protection Aunt Lidia had placed around both places must have blocked their magical activity from appearing on his magical tracking tools.

'And of course, Officer Sobieski is an excellent police officer. She's moral. Has integrity. She couldn't be that way unless she was raised that way. Your aunt has a reputation for being . . . emotional, shall we say? But in my humble opinion she couldn't have raised Kamila to be the way she is if she was one of these *things*. These people have no morals. No kindness. No compassion. They're cold-blooded. Psychotic.' He patted her hand. 'I hope this doesn't change the way you feel about me – because I lied to you. I had no choice. I hope you can see that.'

Alex glanced at her hand in his and suppressed the urge to pull away. No morals? No kindness or compassion? Where was he getting his information from? Was he dealing with dragon descents and mistaking them for all Magicals? She wanted to tell him the truth then, just to stand up for herself and her family and those just like her. The ones who were dedicated to healing and helping mankind.

But she couldn't. She couldn't say one word to him. Her gaze fell to his hand on hers and she summoned a smile. 'I understand why you didn't tell me.'

He exhaled, a puff of relief. 'Good. Thank you, because I care about you, and keeping this from you has really been eating me up inside. I despise liars, you know that.

'It's caused me to hold myself apart from you. But with you knowing . . . well, maybe we can get closer now. I still can't tell you everything I'm doing, but at least it's not all based on a lie now.'

Alex's heart broke just a bit. It broke for how she felt about him before she knew who he really was. And the hopes and dreams she had for them, the ones that could've flourished if she just didn't practice like her mother hadn't with her father. She'd played with the idea of telling Jack. Her mother had told her

250   Esme Addison

father and he'd gotten over it. They'd had a happy marriage. But now? It didn't seem possible with his palpable disgust for Magicals. For her.

He squeezed her hand. 'Once this latest round of testing is complete, the DOD will be able to develop a complete suite of weapons designed to contain and incapacitate these PACs – Practitioners of Anomalous Cognition.'

She nodded, still acting. Still lying to his face, but then his words hit her. 'Wait, you're on board with the unethical testing of human subjects who may have been abducted and studied against their will?'

A deep V appeared between his eyebrows. 'I'm not the monster here, Alex.'

You sure? She tried very hard to hide the revulsion she felt in every bone in her body.

'They are. I mean, are we sure they're even human?' He shrugged, while a wave of nausea rocked Alex's body.

She pulled her hand away, then rose from the couch. Heat flooded her body and beads of sweat covered her forehead. She felt sick. She wasn't sure she could keep this pretense up.

'I was able to access some of the results of past studies and these things are genetically different . . . The Neanderthal is 99.7 per cent similar to human. Chimpanzees share 99 per cent of the same DNA. These PACs share 98.9 per cent of the same DNA as us – as humans.' He looked at her then, searching her face. 'Don't you see? We have more in common with chimps than we do these monsters. They're a different species walking around with us, looking like us but not *like* us.'

She and her family weren't human? Another species? 'Maybe they're not monsters. Maybe they're just like you and me. Have you ever thought of that?'

He didn't hesitate. 'No.' He smiled. Actually smiled. 'You have a big heart. I like that about you. I'm not surprised you'd want to show these creatures compassion, but you can't give these things the benefit of the doubt. They have too much power, and absolute power corrupts. I work with an FBI taskforce that's trying to get a hold of these . . . of this national security issue.'

She, little old Alex Daniels, was considered a national security issue? She couldn't understand it. 'Why are you involved in this?

Why do you care about these people so much? What have they done to you?'

'They – these monsters . . .' His gaze traveled up the stairs and lingered there. 'They hurt my mother. They made her the way she is and I'm trying to find out exactly what they did to her and who did it to her and bring them to justice.'

'How did one of these . . . people hurt your mother?'

He covered his face with the palms of his hands then ran both over his head. When he looked up, his eyes were hard and his cheeks flushed. 'My mother has been the way she is my entire life. Can you imagine what it was like for me to grow up with a mother who was basically like a really happy child?' He wiped an angry tear from his face with a jerky swipe of his arm.

'No, I can't—'

'Always wishing your mother was normal. Like the other mothers. Alert. Smart. Focused. Able to remember things . . . My father couldn't even be bothered to stick around because of her condition.' He huffed in frustration.

'But you do have a mother. And she's sweet and loving and . . .'

'Like a little sister?' he finished for her. 'I grew up taking care of her. Cooking dinner. Helping her pick out clothes. Holding her hand when we crossed the street. Making sure she took her medicine, which she's taken my entire life. She was always in a daze. She's my mother. I love her, but I just . . . I wish she was okay. I grew up scared for her, afraid she'd fall, or walk into the road without looking, or touch the stove when it was too hot . . . I barely had a childhood. I'm in Bellamy Bay to find the monster that did this to her.'

'How do you know it happened here in Bellamy Bay? And that it was one of the people you're looking for?'

'Because my grandparents told me she wasn't born like this. She was fine until she went to college here in town.' His voice hardened as he continued. 'And then she met one of these *things* in this place where apparently these creatures roam around unsuspecting . . . and then she went missing and when she returned . . . she was how she is now.'

Heaviness filled Alex's chest. 'Did she say who she met? What the person looked like? I mean, even if these people do have abilities, how could they give her the condition she has?'

252 Esme Addison

'I don't know. There's a lot I don't know. It's why I took this job as an agent. It's why I joined this taskforce. And that's why I'm here. Investigating. Trying to figure out what happened to my mother. I need to know. I need answers. I need to know why my life has been—'

He was so angry he was shaking. And despite how Alex felt about him, and how he felt about Magicals, she went to him and wrapped her arms around him. He loved his mother. Anyone could understand the motivation of a son wanting to protect his mother. She just wished it didn't come with so much animosity for her and her family and others like them.

He broke the embrace, and looking somewhat embarrassed, he moved away from her. 'I'm sorry. I've never spoken about this aloud to anyone.' He inhaled a ragged breath.

He had to be describing a dragon. One of them had hurt his mother. Maybe. 'Can I help?' Alex asked. 'I love a good mystery, and I've got a little experience in this area. I care for your mother too, and if I can help in any way . . .' And she could probably figure this out before him. Even though he was on a government taskforce destined to track down Magicals, she *was* a Magical. And she knew other Magicals. She had a network and resources he could only dream of.

His face softened. 'I appreciate that. I know you like my mother. She likes you too, and that means a lot to me. It really does. But I don't want you involved with this – with these PACs. I don't want another person I care about to be harmed in any way by these monsters.'

'Even so, what did your mother say about the person who did this to her?'

He averted his eyes, looking embarrassed. 'Sometimes if she doesn't take her medicine, memories come to her, and she says things. Things that don't make sense. And once, just once, when I realized if she missed a dose and I questioned her, maybe I could find out something helpful . . .'

Pain crossed his face. 'I withheld her medicine from her, and she began to remember things. She told me about one of these PACs she met. She didn't know that term, but based on how she described it, I know that's what it was.' His face hardened into anger. 'It had paranormal abilities associated with the water – the

A Brew for Chaos   253

ocean. It's why I didn't want her anywhere near it. My mother said it could stay underwater for long periods of time. It could swim fast. It could emit an electrical charge like an eel, and it could read her thoughts. Among other abilities . . . A monster.'

Alex stared at him, a sick feeling pervading her body. No, that couldn't be right.

'She told me it was a *mermaid*, this thing,' he continued. 'But there are no such things as mermaids. That's just a romanticized version of what these monsters are.' His eyes swept the room, falling on several mermaid-decorated throw pillows. 'There are only these PACs – these creatures.'

A thickness filled Alex's throat, and she could barely find the words to speak. 'Your mother said a mermaid did this to her?'

His laugh was harsh. 'No. But she told me she met one. Actually saw one. Fins and all. And then my mother went missing from school . . . Returned a completely different person.' He shook his head. 'Not hard to put two and two together.' He stood, the memory of what he did upsetting him.

Alex's cell phone chimed, but she ignored it.

'But I pushed her too hard. She got a massive migraine. Got sick. Dizzy. Started seeing lights . . . Throwing up . . . It was bad. I never withheld her medicine again, never asked her any more questions. The doctor was right when he said to keep giving her her medicine and not to try and jog her memory. It's too upsetting.'

'I'm so sorry you had to go through that.' And she meant it. No matter how revolting Jack's feelings were about Magicals. But she needed to get away from him. She stood, grabbing the folder and her purse, refusing to meet his gaze.

'I've said too much,' he rushed out. 'I've scared you away.' He followed her as she headed to the door.

'No. I mean, well, I'm surprised, yes, but it's not you. I need to go.' She opened his front door.

She pushed the screen door open and ran down the porch stairs without looking back.

FORTY-THREE

Not ready to go home and face her family, Alex stopped by the shop.

But first she called Celeste and told her everything. When Alex was done talking, there was a long silence. So long, Alex wondered if Celeste was still on the phone. But then she spoke, her voice firm. 'I'll be right over.'

After the call, Alex arrived at the herbal apothecary, which was bustling with customers. Tanner was working, and she picked up the dry herbs Caroline requested for her tea then drove home. She'd hoped the short detour would help her process everything Jack had revealed to her. Talking to Celeste had helped, but her head was still swimming when she entered the house.

She took a moment to pet Athena, who stood at her side, tail wagging. Sensing something was wrong, Athena whined softly and nuzzled Alex's thigh until she kneeled and buried her face into Athena's fur for extra cuddles.

Then she rose, determined to put on a good face for her aunt. She went to the kitchen where she could hear her cooking, pushed on the swinging wood door, and saw Lidia baking her anxiety away by pounding on a mound of dough. Inhaling deeply, Alex allowed the scent of yeast to fill her lungs.

Alex presented the bag of herbs. 'I picked up Caroline's herb list.'

Lidia took the bag, dumped the packets of labeled herbs out and began sorting them. 'Thank you. She guzzles the tea down so fast I can barely keep up with her appetite.'

Alex leaned against a counter, happy to be distracted by something else. 'It's an interesting mix of herbs. How did you create it?'

Lidia was organizing the packets, placing them in a cabinet when she turned to look at Alex over her shoulder. 'I didn't create that list of ingredients.'

'But I thought . . .' Alex frowned.

Lidia closed the cabinet. 'Caroline already knew what she wanted. Said it would help her feel better.' She crossed her arms. 'It's a nice sound recipe for immunity building. And seaweed among other benefits strengthens the thyroid, which regulates the body's immunity and inflammation response.'

She flipped the ball of yeast over, folded it and began kneading it. 'I keep it in stock, but no one ever asked for it but Jonah . . .' Lidia shook her head. 'I thought the blend was random. But after her hands were healed, and she could write out a list for me, I saw that it was very specific, and she wouldn't accept any substitutions. I keep making great big jars of it, and she gulps it down like it's manna from heaven.'

'With seaweed,' Alex prompted. 'Jonah's secret ingredient.'

Lidia nodded. 'She's been drinking several cups of it every day since she got here.'

Was Spencer looking for a beer recipe? Or instructions for brewing an herbal remedy? 'What health issue would those herbs address?' Alex pressed.

Lidia cleaned her hand on a towel and set it down. 'Astragalus is anti-inflammatory and strengthens the immune system, olive leaf has antioxidants and is, again, anti-inflammatory. So right off the bat I'd say we were dealing with some sort of infection or a situation where the body is fighting off something.

'Horsetail strengthens bones and is also anti-inflammatory, so I'd guess we're dealing with a malady of the bones and/or joints. Maybe arthritis? Ginger can help with nausea but is also anti-inflammatory. But because of the horsetail, I'm leaning towards a tonic for osteoarthritis – because of the amount of anti-inflammatory herbs plus immunity strengtheners, I really feel like this is for a severe issue with the bones, joints and cartilage.'

An image of Caroline in her wheelchair floated in Alex's mind. 'What about the other ingredients?'

'Turmeric for osteoarthritis. The herb bergamot is an interesting choice. It's prescribed for osteoarthritis, but it also addresses emotional issues like depression and anxiety.' She went to a bookshelf in the kitchen and retrieved a slim volume, flipping through it. She nodded. 'Just as I thought. Depression is significant among patients with arthritis and musculoskeletal illnesses. A severe and chronic musculoskeletal illness sounds about right.'

Alex referred to the list again. 'How about milk thistle and echinacea?'

'Normally milk thistle is prescribed to support the liver, but in this context, I'd guess its ability to cause remineralization of bone and protect against bone loss. Echinacea with this blend I think would be to support a strong immune system.'

Alex was just about to leave the house when she received a call. She didn't recognize the number, so she let it go to voicemail. But a moment later a notification appeared, and she listened to it then set down the phone with a satisfied grin. 'Looks like Pepper came through.'

Her aunt planted a hand on her hip. 'How so?'

'I've been searching for a microfiche reader for documents Pepper and I found in Jonah's house, and she's finally tracked one down at the town hall.'

There was a knock on the front door, and Athena trotted alongside Alex as she opened it. Celeste entered the house, her curly hair tousled by the wind. And without speaking she wrapped her arms around Alex. 'Are you okay?'

Lidia stood by watching, lips pursed. 'What's going on?' She looked at Alex, crossing her arms across her chest. 'You didn't mention anything. We were just talking, and—'

Alex soldiered a smile. 'Stuff with Jack. Nothing you'd want to hear about.'

Her lip curled. 'You're right about that.'

Alex exchanged a look with Celeste. 'I have a few errands to run. Want to come with?'

Celeste grinned. 'Let's go.'

On their way to city hall, Celeste paused on the sidewalk outside the bakery. Then Alex heard Celeste's stomach growl and laughed. 'I guess you're hungry?'

She nodded. 'I could really use a bowl of warm soup and a hunk of their bread right now. Do we have time?'

'Sure.'

They entered the bakery, ordered their food and brought it to their table a few minutes later. Celeste hovered over her bowl of spicy peanut soup, allowing the steam to warm her face. 'Oh yeah, that feels and smells wonderful.'

Alex was picking at a slice of smoked maple bacon quiche when someone caught her eye. She discreetly pointed with her fork. 'Look who's over there crying in her soup.'

Celeste turned around and saw Spencer, tip of her nose red and eyes puffy.

'Should I check on her?'

Celeste laughed. 'After she threw a smoothie at you? Proceed with caution, that's all I have to say.'

Alex stood. 'I will. Be right back. Enjoy your soup.' She made her way over to the woman.

Spencer scowled at her when she recognized her. 'What do you want?'

'Nothing. Just checking on you.'

'I can take care of myself.'

'I know. I saw you arguing with someone on the street earlier. Guy named Leith? You seemed to handle that too.'

She bowed her head, shoulders drooping as if all the anger she'd just felt melted away. 'It's nothing.'

Alex leaned forward. 'Was he bothering you?'

'I can't talk about it.'

'Why not?'

She looked up then, her face hesitant like she wanted to speak, but then she shuttered again. 'He was complaining about his experience at the tavern. Nothing I can't handle.'

Alex watched her, feeling that she wasn't being completely honest. 'Okay, well. I saw you were upset . . .'

'Just leave me alone.'

And Alex wondered if she was about to get the remains of a grilled cheese sandwich tossed in her face and took a step back just in case.

'You can't help me. No one can.' She had begun packing up her things when her tote fell in the scramble and Alex saw the spine of a book in her leather bag. She recognized the title. Her

258   Esme Addison

aunt had the same book in her kitchen on a bookshelf. *From Ale to Ailment: Exploring the Medicinal Properties of Beer Throughout History.*

Spencer grabbed her bag and tray and brushed past Alex.

A few minutes later, Alex and Celeste were back on Main Street and in front of town hall. As they ascended the stairs, Alex went over what they'd learned about Spencer. 'Maybe the recipe she's looking for is not for the brewery but for Chandeuz's pharmaceutical business.'

Celeste opened the doors, and they entered the colonial brick building. 'But why would she think Jonah's recipe is for a medicine versus an actual beer?'

They stopped to stand in front of the receptionist's desk, and she led them to the basement level, passing old furniture, crates of documents and even one old statue in the corner. She showed the women how to turn the machine on and enter the films for view. She did the first one, and a document appeared.

'Thank you.' Alex nodded at the woman as she moved past them to the stairs.

They waited for the sound of her heels to go away and the door to click closed before they returned to the screen.

The first page had the words *Top Secret* in bold red font stamped across the top. And then a purple M-Level stamp in bold. Another stamp in black read *For Internal Distribution Only.*

Celeste shared a glance with Alex. 'What in the world are we about to see?'

'*Project Oannes,*' Alex began reading tentatively. '*January 12, 1963. Headed by Dr Alasdair Frazier.*' Alex's throat tightened. '*Naval Intelligence.*'

'Frazier?' Celeste echoed.

'Yeah. As in the same person who said he was Maisie's husband and removed her from school.'

'And presumably fathered Jack,' Celeste stated.

Alex blinked. 'None of this makes sense. The man who headed up this study married Maisie, fathered Jack, then left them both?'

Celeste held up her phone. 'If this is the right Alasdair J. Frazier, it says he died twenty years ago of natural causes.'

Alex read the obituary. Naval officer, born in New York, married

A Brew for Chaos   259

with one son, same middle initial . . . 'Seems like the same guy. I wonder if Jack knows? He said he left them when he was just a toddler. He joked that he was probably dead.'

'Let's keep reading. Maybe it will all click,' Celeste suggested.

Nodding her agreement, Alex began to read the file. '*The study began after a relationship was discovered by scientists between the lungfish, the tetrapod – four-legged creatures – and Homo sapiens,*' Alex read. '*A secondary study looked into the development and evolution of the pelvic fin, which led to studying an animal called the tetrapod in the Devonian Antarctic Circle, that would have resembled a cross between a crocodile and a fish, with a crocodile-like head, stubby legs, and a tail with a fish-like fin. It represented the link between fish and human evolution.*'

Alex stopped reading, and Celeste made a face. 'That sounds gross. Fish to reptile to humans?'

'Some seventy million years ago, I guess so,' Alex said, then paused. 'Why does Jonah have this? How did he obtain it? It's clearly classified material.'

Celeste shrugged. 'He's a journalist. Maybe a whistleblower sent it to him?'

Nodding, Alex thought of Tanner and his blog, which was fueled by anonymous tips. 'That makes sense.' She returned to the screen. 'And the Navy was studying this . . .' She swiped through several pages analyzing the various studies and diagrams of lungfish and tetrapods, sightings of ancient fossils. Alex shook her head. 'I don't know what this has to do with—'

'There,' Celeste said with excitement. Her finger jabbing towards the screen. 'Go back to that last screen.'

Alex went back one slide, and they both reread the page. She gasped.

'Holy . . .' Celeste murmured to herself.

The page showed an image of a human, not unlike the famous Leonardo Da Vinci drawing *The Vitruvian Man*, but this one was a woman with words written all around it extended by lines pointing to certain parts of the body.

'What the . . .' Alex said as she read the page. 'They're comparing the human body to its genetic source in tetrapods and lungfish. I don't . . .'

'Turn the page,' Celeste said.

260 Esme Addison

Alex did and they kept reading. The page had turned wholly scientific with listings of DNA codes and analyses.

Celeste began reading. '. . . *our findings concluded that humans share 60 per cent of their DNA with fish, with the coelacanth, a fish once thought to be extinct, sharing up to 96 per cent of the human genome. Humans have forty-six chromosomes. The coelacanth has forty-eight chromosomes. The DNA of humans is more similar to the DNA of fish than to the DNA of any other type of organism.* I should've paid more attention to science class and not marketing,' Celeste said. 'This is a lot of data, and it's interesting, but I'm not sure where they're going with this.'

'Here, another study was completed in 1974, where they discovered that the same cells in fish and in tetrapods either ask the body to develop dermal bones or endochondral bones.' She paused. 'The result is either hands and fingers . . . or fins.'

'Wow, it's a wonder we're not all walking around with fins.'

Alex rubbed her eyes. 'If we're mermaids genetically, have you ever wondered why we can't . . .' She shrugged, feeling silly. 'Become, you know, actual mermaids?'

'With purple hair and pink fins? Are you kidding me?' Celeste laughed. 'Like every day. When I was a kid, that is. I mean, what little girl doesn't want to be a mermaid? And knowing we have the genes for it.' Her face lit up. 'I can't tell you how many times I tried to wish myself into a mermaid. Or days when I'd go to the beach and just stay in the water trying to shift into my Mer form.' She poked out her bottom lip in mock despair. 'But nothing ever happened.'

'And no one knows why we can't just snap our fingers and have fins?'

'Whatever the process is, it's been lost to time. Or maybe God took it from us.' Celeste's face went wishful. 'I would love to experience being a mermaid – a real mermaid. Just once.'

Alex returned to the screen. 'In 1976, the next study examined the genes that created hands and feet in humans or fins in fish.' There were more diagrams of the genes, then drawings of hand, feet and fin skeletons. These images devolved to x-rays of hands, feet and fish fins with portions circled and tagged with Latin terminology. She clicked on the next screen, which was a solid black square that filled the projector viewer. 'That's it?' She stared at the black slide in confusion.

'I guess we can assume that Project Oannes was a series of tests the Navy concluded on the evolutionary link between humans and fish and reptiles.' Alex steepled her hands and pressed them together, stretching her fingers. 'Interesting, but not sure why it was so hush hush.' She retrieved the film from the reader and slid it back into the envelope then stopped. 'Hey, there's another page in here. Not sure how I missed it. Should we view it?'

Celeste groaned. 'No more fish DNA.' She laughed. 'Yeah, we have to at least give it another look. But first, coffee. I'm going to see if the receptionist has a pot brewing somewhere.' Celeste began walking to the stairs. 'But don't start without me.'

Alex promised she wouldn't. She stared at the reader. Then tapped her fingers on the desk. She checked her phone. No messages.

Alex looked up when she heard Celeste descend the stairs with two steaming cups of coffee in to-go cups.

'I have coffee-e-e-e,' she sang out with glee. 'We are officially fortified to continue our deep dive into fish DNA.' When she reached Alex, she handed her a cup.

Alex took the coffee. 'Thank you. After all this' – she waved a hand towards the microfiche reader – 'I need some caffeine.' She took a sip and sighed contentedly.

Celeste held her cup tight in her hands. 'Sounds like they began Project Oannes right around the time the other testing ended.'

'I wonder if they heard about dragon descents from Dylan's father and tried to create their own. And failed miserably.'

Alex sighed. 'And then the testing on mermaid descents began.' She picked up the last microfiche and fed it into the machine. 'Ready?'

Celeste nodded.

Alex turned knobs, bringing the first slide under the viewer and then maximizing it until they could read it. 'Looks like they began a new study. *Researchers report that memory in the form of "DNA methylation" is preserved between generations of fish, in contrast to humans where this is almost entirely erased.*'

'Wait, what is DNA methylation?' Celeste asked.

Alex skimmed the page and found the definition. '*DNA methylation is the process that controls how our DNA is expressed, in effect, by turning genes on and off.*'

Celeste nodded. 'Got it. I think.'

'*Methylation sits on top of DNA and is used to control which genes are turned on and off. It also helps to define cellular identity and function. In humans and other mammals, DNA methylation is erased at each generation; however, we found that global erasure of DNA methylation memory does not occur at all in the fish we studied.*'

Celeste read ahead. 'Okay. So . . . they're trying to figure out how to turn the genes that create hands and feet in humans and fins in fish on and off?' She frowned. 'Wait, I'm getting mad scientist vibes right now. You?'

Alex nodded. '*The next study commenced twelve months later on the Early Tetrapod Fossil.*' She kept reading. '*They were trying to figure out how the four-limbed, land-walking tetrapod evolved from the fish that had lungs . . .*' She went to the next screen.

Celeste wrinkled her nose. 'I don't think I like where this is heading.'

Alex looked over her shoulder at Celeste in concern, but Celeste's gaze remained fixed on the screen. Frowning, Alex turned around to see what had upset Celeste. And then her mouth fell open too.

They both stared at a faded color image of a woman. She floated in a large tank, almost like a fish tank but at least twelve feet high and twelve feet wide. Her dark hair fanned around her face. Her eyes were dark. Flat. Hollow. Angry. Her face twisted into a mask of hate as she glowered at the photographer.

Her waist flowed seamlessly into a long silvery fin. Metallic in sheen with blue undertones, it curled under her while a large fin flared behind her.

Caroline.

Both Alex and Celeste recognized her immediately. But here in this photograph, that's not what they were calling her.

Caroline was a mermaid.

FORTY-FOUR

'Caroline is a mermaid,' Alex said, when she could find her voice.

They both stared at the image in silence.

'Like a *real* mermaid,' Celeste whispered, her voice in awe. 'Not just a carrier of the genes like us . . . But how? I mean . . . she's got legs.' She frowned. 'Right? I'm not making that up.' Her eyes remained focused on the image.

'Not unless this is a group delusion.' Alex couldn't take her eyes off the screen either. 'And how and why was she a student at Bellamy Bay College? I mean, did she wake up one day and trade her fins for feet so she could get a college degree? Or was that a movie I saw.' Alex almost laughed. 'I-I-I don't understand.

'When Maisie went to college, she was a marine biology student. She said she used to go to the beach, ocean watch and collect shells and specimens. She also told Jack that she saw a mermaid. She wasn't making it up. She must've seen Caroline in her Mer form.'

'And what?' Celeste interrupted. 'She shifted to her human form, swam ashore and made friends?'

'Yes, that's exactly what I think happened. And somehow Caroline became her roommate and went to school with her. That part I just don't get.'

'All this time we assumed Caroline was a genetic mermaid like you and me . . .' Celeste mused aloud.

Alex remembered Caroline's sharp retort and winced. *I'm not like you.* 'No, she's different. She's a real mermaid who was tested on by the military . . . How convenient that Maisie was diagnosed with dementia and couldn't remember meeting—'

Alex gasped. 'No . . .' Her eyes widened and she shook her head. Jack was right. Someone had done that to her. She'd hoped he was mistaken. But . . . He had it wrong.

It wasn't a Magical who'd hurt his mother. She thought of the similarities between Maisie's symptoms and Minka's, a sick feeling permeating her body. 'I think someone from the project used the Zombie Maker on Jack's mother when she was abducted to wipe her memories and scramble her brain. That was done to her.'

Tears pushed against the back of her eyes. 'She didn't have to be like that. Jack didn't have to grow up with a mother like that . . .' Slowly, Alex turned back to the screen. 'I'm afraid to see what's next.'

'Caroline is a real mermaid,' Celeste emphasized again. 'And now she has legs. How did she do it? I want to know her secret – how did she shift between Mer and fully human? And more importantly, can she teach me?'

Alex scrolled through several pictures that showed Caroline in and out of the water. Strapped to a raised pallet-like bed, fins and all, and then back in the water. 'You notice something about these pictures?' Alex asked.

Celeste still couldn't take her eyes off the screen. 'You mean besides the fact that there's a real mermaid in them?'

'Her face,' Alex said. 'She looks . . . angry.'

'Enraged might be a better word.'

More pictures scrolled by. Caroline sitting up. Caroline with her hands on her throat, gasping for air. Caroline looking calm, eyes icy. Or eyes like daggers. In one picture she appeared to be lunging towards the photographer.

'She must've hated whoever was taking the pictures of her.'

'I was just thinking that. Like, why isn't he helping her instead of . . . documenting her pain.'

'According to the notes,' Celeste read, 'I think they were training her to stay out of the water and breathe air.'

'Torturing her was more like it.' Alex noted the stamps. Dates and times with each duration getting longer by a few minutes. 'She must've felt like she was suffocating. Inhumane.' But if Jack was any indication, these government types didn't consider her human.

'And keeping her in a fish tank like an animal,' Celeste said with a sour tone. 'When she was used to roaming the sea.'

The images progressed over a two-year period to Caroline being strapped to her bed, no more aquarium, and eating fish and drinking something out of a large black tumbler. She was no longer angry, but she wasn't happy either. The expression on her face was nonchalant like the tests bored her. She still had her fin though.

They showed her getting shots. Each time, her face was stretched in pain. Or fear. *'Gene therapy based on their DNA methylation research,'* Alex read aloud as she stared at the images. Each one showed her getting a shot with the amount and a report on her response. The shot stung. She felt sleepy. She was hungry. She slept for sixteen hours straight. She was nauseous.

The note-taking was meticulous, and she wondered what kind of monster had the stomach to observe and then document the testing without one ounce of compassion for this . . . woman? Mermaid. 'They're tweaking her DNA, trying to shut off the . . . what was it? The Hoxa-13 and Hoxd-13 DNA that decides on feet or fins.' A tear slid down Alex's cheek. 'They're trying to change her fins to feet.'

'They're forcing it,' Celeste said with a frown.

They stared at the images as they saw her fins go from a beautiful shiny silver to a dull matte gray of a dolphin, and then to a mottled purple-brown like a banana spoiling. And then a depression appeared, running the length of the fins, as if the fins were trying to divide but hadn't quite made it. Then they were separated.

The two fins had a matte finish and had turned an odd gangrene-looking purple-green, as if they were rotting. Over a period of three months the color lightened into an odd muddy gray color and then to her pale flesh color that matched her upper body. And then those two fins morphed into feet. Caroline no longer looked calm or serene in the pictures.

Her face was twisted in pain, or there were dark hollows under her eyes as if she'd endured pain. She'd lost weight, her skin tone had grown sallow and all the while she was pictured eating plates of fish and seaweed and drinking something in a tall dark thermos.

'They did it,' Alex said. 'They changed a mermaid to a full woman with gene therapy.' She checked the time stamps. 'And it only took three years of torture.'

Celeste wiped a tear off her cheek. 'How did she bear it

266 Esme Addison

without going mad? If it was me, I'd have so much hatred in my heart.'

They were both silent, processing what Caroline had gone through.

Then Alex leaned forward and tapped the screen. 'What's that?' She zoomed in on an item on the floor.

'Looks like beer bottles?' Celeste squinted at the image.

Alex nodded. It was a case of dark brown glass bottles. 'I don't understand. Who would be drinking beer in that environment?'

'I think I've seen enough,' Celeste said. 'There's one page left. I'm not sure I can bear to see her in pain anymore.' She looked away from the microfiche reader.

Alex sighed. 'I know, but we need to read everything.' She switched to the last slide. 'Look, it's just text. No images.' She looked at Celeste, who'd closed her eyes tightly. 'You can open your eyes. It's just . . .' She began reading. 'A recap of the proj—' She stopped talking. Her throat tightened.

Celeste opened one eye. And then another. 'What's wrong?'

Alex pointed to the screen. To the last sentence. She began to read. '*Project Oannes was documented in words and pictures by Lieutenant Jonah Fox, US Navy.*' The date was January 17, 1981, and his signature was scrawled under the name.

FORTY-FIVE

'Jonah was a horrible person.' Alex opened the car door and slid inside. 'And Caroline clearly had motive. I'm not sure where she's been all this time, but it looks like she came back set on revenge. And I'm not sure I blame her.'

'Agreed.' Celeste stepped into the car and closed the door. 'But the police have determined that someone else killed Jonah. And attacked her. Remember, she was found alongside Jonah. Assaulted.'

'But was she?' Alex asked, starting her car. 'Assaulted, I mean. I don't recall Dr Crow finding any signs of a recent attack. She was just passed out. Maybe she was exhausted from fighting with Jonah – he'd been on the phone with someone prior to him going to the beach. Maybe they were arguing. She lured him to the beach and killed him.'

'And her legs?'

'Aunt Lidia speculated she had some sort of chronic condition related to her bones and joints. And the tea she's been drinking may have helped her with the symptoms. Those beer bottles we saw in the image – really just dark glass bottles to prevent oxidation by the sun, same as we use for our essential oil blends and tinctures, and hermetically sealed to prevent spoiling – they must've held the drink in the thermos she had. And it's the same blend she's had Aunt Lidia make for her.'

Celeste pressed a palm over her mouth. 'What if Caroline somehow found Jonah and demanded he give her the herbal brew, like she needed it or she'd get sick and die? And when he refused, she killed him. Then pretended to be a victim on the beach?'

Alex thought back to Jonah's basement where he'd housed his beer. Mermaid Magic. The instructions like medicine. 'Jonah wasn't brewing a novelty beer for our mermaid festival. Or for the café at the aquarium. It was the medicine Caroline needed to keep her from getting sick. There were cases and cases of it, enough to last Caroline several months at least. Maybe a year even . . .'

Alex closed her eyes, thinking. 'Caroline was suffering from the side effects of the gene therapy forced upon her. Jonah had the medicine, which Spencer has been after for the past year, and now he's dead. I feel like we're missing something,' Alex said as she turned off Main Street.

Celeste pulled down the passenger mirror and checked her makeup. 'What can I do to help?'

Alex retrieved the folder of documents Jack had given her from her purse. 'Take a look at these. I haven't even had a chance to review them yet.'

On the third page, Celeste sucked in a breath.

'Found something?' Alex asked, turning at a light.

She held up a page. 'I found the RFP for Project Oannes. The name of the company who was awarded the contract: One guess.'

Alex stopped at a light, she turned to Celeste. 'No way. Not Leviathan . . .' She thought of the Sumerian idol Montgomery had on his desk and sighed. 'I guess all of the Sumerian names make sense . . .'

Celeste held up another page. 'Here's the budget. Signed off by someone at Leviathan. It's a scrawl, can't make it out. But he was paying the salary for Alasdair Frazier. The other members of the team have been redacted, but I'd guess they're Jonah Fox and Carson MacInnes.'

'And Montgomery wants the recipe . . .' Alex leaned forward, massaging her forehead with her palm. 'Montgomery bankrolled the study and had the government contract for the testing.' Eyes wide, she met Celeste's horrified gaze. 'If he needs the recipe, it's because they're going to try and find more women with the mermaid gene and reverse engineer them into mermaids. Jonah must've refused to give them the recipe for a second round of testing.'

Alex recalled the heated conversation Jonah had in her shop. The caller who found it hard to take no for an answer. Had that caller killed him when he refused to give up the recipe?

Celeste reached for Alex's hand and squeezed. 'We have to tell Jack.'

Alex shook her head. 'I'll call Kamila.'

'Right. I keep forgetting he's only pretending to be a cop.'

Alex's phone rang. It was Minka.

A Brew for Chaos 269

'I discovered something.' She hesitated, and her voice wavered. 'Only it doesn't make sense.'

Alex glanced at Celeste, who leaned forward, listening with interest. 'Hey, you're on speaker, and Celeste is with me.'

'Bring her.'

'Where are you?'

'The shop. In the backroom on Mom's computer. She has the VPN, so I thought it would be safer if anyone was tracking our IP address. Remember, you said I need to be somewhere safe, and Mom has the protective field over it, so—'

Alex and Celeste entered the shop, waved at Tanner, who operated the register, and went into the backroom where Minka was sitting in a makeshift office, really just a corner free of soap and candles with a small desk and chair and a desktop computer her aunt used for shop business.

Minka rose and grabbed Alex into a tight embrace.

Alex didn't hesitate. She hugged her back, remembering a time not that long ago when such a gesture had made her feel awkward. 'What's wrong? Are you okay?'

She shook her head, her brown curls flailing around her as she did so, then hugged Celeste. With a shuddering breath Minka fell back into her chair, a look of hopelessness on her face.

Alex pointed to the screen. 'You said you figured something out?'

She nodded, quiet for a moment. 'Not where I was taken. And not what I discovered the night I was abducted . . . something else.' She pointed to her screen. 'This is the software I used to track the dolphins I was reporting on.'

Alex looked at the screen. It was a satellite-like image of the ocean, the area extending beyond Bellamy Bay specifically. She could see different shades of blue and gray delineating the changes in depth. And occasionally a white dot would swim by.

Minka hovered over one and a set of numbers appeared. 'See this?' she asked, and Alex nodded. 'This is the number associated with each dolphin. If I click on the number' – she did so – 'it shows tracking analysis associated with the number going back a year.'

Alex read through the information. It showed the average

speed. Latitude and longitude updated every sixty minutes with additional analysis on their swim patterns. 'Okay. I don't know much about dolphin tracking, but it seems pretty par for the course, right?'

A pained look crossed Minka's face and she squeezed her eyes tight before opening them. 'Something kept bothering me, kept niggling in the back of my brain. So, I made an appointment, and I went to see the doctor again.'

'What did Dr Crow say? Are you okay? Do you feel all right?' Alex's worried gaze raked her cousin's face. Come to think of it, she did look rather pale with a sheen of sweat on her face, but Minka brushed her concerns away with a dismissive hand.

'I'm fine. I just said that so I could go back to his office – the same one you and I went into?' Alex nodded, confused about where Minka was going with this. She picked up her phone, typed the passcode and swiped the screen. 'I wanted to get a picture of this.' Minka held the phone up and Alex looked at the image, not understanding. 'Isn't that—' She stopped, shaking her head.

Minka nodded, swallowed with difficulty. 'The number on this' – she pointed to the image on her screen of the device removed from Caroline's neck – 'matches the format of the numbers here.' She pointed to the screen with the floating white dots. 'One letter. Three numbers. Two letters. One number.' She bit her bottom lip so hard a drop of blood appeared as Alex watched. 'It can't be a coincidence, can it?' she asked, her eyes on the screen, watching the dots move around. Some solo and some in groups. Some zipped around while others were more sluggish.

Alex shook her head as a sick feeling coiled in her stomach.

Minka covered her eyes with her hands and bowed her head, her voice full of tears. 'I don't think I've been tracking dolphins, Alex.'

Horrified, Alex stared at the screen of moving dots, remembering the image of Caroline in the tank. The tracker in her neck. Minka was right.

'No, they're not dolphins,' Alex agreed. 'They're mermaids.'

FORTY-SIX

'**M**ontgomery is a monster. And I've been helping him,' Minka said, her voice thick with tears. 'I'm complicit in the abuse of these women.'

She looked from Celeste to Alex, searching their eyes for condemnation. She didn't see it there. Only compassion and understanding. 'I'm no better than him. I mean, why did he hire me – me of all people? Is there really a dolphin project? Or is he just a sicko who thought it would be funny for a mermaid to track other mermaids?' A loud sob erupted from her lips as her face crumpled.

Celeste reached out and touched her hand. A stream of tranquility flowed from her fingers into Minka's palm. The room chilled, and the smell of ozone wrapped around them.

'Don't say that,' Alex said, her voice firm. 'You obviously figured this out once before. And this is why you were taken. You were trying to stop it.'

Celeste nodded, pulling her hand back with a gentle smile. 'You're okay.'

Minka nodded slowly, wiping her tears. 'If I did figure this out before, I would've called Pepper, and then gone straight to Montgomery. I didn't want to believe this about him. He really has been kind to me.' She closed her eyes, rubbing her temples. She opened them. 'But I must've told him, and he had me removed.' She shook her head slowly. 'But he wouldn't have been the one to actually take me. So who could've done it? And where was I taken?'

'Any memories coming back?' Celeste asked. She grabbed her hand and patted it reassuringly. 'Try. Try to remember.'

Minka closed her eyes, her face wrinkled in concentration. Then she opened them. 'Nothing. I've got nothing.'

'Let's try and heal her again,' Celeste said, voice determined. She grabbed Alex's hand. 'Now. Right now.'

Eyes shut, healing energy coiled around them, a shimmery

272   Esme Addison

halo of gold. Sweat appeared on Celeste's forehead. Alex's face flushed with color while Minka took deep calming breaths, allowing the healing to filter over.

A moment later it was over. Celeste opened her eyes, her hair wet and lying limply against her scalp. Alex looked the same.

'That Zombie machine is really powerful. I could literally feel Minka's mind fighting against us.'

Minka sighed. She looked pale, though her eyes shone brightly. More alert than before.

'Well,' Celeste said, 'do you remember anything?'

'I'm sorry, it's still really foggy. Very vague . . .' She closed her eyes then opened them. 'Wait.'

Alex leaned forward, hands on her knees. 'What is it? You remembered something, I can tell.'

'I'd been texting someone all night,' she said slowly. Then nodded. 'Yeah, I . . . was talking to a guy. He wanted to meet up and I told him I couldn't – not that night. I made an excuse, because we were going to try and heal Caroline . . .' She looked up, confused.

'What is it?' Celeste asked.

'Who was he?' Alex asked. 'Who were you talking to?'

Minka stared off into space, a smile playing on her lips. 'It was . . . Leith.' She turned to Alex and Celeste, her smile turning into a frown. 'Leith?'

'I've met him a few times. He seems like a nice guy. Really nice,' Alex said. She searched for her phone in her purse. 'He was the last person to speak with you before you were abducted?'

'I don't know. Maybe.'

'But you're not sure he was the one who took you?'

'I-I can't remember. But I don't think so – I mean, why would he?'

Alex dialed the bed and breakfast, and Mac answered on the second ring. She asked to speak with Leith and was told he was out playing golf.

'What do we know about him?' Celeste asked. 'I never met him.'

'Leith is the grandson of Forbes McDonald. And we know that Forbes came to town in the eighties under an assumed name, pretending to be a policeman, but was really a member of naval intelligence.' She frowned. 'I thought it was a coincidence that

A Brew for Chaos 273

Leith came here just as Jonah was killed and Caroline appeared . . . I spoke with him several times and thought I had a sense of who he was.'

She explained to them that Forbes was in failing health and came to town looking for some sort of closure and Leith had accompanied him on the trip. A last grandfather-grandson trip. 'I thought it was sweet,' she said, wondering if she'd gotten it all wrong.

'Is he really sick?' Celeste wanted to know.

Alex nodded. 'I read his aura. He's beyond sick.' Both Minka and Celeste stared at her.

'Yeah.' Minka gasped. 'You're coming into your own powers.' But then she looked thoughtful. 'If the granddad was really sick, then maybe Leith isn't involved. And it's just a coincidence.'

Like Zane leaving town at the same time Minka went missing? Alex thought to herself. And he still wasn't back. 'Leith *was* very concerned about his grandfather . . .' Alex said aloud but stopped. Now she wasn't so sure. She was beginning to think there were no such things as coincidences.

'We need to find Caroline,' Alex said, rising from her seat. 'She made us think she couldn't talk, and then she could. She said she couldn't remember anything, but I think she's lying. Why didn't she tell us she was an actual mermaid? A lot about her isn't adding up. I'm not sure she can be trusted.'

She grabbed her purse and slung it over her shoulder. 'She has a lot of explaining to do. Like what really happened on that beach and why she was there in the first place.'

Minka nodded. 'And where are those mermaids I've been tracking? And why is Montgomery surveilling them?'

'I think they might be a security force for the Navy,' Alex said slowly, but hoping she was wrong. Then told them what Tanner had shared with her on the subject.

Celeste looked at Minka, a question on her face. 'Let's say we do find them. Then what?'

'We have to help them, of course. It's too late for the victims of the Fisherman, but we can help them.' She pointed to the screen. 'Look at them. They're right there. We have to get those trackers removed and set them free back into the ocean. Who knows what is still being done to them.' Her eyes lit up. 'We

274   Esme Addison

thought that only the mermaid gene had survived through the centuries, but mermaids are real and are swimming out there. They're our sisters.'

'But where do we look?' Celeste pointed at the moving dots. 'Where are they going when they disappear? Where are they kept?'

Alex's brow furrowed. 'Let's update Aunt Lidia. Maybe she'll have some suggestions.'

Tanner entered the room, and Minka scrambled to shut the computer off like she had something to hide. Tanner's eyebrows shot up. 'Sorry to interrupt, but there's a customer. He's asking for Alex.' He looked at Minka then at Alex. 'Is she okay?'

Alex nodded. Smiled. 'I'll talk to him. Thank you.'

After he left, Alex placed her hand on Minka's shoulder. 'Go home. We'll figure this out.' She glanced at the now darkened screen as anger began to bubble deep within her. 'I promise.'

She followed Tanner into the shop and stopped when she saw Mac.

He dipped his chin. 'Can we talk?'

'Yeah.' She told Tanner she was going to step outside for five minutes, and Mac followed her to the street. 'Suddenly remembered something?' she asked, her tone sharp.

His cheeks reddened. 'It's not easy for me to talk. I'm not supposed to, okay? I've given my word, taken oaths . . . It's not something I take lightly.'

Main Street bustled with customers and across the street, city workers attempted to blow the orange, gold and red leaves off the sidewalks. The air was cool and smelled of cinnamon sticks from the local apple cider vendors on every corner.

Alex had forgotten to take a jacket with her and rubbed her hands together for warmth. 'I'm listening.'

He looked up and down the street, forever on guard for listening ears, it would seem. 'I have an M-Level security clearance. And that summer, the government was looking for a certain demographic of women for testing.'

'Do you know what marked this demographic?'

He shoved his hands in his pockets and stared straight ahead, eyes fixed on a city worker hanging gold and burgundy banners celebrating autumn from flag poles. 'I do.'

A Brew for Chaos   275

She gave him a sideways glance, wondering if he thought they were monsters like Jack did.

'Tell me.'

He swallowed slowly. 'A set of genetic markers that the US military found desirous.'

'And?' She turned to look at him then.

'There's a whole world of information behind this topic, Alex, nothing I can share with you on the street corner like this. But . . . about a year or so previous, the government had reached out to many women in this group, asking them to be part of a study, offering to pay them generously for their time. But there were complications.'

Alex saw that this conversation was genuinely difficult for him, and she sighed. 'Let's walk. I'll get you a sweet potato hand pie, okay?'

He nodded, and they began walking. And talking. 'Most women in the target group had no idea about their genetics and had to be educated on their own biology, which required time. And often once this was done, skepticism turned to resistance with the subjects either refusing to go further with the projects, wanting more money, threatening to go to the media . . . It was spinning out of control and a lot of time, money and resources was allocated to covering and cleaning up the mess.'

They stopped at a vendor and Alex asked for one hand pie and two sweet potato lattes. When they were ready, Mac surprised her by paying for them. They continued walking.

'What happened to the study?'

'It stalled for a time. And then it returned under a new name and new guidance.' He bit into his pie, a crispy brown semi-circle with tined edges and glistening with butter and brown sugar and cinnamon. 'I'd worked on the first iteration of the study. When it was above board and 100 per cent voluntary. I'd been a hospital corpsman in the Navy, like a medical tech. Taking blood, helping with medical tests and such . . . so I was working intimately with the subjects when it came time to testing.' He wiped crumbs from his mouth. 'The second time around, they brought in this guy, a real hard nose, ready to get results no matter what it took. And he told us the testing had become a black operation – absolutely no transparency, no senatorial oversight, no media gaze,

276 Esme Addison

nothing, as this was considered a priority for national security.' He paused to shove the rest of the pie in his mouth and swallow it down with coffee.

'This was a significant change from the first time when it was considered medical research for possible utilization in biological enhancements that could benefit our troops.' He wiped his hands on a napkin and tossed it and his empty cup into a nearby trashcan. 'Originally, I felt good about what I was doing. I thought I would be a part of a project that would help our armed forces.

'Then it changed to trying to understand the enemy and turning their abilities against them. Or trying to figure out how to contain them . . . There was a complete 360 in how we spoke about the subjects, a whole type of indoctrination for the new staff brought into the project. I didn't like it. It was getting ugly, with the people in charge dehumanizing the subjects. And these were women you'd see on the street or in the shops. I no longer wanted any part of it, and I not only left the project but got out of service. But they found me anyway here in Bellamy Bay and told me I had to help them or else.'

'Or what?'

'You name it. They threatened me. Said they would hurt my mother. Burn down the B&B . . .' He shrugged helplessly. 'I had no choice.'

'What were you doing for them?'

'They'd created a quick blood test to confirm that the subject had the markers. When they brought in a new test subject, I had to do the test and confirm the results before they took them to the testing site. And I—' He paused to gather his courage. 'Sometimes I had to go to the testing facility to help with medical situations. The man in charge was a doctor, but he occasionally needed help.'

'Jesus, Mac,' Alex said, voice rising in anger. She took a step away from him. 'You're complicit.' She lowered her voice, but it was no less harsh. 'You're an accessory to those women's deaths.'

'No,' he whispered, grabbing her arm. 'You don't understand.'

She glared at his hand on her arm and yanked it away.

He stepped backwards, both hands up. 'Hey, hey, just trying to get your attention.'

She took a breath. 'You're no better than them. Maybe you

did kill Jonah.' She looked up and down the street as if she wanted to sprint away from him.

'Listen. Sacrifices had to be made.'

'Sacrifices,' she hissed back. *Jack. Forbes. And now him?* 'Why does everyone keep saying that?'

'Because it's true. I did what I had to do to save the people I cared about.' He closed his eyes, and he blinked away tears. 'Please listen.'

Alex stared at him, jaw clenched. 'I'm listening. You've got two seconds.'

He held up both palms. 'Okay, okay.' He took a steadying breath. 'One day, I accidentally saw the list of the subjects that were going to be taken.'

The list Neve had warned her about before she died, Alex thought with a twinge of regret. The list of names Dylan's grandfather had shared with the government. 'And?' she prompted, impatiently.

'Your mother was on the list.'

She blinked. 'What?'

He nodded. 'And your Aunt Lidia. And Daphne and her mother . . .' He took a step closer to her. 'Do you understand what I'm saying?'

'No,' she whispered. 'I don't.'

'I made a deal. That day. I told them I'd do what they wanted but they had to keep hands off the people I knew from town and cared about.' He gently grabbed both her hands and leaned down so he could see into her eyes. 'I sacrificed others so I could keep your family safe.'

'Oh,' Alex said.

He took her by the arm and guided her to a nearby bench. 'I went to school with Lidia, I was a couple years ahead of her, but we were always good friends. I didn't know your mother that well, but I knew she was your aunt's sister, a Sobieski. I knew Daphne's older brother; we hung out and that's how I became familiar with her and her mother.' He shook his head slowly. 'I saw those names on that list, and I thought there's no way I can let what is happening to these other women happen to them.

'And I know it was wrong. But I couldn't stop it. If I'd taken one wrong step, they would've harmed someone I cared about. I could not go against the military, the Department of Defense, the US government. I could only do what I could do in my very small way.'

Tears ran down Alex's face. 'I'm so sorry, Mac. I had no idea.'

'How could you? And you weren't supposed to know.'

She wiped the tears from her eyes. 'But you do know. And you don't think we're monsters . . .' She thought of Jack and everything he'd said about those like her.

'Of course not. I've grown up in this town. I know Bellamy Bay is not like other places, that we've got people different from others and yet, this is one of the best places to live. I traveled the world when I was in the Navy, and I always looked forward to coming home. To Bellamy Bay. Good, decent people. Kind. Generous. Honest . . . We're all the same here. And this ugliness that has set upon our town, it eats me up knowing the part I've played in it. And knowing the cancer that was here is still here and I don't know what I can do about it.'

She reached for his hand, squeezed it. 'You've done enough. You've done everything.'

'I wish I could've done more.'

'And to go through the humiliation of being questioned for the actions of those . . . they're the monsters, right?'

'Yeah,' he said quietly. 'That's the rub right there.'

'You're not a killer. And you didn't kill Jonah.' She tried to smile. 'Though I bet you're not sad he's gone.'

'Haven't shed a tear. You're right about that.'

They stood, and Alex hugged him, right there on the street and surprising the heck out of Mac. 'Thank you. Thank you for saving my family. Can I tell them what you did for them?'

'No.' He shook his head. 'Please don't. Let this ugliness die with me if it can.'

'Okay. Well, I'm going to think about how I can repay you for what you've done.'

He chuckled. 'Free joint cream for life?'

'Absolutely.' She grinned and they began walking back to the shop in silence. When they neared Botanika, Alex turned to him. 'You were at the testing facility. Can you tell me how to find it?'

A Brew for Chaos 279

'Why would you need to go there? The project ended decades ago. Nothing we can do to help those poor women now.'

Alex thought of the white dots moving on Minka's screen. No matter how difficult, she had to try and find them. 'Even so. Anything you can tell me would be helpful.'

'A wrap was placed over my head when we traveled to the testing, and I was knocked out with a sedative – the same one I gave the women.' He ducked his head, embarrassed. 'I'd just wake up there.'

'And the facility, what can you tell me about it? You must remember something,' Alex insisted.

Mac squinted his eyes, trying to recall. 'Nothing really . . . Once I thought I might try to save a girl, and I pretended to give myself the sedative. Head wrap was on, and I pretended to be asleep. But I changed my mind. There was always armed security around.' He averted his eyes. 'Lost my courage, I'm ashamed to say. But towards the end of the ride, the road got bumpy.'

'Bumpy?'

'Yeah, like we were on a dirt path or a road that wasn't paved. And I think we used a tunnel. I recall it was real hot and humid in there, right before we reached the facility.'

'What areas around here are unpaved? And where are there tunnels?'

'That's the thing. It's all paved. Wouldn't be good for tourism if we had bad roads. The mayor saw to that when he first came to office. And as far as tunnels? I think the Shashanoke tribe may have had tunnels, but it's all myth at this point.' A look of regret flashed across his face. 'You probably heard I had a drinking problem when I was younger?'

Alex nodded.

'This is why. I couldn't live with what I'd done. Or rather what I didn't do. It's why I started going to church, getting involved with the ministry. I was trying to do better, be the man my mother could be proud of . . . Been sober for over thirty years.'

'That's wonderful.' Alex smiled at him, sad for what he'd gone through. 'Why do you think they decided to make you the patsy for this operation?'

He barked a laugh. 'Because I was always questioning my orders. They were afraid I was a liability. It was a punishment.'

She nodded. 'Last question. Who helped move the girls?'

He looked up and down the street like he was afraid to be seen talking to Alex. 'I gotta go.'

'You're still afraid of the Fisherman? Why can't you tell me who he is?'

Just then, a car honked on the street and Alex turned to look.

When she turned back to thank him, he'd disappeared into the crowd.

FORTY-SEVEN

Lidia flipped over a sizzling potato cake while Alex brought her up to date on everything except what Mac had done for their family. The smell of fried potato and onion filled the kitchen, causing Alex's stomach to rumble. It had been a while, she realized, since she'd eaten.

'So, we have Alasdair Frazier running the testing. Jonah was photographing and documenting, and Mac was the medical tech on the project. What am I missing?'

'Well, for starters,' Lidia pointed out, 'who was bankrolling everything?'

'One guess.' Alex rolled her eyes.

'Montgomery?' Lidia's face twisted into a disagreeable expression. When Alex nodded, she continued. 'I should've known he was involved.'

'We're still missing a crucial piece of the team. How did they coerce the women from their homes and schools and work? First they had to get them to the beach. And then somehow to this super-secret testing facility,' Alex mused aloud.

'One more member of the team?' Lidia plated one cake on a platter already piled high, covered it with foil and then added sliced kielbasa to the pan. 'Best way to catch a woman is with another woman.'

Alex gasped. 'Right?'

Her aunt nodded. 'Friendly face. A kind word. Next thing you know, you're kidnapped.'

'Spencer was hanging out with them when she was in college. She dated Jonah. Maybe she's the fourth member of the crew.'

'I didn't know her,' Lidia responded. 'Hard to say if she was capable of such.'

Alex watched as Lidia reached for another onion, set it in the center of the chopping block then minced it within an inch of its life. 'And then, there's still the question of the mermaids – if they *are* mermaids. I'm really hoping Minka is wrong and they're dolphins.' She swallowed. 'Where are they?'

The knife stilled and Lidia turned to Alex. 'Don't you have that information? If the mermaids are being tracked, isn't it as simple as following them and seeing where they go?'

Alex nodded. 'You'd think. But that was the initial issue – at least that's what Minka thought was the issue. When the dolphins – or mermaids' – Alex shook her head, still trying to understand that those dots could actually be real live mermaids – 'would swim to a certain area, the tracker would stop working.'

'Like where they are actually being kept is . . . cloaked?' Lidia raised an eyebrow, then picked up a saltshaker and began seasoning the batter.

Alex nodded slowly. 'Like how you cloaked this house and the shop, which prevents Jack from knowing we're practicing magic.'

Lidia set the shaker down and propped a hand on her hip. 'Is that so?'

Alex nodded. 'Saved our bacon. I think I know who can help me with this. I'll call Dylan. But first . . .' She looked around the kitchen. 'I need to speak to Caroline. I don't think she's been honest with us.'

'Really? That poor girl.'

Alex filled her in on Project Oannes.

'There's so much I'd like to ask her. If Jonah was the one taking pictures and documenting the project, she must've really hated him . . . enough to kill him. Have we been harboring a killer all this time?' Lidia wiped her hands on a towel. 'I'll go get her. I agreed to bring her into this house, it's my responsibility to find out what's going on with her.'

Alex watched her go, wondering how Caroline could possibly spin the situation.

A few minutes later, Alex heard footsteps on the second floor. Then down the stairs. Lidia ran back into the kitchen. 'Have you seen Caroline? Did she go into the gardens?'

'I don't think so. Is she not in her room?'

Lidia looked concerned. 'You check outside, and I'll check the rest of the first floor.'

They reconvened a few minutes later. 'She's not here,' Lidia said. 'And there's no note. We all agreed she wouldn't leave the house for her own safety, and she said she didn't *want* to go anywhere because she was afraid that whoever assaulted her might try again.' She moaned. 'This is my fault. I'm the one who left her alone. But she was resting in the library, and right before you got here, I just ran to the post office to ship off some online orders. I couldn't have been gone more than twenty-five minutes.'

'It's okay, Aunt Lidia, maybe she—'

Alex's phone rang.

It was Jack.

His mother was missing, and he wanted to know if she was with them.

FORTY-EIGHT

J ack arrived a few minutes later, the siren on his truck blaring as he parked.

Alex opened the front door, and he ran up the stairs two at a time, eyes wild. 'How can she not be here?' he said when he stepped inside.

Lidia frowned at him, but Alex shot her a look then telepathed a message. *Be patient, his mother may be missing.* She went to him and reached for his hands. 'I understand you're worried. Might she have just gone for a walk?'

He jerked his hands away from her and held up a piece of paper. It trembled in his shaking hands, and he pushed it under her nose. 'Not after seeing this. No.'

Alex gently removed the paper from his hands and read it.

> *Jack,*
> *Don't worry. I've gone with a friend to see the mermaids.*
> *Mama*

Heat crept over her face, and she felt sweat beading on her forehead. *Oh no.* She looked up from the paper and into his worried eyes.

'This is your doing. I know it is.' His chest heaved and his face was flushed. 'You're the only one she's spent time with, you took her out. Who did she meet? Where could she have gone?' His voice rose with each question. 'What have you done?'

Alex glanced at her aunt, worried she'd fling Jack against the wall with the flick of her hand, but Lidia only glared at him, her arms tightly crossed at her chest.

'Calm down, Jack. We'll find her. Are the police looking for her?'

'Of course they are. There's a search team with dogs in my neighborhood. And an APB and a Silver Alert, but what did you do? When you brought her here?' His eyes darted around the house. 'What happened? I've kept her safe for years, and then a few weeks with you and—' He suddenly sank into a chair behind him, bowed his head and covered his face with his palms.

Lidia's scowl softened. Slightly. 'I'll get some tea.'

Alex nodded, knowing it would be an extra-large glass of their Calm Down blend. She sat down beside him, giving herself a few moments to gather her thoughts. 'Our Jane Doe is missing too.'

He raised his head. 'And?'

'I'm guessing that your mother is with her.'

He sat up then. 'Why would you think that?'

She swallowed. 'There's some things you need to know about our Jane Doe – and about your mother.'

Lidia entered the room then and handed Jack the glass.

He took it then raised it up to the light and inspected it. 'What's in it?'

Lidia rolled her eyes and planted a hand on her hip. 'Arsenic.'

Alex playfully nudged his leg with her knee. 'She's yanking your chain. It's just lavender. And chamomile.' That wasn't quite true, but he didn't need to know that. And hopefully he'd recognize two of the most popular and innocuous herbs.

He nodded slowly. 'Okay.' Then drank the entire cup in several large gulps.

Alex knew the waves of calm would wash over him immediately, and she saw him blink several times as if he was fighting sleep and then settled into the frequency of calmness and tranquility the enchanted blend provided.

And then she told him about his mother.

When she was done telling him everything except that Caroline was actually a mermaid, he looked relieved. Exhausted but relieved.

'So you think someone working on this project did something to her . . . not a PAC?'

'That's right.'

He stared at the wall in front of him, his gaze slightly unfocused. 'I don't know what to think anymore.'

Despite her anger at him for lying to her, betraying her, deceiving her, she still cared for him. And although she hadn't known her long, she already loved his mother. 'Let us help you find your mother. Okay?' She looked at her aunt, who glared at Jack, a mixture of anger and pity on her face. She and Alex were both seeing another side to him. A son who loved his mother. Needed her. Was afraid for her. And the last bit of anger in both of them melted away.

Lidia's expression softened and she uncrossed her arms. 'I was friends with your mother in college, Jack.'

He stood, wiped his eyes, blinking as if he'd come out of a dream state. And frowned. But Lidia and Alex smiled back.

He reluctantly returned the gesture, then sighed. 'Where do we start?'

'We have to figure out where the testing took place. Mac said the drive to the testing facility was bumpy. That there might be a tunnel. It's the only thing he remembered . . .' She paused. 'Wait . . . I discovered that one of the renovation projects Montgomery funded for the town when they agreed to hire Jonah was to pave roads around the Maritime Forest.'

'I remember that,' Lidia volunteered. 'They used to be dirt roads that led to the hiking trails. It got really bad. Especially when it rained. Sinkholes and the like.'

'So . . . let's say it was a road around the forest that led to a tunnel. Who would know about tunnels around here?'

Lidia shook her head. 'Those tunnels are the property of the Shashanoke tribe.'

'There's a map of the tunnels at the history museum as part of their exhibit on their history in the area,' Alex said. 'I wonder if the exhibit is also online?'

Lidia had already gone to get her laptop. When she returned, she went to the museum website and began a search. She found the map and Jack and Alex peered over her shoulder, waiting for it to appear.

The map, a black and white depiction of the town, showed numerous bisecting tunnels that ran along the coastline and aligned with many of the streets in the downtown area.

'Unbelievable,' Lidia murmured. 'I had no idea they were so extensive.'

'And for what purpose?' Jack said. 'These are perfect for hiding criminal activity. They should be closed.'

A Brew for Chaos

Alex scowled at him. 'Or studied for their historical value?' She returned to the screen. 'We're looking for a tunnel that could lead to a location that could hide secret testing.'

Lidia shook her head, pointing to the image. 'I don't know. This one leads to the town hall. This one leads to the library.' She reached for her phone. 'Mayor Bellamy knows the history of the town. Let's see if he can help.'

Lidia waited for the call to be answered, while Jack and Alex looked at each other. Lidia explained the situation and what they were looking for, then asked if she could put him on speaker phone.

'Pepper will hate she missed the opportunity to cover this story,' the mayor said.

'Where is she?' Alex asked.

'Quick trip to Atlanta. An exec at the cable channel HQ wanted to see her in person. I suggest you check the aquarium.'

Alex swallowed slowly. 'The aquarium? But . . . It's open to the public. It would be impossible to—'

'There is a massive underwater aquarium on the bottom floor that hasn't been used since . . . I don't know when. It runs the length of the first floor, which has to be at least a hundred feet? Eighty feet in width and about forty feet deep. It was quite something when it was first built, but there was water damage after a hurricane and the town couldn't afford to both repair the underwater aquarium and manage the one on top, so it went into a state of disrepair for ten or twenty years.

'But then my father who was the mayor at that time reached out to the military to see if they wanted to use the tank for deep sea training for their troops. A deal was reached, and they covered the repairs and began using it for a time, and then I guess they stopped. Or at least I didn't hear anything about it.'

Alex was on her phone swiping through screens, and then she gasped. Looked at Jack and her aunt, then began reading. '*The Bellamy Bay Aquarium was originally built in 1947, designed to be a four-floor aquarium with the lowest level an exhibit of natural beauty and splendor. Existing tunnels and sea caves created by the Shashanoke tribe were utilized to create aquarium exhibits that ran underground with a tunnel system that leads to the bay.*'

288   Esme Addison

'That's correct,' the mayor said. 'Because the aquarium is located near the coastline, there's a level beneath the basement that was supposed to be part of the aquarium, completely created from the tunnels and caverns underneath. Exhibit venues carved from the very earth. Natural formations of coral, salt caves. I've never been there, but I heard it was beautiful.

'The military commandeered the bottom half of the aquarium for their own use, the tunnels were sealed, and the exhibits were closed off to the general public.'

Lidia thanked Oswald and ended the call.

'That has to be it,' Jack said. 'I'm calling the station—'

'No. Wait,' Alex said. 'If we come in with sirens blazing, a parade of patrol cars and SWAT vehicles, something could happen to your mother before we find them. I have a better idea.'

FORTY-NINE

Alex made a few calls, gathering as much firepower as she could. Both figuratively and magically.

They arrived in separate cars, and at different times over the course of two hours. All seeming to be visitors to the aquarium.

All except Minka, who returned to her office for work. She waved to the security guard on her way in, reached her office and settled at her desk. Once in she was able to find a map of the aquarium on the work intranet and send it to Alex, who passed it along to Harrison.

Celeste arrived with Kamila, who appeared to have showed up to have lunch with her sister. But first she stopped by the security office to chat up Gus and discovered that Leviathan had a private security force of which he was not a part of. He and two other retired veterans from the Vietnam War patrolled the main aquarium, but a younger, leaner detail guarded basement level for reasons he never quite understood. Since there was nothing down there but chemicals.

Alex and Jack arrived, bought two tickets and began touring the aquarium.

And then Dylan arrived with Harrison. They strolled through the enclosed park while Harrison noted all of the security cameras, hidden and in plain sight.

Lastly, when Kamila was able to confirm that four security guards patrolled the basement floor, four young men who all happened to be former Marine Raiders turned armed security guards at Wesley arrived. They were dressed casually in jeans and t-shirts for the day with backpacks filled with non-lethal weapons. One more man, a friend of the other four, stayed behind in his car, playing a game on his phone but keeping an eye on the parking lot and any visitors who may be of interest.

Alex held Jack's hand as they walked around, scouting for doors leading to the basement floor. Hoping to confirm the map

Minka had sent was accurate and up to date. She worried that she may have to use magic in front of Jack to rescue his mother.

While Kamila and Celeste discussed the best donuts in town with the security guard, Harrison, using an app on his phone, had hacked into the security camera network and replaced the live feed with a static hallway scene. Alex and Jack contrived a lovers' spat that caught the attention of the guard, who left his office to talk to the lovebirds. When he left with Kamila and Celeste still hovering at the entrance, Kamila searched his desk and found a stack of key cards to open the basement doors.

She passed Harrison in the hallway and slipped the cards into his hand without anyone being the wiser. Then joined Minka in her office.

'I knew there was a basement with the wreckage of an old aquarium and cleaning materials,' Minka was saying to Celeste and Kamila. 'But never thought to go down there.'

'Maybe you already have been,' Celeste pointed out. 'We think that's where you were kept.'

'But why was I wet, and found at the Maritime Forest?'

Kamila shrugged. 'Maybe the tunnels cut across the entire town and end up at the beach. Or maybe they just left you there to confuse you and throw anyone off the scent of the real location.'

Alex had taken pictures of all of the basement-level entrances and texted them to the team, and Dylan, Harrison and his men were positioning around them.

When they were ready, Alex established a telepathic group chat as it were, linking up to her cousins and Dylan so they could communicate incognito. When the former special forces Marines were in place by each door, Bluetooth-enabled earpieces in place, and a second confirmation assured that Gus was eating fried peanuts, drinking a Pepsi and staring at a security feed hacked to reflect a fake status quo, each former Marine used their key cards to open the doors.

They retrieved weapons from their backpacks and slid into the passageways, notifying Harrison in whispered tones when the coast was clear.

One of the men, Jones, with short curly hair and a green t-shirt,

A Brew for Chaos 291

spotted a guard walking down a dark hall. 'First hostile spotted. He's by himself and armed.'

Harrison, who was pretending to gaze at a swordfish swimming by, spoke discreetly. 'Jones, confirm no one else is around, and take him out.'

'Roger that.'

As directed, Jones shot the guard right in the larynx with an Octodart, assuring he wouldn't make a sound. The short, stocky man dressed in a black shirt, pants and boots with a knife strapped to his thigh and a pistol on his waist band slapped at his throat before falling to the ground. Jones approached him quiet as a cat, grabbed his arms and dragged him out of sight.

One by one, each of Harrison's men disabled the aquarium's security guards.

When the first floor was secure, Harrison and Dylan entered the basement with Dylan sending a telepathic message for everyone to join them. When Alex received her message, she pretended to receive a text for Jack's benefit and told him it was time to go.

One by one they made their way to the entrance and slipped inside.

FIFTY

Alex looked around the large space. It was dark but lit with bioluminescent strands of seaweed draped across the cavern's ceiling. The floor crafted from limestone was spotless, buffed to a high shine, and anyone looking down could've seen their reflection in the tile.

'It smells like the beach,' Jack said, squinting into the dark. 'But I can't see a thing.' He turned on the flashlight on his cell phone and held it up.

The smell of sea salt was strong in the underground aquarium, and as the group moved around, their feet created echoing sounds.

Alex went to Dylan. 'What do you think?'

He shook his head. 'Hard to say. Is there an aquarium down here? Is it filled with water?' His cell phone flashlight only illuminated several yards around him.

'Maybe there are offices down here. Locked rooms.' She shook her head. 'Where *are* they?'

Kamila turned to Minka. 'Anything look familiar?'

She shook her head. 'No, sorry . . .' But then she began to walk forward into the darkness.

Harrison instructed his men to fan out with flashlights and report what they found. He turned to a man with a crew cut. 'Bosko, see if you can find lights or a dimmer, anything to increase our visual. They had to figure out a way to bring electricity down here.'

'Yes, sir.'

'Guys,' Minka called out, an odd tone to her voice. 'I found something.'

Everyone clustered around her.

'What is it?' Kamila asked, voice rising with excitement.

Minka's palms were pressed against a glass wall. They hadn't been able to see it because of the darkness, but the glass was there, and it was warm. 'There's something in here. Life. I can sense it.'

A Brew for Chaos 293

Alex glanced at Jack in the darkness, hoping he didn't hear anything strange in Minka's words, but he only walked forward to stand beside her.

Harrison touched his earpiece. 'Heads up, one of the team has found a panel of light switches.'

There was the static sound of lights being turned on, and then the aquarium was lit from within.

'It's beautiful,' Kamila said, her words breathy and reverent.

The aquarium approximated the ocean floor with multi-colored plant life waving on the current. Schools of tiny brightly colored fish floated. Mountains of neon-colored coral accented the sandy floor.

'There's a baby turtle.' Celeste gasped in delight, and Harrison turned to look at her with a hint of a smile on his lips before returning to his men.

'Find anything else?'

Jones nodded. 'Yes, sir. Couple of locked rooms. A few were open. Storage closets. Normal office stuff.'

Minka was mesmerized as a bloom of jellyfish drifted by. 'All of this has been down here . . . and I never knew. It's so beautiful.' She turned to the group, who could now see each other illuminated by the lights inside the aquarium. 'But I don't see . . .'

Alex took a step towards the aquarium, pressing her palms against the glass. She searched the farthest reaches of the water, until she saw a brightly colored fish, yellow and purple, flitting by. She reached out to it with her mind, not sure if it would work, and asked it to come to her.

A moment later she opened her eyes, and it was floating before her.

It worked.

A fluttery feeling of elation filled her chest, and she giggled like a little girl, turning to Kamila and Minka. *I told it to come to me and it did.*

You can talk to fish, Minka telepathed, a look of pride lighting up her face.

Jack moved to her side, his scowl evident in the bioluminescent light. 'What are you doing? We need to figure out if my mother's down here.'

She ignored him and returned to the fish, whose flat, dull black eyes belied its intelligence. She felt a little silly, but . . . *Do you know what a mermaid is?*

Her mind was open, clear, and she knew all the Magicals around could hear her. That Jack was watching her. But she didn't care . . . An image came to her mind, a fuzzy image of the water with vague bright colors in the distance. And then there was a feeling of coldness, numbness. She blinked. The fish was showing her its underwater world through its eyes.

Then she saw the same image zoomed in, everything coming into focus with various types of sea creatures drifting by. The fish, Alex realized, was showing her different types of creatures it came in contact with.

She understood and tried to recall images of mermaids, finally conjuring the images she'd seen in movies.

The little fish appeared to wag its tail and did several loops.

'It looks excited,' Kamila observed, her tone wry.

She could feel the weight of Jack's stare on her. 'What are you doing?'

'Leave her alone, Jack,' Dylan said.

Jack squinted, gazing at the people around him, a look of suspicion casting his features into shadows.

The fish did a twirl and then disappeared into the depths of the waters. Alex took a step backwards, not sure what had just happened. Had she truly communicated with the fish through images or imagined it? She stared into the water as a myriad of sea creatures moved in front of her. A few moments passed, and she wondered what she was waiting for.

Sighing, she looked at Jack, whose face was pinched with a mixture of anger and fear.

She turned to look at the group. 'I'm sorry. Maybe I've led you all on a goose chase.' She ran a hand over her hair. 'There's nothing down here . . .' She moved away from the glass, a sinking feeling in her chest.

Then she heard a gasp. It was Celeste. 'Alex, wait . . .'

'Oh my God . . .' Kamila breathed, her voice low and awe-struck.

Alex felt a hand on her arm. It was Dylan. His voice was low and in her ear. 'I think it worked, darling. Whatever you did . . . it worked.'

FIFTY-ONE

Her back to the aquarium, Alex looked at the faces around her.

They were all staring at the aquarium, eyes wide, mouths open. The young men had silly grins on their faces, while Minka and Celeste looked as if angels were descending from heaven. Kamila stood next to Harrison, a puzzled look on her face, while Dylan couldn't stop smiling.

She found Jack, his posture stiff, and his features twisted into a mask of so many different emotions. Fear, anger, disgust . . .

Afraid to look but unable to stop herself, Alex turned around and gazed into the aquarium.

She blinked several times, not sure she was seeing what she was seeing. But she was, and when it registered . . . The muscles in her face slackened and her mouth fell open. The ocean tank was filled with mermaids as far as the eye could see. Creatures with the heads and torsos of women and the lower half of a fish.

Their hair was a rainbow of colors. Not just black, brown, red and blonde, but varying shades of blue, green, purple and yellow. Their skin tones reflected the humans above ground, but there were also women with pastel shades of blue, green, pink and purple skin, and deeper hues of teal, mossy green, dusty rose and burgundy.

Many were bare-chested, but some wore scraps of seaweed, pearls and shells as decorative tops. Their hair was straight, wavy, afro-curly and braided in so many intricate styles, studded with pearls, coral and shells.

Their fins were varying colors with a few standing out for having muted shades of silver, but the majority of them glistened with iridescent shimmer. No wonder Minka loved glitter.

Alex went to the glass, her palms pressed against it. Her nose too, like a child looking into a candy store. 'I can't believe it.' Tears came to her eyes. 'They're real. They're real . . .' Her vision blurred, and she wiped at her eyes as Minka, Kamila and Celeste crowded around her.

'Ho-ly cow . . .' Jones murmured to the other guys. 'Now we know what the M in M-Class security clearance is for.'

'You're the ones I've been talking to,' Minka murmured through the glass. 'Telling me about the pretty pearls you found . . . And you're the ones that went silent.'

She turned to the group. 'They must all have trackers in them. They are who I was tracking.' She whirled around. 'I'm so sorry. I thought you were dolphins.' Tears splashed down her cheeks. 'How do we get them out of here?' Her gaze went to Dylan. 'What can we do?'

Jack scowled at them. 'Have you all gone mad?' His voice rose in the echo chamber, his words ricocheting around them. 'Why are you all swooning over these monsters?'

Dylan searched the area, ignoring his outburst. 'There must be a tunnel connected to the aquarium with access to the sea that allows the mermaids to swim in and out.'

Jack exhaled loudly, searching the darkness.

'There is.' Harrison held up his phone. 'Look here on the map.'

Dylan studied the image, while Jack grew more agitated.

'Whoever snatched Minka just brought her down here?' Kamila said, anger hardening her voice. 'We were looking everywhere for her . . . And she was right here the whole time.'

'And I must've been sent through the tunnel back to the ocean when they let me go.' She shrugged. 'I guess.'

'But if they can swim out, why would they return?' Celeste asked, her eyes pinned to the mermaids floating in front of them.

'It's because of their trackers,' called out a voice from behind. Her voice echoed in the room around them.

It was Caroline, and she had her arm tightly looped around Maisie Frazier's waist.

FIFTY-TWO

'There's a device in the tracker that acts as a remote control and returns them to this place. To their prison.' Caroline glared at the group. 'And since they've gone operational, their telepathic abilities have been restricted to a Mer frequency only.' She gave Minka a pointed look. 'Blocked to all other interference.'

Jack lunged forward. 'Mom.'

'Not so fast,' Caroline warned, her voice low.

But Maisie's face lit up. 'Jackie, what are you doing here?'

Minka interrupted before he could speak. 'Operational?'

Caroline nodded. 'They've been going out on patrols, doing security work for the Navy in international waters.'

Jack took a deep breath and tried to control his emotions and his body. 'Mom, are you okay?' His fists were clenched at his sides, his eyes locked on hers.

'Of course I am. I'm with Caroline. She's my friend from college.' Her voice was warm, and a secretive look came over her face. 'I told you I saw a mermaid, but you didn't believe me.'

Jack's gaze slowly moved to Caroline's face. 'You're a mermaid?' His gaze went to her legs and back to her face. 'I don't understand.'

Her laugh was sharp. 'Confusing, right? I was tortured into human form.'

Jack's eyes widened as apprehension dawned on him. 'The testing? That's what they were doing?'

She nodded as tears filled her eyes. But she wiped them away, replacing the emotion with anger.

'That's why I couldn't find you in any of our databanks . . .' He softened his stance and tried to smile, nodding encouragingly to his mother. 'If you're her friend, is she free to leave?'

Caroline looked at Maisie and they exchanged grins. 'Not sure she wants to leave, Jack. You've kept her hidden and locked away.' She pointed to the aquarium. 'Like these ladies here.'

298   Esme Addison

The mermaids, all fifty or so of them, were watching from behind the glass. With their multi-colored hair flowing on the current and their tails occasionally wiggling as they treaded water.

Caroline mock frowned. 'And you call yourself a good son.'

Alex saw fear and anger war on his face as he tried to figure out the best way to proceed. 'I *am* a good son. The best son. I've cared for her, loved her, protected her from you.' And just as quick, all compassion bled from his face, replaced with more fear. More anger. 'You did this to her.' He took a step forward, and Caroline raised her hand. Electricity sizzled from her fingertips, crackling in the air.

'What the—' Jack, skittish with adrenaline, leaped back.

The mermaids in the tank jostled with activity. Several pressed their hands against the glass, bubbles floating from their mouths like they were talking or making sounds.

Maisie turned to her, mild alarm registering in her eyes. 'Caroline, you don't need to do that.' She touched the raised arm and gently pressed it down.

Even so, the group collectively took a step back, while Harrison searched for tactical weaknesses. His men looked at him, and he gave them a slight nod then whispered in his comm for them to stand by for instructions.

Alex's breath caught in her throat. 'You killed Jonah. You electrocuted him . . .' She paused, trying to make sense of it. 'Then what? Laid down beside him and pretended like you were a victim when you heard someone coming?'

Caroline's lips twisted into a sneer. 'That man watched my torture for years. *Years.* And did nothing about it. Just snapped pictures and wrote things down while my fin was turned to this.' She pointed to her legs. Her eyes flashed in anger. 'He got what he deserved.'

A low vibration emitted from the tank, an empathetic guttural sound. Some of the mermaids slapped the glass with their hands while others angrily swished their tails.

Maisie's eyes widened. 'You look different from when I first saw you, but you're still lovely.' She looked to her son. 'Her tail was the color of a lemon-lime soda. With sparkles. So pretty.'

For a moment, Caroline's face softened when she looked at Maisie and she pressed her forehead against her own. 'And that's

why I came for you, Margaret. You're the truest friend I ever had.'
A tear ran down her face. 'And when I found out you were alive,
here in Bellamy Bay, I knew I had to find you. Help you . . .'

Jack had inched closer when Caroline looked away. 'Help her
how? You're a monster. You did something to her.'

Caroline screeched like a wild animal and flung her hand at
him, a wave of electricity barely missing him when he jumped
out of the way. 'I'm not the monster.'

The aquarium vibrated with noise, the mermaids moving in a
frenzy.

She looked at the group, her gaze falling on Bosko, whose
right hand hovered at his gun belt. 'Why are you afraid of me?
What have I done?'

'You're crazy,' he said and turned to Harrison. 'Sir, we need
to do something before someone gets hurt.' Bosko twitched his
hand, but before he could reach for his gun, Caroline zapped
him with a bolt of electricity, just like an eel would.

He cried out in pain as the bolt grazed his arm, and he fell to
the floor, jerking with convulsions. The smell of singed flesh
filled the air, and Jones fell to his knees, checking his friend's
vitals.

Harrison stepped forward, hands out in a gesture of submis-
siveness. 'Okay, okay . . . let's all calm down. No one else gets
hurt. Caroline, we don't think you're a monster. You're among
friends here.' He nodded towards Alex and Minka, who'd gone
to the injured man.

Kneeling over Bosko, Minka waved her hands over his burned
arm, allowing waves of healing energy to emit from her palms
and redirect the flow of electrical pulses in his body which quelled
the convulsion.

'The Sobieskis took you in,' Harrison continued. 'Healed you.
We're here to help, not harm you.'

Minka laid her hands on his chest and sent a low frequency
of energy through his body to relax his muscles. She looked at
Jones. 'He'll be okay. His arm and chest will be sore, but he'll
live.'

Jones stared at her, in awe of her healing ability and also her
beauty. 'Thank you,' he whispered. 'You just saved my best
friend's life.'

300 Esme Addison

She shot him a smile before returning to Kamila's side.

Caroline pointed to the group of men. 'All of you soldiers sit down, legs crossed, hands behind your head.'

'They're Marines,' Harrison pointed out, voice still calm. 'Not soldiers.' He then nodded for the men to follow the order.

'Caroline,' Alex began, 'you said you heard Maisie was alive. What did you mean?'

She looked around the space. 'I've been here, locked in this place for decades, and I overheard them talking. The men who run this prison. And one of them mentioned her.' She looked at Maisie. 'But he called her Margaret, which is how I know her . . . He said he wanted to see her one more time . . . and that's when I realized she was still alive. They hadn't hurt her. And for the first time, I felt like I had a reason to live . . .

'I'd never tried to leave before because where would I go? But I knew what to do. When they unchained me for a few minutes a day, I zapped a guard, stole his card, made my way upstairs and ran.'

Her shoulders heaved a sob. 'I wanted to go to the ocean. To smell it. Taste it. Feel it . . . not this fake aquarium but the real thing. So I went to the beach . . .' She shook her head. 'I knew they'd be after me, that they'd send someone. And they did – Jonah. Which is what I wanted. I wanted to ask him where Margaret was, and if I could talk to her. I had to warn her . . . About *him*.'

'Him?' Jack repeated.

But Caroline ignored him, the words she'd wanted to tell anyone for so long rushing out of her. 'I wasn't sure why he was coming. But knowing him, it couldn't be good.'

'Let my mother go,' Jack said, voice slightly above a plea. 'And then we'll listen to whatever you want to say.'

Caroline narrowed her eyes at him. 'You think I'm holding her against her will? She wants to be with me. Before they scrambled her mind, she wanted to study us, learn from us. She respected us in our true form.'

Jack gazed at his mother. 'I can't believe that.'

'Of course you wouldn't,' she seethed. 'Because you're just like him. You even look like he did at your age.'

Jack frowned, glancing nervously around the group. 'Who? What are you talking about?'

'I'm talking about the man who did this to me.' Her voice rose in a jagged wail. 'The man who did this' – she pointed to Maisie's temple – 'to her.'

Maisie looked at her, confused. 'Caroline.' Her voice was soft and childlike. 'You know who made me this way?'

Caroline glared at Jack, bursts of electricity sparking from her fingertips. 'Yeah, I do. It's his father. You know him as Alasdair Frazier. But he goes by another name now.'

Alex's throat tightened. 'Who?'

Caroline's facial features shifted in revulsion. 'Forbes McDonald.'

FIFTY-THREE

'Forbes McDonald?' Jack asked, pain etched across his face. 'The detective who investigated the Fisherman case under a fake name?'

'Oh, I remember that name. He was the nice man who bought us donuts when we went shopping,' Maisie added.

'You know him?' Jack asked Alex, his eyes still on his mother.

'I've met him a few times. Look, Jack . . . he told me he was dying, that this visit was something he needed to do.'

Caroline's face hardened. 'Did you hear me? Alasdair Frazier is not his real name. And neither is Forbes or Gordon Clarke. They're aliases, you should know that.' She looked at Jack. 'He was in charge of the study. Everything that happened was his fault, his doing, do you understand?'

Jack barely nodded. 'Go on.'

'I used to look like them.' She pointed to the mermaids. 'We knew there were vessels in the bay, on the ocean, looking for us. And we were able to evade them for a long time. It became a game for us at times, but then they figured out how to create a type of frequency that startled us, confused and stunned us.'

Dylan shook his head in disgust. 'Sounds like they've been using sonar systems in ways that are patently illegal, not to mention unethical.'

'And that's how they caught me. I was the first – they only needed one at the time. Wanted to perfect their process fin-to-legs before they tried it in reverse. They tortured me until I developed legs.' She screwed up her face to stop the tears. 'And then they put a tracker in me, which they used to control and punish me.'

Celeste looked close to tears. 'I'm sorry to say Alex and I saw the files. Project Oannes.' She turned to the group. 'It was brutal. Inhumane.'

'She's not human,' Jack muttered to himself, but Alex heard and side-eyed him.

'They figured out how to activate my electric shock response

A Brew for Chaos 303

against my will. So anytime I didn't do what they wanted, they shocked me. And they shocked me until I had no more freewill. I did whatever they wanted.'

A deep scowl crossed Jack's forehead. 'And what did they have you do?'

She paused, sighed deeply and looked at Alex before speaking. 'They sent me to town, to Bellamy Bay, to find women with a certain gene.'

Dylan stepped forward, a look of incredulity on his face. 'You were working off the list?'

'Yeah, one Forbes gave me. And he got it from somebody in the government. The military.'

Dylan exchanged a guilty look with Alex before continuing. 'So you were the one abducting women. You were the Fisherman.'

'There was no *one* person. It was a team effort.' She rolled her eyes. 'One that Forbes put together.'

'Jonah, Mac.' Alex ticked off. 'And you.'

'You figured it out.' She gazed at every single face in the group. 'I was *the bait*. And you all probably think I hated what I was doing or felt guilty . . .' She shrugged. 'I didn't. After the physical abuse, I spent ten hours a day learning how to talk, learning the language, learning how to be a young woman, not weird, not awkward being on land . . . I'd been so abused at this point that going to the beach, hanging out with friends . . . it was fun. It was a getaway from my real life, which was an actual nightmare.

'I was learning how to be a real girl.' She laughed bitterly. 'And I just didn't think about what happened to the women that I passed off to the guys on the beach. All I cared about was being free from the pain . . .'

'Where does my mother fit in all of this?'

Caroline glanced at Maisie before continuing. 'Part of my role was to blend in wherever I could. And there were a few targets at the college. Forbes told me to hang around the campus and try to befriend some of the girls. And one day I was on campus and this really vibrant girl came up to me, and she said she knew my face. She recognized me . . . She asked me pointblank: *Are you a mermaid?* Totally floored me, and I flustered my response so bad she just laughed when I finally told her no.

304   Esme Addison

'I asked her how she knew. When did she see me? And she said she'd been at the marina when she saw the men pull me up from the sea when she was a freshman, when I had my fins. She had binoculars and was watching dolphins and whales.

'She saw what they did to me. I was shocked. After thinking all humans were heartless, violent psychopaths, here was someone who'd seen me from before, knew my secret and was kind to me. I told her everything about my life in the sea, how I'd been taken and everything that had happened to me.

'She wanted me to go to the police, but I warned her, told her that if she told anyone what she knew, they might do something horrible to her. As a result, she stayed quiet, but I know she didn't want to. She wanted to save me. Protect me. I told her, there was no way she could protect me. I had a tracker in my neck . . . That she should just be my friend. And she did . . .' The smile slid off her face and it contorted like she was in pain. 'Somehow Forbes found out about her. That I'd been talking to her, that I'd told her everything. I think it was Jonah. He wasn't very nice back then. Petty. Spiteful. Just a jerk, and I . . .' She shrugged.

'Next thing I knew, my best friend, my only friend, had been abducted and I knew it was my fault. I knew who had done it. I returned to the aquarium and blasted Forbes. Threatened all sorts of things if he didn't let her go. If he'd hurt her, if he'd touched a hair on her head . . .'

Jack cocked his head, appraising Caroline as she spoke. 'What did he do?'

'He told me that I had created the problem by befriending her, talking to her, telling her things she wasn't cleared for and that he was going to solve the problem, and he made it sound really ominous.'

She blinked back tears. 'I loved her like a sister. Growing up mermaid . . .' She almost laughed. 'Every mermaid is your sister, and I missed that comradery. Those relationships. Margaret was my sister, and I'd put her in danger . . .' A sob bubbled up from her throat.

'Later I found out that Forbes had been hanging out with her and a group of friends, just to feel her out, see what she knew, see if she would be a problem . . . and I think . . .' Her mouth twisted like she'd bit into a lemon. 'I think he fell a little bit in love with her.'

Jack made a face. 'What?'

'Yeah . . . He had this thing that could kind of shock the brain and make you forget stuff. Only she was so smart, so headstrong, he told me he had to zap her several times before she'd forgotten everything I'd told her. Everything she'd seen.'

Jack's face wrinkled in concentration. 'Her condition . . . it was given to her for operational security?'

Alex placed a hand on his arm. 'Sounds like the same thing used on Minka.'

'Something went wrong though, and instead of her simply forgetting certain things, her cognitive abilities were affected in a substantial way. I think he felt guilty, and he decided to marry her.' She shrugged. 'I don't know if it was a real relationship or not, but . . . he did it so he could have the authority to remove her from school.

'Before I escaped, and heard she was still alive, he finally answered my questions. Said there'd been a shotgun wedding, and you were born nine months later.'

'And then he left. He left her and me.' Jack nodded. 'Yeah, that part I got.'

A tear slid down Caroline's face, and she didn't wipe it away. 'I kept asking him about her. How was she? Did the machine hurt her? Was she okay? Was she still in school? One day, he just snapped at me and told me she was dead, and I should stop asking questions.'

'He was heartless,' Minka murmured. 'And after you'd gone through so much.'

'He didn't consider me human. He told me that often enough.'

Alex couldn't help but glance at Jack. *Like father, like son?*

'We'll finish questioning her later. We need to get out of here. Get your mom . . . How does this end, Caroline?' Alex asked. 'We can't stay down here forever.'

'Can't you? I did.' She pointed to the aquarium. 'They have.' Then walked to the glass, hand gently grasping Maisie's wrist. 'You think all of these women were born mermaids?'

Alex followed her to the glass, inspecting the women's faces. There were so many of them . . . but then, one woman with green eyes and brown hair floated by her. She pressed her hand to the glass as if she could fit her hand to Alex's.

Alex was startled to realize she recognized her face. 'Heather Roland?' she said, looking at Caroline. 'From the list. One of the women the Fisherman took?' She whirled around, not understanding. 'These women? They're—'

'The ten victims of the Fisherman are in there,' Dylan finished for her.

Caroline stared into the aquarium. 'They didn't kill them. They tested on them, tortured them just like they did me. They figured out how to turn my tail into legs. And their legs into a fin.'

'I think I'm going to be—' Minka retched, covering her mouth. Then ran to a trashcan at the side of the room.

'You're right,' Jack said. 'The people responsible for this are monsters. Mad scientists, all of them. And they need to pay. I'll see to that. But right now? Just let my mother go.'

Caroline's eyes narrowed. 'You're a police officer, like he pretended to be.'

'Yeah, I'm a cop, but . . . you're not in trouble right now. We'll figure it all out . . . later.'

Caroline shook her head like she didn't want to hear him.

'I'm not him. Okay?' Jack insisted, fighting to keep his voice calm. 'He's my father, but I don't know him. He left when I was a toddler . . . Please.'

Caroline softened her hold on Maisie. 'Margaret?'

She nodded. 'He's a good boy. He really is.'

'We've got to free these mermaids,' Alex said. 'Any ideas how we can do that before someone finds us all in here?' She looked around. 'Who runs things down here anyway?'

'There's the security guards.' Caroline waved an arm around. 'But they're also trained aquarists, specialists in aquatic care and maintenance. And they're supervised by someone remotely. I used to see the guards talking to them on computer calls or on the phone.'

'It must have been Forbes,' Alex said.

Dylan nodded. 'According to the schematics Harrison downloaded, there's a sealed tunnel inside the aquarium that leads to the ocean, comes out alongside the Maritime Forest's coast. That's how we set them free. We have two challenges. One, we need to

A Brew for Chaos   307

manually open the tunnel to let them out. And then we have to deactivate their trackers and the remote-control function.'

'What about the women who had their gene activated?' Minka asked. 'The ones taken from their home and forced to live in a tank?'

'I don't know,' Alex said. 'We'll figure that out once we set them free. We just have to figure out how to deactivate their trackers first.'

'I was tracking those signals,' Minka said. 'I was the one activating them and sending them the message to return home, only I didn't know where their home base was.'

Dylan's grin reached his eyes as he watched recognition flicker in hers.

'Oh my gosh,' she whispered, 'I'm the one activating . . . I can set them free. I turn the trackers off.'

'That's right,' he whispered. 'And we're going to help you deactivate them permanently. You'll need to get back to your desk. Take Harrison. He can look at your software programs and figure out what needs to be done,' Dylan added.

Alex watched her cousin leave with Harrison, then returned to look at the mermaids behind the glass. 'How do we open the tunnel?'

'One of us has to go inside, swim to the gate and open it.'

Alex's eyes widened. 'Not me. I can't. You know that, not after—' After her mother had drowned in the ocean, Alex refused to return to the water.

Kamila shook her head. 'Don't look at me. Numerous crimes have been committed here, and I need to go figure out who can be charged and what for.' She met Jack's eyes, and he nodded.

'This might be above both our paygrades, Officer Sobieski. But we'll figure it out. Someone has to be held accountable.'

'I'm heading to the police station.' She took off in a trot towards the exit.

'I'll do it,' Celeste said, a wide grin on her face. 'I'd love to swim with the mermaids. But are you sure you don't want to? It's your chance to actually be with real mermaids. I mean, how amazing is that?'

But the images of the testing and torture Caroline had gone through were fresh in Alex's mind. 'I can't. I'm sorry.'

308   Esme Addison

Dylan nodded. 'The access door is over there.' He pointed to a flight of stairs that led to a door beside the glass wall. 'But Alex, Celeste here shouldn't go swimming in the aquarium by herself. Buddy system?'

Alex rolled her eyes. 'I know . . .' She took a deep breath and stared at the mermaids, many of whom were still swimming near the glass but had lost interest in the people watching them. 'Okay, I'll do it. If there's one time to break my rule, this is it.'

FIFTY-FOUR

Caroline watched as Alex walked towards the staircase. 'What are you all *doing*? I don't understand.'

'We're helping,' Alex said. 'Women have been kept imprisoned down here for too long. Celeste and I are going to swim inside that aquarium and open the sea access so these mermaids can be free.'

Caroline's face moved into a mask of incomprehension. 'You're going to free them?'

'Of course. Why do you think we're here?'

Her gaze went to Jack. 'To punish me for what I've done?'

Alex shook her head. 'If you help us, we're going to bring the men who did this to you to justice.'

'What?' She broke then. Tears slid down her face and she let go of Maisie's arm. She fell to the floor, her shoulders heaving with sobs. 'Finally? After all this time?'

Jack lunged for his mother, wrapping his arms around her. 'Mom, are you okay?'

She laughed slightly. 'Of course I am. I've seen mermaids.' She patted his cheek, then turned him by the jaw to the aquarium. 'Aren't they lovely?'

Blinking back an errant tear, he allowed himself to really look at the mermaids. He nodded slowly, finding his voice. 'They are breathtaking.'

Alex gathered Caroline in her arms and hugged her tight, sending her heavy waves of love and compassion and kindness and healing. She sent her so much she thought Caroline would explode from the abundance of high vibrations. When she emitted a peel of laughter, Alex knew she could stop.

'I'm coming with you,' she said, a brightness in her eyes Alex hadn't seen before. 'I wish I could go with them. I miss my home so much.' She looked down at her legs, scorn burning her eyes. 'But I'll never get my fins back.' Then her anger subsided, and she looked at Alex, hope lighting up her face. 'There's something I need to get.' She ran to a room and returned with several wetsuits on one arm, and an old, rusted key double the length of Alex's forefinger. 'The suits are from when they had round-the-clock staff tending to the mermaids. And the key is for the tunnel door.'

They changed into the wetsuits, and Alex took the key in hand. She began climbing up the access stairs, with Celeste and Caroline following her.

'Let's set them free.'

They jumped into the warm salty water. The mermaids immediately swarmed them. A jumble of thoughts filled her brain and Alex realized she could telepath with all of them.

Celeste, swimming like she'd been born in the water, took off, zooming around the aquarium with some mermaids challenging her to a race. Of course, the mermaids won. But then they showed her a few techniques, ways to move their legs and arms for faster swimming.

Alex wasn't interested in any fancy moves, she just wanted to survive the mission. As fantastical as it was. With brightly colored hair fanning around her, and shimmering tails flicking past her, she focused on holding her breath, gliding through the water. She had not gone swimming since learning she was a Magical, but she supposed she was a stronger swimmer than she even imagined.

You'll be fine. Celeste returned to swim alongside her, then telepathed to her. *We can hold our breath for a really long time. And swim without getting tired. Our vision is a million times sharper, and you can hear all sorts of vibrations and frequencies in the water.*

Celeste was sending thoughts to her as they swam to the tunnel access covered by a large metal door chained with a massive old-fashioned lock. *Isn't this so cool? OMG, we're swimming with mermaids. Aren't they beautiful? Look at their hair. I wish we could take pictures.*

Alex wanted to take a moment to let the epicness of her situation sink in, really think about the fact that mermaids in actual mermaid form existed, they were amazing, and oh yeah, she was swimming with them – but she couldn't. She was too afraid

A Brew for Chaos   311

Montgomery would figure out what they were doing before she set the mermaids free and got the heck out of dodge.

She looked around and found Caroline swimming slowly behind them, thoughtful look on her face. Sometimes her eyes were closed and other times they were open, and she did slow twirls as if she were acclimating herself to the water.

They reached the door and Caroline swam beside Alex. *It's just not the same, swimming with legs. I feel like a big fat awkward whale.*

Celeste consoled her while Alex inserted the key. It turned with some difficulty, but then the lock released, and Alex pulled on the heavy door. It creaked open, revealing a grate, which they pulled up. The current from the tunnel immediately pulled them in, but they fought the force of the water by hanging on to large chunks of coral protruding from the tunnel.

They turned to the mermaids that had been following their progress and telepathed to them. Alex gazed at them. All of the women who had been taken from Bellamy Bay and turned into real mermaids floated before her. Trapped for forty years with no way to get word to their families. *Is there a way to turn them back to their human form?* Alex telepathed to Caroline.

She looked at the mermaids. *It may be possible, but they wouldn't want to. Most have lost their memories from before. It was the one thing Forbes did at my request. Zap their brain so they'd never know what they once were.*

Alex stared at the women, then waved her arms in the water. *You're free. Swim away. Don't come back. You don't have to come back . . .*

One by one, the mermaids swam through the tunnel. Several stopped to thank them with telepathic messages, allowing their fingers to touch theirs as they swam by. A mermaid with purple hair and eyes swam close to Alex.

There's something on my neck.

She lifted her long hair, and Alex could see the bioluminescent outline of the tracker at the base of her neck. It glowed green against her skin, which was a pale lavender.

My friend is going to turn it off, Alex told her.

The mermaid looked doubtful. *It makes us come back. We are not free with this in our body*, she insisted.

And then it stopped glowing. Minka and Harrison must've figured out how to turn it off. *Don't worry*, she told the mermaid. *It won't bring you back here again. Promise.*

When all the mermaids were gone, Alex pulled down the grate, Celeste and Caroline pushed the door closed and Alex locked it.

The mermaids would not be returning to the aquarium.

FIFTY-FIVE

When Alex and the rest of the group had climbed out of the aquarium, changed back into their street clothes and descended the stairs, they were met with an almost empty room.

Harrison and his men were gone. Minka hadn't returned from her office, but Jack was there with his mother. Her face was pressed to the glass, palms flat on either side of her face.

'I can't believe I saw them,' she was murmuring to herself. 'So many of them. I thought I'd die before I saw another one . . .'

'Mom, please . . .' Jack looked weary. Exhausted, with dark smudges under his eyes. But he smiled when he saw Alex approaching him with sopping wet hair and clothes. He wrapped his arms around her and held her tight. 'You were amazing. I have no words.'

For a moment, she felt safe and warm, protected in his embrace, and she wanted to pretend like he wasn't tracking her kind and she wasn't a Magical. But she could only delude herself for so long.

She pulled back from him, confused about how she felt. She hadn't had to reveal her Magical heritage to him. He still thought she was a Mundane. The mermaids had been in the water, and now that they were gone, all was right with the world.

He leaned in for another hug while his mother clapped her hands softly as if she were watching a favorite show.

Alex let him embrace her and pepper kisses all over her wet face. She was too tired to figure it all out right now. Too tired to resist his advances.

Tomorrow.

Tomorrow, after she'd had a good night's rest, she'd figure it out.

Someone cleared their throat, and Dylan moved out of the shadows. Jack's back was to him, so he couldn't see the cold look on his face.

But Alex could.
She didn't know what to say or do.
So she said nothing.

FIFTY-SIX

Dylan volunteered to take Celeste home, and Jack and his mother were driving Alex and Caroline back to her house when Alex's cell phone rang.

It was Kamila. She picked up the phone. 'Hey, we've left the aquarium and are heading back to the house.'

'That's great, but that's not why I'm calling,' she began. 'Are you with Jack?'

Alex slid a glance his way. He was driving and looking straight ahead with both hands on the steering wheel. 'Yeah.'

'Put me on speaker.'

Alex did so.

'Hey, Jack, Sobieski here.'

He raised an eyebrow. 'What's going on, officer?'

'Got some bad news, sir. Just heard it on the scanner and wanted to make sure you knew . . .' Her voice trailed off, and Alex shot Jack a worried look.

'Spit it out.'

'It's your father, sir. The man known as Forbes McDonald? He's been rushed to the hospital. Organ failure.'

Jack's fingers tightened on the steering wheel. He looked at Alex. 'Back at the aquarium you said he was dying?'

'Yeah. Liver cancer. I'm sorry.'

'Don't be. I don't know him. And from the sound of it, it was a good thing.' He glanced at his mother. 'She might feel something . . . Mom, do you remember my father?'

'Yes, he was a lovely man. Very kind to me.'

Kamila hesitated. 'He's at the hospital if you want to see him.'

Jack's face hardened. 'I don't want to. But I need to.' He looked at Alex. 'You mind?'

'Of course not.'

He did a U-turn at the next light and sped down the street.

* * *

316   Esme Addison

When they arrived, Alex stood outside Forbes' closed hospital room with Jack and his mother. Jack's expression was solemn, his face pale. She reached for his hand. 'You okay?'

He grunted in response, then nodded. 'Yeah. It's just . . . a lot.' He glanced at Caroline, who sat alone a few yards away on a row of plastic chairs.

'I know you want to see him alone, so I'll just—' Alex frowned. Looked at the closed door. 'Someone needs to call Leith.'

'Who?' Jack scowled.

'Leith . . . I don't think you've met him. He's here in town, and he's Forbes' grandson . . .' Her eyebrows lifted. 'And I guess . . . your nephew?'

Jack crossed his arms. 'Which means my *father*' – he said the words stiffly – 'had another kid that he raised. Somewhere.'

Alex sighed, wanting to take Jack's pain away. 'I'm so sorry. He's staying at the B&B in town. I'll call him.'

Nodding, Jack put his hand on the doorknob, took a breath then went inside.

After Alex left a message at the Seaside for Leith, she sat down beside Caroline. She looked around the waiting area with distaste. 'I hate hospitals. And doctors. And needles.' Her eyes narrowed as she observed her surroundings. 'I hate a lot, generally.'

'I can imagine,' Alex replied, trying not to envision what must've happened to her in the aquarium's testing facility. And then a thought occurred to her. 'Is Caroline your real name?'

She laughed. 'No. Of course not.'

Alex nodded. 'It just occurred to me that your placement on the list of victims was . . . an inaccuracy. Caroline Bracy never existed.'

'No. She was made up by Jonah. In case anyone at the college remembered me and may have wondered what happened to me when I disappeared. He came up with the name and her backstory. Published it once in the papers and the other periodicals picked it up. Insta-truth.'

Alex stared at her, fascinated. Realizing that she was looking at and talking to a real mermaid. 'So, what's your real name?'

'Hulla,' she said with a slight accent.

'That's pretty. What's it mean?' Caroline shrugged and Alex

A Brew for Chaos   317

searched the name on her phone, then looked at her in surprise. 'It means joyful. Its origin . . . ancient Sumerian.'

'You and everyone else can just call me Caroline. Easier that way.' Sadness tinged her features, and Alex placed a hand on her forearm to push the sorrow away. When she did, an ethereal glow of lavender emanated from her body laced with puffs of white. *Her aura.* Caroline was naturally kind and loving. Alex blinked and her aura was gone.

She looked away as a tightness pulled the muscles across her chest.

Caroline's anger and hatred were justified. But Caroline had been a victim the entire time.

Not a killer.

She turned to look at Caroline. 'You know, Spencer's been after Jonah's recipe and you've had it this entire time, drinking it at the house. How did you get it?'

She shrugged, hardening her jaw. 'It used to be kept on a sticky note in the laboratory when they were transitioning me.' She blinked away a tear. 'And I'd just stare at it while I was strapped to my bed.' She tapped her temple. 'It's been up here the whole time.'

Alex shook her head, trying to push the horrific image of Caroline being tested on out of her mind. 'I am so sorry that happened to you.' She reached out and touched her hand. 'You are so strong to have—' She stopped, something occurring to her then. 'Wait. You didn't kill Jonah, did you?'

'I never said I did.' She tilted her head in surprise. 'I said he deserved it, but not that I did it.' Her lips moved into a frown. 'Just because I helped Forbes abduct those women, doesn't mean I'd take a life.'

Alex sighed, realizing their ordeal was far from over. 'What happened that night on the beach?'

Pain flitted across Caroline's face. 'One of the guards from the aquarium must've called Jonah and told him I'd escaped.'

Alex thought back to the Oktoberfest food tasting, when Jonah had run out of the tavern, almost getting hit by a car in the parking lot. That must've been the call.

'When I first broke free, my priority was to procure a supply of Jonah's brew, his Mermaid Magic, to prevent the side effects

318   Esme Addison

of the gene therapy. I've been drinking thirty-two ounces of it
every day since I transitioned to a full-human. And I had to be
strong and healthy to do what I needed to do. So, I found his
address online and tried to break into his house, knowing he had
to have a stash somewhere and I had about twenty-four hours
before my body started to fail me. But I couldn't get inside, so
I spent the night in hiding.'

'That was the night my aunt gave a presentation at our shop.
Jonah received a house alarm notification and had to leave early.'

'The next morning, I knew my escape would be discovered
when the guards opened my room for breakfast and the day's
first dose of Mermaid Magic and found me missing. From my
hiding spot on the beach, I saw the guards dressed as civilians
looking for me. But then, I thought I'd lost them. That's when
I called Jonah and told him to meet me.'

Alex recalled Kamila taking a call about a puzzling break-in
where nothing had been stolen. 'You broke into a bar on the
beach and used their landline?' Alex guessed.

Nodding, Caroline blushed. 'And then we met, and I had so
many questions. Where was Margaret? I begged him to help me
find her. Protect her. Protect me.' Her face twisted in pain. 'So
many ways he could've helped me, righted the wrongs of the
past . . . but he wouldn't. He said I was a reminder of what he'd
done, and that I shouldn't be in Bellamy Bay, but he knew I
couldn't go back to the ocean . . . He looked genuinely conflicted
about what he'd done, but my compassion for him ended when
he called the security forces on me.' Her face hardened. 'Said
imprisonment was the best option for me. And I realized he was
trying to stall me until the security team could get me and take
me back to my jail.'

'The guards at the aquarium?' Alex guessed.

Caroline scowled. 'My jailers? Yeah.' She gritted her teeth. 'I
saw two coming for me on the beach, and even though I was
weak, I was able to defend myself against one. Tried to zap him,
but I think I only singed his arm. His buddy left when he saw
his mate go down.

'I got away from him, but someone else came for me, someone
I didn't know . . .' She blinked back tears. 'All I wanted was the
truth. Was Margaret okay? Could I see her? Jonah wouldn't

answer me and then this other person approached us . . . So angry. They argued. Then they asked for the recipe for the brew. And when he refused . . .' Her eyes widened. 'He was killed.'

'And you?' Alex pressed.

'I hid while they were arguing. After Jonah had been dealt with and they left, I went to Jonah to see if he was still alive. Despite what he'd done, I was still going to try and heal him if I could. But he was already gone. And I couldn't do anything for him. And then I got faint and passed out.'

'And you have no idea who this person was?' Alex asked, chest tightening with anxiety. 'Man? Woman?'

'It's still very foggy. I hadn't had my medicine, I was growing fainter by the minute . . . I'm sorry.'

'It's okay. You've done enough.' And it *was* okay. Because Alex had an idea . . . She pulled out her cell phone and texted Kamila. Asked her to check on something for her.

Alex looked up when the door to Forbes' room opened and Jack appeared.

He looked slightly dazed and searched the area until he found Alex. 'He's awake and he wants to see you.'

Alex rose slowly. 'Me?' She glanced at Caroline, sliding her cell phone back into her purse. 'I'll be right back.'

Alex entered the room. It was stark and cold, white walls and floor. Forbes lay in the bed, seeming to have shriveled a bit since she last saw him. His eyes, sunken into his face, were open and tracked her movements.

'Alone,' he rasped, his voice barely above a whisper.

Alex looked behind her at Jack and Maisie. Jack nodded, arm around his mother, and ushered her out. She closed the door and then went to his bedside.

'No offense, but you're not looking too good.' She tried to smile but suspected he was not long for this earth.

He shook his head, let out a long sigh. 'I finally saw my son. After all this time.'

Alex stared at him, feeling pity and repulsion at the same time. 'You wanted to see me?'

He nodded slowly, reached for a plastic cup of ice chips and wet his throat before speaking. 'I told you I wanted to return to the place of my greatest sorrow . . .'

320   Esme Addison

Alex's eyebrows lifted. 'You regret your role in Project Oannes?'

Even sick, his eyes fired with determination. 'Absolutely not. I will die knowing I did everything I could to protect this country from an unimaginable foe.'

Alex's eyes slid to the door. 'You mean PACs.'

'Stupid name. Military gobbledygook. Magicals . . .' His look turned sly. 'That's what you call yourselves.'

Alex took a step back from his bed. 'You told Jack? About me and—'

He shook his head. 'No. I was going to . . .' He tilted his head as he observed her, gaze still sharp. 'But then his mother mentioned you, said he'd told her he loves you.'

Alex shook her head. 'He's never told me that – he couldn't possibly . . .'

'He didn't deny it.' He inhaled slowly, then coughed, a loud, ragged sound filling the room. 'I came here knowing I had a few weeks to live. This visit was my hospice . . . I wanted to see Margaret one more time. I feel . . . guilty about what I did to her. I stole her mind, her vitality—'

'You stole her life when you used the ZIM on her,' Alex finished for him.

'But I didn't kill her.' His eyes narrowed. 'Which was the order.'

Alex's throat tightened. 'You saved her? By scrambling her brain and making her lose her memories?'

He closed his eyes, and so much time passed that Alex thought he'd fallen asleep, but then he opened them, and she saw they were red, moist with tears.

'We all had to tie up loose ends, not a word about Project Oannes could seep out. And she'd befriended Caroline, who told her *everything*.' His eyes flashed. 'This is really her fault; if it wasn't for her, Margaret would've remained untouched. But as it stood . . .' He took a long, shuddering breath. 'I knew Margaret from being on the campus, and I had Mac call her to the beach. But it was me she was meeting. I used the ZIM on her. Once, twice, three times, trying to remove the memories from her.'

Alex couldn't hide the look of disgust on her face, and she rubbed her temples.

A Brew for Chaos

'By the time I was done, she was like you see now.' His features crumbled and he put his palms to his face. 'I didn't mean . . . I just wanted her to forget what she knew.' He wiped a tear from his withered cheek. 'Back then it was an imprecise tool for removing memories. Now? It scans the brain and uses AI to target the exact areas with just the right amount of voltage to accomplish . . .' He looked into Alex's hard eyes and stopped.

'She was like a child, and I couldn't leave her like that. Return her to school and just . . . There was no way she could finish her education. She needed to be removed from her studies and placed somewhere she could be taken care of. It had to be a guardian or spouse, and I wasn't old enough back then to pretend to be her father. So against orders I secretly married her so I could remove her from school.'

'Did you tell Jack all of this?'

'I did. First, I read him in on Project Oannes, so he had context for why I was in Bellamy Bay for starters. I wanted him to understand why I did what I did. The hard choices I had to make.' He grimaced a smile. 'And he, being my son, I think he understood.'

Alex bit the inside of her cheek, hoping he couldn't see the disgust on her face. 'And then?'

'And then, I moved her away from this place, as far from Project Oannes as I could and back to where her parents were. I set her up in a pretty little cottage in upstate New York and played house with her for as long as I could, always afraid someone would find out what I'd done – or rather what I hadn't done. Killed her as ordered.

'I was gone for most of the time with work. I'd visit her when I could. She got pregnant, we had Jack. I tried to be a father to him while taking trips to the submarine base at Kings Bay in Georgia, which is where my work was. But then I had a scare, thought someone had found out about them, so I removed myself from their life in order to keep them safe.'

'What a mess.'

'I know. It's what happens when you don't follow orders.' His jaw hardened, so like Jack's, she could see now. 'If I had killed Margaret, none of this would've happened . . .' He winced then as a strong pain rocked his body. His long fingers gripped the

322   Esme Addison

sides of his bed until the pain passed. He looked into Alex's eyes. 'I know you think I deserve this and maybe I do . . . my penance for all that I've done.'

Alex looked away so he wouldn't see the tears forming in her eyes. Not for him, but for all that had happened to Maisie. And Jack.

'I'm proud of him, my boy. Without knowing it he's carrying on my work. Doing what needs to be done to protect our country.'

'You still haven't told me why you wanted to see me. Or even why you had Botanika on your list of places to visit.'

His eyebrows shot up at her words, and she nodded.

'Yeah, your grandson told me about your morbid bucket list of must-see places in Bellamy Bay.'

His lips twisted in scorn, and he coughed out a laugh. 'He tried to stop me from coming here, and when he couldn't he joined me . . .' His eyes hardened. 'I came to Botanika because it's where I met your mother.'

Something surged in Alex's chest. 'My mother,' she said, suddenly unable to breathe.

He nodded. 'Yes, I came to this town, decided to base Project Oannes here because your mother and her family lived here.' He swallowed with great difficulty. 'Our project needed two things: a biological mermaid like the one we found and named Caroline.' He stopped, held a hand to his waist as pain rocked his body again. 'And a genetic mermaid, preferably with the royal lineage.'

Montgomery had mentioned the same thing. But her aunt had never talked about it. How could he know about her history when her own family didn't?

'You're mistaken. Royal lineage?'

He reached for his cup of ice chips. 'No. I'm quite sure of your genetics. And it's nothing to be afraid of. It just means that you come directly from the Mermaid of Warsaw and her coupling with a medieval Polish king.'

Alex stared at the man. 'I-I've never heard this part of the myth.'

He allowed himself a smile, then took a moment to deposit several chips into his mouth. 'Many have not . . . And of course you know, it's no myth. He retrieved her from the Vistula River

A Brew for Chaos

and made her a court magical along with his astrologer, alchemist, mystic and magician.'

'Her role?'

'Court healer.' His thin, dry lips parted into a smile.

She crossed her arms. 'Like Rasputin was to the Russian imperial court?'

'Precisely. Only your syrenka was beautiful and no charlatan and opportunist. She was truly a creature of magic . . . who eventually became the king's mistress.'

Alex held her breath for a moment. 'And my mother?'

'Has the bloodline of kings and Mer. It's a powerful thing.'

He stared at her so intently Alex fought the urge to scratch at her body and slap away the feeling.

'I wanted your mother for the study. She was on the list, but my team could never quite seem to get her for me.'

Mac. Alex's thoughts went to the man who'd saved her mother. Saved her family. He was getting a lifetime supply of whatever he wanted, that was for darn certain.

'And then . . .' His eyes lit up. 'I caught her.'

Startled out of her reverie, Alex leaned forward. 'What? When? How?'

He took another deep breath, and Alex wanted to grab the man by his shoulders and shake him, force him to speak faster. Tell her what she needed to know.

'Twenty or so years ago, your mother returned to Bellamy Bay, and she'd been spending time on the beach that summer.'

Alex frowned at him, her hands curling into tight fists.

'I had an operative in town and he notified me.'

An operative? 'Montgomery?'

But he only smiled, not answering her.

'I thought Project Oannes had ended.'

'That's what we wanted everyone to think.' His voice was pensive. He shrugged. 'So I told the operative to follow her while she was in town, and if she stepped one toe into the water . . .' He chuckled.

Alex felt energy welling in her hands, causing them to heat, her fingers to tremble.

'What did you do?' she leaned forward, voice low. The life-saving equipment around him began to shake ever so slightly.

'Waited for her to go swimming, which she did. It was a hot day, one of the hottest on record. High nineties, humidity was like pea soup, and she swam out into the cool ocean water where she was caught on a rip tide that pulled her out to the center of the bay and then under where I had a team waiting.'

He looked up briefly to note the fluorescent light panels in the ceiling were flickering. Then turned to gaze at Alex, an impressed look quirking his lips. 'They had a very large net ready to capture the biggest prize of my life.'

Alex could barely contain the stream of rage that flooded her body. Her entire being trembled and the heart monitor attached to Forbes' chest shut down with a shrill whistling sound.

The door flew open, and a team of nurses rushed in, pushing Alex out of the way. Up against the wall, she watched as they checked his vitals and then the machine. Jack joined her, watching his father with a mixture of anger and concern.

Forbes' eyes had lolled back in his head, though his chest still rose with difficulty. Several minutes later, he was stabilized, and his yellowing eyes searched the room until he found Alex.

He lifted his hand to her and gestured for her to come closer. Two nurses were left, and one tried to shoo Jack and Alex out of the room. 'He needs to rest.'

But Alex went to him, needing answers. She glanced back at Jack, who stood by the door, his face a hard mask against anything he might be feeling. 'What did you do to her?' Her voice was low, and she leaned towards him so only he could hear her. *'Where's my mother?'*

He lifted his bony shoulders. 'I don't know. She's the one that got away.' His lips lifted into a sad smile. 'It's the biggest regret of my life.'

Jack stood beside her. 'What did he say?' He wrapped an arm around her, pulling her to him. 'You look upset.'

Coldness sluiced through her body, and Alex stared at him, a heaviness weighing down the muscles and bones of her body. And she realized that *he* was the actual Fisherman. Tears ran down her cheeks and she couldn't stop shaking. So, her mother didn't drown? She'd been kidnapped. But . . . *If her mother got away, where did she go?*

Jack moved her away from the bedside, wrapping both arms around her, trying to quell her tremors. 'You okay?'

When she still didn't speak, he pulled back and looked into her stunned face. 'Let's get out of here.' And he gently guided her out the room.

They both heard the heart monitor flatline as they stepped into the hallway.

FIFTY-SEVEN

Alex sat in the waiting room while an emergency team tried to save Forbes' life. Caroline sat on one side of her and Maisie on the other.

'You okay, dear?' Maisie patted her thigh. 'You seem troubled.'

She shook her head, unable to speak. She was struggling to understand what Forbes had told her. He was responsible for her mother going missing, but he'd lost her?

How? Where?

Did she drown? Had she somehow activated her gene, turned into a biological mermaid and escaped into the ocean?

And how could she tell her family? She looked up and saw Jack standing outside his father's door, keeping one eye on his mother, the other on his father. She turned to Caroline, her voice low. 'Maisie's life is still in jeopardy. The same person who attacked you and killed Jonah will probably come after her. Seems like someone was sent to clean up behind the Fisherman.'

Caroline nodded. 'Now you see why I took Maisie?'

Alex glanced at Jack. 'He owes you an apology and a thank you. Though I doubt you'll ever get it.' Alex's phone pinged with an incoming notification.

It was Kamila responding to her request for information. She read the message, and her heart thrummed with adrenaline.

Her hunch was correct.

FIFTY-EIGHT

Alex turned to Caroline. 'If anyone asks, I'll be right back.' She rushed past Jack, who caught her arm. 'Where are you going? My father—'

'I have something to do. Stay here with Caroline. And if you have to step away, let her stay with your mother.'

'*Caroline?*' His features twisted into a scornful expression, and he stared at the woman before returning to look at Alex.

'She can protect you if—'

His forehead creased, and he stared intently into her eyes. 'If what? I should be arresting her. For all I know . . . What are you up to?'

Alex couldn't take it anymore. The pretending like everything was fine. Like Jack's lies didn't hurt her. Like she was okay with his witch hunt of her friends and family. 'You still think she killed Jonah? After everything you've learned?'

His eyes widened. And blinked once. Twice.

'Have you considered that it could be someone else?'

Shocked by her words, he stuttered, 'Who else could it be?'

'You haven't even looked, have you?'

'I've just—'

She shrugged his hand off her arm. 'I don't need your help. You're not even a real cop.' She hurried down the hallway, knowing she wouldn't tell him anything. Ever again.

When she got to the elevator, she took a breath, stepped inside and watched Jack watch her until the doors closed.

A moment later, she was in the hospital parking lot, keys out and a few yards from her car when she felt someone behind her. The hair rose on the back of her neck, and she began to walk faster, but they were quicker.

An arm snaked around her waist with something hard pressed against her back. 'Not so fast, Alex.'

She twisted her neck around to get a better look. And she snorted. 'I knew it was you.'

FIFTY-NINE

L eith grinned. 'How? What gave me away?'

'When I discovered that Forbes' name was an alias, I wondered about you and your real relationship to him. I didn't know your last name though, and I couldn't just assume it was McDonald.' She tried to pull away from him, but she felt the device on her back heat up, and she stopped struggling. She glanced around the parking lot, hoping someone would notice them. When she didn't see anyone, she focused on him.

'I discovered you *were* registered at the B&B as Leith McDonald. Which meant you were here under an alias as well.' Despite the device, she tried to jerk away, but his grip was too tight. 'I know you've said you're prior military. Forbes was knee-deep in the Fisherman case and the testing. You're not family, you're . . . colleagues. You work together.' She paused, eyes widening slightly. 'You have an M-Class clearance.'

He grinned, tightening his hold on her. 'And you . . . are a mermaid.'

He knew about her? Alex tried to hide her surprise, but her breath caught in her throat.

He pressed the device against the base of her skull. She felt a slight vibration on her skin and a buzzing sound in her ears.

Panic coursed through her and she tried to send a stinging bolt of energy into his body. But nothing happened.

He shook his head. 'This device temporarily disrupts the function of the ion channels in your cells, which prevents your neurons from building up and releasing an electrical charge.'

A wave of dizziness washed over Alex. 'Wait, you understand how my magic works?'

A look of disgust crossed his face. 'You're not special. A freak, sure, but there's nothing about you we can't replicate in a laboratory. We just need to study you.'

For the first time since discovering Jonah's true killer, icy fear crept down her spine, freezing her in place. She realized she was truly afraid. 'Who are you, really?'

'That's enough.' He glanced around quickly, then moved the device from her back and pressed it to her temple for a moment and she felt a tingle vibrate through her skull, a wave of vertigo that caused her to sway on her feet. 'Easy now,' he murmured into her ear. 'Just another love tap to scramble your thinking. I know you can telepath and I gave you just enough of a jolt to prevent you from calling for help until I can . . . well . . .' He grinned, then glancing around to make sure no one was watching, he pushed her towards her car. 'Go ahead and unlock it, nice and slow.'

Blinking several times to focus her vision, she pressed her key fob. 'I can't drive after you used that thing on me.'

The car door chirped, and he pushed her in. 'You're fine. All I've done is incapacitate your paranormal abilities. I know what I'm doing.' He held up a sleek white device with smooth circular edges. 'Try anything, and all I have to do is zap your skull for a few minutes longer and you won't even remember your name. You don't want that, do you?'

Alex shrank back at his barb, her gaze falling to the device. That had to be the device used on Minka and Maisie. She slid into the car, a feeling of complacency settling over her. She closed the door and waited for him to enter the other side.

He took his time getting settled and latching his seatbelt, his arrogant attitude punctuating every action. She tried to send a thought to her aunt, but her head began to swim. She stopped, waited a moment, then lifted her hands in front of her. Wiggled her fingers. He was right, her body was fine, her reflexes were sharp. She just couldn't focus on the part of her brain she used to telepath with her family. And she couldn't send him a zap of electricity.

Anger hummed through her body as she side-eyed him. That device gave him confidence. But if she could separate him from that weapon . . .

'Drive. Stay under the speed limit and don't try anything funny.'

Alex placed both hands on the wheel and did as she was told. But her mind was racing, trying to figure out the best way to—

330   Esme Addison

'Don't.' He smirked. 'You think because you're a PAC you can outsmart and outmaneuver me, right?'

She tightened her grip on the steering wheel. 'Where am I going?'

'Where it all began of course.' He grinned, and it sickened her. 'To the beach.'

He instructed her to drive to a parking lot that led to public access to the shoreline. Then told her to get out and start walking. He marched her towards a wooden sidewalk that led to a ledge of sand dunes that blocked the view of the ocean, though Alex could hear the sound of the waves.

Leith took off his shoes and Alex followed suit, and they walked through the thick cold sand.

Even though it was October, and an overcast blustery day, there were several surfers in dark wetsuits riding the waves. A couple of college students were bundled up in coats, but had their shoes in their hands as they walked across the sand in bare feet.

He pointed to a flight of wooden stairs at the peak of a sand dune that would take them to the water's edge. 'Move.'

'Really. Walk on the beach?' She glanced at the ZIM. 'Want to hold hands too?'

Leith tightened his grip on the weapon and walked behind her down the stairs until they could see the ocean, a dull grayish-blue rolling in and out. Seagulls circled ahead, and small crabs crawled in the sand.

Using the ZIM he pointed to the horizon. 'See that?'

She squinted against the wind that blew stronger as they neared the ocean. Then saw a gray smudge, a shadow of something in the far distance.

'That's us.'

She scowled at him. 'What are you talking about?'

'I'm doing what Forbes failed to do. Bring you in.'

'You're crazy.' Alex tried to step backwards, but he shook his head with a tsk tsk of his tongue and held the ZIM out. He pressed a touch pad on its side, and it crackled with energy, blue wisps flickering around its tip.

Alex tried not to show fear when he did that. But after seeing the pictures of the torture Caroline had gone through, and how

A Brew for Chaos   331

it had affected Maisie, she was afraid of it. She steeled her expression and hoped she looked tough.

'You come from a line of women who descend from the royal house of Sobieski and Mer. We at Project Oannes have coveted your genome for a very long time.'

Alex licked her lips, which had gone dry, wondering how she could get away from him. 'I'm not a genome. I'm a person.'

'Not to us you're not. You're an organic petri dish that we need to study and test and cultivate so we can create a new breed of naval security, something that can counter what China and Russia are creating as we speak.'

'I see. You think you're a patriot, huh? Somebody to be proud of while you abduct, imprison and torture women.'

His jaw hardened. 'Everything I do is for my country.'

Alex gazed into the horizon, the cold wind whipping her hair into her face. The boat was closer. She could see now it was a ship, maybe a cargo ship? But no way it could come into the bay . . . could it?

'Project Oannes is an ongoing initiative that is being moved to a more secure facility since our Bellamy Bay location has been compromised.' His eyes narrowed. 'And you're coming with.' He pointed to the ship, which was closer, a dark, looming object.

But she didn't move. 'Do you work at the submarine base in Kings Bay, where Forbes used to before he was forced to disappear? That's where you remotely controlled the project?'

'Wow.' He laughed. 'When I say you're nosy, I mean . . .' He nodded, his chin lifting. 'Yes, I took over Project Oannes. Montgomery's company and mine collaborate as a joint venture.'

'You took Minka.' She glared at him. 'Why?'

'Yeah, I did it. Our own security team had access to the camera footage in her office. And there was a recording device in the flowers I sent her . . . That is why I was seeing her. Montgomery mentioned her penchant for nosiness, something that must run in your family. And I thought I'd better do a threat assessment on her. When it was clear she'd figured out what we were up to, I stopped by for a visit to confirm.' He shrugged. 'Good thing I did, too. Otherwise, she would've blabbed to your reporter friend, and I would've had to get rid of her, like I did Caroline.'

Thank goodness he never found out the truth. Caroline was alive. Safe. 'Did Montgomery know what you were planning?'

His look was shrewd, but he hesitated. 'No. How I handle my business is not his concern. He just wants results. But he did ask me if I had her. By that time, we'd removed her memories and were conducting a little testing on her DNA.'

Alex's hand trembled. She wanted to send him a jolt of energy so bad . . . but he shook his head, looking at her twitching fingers. 'Wouldn't do that if I were you.

'Testing Minka wasn't part of the plan, but since I had her . . .' He shrugged again. 'When I realized she wasn't what I needed . . .' He tilted his head back and laughed. 'I guess you could say I threw her back – at Montgomery's request. But you have him to thank for why I didn't start our Mermaid Magic protocols on her, because I wasn't going to let an opportunity to test a prime subject pass me by.'

'Mermaid Magic protocols . . . Nice,' she spit out. 'So that's why Jonah named his medicinal brew . . .' She shook her head.

'We'd already tested your other cousin's DNA for the special marker. It's on file because of her job. She didn't have it either. So that' – his eyes narrowed – 'left you.'

And then, he began to undress, right there on the beach.

Not sure what to think, Alex averted her eyes.

'Your mother's DNA was tested years back, lifted from a visit to her doctor, so we know she had it.' He removed his shirt, kicked off his loafers and then his pants, revealing a black wetsuit with red paneling on the torso and arms. He left his clothes on the beach. 'And we also know it's passed down through the matrilineal line.'

Alex stared at the ship. It loomed closer, no longer a shapeless dark mass. She could see all of its angles. Its gunmetal gray color. 'This special marker is different from the mermaid gene?'

He nodded.

'What is it?'

'You have a mutation on the FBN1 gene that presents as Marfan syndrome . . . a genetic disorder that effects connective tissue like joints. But it's not.'

Alex was irritated by his arrogance as he casually talked about abducting women and destroying their lives. 'And?'

A Brew for Chaos

'Without it, the process of turning a woman with the mermaid DNA into an actual mermaid is lengthy and arduous. We'll need samples of your DNA. Then, using advanced gene-editing techniques, we can develop a treatment for our subjects that will expedite the process. But we'll need you to stick around. In case we need more samples. And then there's just so many tests we can run on you.'

Alex looked away, feeling sick.

Leith's phone chimed and he glanced at his screen, rolled his eyes. 'The old man's dead.'

Thank goodness Leith wasn't really related to Jack. Alex searched his face. 'I know he wasn't an actual relation, but you didn't care for him at all?' She glanced down at her blouse and pants. Was he expecting her to go into the water?

He laughed. 'He violated so many regulations, breached security in a million different ways. When I took over the project last year, I discovered, quite accidentally mind you, that he had a whole secret family, with a woman declared a security breach no less.' He shook his head. 'I knew I had to take care of this personally.'

'He had to have been retired for years. How did you know he was planning a trip down here?'

'Once I learned of his transgressions, I had him surveilled. Bugs placed in his home and devices—' He stopped when he saw the look on Alex's face. 'Don't look at me like that. He remained a security threat, and the subject of an investigation that would remain open until I was assured all threats had been mitigated – or he died.'

He looked towards the ship and smiled. 'Looks like they're ready for us.'

Alex looked past him and saw a ladder roll down the side and several men in wetsuits descending the rope and climbing into a smaller boat that floated alongside the ship.

'There's our ride.' He gripped her arm tightly and began dragging her towards the sea.

Panic seized her chest, and she looked over her shoulder towards the direction of her family, of the town she'd grown to love. She tried to telepath a thought to Kamila, to Minka, to anyone, but she couldn't. She got dizzy when she tried. *Would it really end*

334   Esme Addison

this way? She turned back to the sea. The small engine boat was coming towards them while Leith quickened his step.

'Leave your shoes,' he directed.

She did it, leaving the running shoes in the sand.

He noticed her eyes lingering on the footwear and chuckled. 'Don't worry. Where you'll be going you won't need them.'

'Why do you need me? What are your plans?'

'A little testing . . . like we did with Caroline. But at this stage, we know so much more than at the start of the project. And our tools are advanced.' He licked his lips. 'I can't wait to get started. You have the marker – this should be fun.'

Uneasiness washed over Alex.

'You let my girls go.' He raised his voice over the crash of the waves as they walked into the surf.

Girls? Alex wrinkled her nose. 'You mean the women you tortured and imprisoned.'

He jerked her further into the water, the tide running over his bare feet. 'My security *team*. My girls have been trained to protect our ships and submarines and act defensively when called upon . . . I was so close. All you've done is require me to start all over with a new crop of women, unless I can somehow recapture the mermaids you set free.

'Now that we've perfected the process, and successfully trained a team with proof of their accomplishments in the field, we can replicate the procedure and begin selling security teams to our allies.' He gazed across the ocean, admiring the view. 'Only now we don't have to waste time scouring the oceans looking for mermaids. We can just pluck them off the land. Our database of women with the mermaid gene is expanding every day.'

The water was at their thighs now, and the boat was approaching. The man piloting the boat cut off the engine and floated towards them. He held out a hand to help Leith into the boat.

Alex searched the choppy waves, wondering where the mermaids were. Were they still in the bay? Or did they escape into the ocean? She hoped so.

The salty wind filled her nostrils as a breeze whipped her hair around. And where was her mother? When she got away from Forbes, did she drown? She raised her voice over the waves. 'What do you know about my mother?'

He snorted. 'Another of Forbes' failures.' Leith held out his hand, eyes on her. 'Get in.' He held up the device, activated it so that a crackle of electricity flickered above it.

She took a deep breath, searching the water around her, looking for inspiration. Alex knew that if she stepped into that boat, the odds of her escaping were slim. Four men, each with goggles over their faces and dressed in solid black wetsuits with fins, stood on the boat. They had air tanks on their backs and rifles slung over their shoulders.

'You're no good to me hurt,' Leith said over the crashing waves, 'but I'll do what I must.' His eyes narrowed. 'Get. In.'

Alex regarded the men. 'That's the security team from the aquarium?'

'My boys.' He grinned.

She inhaled sharply. 'The guys you were having drinks with at the tavern?'

'The one and only.' His grin transformed into a sneer. 'You almost caught us having a meeting with Montgomery that day. When Caroline escaped, I sent them to find her.'

She remembered the one who'd winked at her, his burn scar. Caroline said one had come after her and she'd singed his arm.

'So, who actually killed Jonah?'

A look of pride crossed his face. 'When they found Jonah and Caroline, they called me. It was me who confronted them. It was me who electrocuted him when he threatened me and all I've been working for. The nerve of that guy.' He made a tsking noise with his teeth.

'I'd planned on taking Caroline back, but she began making a scene. I only tried to silence her, but in my zeal I'm afraid I shocked her too hard. She should've been used to it, since it was the way we disciplined her – there was a tracker . . .' He waved a hand. 'Anyway, she fell to the ground. By then I could hear people coming.' He shrugged. 'So I left her. One less problem.'

Alex couldn't hold her tongue. 'You're a monster.' She didn't have her powers, but she could still do something. With both palms she shoved him in his chest as hard as she could. He stumbled backwards into the water, fell on his bottom with a flail of arms and a loud splash. But he quickly scrambled to his feet.

336   Esme Addison

She began running away, but the water slowed her gait.

He crossed the distance with ease, grabbed her forearm, and jerked her forward so hard she almost fell into the water. And then he dragged her back to the boat.

A moment later, the engine was a roar in her ears, and spray erupted in their wake as they piloted back to the cargo ship. The vessel loomed larger with every passing minute, until at last they drew alongside its towering hull.

One of the security men went up first, then positioned himself at the top of the ladder, rifle directed at her. Leith went up next, and then he called down to her.

'You're next.'

She paused, feeling a tingling in her fingertips. Were her abilities returning? She tried to create a tiny wave of electricity, felt the surge of energy move through her arms to her fingers then fizzle out. But she did feel something. A tug in her fingers caused a slight jump in the waves around her. She casually looked at the men, but no one noticed.

'Today,' Leith said, tone heavy with warning.

She nodded like she'd accepted defeat. Shoulders slumped, she moved away from the guard to her right, whose barrel was pointed at her head, noted the location of the third and fourth, whose gun still hung loosely across his torso, but his brown eyes were sharp, his lips pressed into a grim line.

She moved like she was going to climb up the ladder, but in the last second flung her hands out. She couldn't create a charge within her body, but she could command the water. A tall wave of water knocked the gun out of the second guard's hands, and another wave knocked the third off his feet.

A guard glanced over the edge of the boat for his gun, then lunged for her.

She threw herself over the side of the boat and landed on her back with a hard *thwack*.

'Shoot! Shoot! Don't let her get away.'

She heard Leith directing the guard at the top of the ladder to injure her but not to kill, and she took a deep breath and allowed her body to sink under the water.

SIXTY

S he knew from her time with the mermaids that she could hold her breath for a very long time. She could also see without the salt burning her eyes.

Blinking several times, she adjusted to the feel of the water on her eyes, quickly swimming as deep as she could go. Alex could still see the shadow of the small boat hovering above her, and she wondered how she could get away from them. She hadn't fully thought this plan through – she only knew that she couldn't get on that ship.

Splash.

Startled, she looked up and saw two dark objects sink into the water.

And then another. And another. A few minutes later, one more dark object descended into the water.

Her chest muscles pulled taut, and she felt like her heart would explode. The men were coming after her. She quickly hid behind a large boulder, then peeked around in time to see the men carried something like harpoons, steel tools with sharp hooked ends.

They would not allow her to escape.

But she could swim. Fast. Faster than they could, and she remembered the techniques the mermaids had shown her. She streamlined her posture and kicked her feet in a flutter movement, while her arms used the front crawl, making sure to use her core and arms for the strongest pull.

Out of the corner of her eye, she saw one of the men aim his spear gun at her, and the spear zoomed towards her. She bobbed out of the way, then kicked off, launching her body several yards away from him.

But then she saw another man, and he held a weapon like a bow and arrow, something he could lob at her. She jerked out of the way as the sharp arrow sailed by her.

How could she get away from these men? And then a thought came to her. But it would only work if . . .

She swam out of sight, closed her eyes and tried to telepath, hoping the effort wouldn't make her nauseous. Then she sent her message in images. She opened her eyes and imagined she could see her cries for help floating away on bubbles of water.

She glanced up at the light shimmering above the water. She needed to break the surface and get lungs of fresh air before she dived back down again. She dived lower, holding on to long weeds. She stayed close to the sea floor, hiding behind sea fauna.

Like the predators they were, Alex could see the four men nearby, weapons at the ready, trying to find her. She launched her body in the opposite direction, swimming as fast as she could then propelled her body *up, up, up* until she arced out of the water.

She breathed deeply, quickly looking around to orientate herself. She was about three hundred yards away from the ship. She was a strong swimmer with the mermaid gene. Maybe she could swim back to the shore . . . though it looked to be a good ten or fifteen miles.

As she treaded water, a wave of desperation swept over her, and for a moment she felt like crying at her situation. But no, she couldn't let them win. They tried to take her mother and failed. They would not get her.

Taking another deep breath, she set her mind to swim back to shore no matter how long it took. She pushed forward, kicking her legs – and then she felt something grab her right ankle.

It pulled her backwards and then down. She looked around in the murky water, unable to focus on one object. The inability to see caused her confusion and fear to increase. Alex tried to still the racing of her heart. Maybe a long string of seaweed had wrapped around her leg.

But then she felt something cover her body and tighten. Blinking rapidly, her eyes finally adjusted to the lack of light and the movement of the water. She looked down at her body and saw she'd been covered by a net.

If she could've screamed, she would have. Instead she tried to quell the panic that blossomed in her chest and threatened to make her open her mouth and nose in the water and drown herself.

She grabbed at the net, pushed at the rope, struggled against it, but it only settled tighter around her. *She was trapped. Caught. Like a fish.*

A few yards away, a dark figure hovered by, watching as another man yanked on a rope attached to the net. Three other men treaded water, their weapons trained on her.

She glared at the man closest to her, wondering if she could reach him with a jolt of energy but worried the flow of water would skew her aim with her being so far away from him.

The first man lifted his hand in the water and twirled his fingers in a *let's-go* movement, and the man holding the net jerked the rope and began to drag Alex back to the ship.

SIXTY-ONE

H *opeless.*

That's what Alex felt, being dragged through the ocean like a captured sea creature. There was nothing she could do. She couldn't tear the net apart. The men stayed far away from her and out of range of her hands. But when they pulled her up, and out of the water she—

The net stilled, and Alex looked around. Saw a glimmer of lavender. One of the men in a dark suit's body jerked. He let go of his weapon, and it drifted away from him while he began to float, his arms floating before him, legs not moving.

What happened to him?

A flash of pink from Alex's peripheral, and Leith – she could tell by the red marks on his suit – was hit from behind with a swish of a mermaid tail. The impact flung him several yards, and the spear gun in his hand sailed past him and into the waiting hands of another mermaid.

She didn't hesitate and launched the weapon at his torso. The sharp projectile hit its target, and a trail of blood bloomed around him. He began swimming away with jerky movements then abruptly stopped, his body drifting on the current.

Alex felt the rope of her net go slack and she was floating. The last two men were swimming to their colleagues, wrapping arms around them. Then they both deployed some sort of device on their backs that propelled them forward with force, leaving a white trail of foam in their wake.

What was going on?

And then the net was torn away, two faces peering above her.

Are you okay? The words flittered through her mind. Alex blinked, confused. Her vision cleared and she was surrounded by mermaids. Ten or so.

They had come back for her.

She recognized one of the mermaids from the aquarium. *We got your message. Heard your screams for help.*

A Brew for Chaos   341

If she could've cried underwater, she would have. *Thank you. Thank you for returning for me. Thank you for helping me.* Dizzy with gratitude, the words tumbled through her mind.

The mermaids swam around her, their colorful tails slicing through the water.

Let's get you to the surface. Another mermaid, pale-skinned with a blue-ish undertone and wavy cotton-candy-pink hair swam underneath Alex. Thick strips of seaweed crisscrossed her torso in the approximation of a strapless top similar to a bandeau and studded with seashells. *Lay on my back and wrap your arms around my waist. I'll bring you back to shore.*

Alex glanced at her teal-colored tail. *Are you sure? I don't want to hurt you.* Alex searched the mermaid's face. She looked ageless – twenty or fifty, she couldn't tell.

Alex heard titters of laughter all around her.

It's fine, the mermaid said. *This is how mothers carry their young around. Or how we help injured mermaids . . . I can swim much faster than you can. It's the best way.*

Treading water, her dark hair floating around her, Alex marveled at the sight. A group of mermaids – what did one call a grouping of mermaids?

A glitter, a mermaid with silver hair, a lavender tail and violet eyes with an epicanthic fold telepathed to her.

Alex hadn't realized she telepathed that but smiled. A glitter of mermaids sounded perfect. *Thank you.* She swam over to the mermaid with pink hair and settled on her back like one might ride a dolphin and gently wrapped her arms around her.

Tighter, the mermaid said. *You don't want to fall off.*

More laughter, sounding like hundreds of bubbles popping around her.

Alex tightened her embrace around the mermaid, then looked over her shoulder at the others. *Before I go . . .*

She telepathed an image of her mother. Every image she could recall of her to the mermaids.

In jeans, a coat and ice skates. In her robe making pancakes on Saturday morning. Beside her in bed reading *Winnie the Pooh*. In a glittering black dress for a New Year's Eve party.

The rush of memories was so strong she was suddenly racked with emotion. Sadness. Loneliness. A craving for her lost mother. All the time apart. A child needing her mother.

The mermaids moved closer to her, their words a jumble in her head.

I'm so sorry. You lost your mother. You poor little girl. Don't cry. Be strong. You'll be okay . . .

I don't even know if she's here or what happened to her, Alex telepathed. *But if she is . . . please. Tell her to contact me. Let her know I'm looking for her. That I love her. I miss her . . .*

She pressed her face into the neck of the mermaid.

I'm ready to go.

SIXTY-TWO

Faster than the black marlin or swordfish, the mermaid cut through the water at speeds of seventy miles per hour.

It was a blur of blue and green, the force on Alex's body reminding her of being on the back of a motorcycle with a college boyfriend. She tightened her grip on the mermaid's waist and held on for dear life.

And then she slowed down to about ten miles, a pleasant drift when they neared the shoreline.

Will you be safe once you reach land?

I think so. I hope so, Alex replied as they broke the surface of the water. She took a deep breath of fresh air. *I'm tired, but I can defend myself on land.*

The mermaid floated beside Alex, both of their heads just above the water line. *Good. We can't help you on the sand. But in the water, you will always have sisters.*

Alex searched the shoreline. It was thankfully empty. No Leith. No armed guards.

I can take it from here. Thank you so much.

The mermaid flicked her tail so that it broke the water and arced in the sky, creating a brilliant beam of shimmering color before she dived down, leaving a trail of sea foam.

A mermaid's farewell.

And Alex began to swim the few yards back to dry land.

When she finally reached it, despite the help from the mermaid, fatigue had left her arms and legs leaden. She crawled through the sand until she couldn't feel the tide lapping against her body, rolled over onto her back and closed her eyes.

When she came to, Alex was in a hospital room. She heard a machine beeping, and the smell of pine trees or lemons or maybe both filled her nostrils. She saw her cousins sitting in chairs around the room.

344   Esme Addison

Aunt Lidia rushed forward. 'She's awake. Call the doctor.'

A moment later, Dr Crow arrived, and after checking her vitals, he grinned. 'Considering the length of time she was underwater without a wetsuit,' he directed his comments to Lidia, 'I'd expect her to have hypothermia, signs of respiratory distress and skin irritation due to the prolonged contact with seawater.' He regarded Alex with interest. 'But she's fine. Dehydrated.' He pointed to the bags of saline dripping into her IV. 'But she'll soon recover and be good as new.'

'When can she leave?' Lidia asked, concern still darkening her eyes.

The doctor nodded. 'Overnight for observation. Then she can leave first thing in the morning.'

When he left, Kamila, Minka, Celeste and Daphne surrounded her, a jumble of questions filling the air. She tried to smile, thinking they reminded her of a glitter of mermaids without the ocean water.

'What happened? Are you okay?' Minka asked.

'The mermaids, they saved me,' Alex finally said.

Kamila moved forward. 'Give her room.' She handed her a cup of ice water. 'Here, drink this.'

She did, and then told them everything that had transpired.

'I can't believe it was Leith this whole time,' Minka mused, her lips downturned in a pout. 'He was so sweet, and I thought he genuinely liked me.'

'I swear,' Celeste chimed in with a roll of her eyes. 'The men in this town.'

'The most important thing is that you're okay,' Daphne said, wrapping an arm around Lidia.

'And neither Forbes nor Leith will be harming any more women.'

Alex shifted against her pillows. 'What happened to Leith? Did Jack arrest him?'

'Leith didn't make it.' Kamila shook her head. 'A group of men in baseball caps and sunglasses were seen on security footage dropping him off at the hospital. Left his body in a wheelchair at the entrance.'

A Brew for Chaos

Alex settled against her pillows and sighed. 'Death by spear gun.'

Lidia sniffed. 'A fitting death for the man who would be the next Fisherman.'

SIXTY-THREE

Oktoberfest was in full swing.

Beer trucks filled the parking lot of the tavern, with female servers carrying large trays of food and pitchers of beer, dressed in dirndls: the traditional German dress that gathered at the waist, with an apron, and a vest. A band played festive music on a stage in the parking lot, and the mayor walked around with a microphone, sharing tidbits of information about each local craft beer entered into the contest.

Pepper leaned over the table, fork in hand and reaching for another potato cake sizzling on the tray shared between everyone at the table. Alex, Celeste, Minka and Kamila were crowded around a rectangular wooden table filled with food and drink. 'And then they called me and said they want me to produce a documentary on the Fisherman and how the case dovetailed into the search for Jonah's killer.'

Kamila gave her a knowing look.

'Unfortunately . . .' Pepper pouted. 'Somebody from' – she made air quotes – '"the government" got wind of the assignment and said it touches on classified information and it can't be aired.'

Minka's eyes widened. 'Is that even legal?'

Pepper shrugged. 'Doesn't matter. WNN refused to move forward with the assignment. But there is some good news.'

Alex speared a slice of brats before popping it into her mouth. 'What's that?'

'Even though I was never able to figure out who the Fisherman actually was, they were so impressed with my coverage of the case they've decided to occasionally send me news assignments that will be aired through their DC station.' Her lips quirked into a sad smile. 'But more importantly, we got justice for Jonah. To think, it had nothing to do with the case.'

Alex shot Kamila a glance, hoping the lie they'd come up with would give Pepper the closure she needed.

'I can't believe that guy Leith killed Jonah over a decades-old

A Brew for Chaos

gambling debt he owed to his grandfather when they served in the military.' She made a face. 'It just all seems so senseless.'

Alex turned to watch her Aunt Lidia and Daphne chat up the mayor. It was nice to see everyone having a good time. Alex smiled at Daphne when she caught her eye, wondering how she'd react when she realized Caroline was the woman she met on the beach that night. The one Mac had protected her from. He'd saved her life.

But then her eye caught sight of Dylan. He was sitting with Harrison, who had somehow managed to both find the anti-Zombie Maker device, and win first place in the craft beer's overall competition. They were sharing a pitcher of dark ale and a plate of pretzels. Dylan caught her eye and smiled. She returned the gesture, but quickly looked away.

'I have some news,' Kamila tossed out before sampling a foamy maple pancake milkshake IPA. 'I'm taking the detective exam in a few weeks.'

Everyone at the table cheered. 'That's great news.' Minka elbowed her sister good-naturedly. 'What brought this on?'

Kamila slid a glance towards Alex. 'Detective Frazier put in his thirty-day notice. I figured that was my sign.'

Celeste touched Alex's hand. 'Did you know?'

Alex reached for her drink and took a sip. 'I haven't seen or talked to him since—'

A shadow crossed the table, and Spencer was standing beside them, a hesitant look on her face. 'Alex,' she began with a shy smile, 'can I talk to you for a sec?'

Alex rose slowly. 'Sure. But I'll need to see your hands at all times,' she joked.

'I deserve that.' Spencer led her to a spot near a wall. 'I just wanted to apologize for the smoothie and just being such a jerk to you.'

'Okay.' Alex shrugged, keeping her face neutral. Though not one to hold a grudge, she also wasn't willing to give her forgiveness so easily.

'I've been dealing with a lot of stress lately.' She raised her voice to be heard over the din of noise in the tavern.

'Haven't we all?' Alex looked past her, effecting a bored countenance.

348   Esme Addison

'Yeah, but mine . . . Well, look, I'm just going to tell you, since Leith McDonald is dead.'

'How did you get mixed up with him?'

'It's a bit of a circuitous story . . .' Spencer scanned the packed dining area before answering. 'It begins with Jonah. My senior year of college, we had a thing. Nothing serious. Just fun. Lots of partying. One day, I overheard him talking to his friends about the shady stuff they were doing for the government. Stuff I wasn't supposed to hear.'

Alex turned to look at her then. Did she know about Magicals? 'What kind of stuff?'

'Just stuff like they were doing some testing . . . I never knew the specifics, but my guess is aliens.' She shrugged, and Alex coughed to cover a laugh.

'He told me about debts he had, and how if he didn't pay them off, something bad might happen to him. I think he hoped I would offer to pay them off for him – I didn't. Because at this point I was wondering if he was only with me for my money.' Spencer paused to catch the attention of a waitress and direct her to a table needing to pay their tab. 'Later, he said he'd found someone to help him pay his debts. Which made me happy, because I thought he must actually care about me and not my bank account, right?'

Alex nodded, moving closer to Spencer as a group of rowdy partygoers walked past them.

'Whoever paid his debts had to be highly placed in society, because they got him hired at the newspaper, where he wrote whatever he was told.'

Alex recalled all of the articles blaming Mac for the abductions. *Paid propaganda.*

'One day, he was really upset.' She stopped when a brass band began playing on the stage. Then raised her voice. 'He had a lot to drink and was complaining about how he'd never repay his debts. Told me that he had to create a medicine for a very complicated health issue that could be bottled and last a long time. It needed to be done under the radar and without laboratories or manufacturing facilities.'

'They must've known about his background studies in pharmaceuticals,' Alex pointed out.

A Brew for Chaos

'Yeah, he mentioned that . . . but the guy – he was obsessed with Sumerian history and mythology for some reason and believed if they could create medicinal beer in ancient times, so could he. But he still needed more help, so he visited your aunt to learn about herbs. After several months of trial and error, he found the perfect brew.'

For chaos, Alex thought to herself. If it wasn't for his brew, the summer of chaos would have never happened. 'What does this have to do with Leith?'

Spencer rolled her eyes. 'I'm getting to that,' she snapped, then she sighed. 'Sorry, I need to work on my patience. After my father died, I was dealing with the mess he left behind – and several corporate attacks – when I received an offer.'

Alex glanced over at her family having fun together. A smile appeared on her lips, happy to see Minka and her mother at peace with each other. 'An offer contingent on you providing the recipe for Jonah's brew.'

She swallowed, suddenly looking miserable. 'Exactly. I had twelve months to procure the recipe or they'd back out. It's why I've been so aggressive about finding the recipe. And with Jonah gone, what did it matter if I had it?'

Alex shook her head. *It mattered more than she could ever know*. With that recipe, women would've been abducted and tested on. 'That day I saw you near his townhouse?'

'I was desperate.' Her cheeks reddened. 'I was going to try and break in. But cars kept driving by, he had this crazy security system, and I really didn't want to . . . I left when I saw you two.'

Alex crossed her arms. 'And your argument with Leith?'

She snorted. 'That guy? He was the one badgering me to find it. His company was connected to Leviathan, I guess, and at first, I received a few emails from him, and then letters. When I found out he was in town, I really freaked out. And one day, he just came up to me on the street, accosted me really, and was like, if you find it, you have to give it to me. And then proceeded to threaten me and my family. I told him I didn't have any family to be threatened with and he needed to get out my face. That I'd do what I wanted when I wanted, and he had no say.'

'That was brave.' Alex tried not to think about her last moments with Leith. He'd been a dangerous man.

'And stupid.' She laughed. 'I was scared out of my mind, but I wasn't going to show him that. That type of bluster usually works.'

'What will you do now? You never found it, did you?' She thought of the ingredient list Caroline had given her, and the knowledge that Jonah's secret ingredient was seaweed. Had she had the recipe with her all along?

Spencer looked around the festival. 'I'm over it. Done stressing. They can have the company. Or not. I'll let my business managers figure it out. In the meantime? I think I've met my next husband online. He's an Italian count with a villa that needs a woman's touch.' She air-kissed Alex's cheeks, then looked around the festive environment, her gaze landing on her manager. 'Zane does a great job running this place. I'm ready to let him do it.'

Alex followed her gaze. 'He's a good guy then?'

'A real Boy Scout. If I had a daughter, I'd set them up.'

Alex smiled, wondering if Minka would give him a chance.

'Time for me to get out of this little hick town.' She grinned. 'No offense.'

Voices were loud, mugs were clinking, and everyone was having a good time.

Alex gazed around the room, a smile playing on her lips. 'None taken.'

Her life wasn't perfect. But she was grateful that Minka had been found. And grateful she was back on good terms with Aunt Lidia.

She had her family back, and that was all that mattered.

EPILOGUE

Jack stared at the device.

Alex was tired of holding her hand out. 'What do you have to lose?'

He picked it up and inspected it while his mother set out tea and shortbread cookies – cookies Alex now knew had been Forbes' favorite.

She smiled at them. 'Have one, Alex.'

Nodding, Alex selected a cookie while Jack watched his mother with concern.

Maisie returned to the kitchen, and Jack looked at Alex. 'Tell me again how you found this?'

'Dylan,' was her one-word answer.

He narrowed his eyes, studying the device. 'What if it makes things worse?'

'How can it be worse?'

He closed his eyes and took a deep breath. 'Okay. Just, if I say stop, then stop.'

'Of course.'

Maisie returned and joined them on the couch, a sweet smile on her face. 'Alex, it's so nice to see you. What's that doodad in your hand?'

Alex showed her the device. 'It's something to help you retrieve your memories. Would you like to remember things you've lost, Maisie?'

She cocked her head, an amused look on her face. 'Not especially. I'm fine.'

Jack swallowed slowly, a disturbed look on his face. 'You won't feel anything, and it will just take a second. Maybe it won't do anything. Can we try?'

'Of course, Jack. If it will make you happy.'

His brows dipped down as he struggled to keep his expression off his face. 'Yes, Mom. It will make me happy.'

352   Esme Addison

Maisie nodded, then turned to Alex. 'What do I need to do?'

'Just . . . Sit there. Close your eyes.' She held out her palm. 'I'm going to place this on each temple for a few seconds and it will send healing frequencies into your brain. Okay?'

Eyes already closed, she nodded.

Taking a deep breath, Alex recalled the directions Harrison had given her after he'd found her at the festival. Hit the wrong button too many times, and the device went into kill mode, exactly what Leith had done with Jonah.

Swallowing slowly, she positioned the device beside Maisie's right temple, close but not enough to actually touch skin, and activated a touchpad on its side. There was a delicate chime and a blue glow emitted from the half-globe. Alex could feel a vibration in her hand, but that was all. According to Harrison, the device was mapping a part of the brain and identifying the areas that needed repairing. There was a second chime, a slightly lower tone and the globe turned green, indicating it was in repair mode. Then the device powered down, and Alex moved to the other temple and repeated the procedure.

She turned to Jack when it was done. 'Bring her some water. Or something with electrolytes. She'll need it.'

'Lemonade?' he asked, pausing at the kitchen door.

'Even better. Add a dash of sea salt.'

He returned with the glass, and Maisie drank the entire beverage in several large gulps.

She looked around and giggled. 'Oh my, but I was thirsty.' She set it down and smiled at the pair.

'She seems the same,' Jack murmured under his breath.

Maisie yawned. 'I'm tired.' She blinked several times. 'I can barely keep my eyes open.' She pressed a palm on Jack's leg. 'You don't mind if I take a nap, do you?'

'I'll walk you up, Mom.' He rose, took her arm and guided her up the stairs. He looked over his shoulders. 'Don't leave,' he told Alex. 'We need to talk.'

When he returned, he sat beside Alex on the couch.

'I'm sorry, looks like the device didn't work.'

He took her hand but didn't look her in the eye. 'It's okay. We tried. It was silly of me to want her to be different. Let's

A Brew for Chaos 353

face it, if she were to change, it would be like having a stranger for a mother. Maybe this is for the best.'

Alex glanced down at their hands intertwined, not sure how she felt about him touching her.

Silence bloomed around them, awkward and a bit painful. He cleared his throat. 'I'm leaving the force.'

'I know.'

He turned to her. 'Officer Sobieski?' She nodded, and he sighed. 'I've made a mess of things here, haven't I?'

Alex didn't answer.

'My cover's blown. You hate me . . .' He turned to look at Alex. 'You do, don't you? For lying to you.'

Alex bit her lip. *No, not just because you lied*, she wanted to say. *But because you're out to get me, my family and others like me*. She couldn't admit that though. 'It's a lot . . . What will you do?'

'I'm not sure. I'm not leaving town, just the force. Maybe I'll be reassigned. At least for now I was hoping we could work on us.'

Yeah, about that . . . Alex stood, gently moving her hand away from his. 'I think we need a break.'

He followed her to the door. 'Please. Wait.'

'Why?' Alex whirled around to face him. 'Do you have real feelings for me? Or was that a lie too?'

He paused, his jaw tightening. 'No more lies?'

Her eyes widened. *There were more?* 'No more lies.'

'At first, I wanted to get to know you because your family was on my list for possible PAC activity. That day when we met jogging? It was planned. I'd been watching your family's house and when you showed up . . . it seemed the perfect in.'

Alex huffed in disbelief and tried to leave, but he blocked the door with his arm. 'Please, hear me out?' When she nodded, he removed his arm. 'But then I got to know you and your family – I mean your aunt.' He shook his head. 'She's different. But they're not the freaks I've been tracking down. And I've come to like them. I've come to care about you. More than care about you.'

But Alex was through with him. *Freaks?* 'You still think they're monsters? You saw the mermaids, they were beautiful. And they didn't hurt your mother. Your father did. Why aren't you angry with the government? Why are you still working for an agency that's party to the torture of women?'

'They're not women, Alex.' His eyes flared. 'They're creatures.'

'What about the women that were abducted, the ones with the mermaid gene that were turned into mermaids and are now forced to live in the sea? This was done to them – they're monsters too?'

'It's complicated. I mean, I'm sorry those women were taken, their families lost mothers, daughters, sisters . . . but with that gene?' He shook his head. 'They were just pretending to be like us. That's what's scary, that they can be among us, pretending to be like you and me, but they're not.'

A part of Alex wanted to shock him and tell him the truth about her Magical heritage. Destroy his delusions. *Hey, Jack, guess what? You've been so-call in love with a Magical all this time. What does that make you?* But she wouldn't, wouldn't out her family in that way. Ruin Kamila's career. Possibly destroy the business. No, she'd say nothing.

'I can't get past the lies, Jack. We're not right for each other, and we never will be.' She pushed past him, stepping onto the porch, and he grabbed her hand.

'Alex, don't leave like this.'

'Jack, let go of her.'

Alex looked past Jack into the house.

He turned around, and Maisie was descending the stairs, a firm look on her face. She was changed. The vacuous look of complacency was gone. Her green eyes were sharp, focused and bright. Even the set of her face was different. Her jaw was firm, no more slackness around the mouth, and her arms were crossed at her chest. A look of disapproval in her eyes.

'Mom?' Jack's voice cracked like a thirteen-year-old boy.

Maisie reached the landing, and her eyes softened. 'Yes, Jack. It's me. It's finally really me.'

Jack let go of Alex's hand and went to his mother, squeezed her in a bear hug, lifting her feet off the ground. 'Mom,' he repeated, voice hoarse with emotion.

She pulled back from him. 'We have a lot to talk about, you

A Brew for Chaos 355

and I.' She looked over his shoulder at Alex. 'Thank you, dear. For all you've done. You gave me back my life.'

'I'm glad.' Alex stared at the woman. She was no longer Maisie Frazier, the woman Forbes McDonald had assaulted with a device that scrambled her brain, or the woman he'd married under false pretenses and removed from school.

This was Margaret Dunsmore, the smart, vibrant, confident young woman that her Aunt Lidia knew, that Caroline had befriended and Tobias had cared for.

The device had worked.

Jack hugged his mother again, with tears running down his face.

It was the perfect time for Alex to slip away. She wiggled her fingers to Margaret in a farewell and closed the door quietly behind her.

As she sat in her car, and began to drive, she was happy that at least someone she knew had reconnected with their mother.

She didn't realize it, but her eyes were filled with tears as she drove with no direction. Minutes later, she found herself at the beach. Today there was a chill in the air, but the sun was high in the sky.

She stepped out of her car, walked up the dunes, down the stairs and took in deep breaths of sea air. A place of tranquility. Her happy place. A slight breeze lifted her hair on the wind, and the sun shone brilliantly on the cold sea, creating slicks of silver shimmer on the surface.

She took off her shoes and socks, allowing her toes to grip the cold sand. She walked close enough for the tide to wet her ankles. The last few days had helped her get over her fear of the water. It was home for people like her.

Once Dylan had told her the ocean had a feminine energy. That it was generous and that if you asked it a question, it would answer. That you could talk to it. She wasn't sure she believed that, but she no longer believed the sea was her enemy.

She stared into the horizon, both feet covered in water, and tears filling her eyes. Her mother had disappeared without a trace. Her father had passed away . . . had she ever truly dealt with the weight of it all? Or had she tried to stay strong and

356 Esme Addison

soldier through it with a tough attitude and a smile on her face?

No more. The pain was immense, and it threatened to crush her. *Mama*, she screamed in her head. *Where are you? I helped Jack reconnect with his mother. And I'm happy for them. But why can't I find you?*

She stood there for minutes, tears rolling down her cheeks and falling into the ocean. And then she fell to her knees, closed her eyes and wept.

When she opened them, she felt somewhat better. A good cry always did the body good. She looked around, hoping no one had seen her.

No, she was good. The beach was mostly empty, though she could see a couple walking in the far distance. She wiped her eyes with her shirt sleeve, then focused on something in the water. It was small and glistening, drifting towards her.

She blinked, wiped her eyes again and saw an object in the water. A glass bottle made of tinted glass. She stared at it for a moment, wondering where it had come from, but then she began walking towards it lest a current send it down the shoreline or even back to the depths of the sea.

She started running in the water, until it was up to her knees, and she plucked the bottle from the ocean, feeling like a child at an Easter egg hunt. Holding the bottle tightly in her hand, she returned to the sand and inspected it.

A cork was wedged in the top, and it took several tugs before she could pull it out. It opened with a pop. She peered inside the bottle and found a yellowed piece of paper, looking like a scrap of old-timey parchment.

She pulled it out, unfurled the paper and saw there was a note on it. The handwriting looked familiar, maybe? It had been so long since she'd . . .

But it was the message that caused her vision to blur with tears.

If you are reading this letter,
please get a message to my
family in Bellamy Bay.
My name is Helena Sobieski Daniels
and I am still alive.

A Brew for Chaos

Alex stared at the ocean. And for a moment, far off in the distance, she thought she saw the arc of a purple mermaid tail swish in the air.

This was a message from her mother. If the message could be believed . . . She was still alive.

Her mother was alive.